Praise for the
Remy Chandler Novels

Walking in the Midst of Fire

"Sniegoski continues to ramp up the stakes in the entertaining fifth hard-boiled adventure . . . complete and entertaining."   —*Publishers Weekly*

In the House of the Wicked

"Remy and his human friends are engagingly believable characters in a series noted for flashes of humor despite its overall serious tone. Series fans and followers of Jim Butcher's Dresden Files will enjoy this urban fantasy."
—*Library Journal*

"A fun book . . . a thought-provoking book."   —Innsmouth Free Press

"The conflict and situations within this novel are refreshingly personal. . . . The characters are varied and very well-developed, bringing life and humanity into this novel largely centered around the angelic pantheon. . . . A very powerful, very personal tale that is equal parts gut-wrenching, heartwarming, and awe-inspiring."   —The Ranting Dragon

A Hundred Words for Hate

"Sniegoski nicely juggles a large cast and throws in some touching moments (Remy's conversations with his late wife, Madeline, are especially sweet) and humor (as always, provided by Remy's dog, Marlowe) to balance the epic violence. There's more than enough nonintrusive exposition to let new readers jump into the story, while longtime fans will appreciate the development of recurring characters."   —*Publishers Weekly*

"A fun, fast ride that takes advantage of a strong setting and interesting characters. And when a book combines that with serious angel smackdowns, really, what else do you need?"   —The Green Man Review

continued . . .

Where Angels Fear to Tread

"This strong, fast-paced noir fantasy is a treat. Remy is a compelling character, as he constantly struggles to hold on to the shred of humanity he forged for himself by suppressing the Seraphim. . . . This is one of the better noir fantasy–meets–gumshoe detective series on the market today."

—Monsters and Critics

Dancing on the Head of a Pin

"[Sniegoski] nicely blends action, mystery, and fantasy into a well-paced story . . . a very emotional read, with the hero's grief overshadowing his every move."

—Darque Reviews

"Equal measures heartbreaking and honorable; Sniegoski has created a warm, genuine character struggling with his identity and destiny. . . . The fast pace, gratifying character development, and a sufficiently complex plot to hold your interest from start to finish make this one a winner."

—Monsters and Critics

"A fun read. The pace of the book is excellent, and it never has a dull moment. . . . The tale is definitely something that you would read out of a 1930s crime noir novel, and it is engaging, tightly written, and moves along at a rapid pace. You won't find a dull moment."

—*Sacramento Book Review*

A Kiss Before the Apocalypse

"The most inventive novel you'll buy this year . . . a hard-boiled noir fantasy by turns funny, unsettling, and heartbreaking. This is the story Sniegoski was born to write, and a character I can't wait to see again."

—Christopher Golden, bestselling author of *Waking Nightmares*

"Tightly focused and deftly handled, [*A Kiss Before the Apocalypse*] covers familiar ground in entertaining new ways. . . . Fans of urban fantasy and classic detective stories will enjoy this smart and playful story."

—*Publishers Weekly*

A DEAFENING SILENCE
IN HEAVEN

A REMY CHANDLER NOVEL

THOMAS E. SNIEGOSKI

A ROC BOOK

ROC
Published by New American Library,
an imprint of Penguin Random House LLC
375 Hudson Street, New York, New York 10014

This book is an original publication of New American Library.

First Printing, October 2015

For more information about Penguin Random House, visit penguin.com.

LIBRARY OF CONGRESS CATALOGING-IN-PUBLICATION DATA:

Sniegoski, Tom.
A deafening silence in heaven: a Remy Chandler novel/Thomas E. Sniegoski.
pages cm.
"A Roc Book."
ISBN 978-0-451-47002-7
1. Chandler, Remy (Fictitious character).   2. Private investigators—Fiction.
3. Angels—Fiction.   I. Title.
PS3619.N537D43 2015
813'.6—dc23   2015026446

Printed in the United States of America
10 9 8 7 6 5 4 3 2 1

Penguin
Random
House

For my father.
If I end up being only half the amazing individual that you were,
that will still be something pretty darn special.
Love and miss you every day.
Joseph J. Sniegoski
November 20, 1919–April 26, 2013

ACKNOWLEDGMENTS

Intense amounts of love and thanks to my long-suffering wife, and to Kirby for always keeping things interesting.

Special thanks also to my buddy Christopher Golden, the amazing Jessica Wade, Ginjer Buchanan, Howard Morhaim, Kate Schafer Testerman, Thomas Fitzgerald, Dale Queenan, Larry Johnson, Pam Daley, Frank Cho, Dave Kraus (from his La-Z-Boy in Heaven), Kathy Kraus, Mom Sniegoski, and the Filthies down at Cole's Comics in Lynn, MA.

You ain't seen the last of the Boston Seraphim.

What we call the beginning is often the end
And to make an end is to make a beginning.
The end is where we start from.

—T. S. ELIOT

A Deafening Silence
in Heaven

PROLOGUE

A shopping mall food court
Somewhere in the United States

It was a day that seemed just like any other.

The sun rose as it was supposed to, and people woke from their nightly slumber to begin their daily routines: preparing for work, getting dressed for school, walking the dog, retrieving the morning paper from the front walk, making breakfast.

It was all so normal.

All so mundane.

If only they were aware of the event of cosmic proportions and significance that was about to occur.

He who had been called the Son of the Morning sat at a table in the food court of the mall, observing the ebb and flow of humanity.

Leaning back in the metal chair, Lucifer Morningstar saw them at their best and worst: an old woman fumbling with multiple plastic bags unwittingly drops a wad of dollar bills to the floor; a man sidles up alongside her, snatches up the money, and then promptly returns it to her. A teenage girl—a mere child—picks up her phone from the tabletop, her hands shaking horribly as she checks to see if her dealer has called, and bursts into tears when she sees that he hasn't. An overtired and whining child is brought to obvious joy when handed a book to read. A man who is unhappy with the speed in which he received his burrito takes it out on the young girl at the counter. A Benny Goodman instrumental plays over the food court sound system and an old man grabs hold of his wife's hand; they look into each other's eyes and smile, their love still strong.

"Don't tell me that you're still upset with them," said a voice beside him, and Lucifer turned to see an elderly gentleman, dressed in a beautifully tailored dark suit, standing at the table, orange tray in hand.

"I was never upset with them," the Morningstar said, pushing out a chair so the gentleman could sit down. "I was much more upset with you."

The old man sat down and began to disperse the items on His tray. He placed a cup of steaming coffee in front of the Morningstar. "You thought that I loved them more," He said. He took His own steaming cup from the tray, and what appeared to be a container of chicken fingers.

"I wasn't the only one," Lucifer said. He continued to watch the patrons of the mall food court.

"No, but you were the loudest voice."

The old man prepared His coffee: two sugars and three containers of cream.

"I felt I needed to be loud so you would hear me . . . hear us." Lucifer sipped his own black coffee, dark eyes roaming the court.

The old man chuckled, drinking delicately from his cup before setting it down upon the table. "Oh, I heard you, all right."

Lucifer fixed Him in a steely gaze.

"But did you listen?"

The old man did not answer but reached into the foam container and removed a piece of fried food.

"Is that a chicken finger?" Lucifer asked Him, shocked by what he was witnessing.

The old man studied the batter-covered object, which did not resemble any part from a chicken, or a finger, for that matter. "I love chicken fingers," He said, taking a bite. "Horrible for you, but everything in moderation."

Lucifer drank more of his coffee, noticing the euphoric teenage girl from before, walking past them while talking happily on her cell phone, her dealer having finally called. Life was good again. Or not.

"I listened, but I don't believe there was anything I could have said at that time to convince you otherwise," the old man said, picking up a napkin to wipe the grease from His mouth. "You did what you felt you needed to do, as did I."

Lucifer turned his cup ever so slowly.

"Was it worth it?" he asked, feeling a heavy sadness for all that had come to pass.

"That's a question I should be asking you," the old man said, pointing with a chicken finger.

Lucifer continued to slowly turn his cup, a faint trace of steam billowing from the hot liquid.

"It is what it is," he said finally, neither regretful nor content.

The old man finished His chicken finger and licked the tips of His delicate fingers.

"Things happened, and as a result . . ." He made a rolling gesture with His hand.

"Here we are," Lucifer finished. "When it's presented that way, it all seems so simple."

"It's all in how you look at things," the old man replied as He wrapped His hand around His coffee cup. He was watching the elderly couple that Lucifer had been observing earlier. They were talking happily, and for a brief moment even began to dance, which got them both laughing.

"Why are we here?" Lucifer finally got up the courage to ask. "I'm sure you're well aware of the whispers of a new war between Heaven and Hell floating in the ether."

"Yes, I'm afraid I am."

"So?"

The old man lifted His cup and had some more coffee. "I think it's time for something more to happen," He said, speaking over the rim of His cup.

Lucifer leaned in closer. "War?" he asked.

The old man was silent, as if deciding on His answer.

"No," He said after a moment. "The opposite."

"Truce?" Lucifer suggested. "I thought we already had that."

"Peace," the old man corrected.

Lucifer was shocked. "What are you suggesting?"

"I want you to come home."

And for the first time in countless millennia the Son of the Morning was speechless.

"It's time for us to be whole again," the old man told him.

"Do you mean to say . . . ," Lucifer began, and stopped as the old man sitting across from him nodded slowly, a loving smile spreading across His face reminding Lucifer of the very first dawn over the world on the eighth day.

"Unification, my son," the old man said, and then slid the container of chicken fingers toward him. "Chicken finger?"

The Bone Master screamed far longer than Remy Chandler imagined it could have.

When the creature finally fell silent, Remy let its body slip from his grasp. But the fire continued to burn, jumping to the assassin's robes and the flesh beneath; before long, there would be nothing left to show that the assassin had ever lived . . .

. . . except for the physical and mental damage it had inflicted.

Marlowe came to Remy, leaping up onto his chest, stretching his neck to eagerly kiss Remy's face. Remy found it suddenly difficult to remain standing, and dropped to his knees, giving the dog ample opportunity to display his rampant affections.

As Marlowe licked his face, Remy caught sight of Linda staring at him from where she sat, perfectly motionless upon the floor. He wanted to explain everything to her, but the words would not come.

The look of fear in her eyes froze them in his throat.

"I believe," he began, forcing the words from his mouth, "I owe you an explanation." He found his speech strangely slurred and wondered what could be the cause, then realized that his entire body was growing increasingly cold. He could not feel his limbs and suddenly toppled over onto the floor.

Marlowe yelped in panic as he fell, and Linda was at his side, leaning over him, tears in her eyes, her face racked with the beginnings of panic.

"You're bleeding," he heard her say, though the words were strangely muffled.

He managed to lift his head and saw that he was indeed bleeding. The cold realization washed over him—the assassin's bullets had found their target, the venom-infused teeth sending a powerful poison coursing through his veins.

Remy tried to alter his internal chemistry, as he had so many times before, to burn the poison away. . . .

Nothing happened, and the cold continued to permeate his every fiber. He was finding it harder and harder to remain there—to remain with Linda and Marlowe.

Marlowe cried pathetically, pacing back and forth in front of them. Linda was holding him now, gripping him tightly in her arms and begging him to stay with her.

"Remy, what should I do?" she pleaded.

She was panicked, and he wanted to hold her, to tell her that he would be fine, but he could no longer move his arms, and now that what he truly was had been revealed, he did not want to begin another lie.

"I . . . I'm so sorry," he managed to squeak. "Didn't want . . . to lie."

"Remy," she cried, her tears raining down upon his face—tears that he could not feel.

He tried to stay with her, but his eyes had grown so heavy, and he could no longer hold them open. *Maybe if I close them for just a moment. To rest.*

Marlowe howled, his cries reverberating through the room, and Remy thought it was the saddest sound he had ever heard.

Darkness surrounded him, but there was fire in the midst of shadow, a flame struggling to stay alight within the encroaching gloom.

But the flame grew smaller with each passing moment until it was but a faintly glowing ember, and it could fight no more and gave in to the dark.

Is this what it's like to die?

Remy opened his eyes to look upon an eternal expanse of ocean, the color of copper and fire in the light of the sun hanging over the horizon.

He felt a sense of calm as he realized he had been to this place before.

"Is this it?" he asked, shifting in the beach chair so he could see the person sitting beside him, still as beautiful as she had been in life.

Madeline stared out at the ocean, her attention unwavering.

"Do you want it to be?" she asked.

"I . . . ," he began, then hesitated, letting his wife's question reverberate through his mind, surprised that he couldn't answer right away.

"Did you finish?"

He watched her as she continued her study of the ocean.

"What do you mean?" he finally asked.

Madeline turned her gaze to Remy, her dark sunglasses showing the twin reflections of the setting sun in their center as if they were her eyes. "Did you finish everything that you started?"

Again, he had to think about her question, the memories of what he'd left behind already starting to fade. It would have been so easy to just say yes, but he knew he would be telling another lie.

"I doubt it," he said sadly.

She nodded, smiling the way she always had, and he felt a love for her that was so great he was surprised his mortal form could contain it.

And then he remembered another woman who had managed to capture his heart after Madeline's devastating loss.

"Linda," he said quietly, fearing that speaking the name of another would somehow take away from the love he had shared with the woman sitting beside him.

"I bet you two would have told a wonderful story," Madeline said.

Remy held on to the memory of Linda, refusing to let it diminish—refusing to let her go. "Yeah" was all he could say.

"Yeah?" Madeline repeated, reaching out to let her fingertips caress his biceps.

"Yeah," Remy said again. "I'd like to tell that story."

Madeline smiled, and he knew that she was truly happy for him.

A sudden breeze came off the ocean then, a cold sharpness to the air that made him wince as he pulled his bare legs up from the sand. Remy gazed down and saw that he was bleeding. He'd forgotten that he had been hurt.

The sky above the ocean had grown dark, thick, roiling clouds blotting out the warmth of the sun.

"That's going to be a problem," Madeline said, her fingers still gently caressing the skin of his arm, which had now gone cold.

"It looks bad, doesn't it?" Remy said, staring at his wound, not quite remembering exactly what had happened.

"It's even worse on the inside," Madeline told him.

"Do I have a chance?" Remy asked, a sudden despondency washing over him.

Madeline returned her gaze to the ocean. The water was receding, exposing an ocean floor that resembled the surface of some alien world.

"That's not for me to say."

"Something's happening," he said, his body racked with pain as he too watched the sea pull away from the shore.

"He's coming."

There was a sound, far off in the distance, like the blast of a trumpet heralding the arrival of something great, but as Remy listened more closely he realized it was the sound of a giant wave as the ocean rushed back to meet the shore.

The wall of water came toward them with incredible speed, and he reached out, searching for his wife's hand, before—

The wave froze in place as his fingers wrapped around hers.

"What's happening?" Remy asked, eyes fixed on the wall of bluish green water before them.

"I told you He was coming," she whispered as she leaned in to kiss him warmly on the lips. "Your Father."

The water parted like a curtain, and an old man stepped out.

Remy gazed quickly to where his wife should have been but found that she had left him alone on the beach with a petrified ocean and an old man.

An old man.

Remy knew this man, dressed in His fine, dark suit. They had spoken on this very beach, not long ago, about a coming war.

"The war," Remy called out as he stood.

The old man, who was so much more than that, did not look at him, instead gazing off in the distance as if seeing something that Remy was not privy to.

"A horrible thing," He said.

"What are you saying?" Remy was confused. "The war hasn't happened."

The wall of water crashed to the sand behind the old man in a roaring rush that sent water and foam splashing through the air. But it did not touch the man. "Yes," He said, His gaze drifting toward Remy. "And no."

"I don't understand."

"In some instances it did happen, while in others . . ."

Remy still wasn't certain what He was going on about, but who was he to question his Father?

"So many worlds," the old man said. "I wish I could save them all."

"My world?" Remy asked, stepping closer. He could feel the power emanating from this being, and knew he should be on his knees with his head bowed in respect, but his concern was too great. He needed to know if his world was all right.

The old man looked Remy up and down, the hint of a smirk playing at the wrinkled corners of His mouth. Remy took a step back.

"A favorite," He said. "But on the brink."

A nearly overwhelming sense of panic washed over Remy . . . followed by the numbness. Once again, he found it difficult to remain standing and fell to his knees. "Please," he begged. "I need to help them."

The old man stared at him and Remy saw in His eyes an array of infinite possibilities.

And as he believed his question—his plea—was about to be granted, the old man turned His attention to the sky above. The clouds had grown thinner and the stars were beginning to shine down upon them.

"You need to see," He said wistfully. "You need to see what it will be like if you fail."

"Show me," Remy pleaded.

"It is a sad thing," the old man said, His voice quavering with emotion. "A tragic thing."

"Show me," Remy demanded.

The old man turned tear-filled eyes to Remy, extending a hand to gently cup the angel's face.

And Remy saw.

CHAPTER ONE

Time was standing still.

Linda Somerset was afraid to move as she sat, cradling her injured lover in the doorway to the living room of his Beacon Hill home.

What she had just seen—what she had just experienced—tested everything that she had always considered her reality. She was even afraid to breathe, afraid that the up and down of her chest would be enough to cause it all to break away.

Her entire world shattering like an old mirror.

But she had to breathe to live. Carefully, slowly, she exhaled, eyes darting about, watching for signs that the world was about to come apart.

And it stayed as it was.

For the moment, at least.

Linda took in a small, tremulous breath, not sure exactly what she expected to happen. Would there be the sound of something cracking as her world fell apart? Like a frozen lake on a late winter's afternoon, when the sun was at its strongest.

There was a moment of silence, and then the sound of a soft exhalation, followed by the most pathetic of whines. Linda jumped, remembering that she wasn't alone. Marlowe lay on the floor nearby, the black Labrador's brown, soulful eyes locked upon his master's still body.

Reality had remained in one piece after all.

Linda dared to look at Remy as she cradled him in her arms. There was blood on the front of his dress shirt, the expanding stain reminding her of the violence that had erupted in her lover's home.

She saw the fight in staccato images burned into her memory: Remy—her wonderful, handsome Remy—fighting a pale, horrible thing that seemed to have appeared out of nothingness. The memories were as clear as if the events were unfolding before her at that very moment.

But it was really just one particular sight that caused her to doubt her sanity.

Made her doubt her reality.

Maybe it had already fallen, insanity growing like some malignant vine, twisting the normal into something beyond comprehension.

Remy had had wings—powerful, golden wings. She had seen them as clear as day in the theatre of her mind's eye but still doubted their actuality.

Marlowe whined again and shoved his black snout beneath Remy's still hand, attempting to flip it so that Remy would pet him. But the hand just flopped back to the floor.

The Lab's sadness was palpable, and whether Linda believed in what she had just witnessed, Remy was injured, and she needed to help him.

She let his body slide gently to the wood floor, placing her hands on his face, struggling to remain in control of her emotions. His skin was cold and turning an unhealthy shade of gray. She could feel Marlowe's eyes watching her as she searched for signs of life.

"He's going to be all right," she told the dog as she jammed her fingers beneath the collar of Remy's shirt, desperate to find a pulse. "Don't do this to me," she said aloud, panic creeping in as she felt none. "Don't you dare!"

She'd had to take CPR classes when working as a waitress at Piazza and tried to remember what she'd been taught. She placed the heels of her hands, one atop the other, on the center of Remy's chest and began compressions.

Marlowe paced around her, vocalizing his concern.

"It's okay, buddy," she said, breathlessly, still pumping. "We're going to bring him back to us."

She stopped for a moment and checked again for a pulse. Still finding none, she reached into her back pocket for her phone to call 911—and found it empty.

"Fuck!" she screamed in frustration, turning toward the living room, where she had landed when Remy had thrown her inside. Her eyes scanned the room, landing on a small pile of crushed bone smoldering in a patch of sunlight that managed to creep from beneath the pulled shades. She thought of the pale-skinned attacker and the weapon he'd wielded. She remembered the feel of it shattering beneath her foot as she stomped down upon it.

It was real.

She recalled the ferocity of the battle, Remy holding on to his foe as his hands began to burn. And there was the black, oily stain where the pale man had died, eaten alive by the fire that had come from her lover's hands.

It was real.

Linda was suddenly dizzy, but the sound of Marlowe's whines as he licked Remy's ashen face spurred her on. She caught sight of the phone and lunged across the floor, snatching it up.

Just as Marlowe erupted. The dog stood over Remy, staring beyond the open door to the foyer, barking furiously, black hackles raised the length of his back and tail standing out stiffly from his body.

As if yet another threat was about to present itself.

Francis was in the basement apartment of the Newbury Street brownstone that he owned, trying to drown his anxieties in a tumbler of scotch and Sergio Leone's *Once Upon a Time in the West*. But he hadn't even made it to the introduction of Henry Fonda's reptilian villain, Frank, before being forced to switch the Blu-ray player off.

He couldn't banish the look from his mind—the expression of utter disappointment on Remy Chandler's face.

He'd tried to explain his actions to his friend, why he had joined with Heaven's angel elite to execute the offspring of Nephilim whores and archangel soldiers.

"I didn't have a choice," Francis had said. *"Part of the deal I made. He says, 'Jump,' and I ask how high."*

"And exactly how high can you jump, Francis?" Remy had retorted, wearing the look that now haunted Francis' memory.

It wasn't as if he had never disappointed Remy before; the former Guardian angel's penchant for violence had often been a bone of contention between the two friends.

But this time it was different. This time, Francis might have gone too far. He considered just leaving Remy alone, giving him a chance to work through his anger, and maybe in time, they would talk things through.

But the look in his friend's eyes had hurt so much more than harsh words or a knife to the kidney. This was something that Remy wouldn't let go; this was something that had altered their relationship forever.

Even though Francis was sure Remy had already put two and two together. How else could Francis have survived being trapped in a re-forming Hell, if the Morningstar hadn't saved him?

And for that save, Francis owed the former right hand of God and failed conqueror of Heaven. Where had the Almighty and all His angelic legions been as Francis lay dying upon a transforming, hellish landscape? Nowhere. It had been Lucifer who had found him—saved him—lifted him up and made him whole again.

What fucking choice had he had but to once again swear his allegiance to the Son of the Morning?

He'd known how it would go over with Remy, so he'd kept his mouth shut. There was no easy way he could ever have explained himself.

Dude, yeah, not sure if I mentioned this, but Lucifer is my new boss. Let me tell you about his kick-ass benefits package.

He could see that going over like a fart in an iron lung.

But Francis couldn't leave it alone, couldn't let what he had with the former Seraphim wither and die. As much as it killed him to admit it, their relationship meant something to Francis.

And that was why he had to talk to his friend now, whether Remy wanted to hear it or not. Francis was going to come clean about everything that had gone on and was going on.

Francis hoped it would be enough to get him back in Remy's good graces, but one never knew when dealing with the former soldier of

Heaven–turned–private investigator. He could be a little prickly sometimes.

Francis would just have to wait and see.

Wanting to get it over with as quickly as possible, the fallen Guardian angel stood and began to use one of the gifts that Lucifer had bestowed upon him—the ability to walk between realities, to go from here to there in a matter of seconds, even though his wings had long ago been taken from him. He thought of the foyer in Remy's Pinckney Street brownstone and stepped through the rip in the fabric of time as it opened before him.

Francis sensed it immediately; something bad had transpired in his friend's home, and not too long before his arrival, by the feel of it. Instinctively he reached for the Colt pistol inside his suit coat pocket.

A dog was barking ferociously nearby, and Francis recognized it as Remy's dog, Marlowe. One didn't need to be able to speak the language of beasts to know that the dog was upset.

The heavy wooden door into the hallway was wide-open, so Francis began to move toward the sound of the frantic animal, gun cocked and ready to fire. The atmosphere grew even more tainted, a negative energy electrifying the air, telling him that whatever had happened was bad.

Really bad.

But nothing could have prepared him for what he saw as he turned toward the living room.

"What the fuck?" he said aloud, bearing witness to his best friend lying on the floor, dog tensed protectively over him, and a woman, cell phone caught midway to her ear.

"Oh my God," cried the woman, whom Francis suddenly realized was Linda, the waitress from Piazza. "Are you the police?"

Ignoring her question, Francis dropped to his knees beside his downed friend, the pistol disappearing back inside his jacket. Marlowe growled as Francis reached to check Remy's vitals.

"It's all right, pal," Francis said, and the growl turned to a pathetic whine.

"I'm calling nine-one-one . . . ," Linda began.

"Put the fucking phone away," Francis snapped at her, and she recoiled as if slapped. He pressed his hand against Remy's throat. The coldness of the flesh beneath his fingertips and the widening stain on the front of Remy's shirt told him all that he needed to know.

"Give me the abridged version," Francis barked, ripping open his friend's shirt, sending buttons in every direction.

"He was attacked. . . . We were attacked . . . ," Linda stammered.

"By who?" Francis asked, eyes upon the strange injuries.

"It was some sort of . . . thing," she said, trying to find more words but failing miserably.

Francis looked up at her and followed her gaze to a pile of what appeared to be bones smoldering on a greasy stain in the corner. "Is this it?" He sprang up from Remy's side toward the bone pile. "Is this what's left of the thing that attacked you? Did Remy do this?" he asked as he knelt before the remains.

"Yes." Linda nodded furiously. "He did that before . . ."

There wasn't much time. Francis reached for what was left of the creature's skull. There were still bits of skin attached, and he hoped that there might be enough inside its brainpan to read.

From inside his coat, Francis removed a knife with a blade so thin it looked as though it might be able to cut between molecules. Linda was watching him, wide-eyed, and he wondered if he was going to lose her as he positioned the blade above the skull and brought it down with great force, puncturing the skull, like a straw into a juice box.

It wasn't going to be pretty, but he needed to know.

A brief blast of foul-smelling steam escaped into the atmosphere, and Francis wrinkled his nose in disgust.

But the knife found what it was seeking, as it sank into what remained of the attacker's brain, drawing up information and feeding it to Francis in a series of staccato images. In a matter of seconds, he knew about the demonic assassins known as the Bone Masters, how they'd been contracted to kill Remy Chandler . . .

. . . and how they had hoped to use the angel's female to lure him into the open.

Francis pulled the knife from the skull, gazing at Linda, who returned his stare with deer-in-the-headlights eyes.

The angel's female?

CHAPTER TWO

The Old Man had done something—sent Remy to someplace, someplace where he could see the price of his failure.

It had been like falling into a hole, the darkness so all-encompassing that it became the world, and the distance so deep and far that he forgot he was falling.

Until he hit bottom.

Remy landed in an explosion of pain. The world of cold primal darkness that had been with him for what seemed like an eternity was replaced with a jarring agony. From his internal workings, to his bones, to his every joint, muscle, tendon, and ligament—everything was screaming.

A painful reminder that he was still alive—

And under attack.

Remy opened his eyes, and immediately knew that he was in another place—*another reality,* familiar yet strangely different. Winged forms flew above him in a gray, smoke-filled sky. *Angels,* he thought, watching one of the shapes bank sharply to the left, wings spread to their full impressive span as it glided down at a breakneck pace.

But questions of where he was and what was happening would have to wait, for a hissing gout of flame rocketed toward him from the sky. Remy reacted even though his body cried in protest. He rolled across the rubble-strewn ground as the miniature comet struck mere inches from where he'd been, melting the surroundings to glass.

A spark of divine fire landed on the sleeve of his coat, the heavy material beginning to burn as the holy flame sought out the soft flesh beneath. Remy slapped at the fire before it could grow any hungrier, and what he saw on the back of his hand chilled him to the bone.

A tattoo of some kind appeared to be permanently inscribed upon his flesh. He did not know what the mark was or how it had gotten there, but could sense that it was a sigil of some long-forgotten power.

"Move your ass or you're toast!" commanded a gruff, almost animal-sounding voice from somewhere close by. Remy didn't have an opportunity to find the source of the command, but he did what he was told as spears of fire hurtled toward him.

Incendiary blasts struck all around him as he darted and weaved about the blighted landscape. So intent was he on avoiding the Heavenly fire that he did not see the body smoldering on the ground before him, and he tripped, falling onto his stomach, the air punched from his lungs as he hit. Scrambling to rise, he glanced at the corpse, recognizing the dead man as one of Samson's children, somehow knowing that the Biblical strongman and his brood had once again come to his aid despite the near certainty of catastrophic failure.

The air was filled with acrid smoke and the heavy, dusty smell of something . . . *familiar*. It was that intimate aroma that froze him in place. *It can't be. How is this possible?* he thought, his mind racing as he tried to process the overwhelming flow of information into his already addled brain.

An angel dropped from the sky, its powerful wings kicking up clouds of dust and dirt as it touched down before Remy. He stared, hypnotized by the creature he would once have called brother. It was covered in a thick coating of black ash, with fish-belly white skin peeking out from cracks in the filthy covering, but it was its eyes that told Remy a story he did not care to hear. The eyes were filled with madness, what divinity had once pulsed through its holy body having long since fled.

He wanted to ask it what had happened, what horrors had occurred to make it this way, but Remy knew that it was about to kill him.

Twin daggers with blades as black as the soot that covered its body appeared in the angel's hands, and it lunged at Remy, eager to vent his body to the outside world.

Remy tensed the muscles in his back, wishing his wings into existence to evade the blades—

And nothing happened.

He did not have time to ponder this latest insanity. The filthy angel screeched something unintelligible as it thrust with one of the knives. Remy managed to leap back, the edge of the blade catching the front of his shirt and slicing across his belly.

The angel cried out as the scent of Remy's blood perfumed the acrid air. The other blade was eagerly coming around for more of the same. This time, Remy caught the angel's wrist and twisted it back behind it, pulling up savagely until the sounds of snapping bone and sinew mixed with the angel's cries of pain.

The knife fell to the ash-covered ground, and Remy snatched it up. The blade felt wrong in his grip, as if the weapon did not care to be held by anyone other than its owner. The intense burning sensation came next, causing Remy to drop the black-bladed knife to the ground as he gazed at the blistered flesh of his palm.

The angel started to cackle as it came at Remy again, still gripping the other knife, one arm now useless and dangling at its side. On reflex, Remy again called upon his wings, and again he could not summon them. The horror of his new reality grew even more oppressive as he braced himself for the angel's further assault.

Something huge and incredibly fast suddenly moved past Remy in a blur, landing upon the angel and driving it back to the dirt. The air became filled with the sounds of growls and screams of pain, which grew louder and more intense until silenced as the monstrosity standing upon the angel's blackened chest tore away its throat.

Remy stared with equal parts wonder and horror at the great beast that had taken the angel. Two sets of memories—the old and the new—struggled for supremacy, and he thought his skull might split.

The beast's body was huge, the size of a great jungle cat, with short, black fur covered in filth. The color tickled his memory, and he remembered a part of his life filled with the love and loyalty of an animal named . . .

It spun its large square head around to face him, its muzzle shiny with the blood of the once divine.

"Marlowe," Remy said aloud as he looked into the face of the demonic hound.

"What did you call me?" the animal asked, its fleshy lip peeling back in a ferocious snarl. "You're never to call me that!"

And that was when Remy felt it all slide out from beneath him, his brain unable to handle it anymore, deciding that this would be the right time to shut it all down—

To drop the curtain.

To fade to black.

Heaven had the most distinctive of smells.

Everything else Remy had experienced since leaving the Golden City paled in comparison to the scents of Paradise.

Madeline had once asked him what it was like to be in Heaven. At first, he'd been speechless, unable to find words suitable for the human mind to comprehend.

"Okay, we'll make this easier," she'd said. *"What's it smell like?"*

And he'd given it a shot.

"You know how you feel when you walk past a bakery and smell the freshly baked bread, or that delicious aroma of a home-cooked meal, or even the wonder of a freshly brewed pot of coffee?"

He recalled Madeline's magnificent smile.

"Imagine all the wonderful feelings and sensations created by those awesome scents." He'd paused, watching to see if she was doing just that, and the twinkle in her eye had told him she was. *"All right, now multiply all those feelings by a million, and then a million more, and then a hundred million more."*

She'd told him that it must be wonderful.

And he'd remembered that it was—before the war, before he had abandoned his place of creation.

He'd told her that, and then they had made love with a passion far more intense than ever before, almost as if she was attempting to sate a hunger that could never be satisfied, and he trying to recapture a taste of what he'd abandoned so very long ago.

But all it had done was remind them each of what they would never have.

Now, deep in the darkness, Remy was again reminded of the glories he had left behind, the distant memories stirred by an all-too-familiar aroma.

Even deep within the clutches of unconsciousness, he could smell Heaven. The scent had caught him off guard as he'd tried to defend himself against his angelic attacker. Although tainted by other, more pungent odors, such as fear and despair, at the core of it all, Heaven was there.

Drifting in the air, Heaven was there.

The smell drew him up from the darkness, where he became aware of a strange stinging sensation in his lower body. He gasped, snapping his eyes open to the most insane of sights. The giant doglike animal stood by Remy's side, his monstrous head lowered to Remy's bare midsection, a tongue as thick as Remy's forearm lapping languidly at his stomach.

"What the Hell?" Remy managed.

The beast stopped licking, and his massive tongue returned to his mouth.

"You're awake," he growled. "About fucking time."

The dog moved away from him, dropping his enormous bulk to the ground with a heavy sigh.

Remy looked down at his stomach, at where the dog had been licking.

"What the fuck were you doing?" he asked, touching the tender spot with his fingers. It was still wet and quite sticky, with a nasty stink coming from the area.

"I'll let you die from infection next time," the monster dog said indignantly. "Believe me, the taste of your pus is not something that I enjoy." The beast put his large face down between equally enormous paws. "And fuck you very much."

Remy then noticed the additional tattoos, across the taut muscles of his stomach, snaking up his sides and down his bare arms.

"When did I . . . ," he began, struggling to decipher the meaning of the markings but coming up with nothing.

"When did you what?" the beast asked, watching him with curious, blood-tinted eyes. "The sigils? What, did you bang your head or something?"

Remy remembered his wings, or lack thereof. He twisted his head so he might see where they should have been. "My wings. What's happened to my wings?"

"Your wings?" The dog rose to all fours and cautiously approached. Remy could see the animal's coppery hackles rising as he sniffed at him. "Are you all right? Maybe that blast took more out of you than I thought."

Remy almost asked about the blast—what exactly had happened— but decided to wait. "I'm fine," he said instead, getting up from the blanket he was lying on. He could see he was inside a tent, and he was suddenly desperate to head outside for a look at the world in which he now found himself. A world whose very atmosphere smelled of Heaven.

He found a shirt in a pile on the floor next to him. It was torn and bloodied, but he put it on anyway.

"You don't seem fine," the great dog said, continuing to study him.

Remy was saved from replying as the flap of the tent lifted and a dark, bearded man stepped inside. Remy knew at once the man was also a son of Samson.

"What is it?" the demon dog asked.

"You need to see this," the man said, ducking back outside.

"Stay here," the dog ordered Remy as he pushed his massive bulk through the flap and outside.

Remy followed, ignoring the command.

The sky was filled with billowing gray clouds that roiled and moved through the air like protozoa viewed from beneath a microscope lens, and Remy wasn't sure if it was day or night.

The camp appeared to have been set up somewhere inside the crag of a mountain, the edge of the encampment looking down onto a sprawling and unfamiliar desert landscape. But it was the sight beyond the desert that sent a deep, icy chill down the length of Remy's spine, for now he knew why the air was filled with the scents of his former home.

In the distance were shapes that at first glance seemed to be another great mountain range, but the longer he looked upon them, the more familiar they became.

The reason the air of this place was filled with the smells of Heaven was obvious, for it was Heaven—or at least a portion of it—that Remy saw sprawling across the landscape far off in the distance.

It seemed that Heaven had fallen from the sky.

CHAPTER THREE

The angel's woman.

The words were like a spear to the heart. It was Francis who had first noticed the attractive waitress named Linda Somerset, notice that had quickly transformed into a kind of obsession with the woman. That had been totally unlike him. Sure, he'd had human women over the centuries, but, with the exception of Eliza Swan, they'd been little more than playthings.

Linda Somerset was the first woman he had taken note of since Eliza, and he had even gone out of his way to point her out to his friend Remy Chandler.

Francis suddenly felt an odd sense of anger and betrayal wash over him as he looked down on the body of someone he'd thought had been his friend. *What the fuck were you thinking?*

But he would never get the chance to ask that question if he didn't move quickly. Francis could barely sense the presence of the Seraphim's life force. It wasn't much, but it gave him hope.

"He's alive," Francis said to the woman. "But I'm not sure for how much longer."

"We have to do something," Linda said. "We can't just let him die."

"No, we can't," Francis said, pushing past his tumultuous emotions.

"What are we going to do?" Linda asked, panic in her eyes. "Is there someplace we can take him . . . somebody we can call?"

Somebody we can call.

Francis rose to his feet, taking his cell phone from his pants pocket. He scrolled through his contacts, looking for the number he hadn't used in quite some time.

Physician.

He touched the number and put the phone to his ear, listening as an answering machine picked up.

"This is Francis . . . Fraciel," he added, using his divine name just in case. "Call me back. It's a bit of an emergency . . . a matter of life and death. Thanks."

He hung up, turning to look at Linda, who was now sitting beside Remy, gently brushing the hair from his face, her gaze filled with love and sorrow. Francis felt a wave of anger and jealousy begin to rise within him and quickly tamped it down. Now wasn't the time for this.

"Who did you call?" Linda asked.

"Someone who can help," Francis replied, knowing that time was of the essence and hoping that a return call would come.

Before it was too late.

His true name was Assiel, but he hadn't been called that in a very long time.

Darnell rhythmically dragged the broom over the old linoleum floor, picking up the wisps of dust that had formed since he'd last swept the hallway of Five South.

To anyone who was watching, it appeared that Darnell—*Assiel*—was just doing his job, keeping the floors clean at Saint Joseph's Nursing Home, but in fact, he was listening, attuned to all two hundred and thirty-two residents. Darnell knew every man and woman who called this place home. He knew their aches and their pains, and he knew when it was time for them to abandon their deteriorating shells and rejoin the source of all things.

It was quiet here on Five South, the nursing home's hospice unit. There were seven residents on the floor, all at various stages of dying, but one was closer than the others, and she called to him now.

Candace Ransley did not ring a bell or call out his name, but she summoned him just the same.

Darnell stopped outside her room and glanced down the hall to see if the nurse or any of the aides were watching, and, finding that they were otherwise occupied, he stepped in.

It was dark in the room, the curtains drawn to keep the sun away. The strains of fifties doo-wop played softly from a radio on the night-stand. Candace loved doo-wop. She'd often asked Darnell if he'd listened to it as a child where he'd come from—he'd told the residents that he was an immigrant from Nigeria. Occasionally he wondered if those he looked out for here—his patients—would have been in any way comforted to know where he really came from.

Many of them believed in a Heaven, but the reality might not have been as comforting as they wanted to believe.

The war was never far from Darnell's mind, the atrocities he'd seen—and participated in—always there to remind him of his fall from grace. But he had paid the price for his betrayal of the Almighty, first serving time in the hellish prison of Tartarus, and now the remainder of his penance amongst humanity, where he hoped to do some good.

And eventually be allowed to once again bask in the glorious light of the Creator.

But did the Heaven that Darnell remembered even exist anymore?

He stood at the foot of Candace's bed, clutching his broom, listening to the sound of her labored breathing. As he watched her, he could see how far her sickness—cancer of the lungs—had progressed. It would only be a matter of minutes before her physical form finally broke down and ceased to function.

Minutes normally plagued by pain, fear, and loneliness.

Normally.

Are you ready, Candace? Darnell thought. *Ready to leave this moldering shell and join with the stuff of creation?*

Her eyes slowly opened, and she looked at him. In response, he allowed her to see him.

To truly see him.

She watched him with tear-filled eyes as he moved around the side of the bed and placed his hand above her chest, his thoughts urging her to not be afraid. Beneath the cancer he saw what the Lord God had given her and all the others that made up humanity: a spark of the divine.

A piece of Himself.

And, wearing the guise of Assiel, Darnell performed the task assigned to him as a healer. He drew the fire of life that humanity called the soul up from beneath the mire of sickness and out of the frail, rotting husk that could no longer sustain it.

Candace sighed as the spark left her, and then she was still, a look of contentment upon her once pained features.

Assiel held the flame in his palm, a part of him not wanting to let it go. Of all the things that the Lord of Lords had given His human creations, this was what Assiel coveted the most.

This was what had so long ago swayed him to the beliefs of Lucifer Morningstar.

He watched the fire dance above the palm of his hand, holding it there with his will. What an amazing gift He had given them.

Candace's soul felt the pull of the source upon it and began to panic, struggling to be free of his will. Slowly he released his hold upon it, watching as the flame leapt from his palm to disappear in a flash, leaving the material world to join with the Angel of Death, and eventually the stuff of inception.

Assiel returned to his human guise, taking one more long look at the empty casing that had once held something so wonderful before leaving the room as a song about a teen angel serenaded Candace Ransley's corpse.

Outside the room, Darnell began to casually sweep again, working his way back up the hallway.

"Hey, Darnell," a young nursing assistant greeted as she passed him on her way to Candace's room.

He smiled and nodded, counting the seconds until she left the room in a hurry, rushing by him to the desk to report what she had found.

After using a dustpan to pick up what he had swept, Darnell wheeled the gray barrel past the nurses' station to the elevators. It would be quitting time soon, and he would return to his residence and to the other patients whom he had acquired in the tenement where he'd chosen to live.

Mr. Daron was quite close, and Darnell wondered if tonight might be the night.

As he waited for the elevator, he took out his cell phone and saw that there was a message. He wasn't supposed to use his cell on the units, but curiosity got the better of him, and he punched in the code for his voice mail.

The doors to the elevator opened before him as a familiar voice spoke in his ear. It was Francis—Fraciel, to those who had known him in another time.

"Have a good night, Darnell," the nurse called out as he stepped into the elevator and pushed the button for the lower level.

He managed a smile, but it quickly dissipated as soon as the doors slid shut.

A good night? He seriously doubted it, if Francis was to be any part of it.

The Archangel Michael lay upon the cold stone floor of the mountain monastery, pieces of his divine armor strewn, twisted and bent, about him, glistening like dew in the cold Eastern European sun.

It had come upon him so quickly, lifting him up with such force that he had not had the opportunity to react, the intensity of the interaction stripping the armor from his body. He lay there, naked in his human form, his perfectly muscled body shivering.

It took the archangel some time to recalibrate, to remember where he had been and what he had been doing. He had been contemplating his place in the world of man and had concluded that his legions were needed here. Even though there now existed a binding treaty, he suspected that the Morningstar would soon find a way to further exert his will upon the Earth.

And Michael, in service to God and Heaven, would have none of that.

He had been considering his options when the Almighty reached out to him.

It had been too long since he and the Lord God had last communicated, and he had forgotten the intensity of such interaction. One moment he had been there, in the abandoned holy sanctuary, and the next, he'd been violently torn from reality and in the Presence.

In *His* presence.

The memory of what he'd just endured caused his tremors to worsen, and for a moment he felt a kindred spirit with the holy men and saints of old who had lived in this monastery, imagining that this was how they must have felt when they received His blessed word.

Using the ancient stone wall for support, he slowly rose to his feet, collecting his wits as he steadied himself. The archangel wove a suit of clothing from the elements in the air to cover his bedraggled body. But it did not stop his trembling, for it was not only the experience that wreaked such havoc upon him, it was the message that had been delivered.

Michael suddenly realized he was no longer alone but surrounded by the legion of archangels that served him, who were watching him with dark, curious eyes.

It was his second in command, Satquiel, who finally had the courage to approach. "Master?"

Michael braced himself and turned to face his second.

"He has spoken, Satquiel." The reverence in his tone was enough to drive his legion to their knees with bowed heads.

"And what did He say, my master?" Satquiel asked, eyes averted to the stone floor of the monastery chamber. "What has He asked of us?"

Michael could not speak the words. They were jagged and sharp in his throat, threatening to cut and render him speechless as they were uttered.

After a time, Satquiel raised his head to look upon his commander, eyes questioning his superior's state.

Michael wrestled with the message, his mouth attempting to wrap around the malevolent words, afraid to set them free.

"The Lord God commands," Michael finally began, his booming voice so loud in the enclosed room that it shook bits of loose mortar from the walls. But he continued to struggle, fighting the words that he had been charged to proclaim.

"What does He command, Michael?" Satquiel urged, his eagerness a balm, drawing the malignant words from Michael's mouth. "Tell us."

"That we forgive," Michael stated at last. The words took his strength as they spilled from his mouth, and he dropped to the floor.

"Who, Michael? Who does the Almighty wish us to forgive?"

The name left his mouth like a stream of noxious bile.

"The Morningstar," Michael stated, feeling a bit of himself begin to wither and die. "We are to forgive Lucifer Morningstar."

Simeon remembered how he'd first come to entrap the angel.

He'd been attending the wake of one of his children sometime in the early forties. It had been late summer in the South, and the heat had been terrible.

He recalled the image of his son lying puffy in his quilted casket, one of the hundreds of children he had sired as he'd wandered the planet pretending to be a part of humanity. This one had lived close to ninety years, according to the undertaker who'd greeted Simeon at the door.

Simeon hadn't told the dark-suited man who he actually was, for he looked no older than thirty years, thanks to the touch of that accursed Son of God. He'd chosen instead to say that he was just a friend from a very long time ago.

He had known next to nothing about this child of his, not even the mother, but sensing the death of something that had once been a part of him had drawn the forever man there.

How many times had he done something similar to this, bemoaning the fact that something that he'd had a part in creating was no more, and at the same time jealous that they'd had the opportunity to leave the world behind, to escape the confines of Earth and join with the Creator in eternity.

Something that had long been denied him.

As he'd stood above the coffin, staring into the face of the dead man, he'd felt the atmosphere in the room change, as if something of great power had been drawn to his moment of woefulness.

"Who's there?" Simeon had demanded. He'd turned toward the back of the viewing room, where the air seemed to shimmer, and touched the rings that he wore on each hand—one giving him power over the demonic, the other the angelic. "Show yourself."

"That's it," the forever man had said, practically giddy as the angel of Heaven took shape, ensnared by the power of the ring. "Don't waste your strength. Solomon was very thorough with the magick he employed." And Simeon had held up his right hand, showing off the silver ring that adorned his finger, the one that gave him control over God's winged messengers.

The angel had continued to struggle, attempting to disappear from view, but the magick of the ring kept him there.

"Why are you here?"

"I was drawn to your emotion," the angel spoke haltingly, as if trying not to speak, but the words forced their way out anyway.

"My emotion?" Simeon had begun to pace amongst the chairs that had been set up for those who would come to pay their respects.

"I have never sensed anguish so vast," the angel had said. "Sorrow so deep. It drew me to you."

Simeon remembered smiling with little humor. "Let's say I've had ample time to accrue more than my fill."

The angel had looked at him strangely then, tilting his head in that birdlike fashion they had a tendency to do. The Heavenly creature had yet to realize what he was actually dealing with.

"And you came to me to do what exactly?" Simeon had asked. "Soothe a troubled nature with a divine touch upon my furrowed brow?"

"I certainly could bring you some peace—yes," the angel had agreed.

Simeon had laughed, a short barking sound. "It would take far more than that to assuage my tortured feelings," he'd said with a snarl. "In fact, I doubt that all in Heaven could quench my wrath."

He had walked toward the angel then, weaving his way through the chairs, feeling the rage growing within him—a rage that could never be satisfied. For he had been denied the joy of Heaven, had had it painfully snatched away as he was returned to a life eternal by the touch of the holy man from Nazareth.

"I am an emissary of God; let me help you . . . ," the angel had stammered.

But Simeon had simply raised a hand, cutting off the angel's words. "Bleed for me," he'd said.

The angel had tilted his head left, then right. "I don't . . ."

"Bleed for me," Simeon had repeated, putting the power of Solomon's ring behind each word.

The angel had struggled, but it was all for naught. The winged messenger of God extended one of his long, muscular arms, pulling back the diaphanous sleeve of his shirt to expose the pale, marblelike flesh, his gaze begging the forever man to reconsider.

But what would have been the fun in that?

Reaching across with his other hand, the angel had begun to dig the razor-sharp nails on his fingers into the exposed arm, grimacing as he ripped bloody furrows in the bare white skin.

"Isn't that something," Simeon had said, placing his hand beneath the drips of blood raining down from the wounds.

"Why?" the angel had asked pathetically.

And again, Simeon had given him that humorless smile, recalling a similar question he himself had asked of the Son of God so very long ago.

"To show that I could."

A sound from the entrance to the room had distracted them then, and Simeon had turned to see the undertaker standing there.

"I thought I heard voices in here," the middle-aged man had said, not yet noticing that he was in the presence of the divine.

Simeon watched his face, waiting for it to sink in.

"Oh my," the undertaker had said dreamily, his eyes fixed upon the winged being.

"Be not afraid." The angel's voice had sounded like the first notes of the most beautiful of songs.

"Oh no," Simeon had said, his gaze going from the angel to the undertaker. "I think he should be afraid." He'd strode over to the man, raised his hand, and wiped the blood of an angel on the undertaker's cheeks.

The man had simply stood there, stunned beyond movement. "Please . . . ," he'd managed.

Simeon looked back to the angel. "You heard the man," he'd said. "He's begging you."

The angel had tensed, his wings flapping furiously as he'd tried to shrug off the spell that had hold of him.

"Do it," Simeon had commanded. "Kill him."

And the angel had flown across the room, pouncing upon the defenseless undertaker, tearing him apart in a show of preternatural strength.

That was the beginning of a beautiful friendship between Simeon and Satquiel.

A friendship that had continued to this day.

"To what do I owe this unexpected visit?" Simeon asked the angel Satquiel, crossing his legs as he reclined comfortably in the wingback leather chair. He held a snifter of brandy, moving his wrist in such a way that the caramel-colored liquid swirled about, coating the inside of the glass.

The angel stood before the large window that looked out onto one of the Vatican's many gardens, this particular one devoted to roses of every imaginable color.

Simeon's associates in the Vatican had given him this office study to think and to collect his thoughts. If only they realized how hard he was trying to destroy everything that they believed in, but for now what they didn't know wouldn't hurt them.

"The Lord God has spoken," Satquiel said, arms crossed behind his back as he looked rigidly out upon the rose garden.

"Has He now?" Simeon said, taking a sip of his brandy. "And, pray tell, what did the supreme being have to say?"

Satquiel appeared to grow even more uncomfortable, his body twitching uneasily.

"Michael has received a special message from the Lord God," Satquiel said, turning his head from the garden view. He appeared to be concentrating on a patch of deep shadow in the corner of the room, near the floor-to-ceiling bookcases.

"Go on, Satquiel," Simeon urged as he turned the ring of Solomon on his right finger, wanting to distract the angel from the pool of darkness.

The angel turned, visibly shaken by what he was about to relate. Simeon leaned forward in his chair, ready to hear.

"Lucifer Morningstar," Satquiel said, his voice trembling.

"Yes?"

"The Morningstar is to be forgiven his indiscretions," Satquiel at last said, the words spilling from his mouth like vomit.

"The deuce you say," Simeon reacted, slowly bringing his drink to his mouth and draining the remainder of its contents in one gulp.

"Rather than involve the forces of Heaven and Hell in another war that would most assuredly spill over to Earth and humanity, the Almighty has decreed that the Son of the Morning be exonerated from his crimes against Heaven."

Simeon reclined farther into the chair, the gears inside his brain already beginning to turn, the repercussions of this decree immense.

"My, my, my," Simeon said, the scenarios that he was imagining too numerous to count.

"Michael," Simeon stated, capturing Satquiel's attention.

"Yes, what about him?"

"How is the archangel taking the news?"

"The Creator has spoken. The Archangel Michael, as well as us all, will bathe in the glory that has been bestowed upon us with His holy words and prepare to carry out that which has been—"

"How is Michael doing?" Simeon asked.

Satquiel's posture sagged. "Not well at all," he said.

"Wouldn't think so. Can't even imagine God's number one commander against the forces of evil kissing and making up with the adversary. Ouch." Simeon paused, continuing to let the information wash over him. "Poor bastard. Must be so hard for him . . . hard for you all, really."

"You have no idea," Satquiel said. "But God has spoken. We have no choice . . ."

"I get it, and there's that whole working-in-mysterious-ways thing He's known for."

The angel stood before him, the troubles that he'd just related appearing to have taken their physical toll upon the divine creature.

"It is for the good of us all."

Simeon smiled. "Of course it is," he said. "That's what a loving God is all about."

Tired of the angel, and wanting to think further about the situation, Simeon ordered Satquiel away.

Needing another brandy, he rose from his chair, approaching the bar in one of the room's other corners to help himself.

"Did you hear?" Simeon asked as he poured.

He looked toward the patch of darkness where the angel's attention had been drawn earlier. The black moved like liquid, and a shape, followed by three others, emerged to join him in the study.

Constantin Malatesta stood just outside the shadow, while Simeon's three demon lackeys moved to the opposite side of the room.

"The sound was a bit distorted within the shadow," the Keeper agent of the Vatican said. "Did he actually say that God is ready to forgive Lucifer?"

Simeon could not help himself and began to giggle. No matter how long he lived this wretched existence, the unexpected happenings of the day never ceased to amaze him.

"He did," the forever man answered, taking a sip from his fresh glass of brandy.

"Perhaps there's hope for us all, then," Malatesta said, suddenly doubling over in pain as the thing that lived inside of him—the Larva—again tested the constraints of his body.

"Hope isn't something that the infernal really care to hear about," Simeon told him.

Beleeze, Dorian, and Robert watched in amusement as the Vatican sorcerer struggled with the diabolical entity that had possessed him since childhood. Simeon's demonic helpers didn't really care for the newest addition to their dysfunctional family and enjoyed his suffering whenever possible.

Malatesta slowly straightened and from the look upon his face Simeon could see that the Larva had once again regained a modicum of control.

"Personally I've always believed hope to be overrated," the Vatican magick user said, his words tainted by the malevolence of the demonic parasite. "It's so easily taken away."

The Larva smiled behind the mask of Constantin Malatesta.

"So here's the question," Simeon then proposed, the wheels inside his mind spinning even faster, tossing off sparks of fire that only served to ignite more thoughts on the situation. "How do we best use this to our advantage?"

CHAPTER FOUR

Something moved in the sky above the ruins in the distance.

It writhed like smoke, rising up from the crumbled citadels and towers, but it did not drift as smoke would upon the heavy winds that moved across the bleak desert landscape. It collected en masse, like a swarm of locusts, flying over the desert, heading toward the mountain.

"We need to get out of sight," the demon dog announced.

Samson's son was instantly on the move, the dog right behind him, using his large paws to pull down the tent.

"Must have been another scout we didn't see. We'll head to the caves and hold up there until the Filthies get tired of looking for us," the dog said, his paws far more dexterous than Remy would have believed.

Filthies.

The word exploded in his brain, images like jagged pieces of shrapnel tearing through soft tissue, memories flowing like blood as he turned his eyes to the dark, living cloud spreading over the desert toward them.

Remy blinked away the nightmarish vision to see the great demon beast staring inquisitively.

"What the fuck is wrong with you?" the beast asked.

"Those are angels," he said, squinting his eyes, now able to see the twisted mockeries of something once divine as they approached, their disease-ridden wings beating the dust-filled air. "What happened to them?"

The dog stiffened as he stared at him.

"What do you mean, what happened to them?" the demon hound asked gruffly. "*This* happened to them." The dog looked around at their blighted surroundings. "The world is fucked, and so are they. Are you sure that you're all right?"

Remy knew that to answer truthfully would have added another wrinkle, so he decided to play it safe and keep his mouth shut until he had a better idea of what was going on.

"I'm good," he said, the swarm of Filthies even closer now. "We should get to the caves."

The dog hesitated, but only a moment, then spun his muscular body toward a rocky incline. "Take the tent," he ordered over his shoulder.

Remy snatched up the pieces of the disassembled tent and followed the animal down an embankment where others of Samson's brood were quickly heading toward a mountain wall, surrounded by some heavy brush. As he drew closer, Remy saw the jagged crack that resembled a bolt of lightning. He was the last to enter, careful on the unstable, rocky terrain down into the earth. The passage grew uncomfortably smaller as it reached another crack that bisected a wall of stone and led into a much larger chamber.

Remy's head buzzed with what he had just seen above, the bizarreness of this unfamiliar world wreaking havoc on his perceptions of reality. Was this all some sort of twisted hallucination, or was it—as he suspected—something far, far worse?

Setting the tent down upon the ground, he turned toward the gathering, searching for the demon dog, when he was struck savagely from behind, driving him to the floor of the cave.

Remy found himself gazing up into the sneering face of the dog, his eyes blazing as if LEDs had been placed inside his large blocky skull.

"The smell is just a little off. . . . So is the taste," the dog growled, bearing his tremendous weight down upon Remy's chest as he lowered his snout closer. "Almost began to think it was just me, but then I saw the look on your face when you saw the Filthies swarm, like you'd never seen such things before."

The dog's breath was awful, and saliva dribbled from the corners of his mouth onto the Seraphim.

"So who the fuck are you . . . and why shouldn't I eat your face for deceiving us?"

Francis could feel the intensity of Marlowe's eyes upon him as he knelt beside his friend, the dog's gaze pleading for him to do something—*anything*—to bring his master back.

"I'm working on it, pal," Francis said, looking away from Remy's pallid face and into the Labrador's deep brown eyes. Marlowe whined mournfully, moving closer to where Remy lay, the side of his black muzzle now pressed to Remy's cheek.

Francis knew at once what the dog was doing, the physical contact perhaps allowing Marlowe to share some of his strength with that of his master. It was as good an idea as any, Francis thought as he reached down to take hold of Remy's hand.

Linda appeared in the doorway, arms filled with pillows and a blanket she'd retrieved from the bedroom upstairs. "Is he . . ."

"The same," Francis said. "Marlowe and I are just trying to help him out is all."

"This will make him a bit more comfortable," she said, kneeling beside Marlowe, gently lifting Remy's head, and sliding two pillows beneath. She shook the blanket out over him and then knelt there for a bit, watching him. "I feel like I should be doing something, but I don't . . ."

She started to cry again but sucked it up, wiping the tears away.

"This is fine." Francis tried to calm her. "All we can do is wait and hope the physician gets back to us soon." Just in case, he pulled his phone out again and checked for messages. There were none.

The silence in the room was deafening, and he felt his flesh begin to squirm, his muscles twitch, desperate for action—any action. Francis was used to dealing with things in a more physical fashion, but his predilection for violence had no place here.

He was about to look at his phone again, just for something to do, but Linda interrupted.

"He's an . . . angel," she stated, appearing to have some difficulty getting the last word out.

"He is," Francis confirmed. "A Seraphim, to be exact."

"From Heaven . . . He's an angel from Heaven that has come to Earth."

"It's a little more complicated than that, but yeah, basically that's it."

"And you're an angel?" she asked, watching him with a combination of fear and fascination.

"Yeah, but I'm of the fallen variety."

"I thought that fallen angels were bad."

"Who said I'm not?" The admission stirred more emotion in Francis than he would have expected after all this time. "I made some bad decisions a long time ago, and I'm paying for them now."

"Is Remy fallen, too?" she asked, reaching out to gently run her fingers through his hair.

"Not at all," Francis said, impressed with this woman. Most humans would have been quivering in a pool of their own piss by now. "Remy is one of the good guys. He came here by choice—couldn't quite stomach the politics after the war and was looking for some peace and quiet."

"The war?"

"The legions of God against the Morningstar and his armies."

"The Morningstar," she repeated, the meaning starting to sink in. "You mean like the Devil. . . . He's real?"

"Of course he's real," Francis said, unable to keep the irritation from his tone. "Why is it that you can accept that he . . . that we're angels of Heaven, but not the existence of Lucifer?"

"I don't know," she said, shrugging her shoulders. "Wishful thinking?"

"If it makes you feel any better, organized religion has had a field day with his story. Responsible for all the evil in the world? Not even close," Francis explained. "Sure, there were some pretty heavy doings with the Big Man upstairs, but very little fallout ever made it here to Earth."

"But the Bible says . . ."

"The Bible says a lot of things, but not much of it is all that accurate."

Linda looked as though she'd been slapped.

"Look," Francis said. "The Bible was written by a bunch of guys trying to explain what they understood of God's glory and the ills of the world. It's a helluva lot easier explaining why a guy would slaughter twenty innocent people in a McDonald's when there's a supreme boogeyman to lay the blame on."

"I guess that makes sense," Linda said.

"Happy to set things right for you."

"You say that he's one of the good guys," Linda said after a moment, looking down at Remy again. "I knew it the first time I met him. . . . It just came off him in waves. I didn't know how to describe it at the time; I just knew I'd be safe with him . . . that he would protect me." The tears started again, pouring from her eyes to spatter upon the floor beside Remy's head. "Who's going to do that now?" she asked, looking imploringly at Francis. He was about to tell her that he would gladly do that for her, but then his phone vibrated.

"Is it the doctor?" Linda asked, the expectation nearly palpable.

"Yeah." Francis stood and stuffed his phone back into his pocket. "I've gotta go get him."

He headed for the kitchen but stopped. "Stay with him," he said, turning back to gaze first at Linda, and then at Marlowe. "And you keep them both safe."

The dog woofed as Francis stepped into the kitchen and out of sight, opening a passage to the physician.

Linda leapt to her feet, wanting to know if there was anything she should be doing before the physician arrived, but the kitchen was empty; Francis had already gone.

She had no idea how he had disappeared so quickly, but the air appeared to be strangely unsettled in a corner of the room. She moved her hand through the area of turbulence as it dissipated. *Angel stuff,* she thought.

She turned to go back to Remy and caught sight of Marlowe through the kitchen doorway, still sitting loyally by Remy's side. It broke her heart to see the dog so distraught.

But there was no use fretting over something that she could do little about. She had to keep things positive. Right now, Remy seemed to be holding on. She only hoped it wouldn't be too long before Francis returned with the physician, and then they would know.

Good or bad, at least they would know something.

She returned to the living room, staring at Remy's prone form. If she didn't know better she would say that he was just catching a little nap.

Do angels even sleep? She tried to recall if she'd ever actually seen Remy sleeping, but her memories drifted back to the last time they'd made love. She couldn't help but smile. How loved she'd felt since he'd come into her life.

The tears came again in scalding torrents, and Linda rushed down the hallway to the first-floor bathroom.

She turned the water on full blast, then caught her reflection in the mirror above the sink, horrified by the puffiness of her eyes and the blotchiness of her complexion. If Remy should awaken now and see her, she thought, he'd probably scream and crawl back into his coma.

Marlowe joined her, sitting down on the bath mat outside the shower stall.

"I wouldn't want to be alone, either," she told him. "Let me wash my face, and we'll go back to him together."

The dog's tail thumped twice in response, and Linda bent forward over the sink, splashing cool water onto her face in the hopes of somewhat rejuvenating herself.

Then a sudden sound made Marlowe bark, startling her. Standing upright, face dripping, she listened. Marlowe stood in the bathroom doorway at attention, growling softly.

She wasn't sure what the sound was, but thought she heard the creaking of a door hinge.

"Francis?" she called out, grabbing a hand towel and drying her face as she cautiously left the bathroom. "Francis, is that you?" she asked.

Marlowe was ahead of her, growling, the bristled fur on his back somehow darker than his normally black coat. He stopped outside the living room entryway, barked once, and then rushed into the room.

"Marlowe!" she cried, running to the doorway and stopping short. A man stood over Remy, and the Labrador sat next to him, staring balefully up at him.

"Hello?" Linda said tentatively.

The man slowly turned toward her voice, his face scratched and bruised as if he'd recently been in a fight, his eyes filled with emotion.

"I'm too late," Stephen Mulvehill said, his voice quivering as he dropped to his knees beside the body of his friend.

"God forgive me. . . . I'm too late."

CHAPTER FIVE

Francis stepped onto a street that looked like something out of a postapocalyptic nightmare.

It took him a minute or so to remember that he was in Detroit.

"What a shit hole," he muttered as he began to walk the blighted city neighborhood. Miles of abandoned city blocks, the only apparent life being weeds that pushed up through the broken blacktop and swarms of rats and roaches that skittered about in the darkness of the empty buildings.

In a way an apocalypse had happened here; it was just of an economic kind.

He wasn't sure exactly why places like this, abandoned places, places that had once pulsed with life but were now dead, drew the fallen angels of Heaven. The Denizens, as they were called, having served their time in the Hell prison of Tartarus and now completing their penance here on Earth, seemed drawn to these desolate, hopeless places like lice to a healthy scalp.

The Denizen known in certain circles as the Physician was no different from his penitent brethren.

A ragged dog emerged from an alley, its snout pressed to the ground as it tracked what it probably hoped would be its next meal. It stopped when it saw Francis and studied him with dark, bottomless eyes. It looked as though it would turn tail and run when he spoke.

"I'm looking for Darnell," Francis said in a language the animal could understand. "I'm looking for the Physician."

The dog hesitated only a moment before tossing back its mangy head with a woof and heading back the way it had come. Francis did as he was told and followed.

At the end of the alleyway, the dog turned right and trotted through three city blocks before stopping in front of yet another dilapidated tenement building, only this one had a former angel of Heaven sitting on its cracked front stoop, sipping from a bottle of cheap whiskey.

"Fraciel," the Denizen acknowledged.

The dog continued on its way, occasionally pissing on random objects that littered the deserted streets.

"I'd ask if I could have a sip," Francis said, nodding toward the bottle, "but I'm in a hurry."

"I told you I didn't want to ever see you again."

"I thought you were joking. What would a life truly be without a little me every now and then?"

"Whenever you come calling, trouble follows like a bad smell." The Physician was going to take another swig from the bottle but stopped and locked his dark gaze upon Francis. "What do you want?" he demanded.

"I need your skills."

"My skills?" Darnell asked, then laughed. "The last time you needed my skills, you had a hole in your stomach so big I could put my whole hand into it. You don't look hurt to me now."

"It's not me; it's a friend."

"A friend?" he asked incredulously. "I didn't think you were the type."

"Not something I'd like to get out," Francis said. "Will you help?"

Darnell seemed to consider the question, while Francis thought of options in case he refused.

"What's in it for me?" Darnell finally asked.

"Let's just say a nice thank-you card might be showing up in your mailbox. Do they even still deliver mail around here?"

The fallen angel shook his head. "Stopped the same week they cut the power and water."

"Bet the rent is good," Francis said. He studied the front of the tenement, noticing ghostly faces in some of the windows, peering out at them.

"Can't complain."

"Will you come with me?"

"How bad?" Darnell asked as he slowly screwed the cover back on his whiskey bottle.

"Bad enough that this could be a waste of both our time."

The demon dog pressed down upon him with all its monstrous weight.

"Who. The fuck. Are you?" he growled, the stink of his breath like a slaughterhouse on the hottest day in August.

"I'm who I say I am," Remy told the beast firmly, looking directly into his large dark eyes. "But at the same time—I'm not." There, he'd said it—the cat was out of the bag.

"Bullshit!" the dog roared, plunging his enormous head down and sinking his teeth into Remy's shoulder.

Remy cried out, thrashing beneath the immobilizing weight, and he felt something stir within him, something that had been dormant up until now.

Something that moved with a yawn and a languid, catlike stretch. Something that he had not felt since awakening in this strange, twisted world.

The essence of the Seraphim still existed inside of him, though he could feel that it had changed. It felt weaker—tired.

He had no idea what could have happened to weaken it so— weaken *him* so—but at that moment, it was awake.

Aware.

And angry.

Remy felt the power react to the sudden pain, consuming it, using the searing agony as fuel. He felt it upon his flesh, the mysterious sigils coming alive as his angelic birthright began to flow through them.

"Get off!" he bellowed as a blast of sheer power exploded from the markings on his flesh, propelling the great animal backward and giving him a moment to collect himself.

Remy scrambled to his feet, the pain from the bite in his shoulder excruciating. He watched the dog as he majestically rose to all fours, the musculature of his body rippling beneath the tight black fur.

"You're going to tell me who you are—what you are—and it doesn't matter to me if you're doing it sliding down my gullet or not."

Samson's children surrounded them within the confines of the cave. They had weapons in their hands and were ready to use them.

"I told you who I am." Remy flexed his fingers, feeling the altered power of Heaven collecting there. "Just not the version I'm supposed to be."

The dog sprang, his powerful back legs kicking up a barrage of rocks. "My patience is at an end!"

Remy instantly threw up his hands, the power of Heaven flowing from them to erect a shield against the beast's fangs. The beast hit with a grunt, and Remy thrust him away.

"We need to stop this nonsense and try to figure out what the hell is going on."

"I already know what's going on," the dog said, pacing like a caged tiger, his eyes never leaving Remy. "My master has been replaced with a doppelganger—some sort of Shaitan trick, maybe."

Shaitan.

Another name that caused Remy's brain to explode outward in ragged imagery as he remembered foes from what seemed like another life. And this is where it became all the more insane—all the more riling—for in his memory, the Shaitan—the shape-shifting and savage precursor to the angels of Heaven—were still trapped within the confines of Eden, the Garden cut loose from Heaven during the Great War to drift through the seas of reality.

Remy remembered that they had tried to escape, but he had stopped them. . . .

Or had he?

There was another memory suddenly present, one that he was

afraid to look upon. In this memory, Eden had returned, and the Shaitan . . .

The Shaitan had been set free. . . .

Images played before his eyes, flashes of a film that he had no real recollection of seeing, but they were there just the same. The Shaitan, horrible creatures of violence exploding up from the soil surrounding the Tree of Knowledge, their loathsome numbers descending upon a magnificent city composed of purest yellow light.

A golden city that could exist only in Heaven.

The picture of the air above this place filled with the war of angels versus Shaitan, and the Golden City as it burned below temporarily stole his breath away.

Remy blinked away the nightmarish vision to see the great demon beast staring inquisitively.

The dog came at him again, his growl low and guttural and filled with determination.

Remy felt the shield of tainted Heavenly power solidify on one arm and drove it into the face of the oncoming beast. He needed something to defend himself further, eyes darting about the enclosed space for something—anything that he might use.

His eyes locked with one of Samson's brood, a teenage girl with a razor-sharp glint in her eye.

Leila. Her name was Leila.

Suddenly she darted forward, and he saw the short-bladed sword in her hand. For a moment Remy thought he might be defending himself on multiple fronts, but instead she surprised him by tossing him the sword.

"It's only fair," Leila said as her brothers gawked at her. "It's only fucking fair."

Remy gripped the sword, willing more of the sluggish power of divinity into the blade. It sputtered to life, Heavenly fire dancing across the metal surface. He stabbed at the hound, and the great beast leapt back.

"Won't fucking matter," the dog growled. "You'll be gutted before you get the chance to use it."

"That would be too bad," Remy said in a crouch, waiting for the inevitable pounce. " 'Cause then you'd never get the chance to hear my story."

"I know your story," the demon dog spat, pacing back and fourth.

"You think you do." Remy stared at the animal, the shield of divine power on his arm starting to sputter away. "Look at me," he commanded. "Really look at me. Do you seriously believe that I'm some sort of imposter?"

The dog continued to snarl, his fleshy upper lip rippling. "Who knows what the fuck the Shaitan are capable of these days?"

"You said my smell was off, but only just a little. How can that be? I either smell like me, or I don't."

"I'm getting tired of your yapping," the hound roared.

"I smell like me—like Remy Chandler—because I *am* Remy Chandler. I'm just not the Remy Chandler that you know."

The enormous dog cocked his head in a familiar way that caused Remy's heart to suddenly hurt, reminding him of somebody likely gone, but then again . . .

"What kind of shit are you trying to sell?" the beast asked. "Not the Remy Chandler that I know . . . What does that even mean?"

"I know it's a lot to swallow. . . ."

"Oh no," the dog growled, taking a menacing step closer. "I could swallow it just fine."

"Will you just listen . . . please?" Remy begged.

For some reason, this seemed to work, and the demon dog actually stopped his advance.

"Talk," the dog barked, sitting his muscular bulk down upon the rocky floor. He glanced at his small army. "Stand down," he commanded, then returned his attention to Remy. "I'm waiting."

Remy took a deep breath. "Something happened . . . ," he began, digging deep into his memory. "I was hurt—badly. Dying, and then I woke up here, but here . . ." He paused, remembering all that he had experienced since regaining consciousness in this twisted version of his body. "This"—he motioned to the world outside the cave—"this isn't right. . . . I don't know a world like this."

The demon dog made a sound that Remy thought might be a laugh. "That's fucking nuts!"

"Yeah, it is," Remy agreed. "But it's true. . . . It's what I know."

"So you're saying that you're a different Remy . . . a Remy from another time or place, who somehow ended up in this Remy's body."

"Wish I had a better answer, but yeah," Remy said. "That sounds about right."

The beast seemed to think for a bit, then rose to all fours and turned to the children of Samson, who had gathered behind him. "What do you think?" he asked them.

One of the kids, covered in tattoos, with a wiry yet muscular build and a Mohawk, casually pulled a toothpick from his mouth. Remy suddenly seemed to recall that his name was Sid. "I think it sounds like a load of crap," he said, and then shrugged his shoulders. "But that's just me."

The dog turned his head to Remy.

"Yeah, I think it's bullshit, too," he said. "Take him."

The children of Samson rushed him in a wave. The burning sword in his hand throbbed eagerly, but Remy resisted the urge to strike them, holding the blade down as they swarmed.

The spawn of Samson laid into Remy. Fists like boulders rained down upon him until he could no longer stand, and he went down in a heap of numbing oblivion, dropping his weapon as he welcomed the shroud of darkness that gave him respite from the madness that his life had become.

Steven Mulvehill was certain that his friend was dead.

"I'm too late," he said again, reaching out to touch the cold flesh of Remy's hand.

Marlowe stood right beside him, and Mulvehill wrapped his arm around the dog, holding him close. The dog responded with furious licks that wiped away the tears running down Mulvehill's face.

"He's not dead," the woman spoke from the living room entryway.

Mulvehill was certain that he'd heard wrong, immediately stifling the surge of raw emotion that just about stopped his heart. He tore his gaze away from his friend to look at Linda.

"He's not dead," she repeated, managing the weakest of smiles. "He's not doing well, but he isn't dead—yet."

There came a surge of adrenaline through Mulvehill then, his brain immediately kicking into full action as he began to formulate what needed to be done next.

"We have to do something," he said, alarm bells going off in his thoughts as he traipsed through the minefield of what he knew of Remy's true identity and what he could share with the woman.

Mulvehill stood, tempted to use his phone to call 911, knowing deep down that this would not help in the least and would most likely be a detriment to his friend's continued health, but he had to do something.

"Francis has gone for help," Linda then said, and there came the screeching of psychic brakes, and quite possibly the realization that Linda Somerset knew more than he'd imagined.

"Francis?" Steven Mulvehill reiterated.

She nodded. "He said that a special kind of physician was needed to deal with . . ."

Linda stopped, her eyes riveted to the man lying on the living room floor beneath a blanket.

"To deal with . . ." Mulvehill urged her to finish the thought.

"To deal with somebody . . . like Remy."

"You know," he stated flatly.

"I know." She nodded. "I'm not sure what I know exactly . . . but I know that he's . . ."

She stopped again, and Mulvehill knew exactly how she was feeling. He'd felt that same raw emotion that threatened to push him from his small perch of sanity when he'd first realized what Remy really was.

"He's special," Mulvehill finished for her. "He's very special."

Linda could only nod vigorously in agreement as emotion filled her eyes.

"I want to do more, but . . ."

Mulvehill found himself going to her, placing a comforting, supporting arm around her.

"I know there's only so much we can do for him." He squeezed her tighter, hoping that they could somehow support each other then.

"Where is Francis now?"

"He left a while ago," she told him. "He went to get the physician, to bring him back here."

"Okay," Mulvehill said, taking the info and processing it. His eyes kept going to Remy, lying there so still. It didn't seem right for him to be this way. He was a force to be reckoned with, and to see him so defenseless filled Mulvehill with an unnatural panic. What did this mean for the rest of the world? Who was keeping the boogeyman from the front door?

"He's going to be all right," Mulvehill suddenly blurted out, looking to Linda for backup. But she just stared. "He has to be."

There was a noise from the kitchen, and they both looked in that direction, while Marlowe barked and bounded from their side, ahead of them, to check things out.

Linda followed him. When they noticed that Marlowe had come to a complete stop just outside the kitchen, hunched and growling, hackles raised, they stopped as well.

"What is it?" Linda asked Marlowe, about to go around the animal.

Mulvehill wasn't sure, but instinct made him grab hold of her arm, preventing her from going any farther as he reached for the Glock holstered on his belt.

Pulling her behind him, Mulvihill entered the kitchen. The back door was open, moving lazily in the gentle breeze finding its way inside. Marlowe's unease had intensified, the dog barking crazily, his gaze fixed on a corner of the kitchen.

All he saw was a patch of shadow, and he was about to tell the dog to be quiet as he checked out the yard, when something moved in the corner of the room.

It dislodged itself from the shadows, a vaguely human shape wearing a tattered cloak that seemed to change color as the figure pushed off from the wall to come at him.

Mulvehill knew exactly what he was facing, having killed one of the creatures in his own apartment only hours ago. He aimed the pistol, firing on the assassin as it drew its own fearful weapon from beneath its cloak, a gun seemingly made from the skeleton of some freakish animal. The creature was fast, ducking beneath his shots as it aimed its skeletal gun.

He caught sight of Linda, frozen in the doorway, and screamed something unintelligible, hoping she would understand and run for cover. Mulvehill fired again, buying them some time, praying that he might kill yet another of the monstrous assassins, but from the corner of his eye he saw the still shape of Remy Chandler—an angel warrior of Heaven, laid low by one of these very things—and realized that his luck had likely run its course.

The creature flowed to one side, easily evading his shot, the bullet burying itself in the plaster wall behind it, as it aimed its own grotesque weapon and prepared to fire.

Marlowe lunged with a guttural growl, hitting the killer like a runaway freight train, throwing the weight of his eighty-pound body into the assassin's side, causing the skeletal weapon to spit its shot into the ceiling.

The creature screamed something in a foul-sounding tongue as it recovered its footing, lashing out at the attacking dog. Marlowe did not let up, showing a ferocity that Mulvehill would never have imagined. The Labrador sank his teeth into the assassin's wrist, holding on and shaking the limb violently as the creature flailed. Mulvehill brought his weapon up, wanting to take another shot but afraid he might hit the attacking Marlowe.

There was a flash, the glint of light off something metal, and Mulvehill saw that a knife had suddenly appeared in the creature's hand. He screamed the dog's name in warning, still trying desperately to aim his gun, but the shot was not there, and he watched in horror as the assassin prepared to use the knife on its attacker—

But instead the hooked blade fell from his grasp.

Mulvehill was stunned, even more so when the assassin pitched forward and fell face-first to the floor, an axe buried in its back.

From behind, a short, squat figure climbed out of a patch of shadow as if climbing up and out of a hole.

"Sorry I'm late," the grotesque little man said as he stomped over to the body of the assassin and pulled the axe from its back with a horrible squelching sound. "But I always have a bitch of a time pulling myself away from *Law & Order* marathons."

The odd stranger wiped the blood-covered blade on the sleeve of his jacket as Marlowe again began to growl.

"So, got anything to eat? I'm fucking starving."

CHAPTER SIX

The Vatican

Normally Patriarch Adolfi would have had one of his Keeper assistants drive him from his apartment across Vatican City to the Biblioteca Apostolica Vaticana—the Vatican Apostolic Library. But today the seventy-eight-year-old leader of the Keepers decided that it was a beautiful day for a walk.

For the first time in many months the holy man had slept well. Instead of the nightmare of an approaching apocalypse that had plagued his sleeping hours of late, last night, he had dreamed of a single word, spoken in the languages of the world. A single, special word repeated over and over again in every language spoken, or ever spoken, upon the earth.

Unification.

And he'd awakened refreshed and rejuvenated, with a sense that something wonderful was going to happen.

"Good morning, Patriarch," the guard at the door of the library said in Italian as he bowed and pulled open the door.

"Yes, yes it is," Adolfi agreed, feeling the muscles around his mouth stretch as he smiled for the first time in a very long time.

It was a good morning.

Adolfi passed through the doorway into one of the oldest libraries in the world, the smell of ancient texts—*of knowledge*—permeating the air of the beautiful building. He mourned the day that the priceless information contained in one of the most significant collections of historical texts would be stored within a computer. He doubted very much that a computer could produce an aroma so enticing and filled with promise.

Not wanting to taint his mood, he pushed aside the concerns of the future library and strode across the meticulously maintained marble floor, beneath high, curved ceilings adorned with Renaissance art. He spied people at heavy oaken tables here and there, perusing texts and making notes in their pursuit of wisdom.

The Patriarch walked from one building to the next and through a security checkpoint into an area of the library where the Holy See's most sacred and secret writings were stored. At the back of this room was a nondescript wooden door, and that was where Adolfi stopped. From the waistband of his cassock, he produced a key, inserted it in the lock, and turned it, hearing a muffled click.

The door swung open, symbols of ancient power carved into the doorframe glowing white in response to Adolfi's presence. He thought briefly of the recent fate of a reporter who'd been attempting to do an exposé on secret organizations within the Vatican. He had found his way to this very door, managing to pick the lock with great expertise, but the poor inquisitive soul was struck dead by the security spell infused within the frame of the door, his mortal form reduced to ash. Adolfi believed that a votive candle was still lit in Saint Peter's Basilica in the man's honor.

The heavily reinforced door slammed closed with finality behind the Patriarch, and the intensity of the light thrown by the sigils over the door softened but still provided ample light to guide his way.

He headed toward an elevator at the end of the sharply inclined corridor, feeling another security spell wash over him, before the metal door slid open to grant him access. Stepping inside, he positioned himself in the center of the cab as he always did, and waited for the journey, miles beneath the Vatican Library, to begin. The magick of the place flowed around him, like the electrically charged atmosphere before a summer storm. This was a place of great power, and that was why the Keepers had been assigned to police this great and often forbidden arcanum.

Every day Adolfi came to the Atheneum to expand his knowledge, lording over tablets, books, and scrolls, collating and translating the ancient writings of some of the world's most powerful magick users. But today he had another purpose.

Unification.

The elevator came to a stop, and he waited for what seemed like an eternity—it always seemed like an eternity—for the door to slide open into what had been his primary domain for nearly sixty years. The light of a Tiffany lamp, a gift from the United States' ambassador to the Vatican, shone from the desk in his study. Despite his exuberant mood, he felt a sudden spike of anger as he saw an open notebook with a pen resting atop it on his desk. Few members of the Keeper organization were actually allowed access to these archives, and certainly none were welcome at his desk.

The old priest headed toward the rows of shelving where many of the Atheneum's special texts were racked. He was going to call out but decided instead to catch the culprit red-handed.

He heard the sound first, a gentle sigh, filled with the weight of so much sadness. The wave of emotion from this simple exhalation was so great that it threatened to darken Adolfi's mood, wrapping him in a heavy cloak of malaise and dragging him down into the shadows. He could not imagine who within his Keeper fold could contain such misery.

The Patriarch rounded the corner of one of the great bookshelves and nearly collided with the mysterious Simeon. He was holding an old volume, one that Adolfi was pretty certain had been bound in the flesh of an infant from the Bon Secours Mother and Baby Home in Tuam, County Galway, Ireland—a recent acquisition that was said to contain the names of all the children murdered at the home and of the Earthbound demons to whom they had been sacrificed.

The pale, dark-haired figure looked up from the open book, his eyes filled with an anguish as deep as the ocean. Adolfi did not know this man's story, other than the fact that he had walked the Earth for a very long time.

"Simeon," the Patriarch said simply.

"It's missing names." Simeon snapped the book closed, an old and disconcerting smell wafting up from the volume.

"Missing names? I don't . . . ," Adolfi began in confusion.

"The book," Simeon said, practically shoving it in the old priest's face. "It's missing names of children as well as the demonic. It's incomplete. Tell your bloodhounds if they want to find a better version they need to keep searching where the home once stood. If my memory serves me there are all sorts of goodies buried there."

Adolfi took the book as it was shoved into his arms.

"Thank you, Simeon," the old man said, not really sure how to respond. "I'll be sure to pass the information on."

"You do that," the man said, continuing to peruse the shelves.

"I didn't expect to find you here," the priest said, looking for a place to set the flesh-bound volume down.

"I needed to distract myself from some recent news, and thought I'd lose myself in rows of forbidden knowledge," the man said, his dark eyes scanning the titles before him.

Adolfi carefully placed the book upon a wheeled cart with other books waiting to be returned to their shelves.

There was a loud and sudden laugh from somewhere close by, and the old priest turned to see the familiar face of one of his Keeper agents, Constantin Malatesta, who walked toward him, reading a text on the rites of exorcism. The former agent looked up from the book, and a shiver ran down the Patriarch's spine. This was not the Malatesta he had once commanded on so many Keeper assignments.

"Have you read this, Priest?" the thing wearing Malatesta's body asked. "It's hysterical what they believe works."

Adolfi reached into the pocket of his cassock for the blessed talisman he always carried as protection against evil.

Malatesta was cackling wildly as he flipped through the yellowed pages.

"Simeon," Adolfi called out. "Stand beside me," he ordered as he withdrew the talisman that was said to have been blessed with the blood of the first Pope, the founder of the Keepers.

Simeon walked to the end of the aisle, unaware of the danger.

"Excuse me?" he asked.

"Step to my side, please," the old priest commanded.

The thing wearing Malatesta's skin was paying attention now, and Adolfi was no longer sure that he could guarantee Simeon's safety.

"And why would I be doing that?" Simeon asked.

The dark-haired man turned his gaze to look at Malatesta. The possessed Keeper just smiled.

"Should he come, too?" Simeon asked in reference to the possessed man.

"Come away from him at once, or I cannot guarantee your safety," the Patriarch proclaimed, raising the talisman so that all could see and feel its power.

"Guarantee my safety?" Simeon questioned. "From him?" He pointed to Malatesta.

"I will attempt to suppress the demonic forces possessing my agent, but I am afraid that—"

"You'll do no such thing," Simeon stated. "That so-called demonic entity is working for me."

Malatesta grinned a grin that seemed far too wide for his human mouth.

"It works for you?" the holy man asked, shocked.

"The demon as well as the man it possesses," Simeon explained. "They work in tandem most of the time."

"Have you read this?" Malatesta held out the book of exorcism.

"Complete rubbish," Simeon commented. "Not worth the parchment it's inscribed upon."

Malatesta let the book drop to the floor, then opened his mouth, spewing a stream of green steaming bile upon the priceless text. The book began to smolder and burn. "It offends me," he said with a shrug, wiping the corner of his mouth.

Adolfi stood stunned, unsure of what his reaction should be as Simeon stepped from the aisle of books, careful not to tread upon the smoking text.

"I told you that I recently learned something . . . something of a divine nature." The pale man began to pace. "I came here seeking solace," Simeon said. "Or at least some consolation from ancient scholars who have come before." He paused as he gazed around the subterranean library. "But I've found no relief."

Adolfi could not help but ask, "What is it, my son? What troubles you so? Perhaps there is something that . . ."

"They're going to forgive him," Simeon blurted. "The Prince of Lies. They're going to forgive him."

The Patriarch let the words wash over him, their meaning distinctly clear. "How is this possible?" the old priest asked.

"I asked the same question," Simeon said, continuing to pace like a caged tiger. "But the divine being to which I spoke explained that it is the Lord God's wish to forgive His once favorite creation."

"An angelic emissary actually told you that Lucifer was to be forgiven?"

Simeon nodded ever so slowly.

"He did at that."

And then it all began to make a kind of twisted sense.

"Unification," Patriarch Adolfi said quietly. "Of course . . . I understand now."

Simeon seemed to perk up at his words. "What do you mean?"

The Patriarch could not help but smile; it was wonderful.

"I believe it was the early Christian theologian, Origen, who first spoke of it. He called it the final reconciliation," Adolfi explained. "But he wasn't the only one to write of it—Gregory of Nyssa, Ambrosiaster, to name of few. If you'd like, I could put together a list and have someone retrieve the works from the archives. . . ."

The intensity of Simeon's gaze stopped him cold.

"It was the belief that in the end, all would be forgiven and return to God," he explained quickly.

"All?" Simeon questioned.

The old man nodded, wanting to restrain the smile that was upon him again, but he was unable.

"All. There would come a time when the Morningstar, and all the fallen angels that followed him, would be forgiven their indiscretions, and all would be as it once was."

"This is the Unification of which you speak?" Simeon asked.

"I believe it is. My dreams for years have been plagued by visions of a Biblical apocalypse with the Kingdom of Heaven raining down from the sky; there wasn't a night of late that I did not see the horrible sights of a great war between the forces of God and Lucifer, but last night . . ."

He smiled again, and it felt so very good.

"Last night I saw nothing of the sort but heard a word uttered in all the languages of the planet. At first I did not understand and came here to research it, but now . . ."

"And that word, the one you dreamed of, it was—"

"*Unification,*" Adolfi said, barely able to contain his elation.

"And you see this as a good thing?" Malatesta chimed in.

"I do," Adolfi answered. "All will be whole again. . . . Heaven will be whole again. When the Great War occurred, there was not only a split between the Almighty and Lucifer, but Heaven itself became fragmented."

The Patriarch paused, waiting for the importance of his words to sink in. "What became known as Hell was once a part of the Kingdom, as was the eternal garden known as Eden. These places became lost to Heaven with the war, but now they'll be returned."

He watched the eternal man for signs that he understood the wonder of what could be about to happen, but Simeon just stared at the floor, as if attempting to bore a hole through the marble.

"This will not do," Simeon then said, looking up from the floor. "It will not do at all."

"You can't be serious." Adolfi was astonished. "If this is true, it will bring about a new golden age of peace and prosperity. . . . A unity in Heaven will spark a unity of the world itself."

"And I can't stand the thought of things being so . . . wonderful."

"Surely you jest, my friend," Adolfi said. "Just think of the joy our Creator will experience when all of His most divine creations are back with Him."

"Our Creator's joy?" Simeon questioned. "Do you seriously believe that I give a fuck about our Creator's joy?"

Adolfi took a step back from the intensity of the words.

"In fact, I will do everything in my power to see that *our* Creator never experiences anything close to joy," Simeon said, regaining his composure.

The Patriarch came to the sickening realization that he had been wrong about this ageless stranger, that he was in fact a force of discord rather than one of harmony. His eyes darted to the red panic button on the wall near where he stood. Once pushed, it would bring a squad of Keeper elite rushing into the Atheneum.

"Your words are surprising to me, but then I know very little about you—the mysterious Simeon," Adolfi said.

"You know what I wish you to know," Simeon replied. "You and your entire brotherhood are but pieces—cogs—in the great machine of my eventual revenge."

"Revenge? Revenge against whom?" Adolfi asked, fearing that he already knew the answer.

"It has been a long time coming," Simeon said. "And with this Unification, perhaps we are finally about to bring the game to an . . ."

Adolfi sensed that the moment was now and made his move while the forever man went on about the culmination of his plans. He moved as quickly as his old bones would allow, darting toward the wall, extending his arm and reaching . . . reaching. . . .

Something had stopped his progress, and he came to the sickening realization that he was hanging in the air as if by the presence of some invisible tether. He saw that Malatesta had stepped forward, staring with great intensity, fists clenched by his side.

"He's a tricky one," the possessed Keeper said. "Can't be a leader of the Keepers without being at least a little tricky."

Adolfi twisted in the air but was held fast by tendrils of invisible force.

"If any of the man I knew and trained is still to be found in that body, please come forward. . . . Wrest control away from the demonic entity that plagues you and . . ."

"And do what?" Malatesta asked.

"Help me," the priest said. "Help your faith. . . . Help the Lord God almighty and all His servants to—"

"Kill him," Simeon interrupted.

"I was hoping you'd say that," Malatesta said, moving his head from side to side, stretching out his neck.

"Constantin, please," Adolfi begged. He managed to lift his hand, which still held the sacred talisman.

"What's that supposed to do?" Malatesta asked, raising his own hand and splaying his fingers.

Adolfi felt the icon ripped from his fingers and watched it shoot across the room to Malatesta's hand.

The former Keeper closed his fingers around the coin, as an oily black smoke started to seep out from between them.

"That hurts a bit," he said, concentrating on his fist and the leaking smoke.

The old man watched the smoke as it started to collect in a roiling black ball above Malatesta's burning hand.

"Will this be messy?" Simeon asked, a hint of boredom in his tone. "I prefer that it not be."

"It won't be messy," Malatesta promised, opening his fingers and dropping the blackened talisman.

Adolfi struggled in the grasp of demonically controlled magick, sensing that if he wasn't able to do something now, then . . .

Malatesta blew upon the roiling ball of smoke, sending it spinning across the brief expanse of space toward him—toward his face.

The old man tried to turn away, but the magick that held him grew taut, preventing his head from moving upon his neck.

The smoke collided with his face, losing its shape as it struck, tendrils of the foul-smelling vapor flowing into his mouth, nose, and eyes.

"Oh . . . God," the old man managed, as he felt the smoke moving inside, coalescing within his chest. The pressure began to build as the smoke slithered about his inner self.

Simeon put a hand to his ear in a mock gesture. "What was that?" he asked. "Who did you call for?"

The pain was incredible, and Adolfi found his body starting to convulse as he began to cough and wheeze, gasping for breath.

"I wonder if He sees your situation," Simeon asked, stepping closer to look him in the eye. "Or is He too busy elsewhere to hear the plaintive pleas of His loyal servant, perhaps distracted by the coming . . . Unification."

The Patriarch felt his consciousness slipping away as darkness filled him, choking the life—and the light inside.

"If you see the Almighty," he heard Simeon say from far off in the distance. "I want you to tell Him that Simeon says hello, and that we'll be seeing each other very soon."

And with that, Patriarch Adolfi left the mortal world, passing into the darkness of death.

"Does this look all right to you?" the hideous little man asked, his grotesque features eerily illuminated by the interior light of the refrigerator.

He held a wedge of mold-covered cheese out toward Mulvehill.

"It's cheese," Mulvehill answered. "It always smells like shit."

"Yeah, you're probably right." The creature took an enormous bite from the wedge and slammed the refrigerator door shut.

"Who . . . who are you?" Linda asked.

Marlowe had come into the kitchen as well, standing close by, wagging his tail as he watched Squire eat the cheese.

"I'm Squire," he said as he chewed. "Francis called and asked if I'd keep an eye on things here, y'know"—he glanced to the body of the assassin on the floor—"just in case. And it looks like his concerns were justified."

Mulvehill looked back to the body and felt a chill run down the length of his spine, the hair on the back of his neck prickling with fear.

"They must know that he's still alive," he said, almost dreamily. "Sent more to finish the job."

"That's probably what Francis was thinkin', too," Squire said, taking another bite from the moldy cheese wedge. The little man looked past them into the living room.

"Shit," he muttered. He leaned his battle-axe against the kitchen cabinet and moved toward Remy.

"You say he's still alive," Squire said, studying the body.

"Yes," Linda was quick to answer. "Francis said that he was."

"Looks dead," Squire said. "If not, then close to."

"He's still alive," Mulvehill emphasized. "That's good enough for right now."

"Yeah," Squire agreed. "Let's hope that Francis gets back here soon, 'cause I think the clock is tickin'."

"He said that he was going to pick up a doctor, or at least somebody who would know how to take care of somebody like . . ." Linda stopped, staring intensely at the unconscious Remy.

Unexpectedly, Squire saddled up alongside her and put a short, muscular arm around her waist.

"Chin up, girlie," he said. "Ain't over till the fat lady gets her sandwich."

"What happened to her singing?" Mulvehill asked.

"She ain't singing till she gets her sandwich," Squire explained. "Buys us a bit more time." He chuckled, a horrible gurgling sound that made Mulvehill think he was going to spit something onto the floor.

"All this heavy emotion has made me parched," Squire then said, licking his lips. "Do you know where he keeps his whiskey?"

Mulvehill was about to suggest that maybe they should lay off the whiskey when there came a grunt and a scream of rage from behind them, and they all started to turn.

It all happened in an explosion of action, the assassin—whom they'd believed to be dead—was swaying in the doorway, Squire's battle-axe gripped firmly, and ready to strike.

"Oh shit!" Squire exclaimed as Linda let out a short squeak of surprise, and he watched as she threw herself across Remy's body to protect him.

That one's a keeper, Mulvehill found himself thinking about Linda, at that strangest of moments, turning toward the charging assassin as he pulled the Glock from its holder again and raised it to fire.

The subsequent gunshot was like that vicious crack of thunder from a particularly angry summer storm, a sound that seemed to vibrate through the skin, and into the bones. A sound that seemed to temporarily freeze time, until the searing flash of lighting moved it along once again.

But the sound had not come from his gun.

Mulvehill found himself still paralyzed by the sound, dropping low to the ground as his eyes remained riveted to the assassin, who now pitched forward in the doorway to the living room, giving Mulvehill a view of the kitchen behind him, and of the two men standing there, one of whom still held a smoking Colt .45 that looked like it was made from gold.

"Drop the gun!" Mulvehill commanded on instinct.

The man did not drop the gun but lowered it ever so slightly.

"Mulvehill, right?" the man asked.

"Yeah," he answered, but his aim did not waver.

"Francis," he said, sliding the pistol into the inside pocket of his suit coat. "And what the fuck did I have you come here for?" he then shouted, obviously addressing Squire.

"I thought he was fucking dead," the squat figure bellowed as he threw his arms into the air.

Francis and another man stepped over the body in the kitchen doorway and into the living room.

"Is that him?" Linda asked. "Is that the doctor?"

"Yeah, name's Assiel," Francis said grimly, staring down at Remy's body.

Marlowe came to Francis, nuzzling the man's hand with his black snout.

"I know, pal," he said to the dog. "I'm worried, too."

Assiel knelt down beside Remy's body, placing a small duffel bag on the floor next to him. He pulled back the blanket covering the angel, then reached into the bag and removed a bronze canister. He twisted the lid open. A thick, almost musty smell suddenly filled the room, and Mulvehill saw inside his mind's eye a lush, tropical jungle, the imagery so powerful and distinct that he could have sworn he was right there experiencing its primitive splendor.

"What is that?" he asked aloud. "It smells like . . ."

"A jungle," Linda finished, meeting his eyes.

"A garden," the doctor corrected as he dabbed his fingers into the dark contents of the canister and began to apply the muddy substance to Remy's angry wounds. "The soil of Eden. This will stop the infection from spreading any further."

"Is that the problem . . . an infection?" Linda asked, kneeling down to join the mysterious dark-skinned doctor.

"It's one of them," he answered, his voice low and timorous. "I am going to need to examine him further to determine the extent of his condition." He looked up at Francis. "Is there a place where I can take him?"

"You can take him upstairs to the bedroom," Linda said quickly, pointing to the stairway beyond the living room.

Mulvehill made a move toward the doctor. "I'll give you a hand with him," he said.

"That won't be necessary."

And before Mulvehill could reach him, Assiel had gently lifted Remy from the floor and was holding him as if he were weightless.

"Okay, then," Mulvehill said. "Looks like you're good." He picked up the physician's bag and handed it to Linda as she headed toward the stairs.

"It's this way," she said, motioning for Assiel to follow her.

Assiel ascended the stairs behind her as Mulvehill, Squire, and Francis watched without a word. Marlowe looked at them with concerned eyes.

"Go on," Francis said. "You can go on up, too."

The dog trotted over to the staircase and began to climb.

"So," Squire interrupted their thoughts. "Do you know where Remy keeps his whiskey?"

"Not sure about the good stuff," Francis replied, "but I know he had a bottle of Seagram's in the kitchen cabinet to the right of the sink."

"Any port in a storm," Squire said, walking past them and stepping over the body of the assassin in the doorway.

"I didn't know that hobgoblins were such drunks," Francis commented with a shake of his head.

"Hobgoblins?" Mulvehill asked, watching Squire in the kitchen. "Is that what he is?"

Squire had pulled a chair out from the small dinette set and was climbing up onto it to reach the upper cabinets.

"What'd you think, he was just ugly?" Francis asked. Then he kicked the corpse at their feet. "This piece of shit is a Bone Master."

"Of course it is," Mulvehill replied. "But knowing that wouldn't have helped me kill the one that came after me any faster."

Francis looked at him, reaching up to adjust his horn-rimmed glasses. "You killed one of these?"

Mulvehill nodded. "Came at me in my apartment. It was close, but I managed to take it out."

"Outstanding."

"Thanks." Mulvehill thought Francis might be looking at him with a new set of eyes. "So what do you think? Will there be more?"

"That's what I'm afraid of," Francis said.

"Found it!" Squire squawked from the kitchen. Mulvehill looked in and saw the hobgoblin cradling the bottle of whiskey like it was the Holy Grail.

"That's why I had our goblin friend come by," Francis said. "Think I'm going to need to do a little more digging to find out how bad things really are."

He reached down and grabbed one of the Bone Master's legs. "I'll start by questioning this one."

"But he's dead." Mulvehill felt foolish stating the obvious.

"Not quite."

"Not quite? An axe in his spine and a bullet in the back of his head?"

"I asked the bullet to stop short of killing him," Francis explained.

"You asked the bullet?"

"What, you don't talk to your bullets?" Francis asked. "Help me with this," he ordered as he began to tug on the Bone Master's leg.

Mulvehill leaned in and grabbed the other leg; then the two dragged the body down the hallway, past the bathroom, and into a small guest room that Remy used for storage.

"Now what?" Mulvehill asked.

"Now you go have a drink with Squire." Francis gently pushed Mulvehill back and started to close the door. "I'll see to this."

The door closed with a soft click and Mulvehill slowly turned away to see Squire standing at the end of the hallway, whiskey in hand. He raised the bottle and gave it a shake.

Why the hell not? Mulvehill thought, joining the hobgoblin.

Linda watched as Assiel laid Remy's body down upon the bed.

Marlowe had come into the room, his gaze at what was happening to his master unwavering.

"It's all right, boy," Linda said to him. "Lie in your bed and you can keep an eye on us."

The dog responded to the mention of his bed, going to a large cushioned square at the far end of the room and plopping himself down with a heavy sigh, his eyes fixed upon them as they moved around Remy.

As Assiel stepped back from where he'd laid Remy, Linda moved in, placing a pillow beneath Remy's head and adjusting the blankets. Then she stood for a moment, staring at the pale features of the man she'd come to love—a man who wasn't a man at all. She began to feel a weird sense of vertigo, as if the planet had started to spin faster and faster, threatening to send her flying into space. She took a deep breath and turned away, suddenly self-conscious as she saw Assiel watching her.

"I just want him to be comfortable," she said quickly, refusing to meet his gaze.

"That's fine," he told her, but he continued to stare.

"I'm done," she said, gesturing with her hands for him to step in.

"You love him," Assiel stated flatly.

"I do," she said, the words carrying a tremendous weight. "I love him very much."

"And he loves you?"

She smiled and then laughed. "I think he does." She stared back at Remy, remembering the times he'd kissed her face, and the passion they'd shared in this very bed. She flushed with a wave of heat at the memory. "Yeah, he loves me," she said, sure of her answer.

"Interesting," Assiel said as he approached the bed. "Being what he is and all." He began to undress Remy, and Linda leaned in to help him.

"What do you mean by that?" she asked.

"You know what he is?"

"Yes."

"He is an angel—a Seraphim to be exact," Assiel explained anyway. "A servant of the Lord God . . . and in Remiel's case, a great warrior."

"Remiel?"

"That is his true name."

"Remiel," Linda repeated, letting the name roll off her tongue.

They removed his shirt and pants and tossed them on the floor.

"It is not common for one such as he to share such emotions with one such as . . . ," Assiel began, then stopped.

"Go ahead," Linda said, suddenly defensive. "You can say it. . . . Never mind, I'll say it for you: It's not common for somebody like Remy—Remiel—to fall in love with a lowly human. That's it, isn't it?"

The angel healer smiled, his teeth incredibly white in contrast with his dark skin. "I meant no offense."

"None taken," Linda answered. "I think Remy is pretty special across the board, angel or not. I love him and he loves me. So can we stop talking and start making him better?"

"I will certainly try," Assiel said, retrieving his bag and setting it upon the bed.

"You're an angel also?" Linda asked as Assiel sat beside Remy and began to examine his wounds.

"A fallen angel, yes."

"Like Francis?"

"There are not many like Francis," the angel said. "I'm very aware of my sins and am working toward amending them."

"By helping other angels," Linda added.

"By helping any in need of my talents," Assiel corrected.

He took a cloth from his bag and dabbed at the first of the punctures.

"The wounds aren't healing as quickly as they should be. I'm guessing there are still foreign objects inside his body."

She was ready to ask what he was going to do, but he was already acting. He took his bag onto his lap and looked inside, removing what appeared to be a golden scalpel and handing it to her. "Hold this for me."

Linda took the surgical tool from him, surprised by how warm and heavy it felt in her hand. She admired the knife, its thin body etched with beautiful markings that she was certain meant something.

Assiel removed a small metal sphere from his bag and gave it a quick shake. There was a faint, almost beelike buzz, and the metal ball began to glow like a miniature sun, floating in the air above Remy.

"Oh," she said, mesmerized by the strange sight.

"It will provide me with the light I need," he said, reaching over to take the scalpel from her.

She watched as Assiel leaned in closer to one of the stomach wounds. He reached up, took hold of the sphere, and moved it down a bit closer; then he placed the tip of the scalpel into the injury.

Linda wasn't sure if it was a trick of the artificial light, but the surgical tool seemed to become liquid in the angel's hand, flowing into the opening in Remy's flesh. She looked up at Assiel to see that his eyes were closed.

"That's it," he whispered, then slowly drew back his hand. The scalpel's end had become a three-fingered prong, and it held what looked to be a bloody piece of bone.

"What is that?" Linda asked, reaching for it.

Assiel pulled it away. "I believe it's a tooth," he said. "And I wouldn't touch it; it's highly poisonous."

He set the tooth down on the bed beside him and placed the scalpel in another of Remy's injuries.

"Did you know Remy . . . Remiel?" Linda asked, wanting to fill the silence.

Assiel's eyes were once again closed. "I knew *of* him," he said, tilting his head slightly to the right and carefully pulling back on the scalpel. "He was a force to be reckoned with . . . someone to fear on the battlefield."

She laughed sadly. "I can't really see that, but then again, after watching him fight that thing . . ."

"They say that the war—"

"The war?" she interrupted curiously.

"The war between God and the Morningstar," Assiel explained. He dropped another tooth on the bed beside him. "They say it changed him."

"Changed him how?"

Assiel shifted his position to get at the last of the wounds, pulling the floating miniature sun with him.

"They say that he was tired of the violence, and that he hated what Heaven had become. That's why he came here to Earth."

"I don't know anything about that," she said, desperate to know more about the man she loved, hoping she'd be able to ask him her questions someday.

Assiel removed the last of the poisoned teeth and again used the balm made from the soil of Eden to dress the wounds.

"Is that it?" she asked, as he cleaned the instrument with a cloth from the bag before plucking the glowing sphere from the air. He put both items away and snapped the bag closed.

"If only it were," he said, his tone grim.

"What's next?" Linda asked, not sure she really wanted to know.

"The foreign matter has been removed and the wounds cleansed," he explained. "Physically he should heal . . . but that isn't what I'm concerned about."

"What is it, then?" Linda felt her heart begin to hammer.

Assiel reached up and pulled open one of Remy's eyes. "He's still alive, but . . . he isn't here. Remy isn't here."

Linda felt as though she might throw up. "What do you mean? I don't understand."

"His life essence . . . the divine spark . . . what passes for an angel's soul . . . It's gone."

CHAPTER SEVEN

He exists in a sea of memory, pushed and pulled by the tides of past deeds, of successes and failures. His history fills him up, flowing about and into his being, forcing him to see even if he cares not to remember.

Surrendering to the onslaught, he allows them their victory, and, caught in the undertow of the past, he relives the times that made him what he was.

What he is.

They come at him with such force, showing him, reminding him, and yes, he remembers, and yes, he accepts histories created by his actions—or inactions.

It is exactly as he remembers.

Until it isn't.

It is a herculean effort, but Remy manages to slow a particular moment in his timeline. *No, this isn't how it happened at all,* he recalls clearly and grabs hold of his memory of the events as they transpired.

This is how it was. . . . This is what truly happened.

The Japanese island of Gunkanjima—Battleship Island—where the forbidden children of Nephilim whores and archangels were hidden, only to have been discovered after the brutal murder of an angel general by one of these very sires. Judgment had been called down upon these unwanted by-products of illicit couplings, and Remy remembers—remembers distinctly—how he tried to intervene, to save the children from a terrible fate at the hands of legions representing both Heaven and the reconfigured Hell.

He also remembers how he failed, and the sight of the children set upon by the two sects of angels, murdered before his eyes.

How could he forget such a thing? Or the events that followed?

For, nearly crushed by the brutality of his brethren, Remy was elated to find that the children had actually survived by psychically manipulating the legions of Heaven and Hell into thinking that they succeeded in their brutal task.

The children of Gunkanjima had survived . . . hadn't they?

There were new recollections now, hungry memories that wished to consume and replace the old.

In these remembrances, the children did not reveal themselves to be alive; instead, their bodies burned, their ashes carried away by the winds of the storm-swept isle.

They were dead. They had to be in order to make things right.

To bring about change.

To bring about . . .

Unification.

Remy awoke with a scream, rolling onto his stomach and retching on the cold stone floor. He lay there convulsing, his empty stomach desperate to find something to eject but providing only painful spasms.

It took more than a moment, but eventually he was able to calm the contractions, gasping for breath, slowly acclimating to the fact that he was surprisingly still alive. As the fog cleared and the pain of his beaten body dulled, he recalled two memories of one event, one of them growing fuzzy and less distinct. The more desperately he tried to hold on to that memory, the sicker he became, his body on the verge of revolt once again.

"Something you ate?" a grumbling voice asked from somewhere nearby.

Remy immediately knew who the voice belonged to, pinpointing its location across the patch of inky blackness. "Something that I . . . remembered," he said, pushing himself up on his knees.

"Not anything good, I'd imagine, to get that kinda reaction," the great demon hound said. "Probably better to forget it."

"No." Remy vehemently shook his head. "I'll hold on to it."

"Suit yourself," the great dog said with a shrug of his powerful shoulders.

Remy carefully sat, amazed that even his butt hurt. "Why am I still alive?" he asked, wincing with each new tweak of pain.

The beast was silent, and Remy was about to repeat his question, when the dog finally spoke.

"A difference in opinion," the dog growled. "I thought you should be put down, while another—"

"Anybody I know?" Remy asked. "Never mind; forget I asked that. I'm not sure I know anybody in this fucked-up place."

"Still sticking to that?"

"If nothing else, I'm persistent," Remy said. "And since I've already put so much effort into lying to you, why start with something new?"

The hound made a sound like the rumble of a car engine before rising to his feet. "I'll give you this—you're certainly as annoying as my Remy is."

"There's a reason for that," Remy said.

"As you've explained," the dog answered. "I'm just not sure I'm willing to go for the ride yet."

"So what will convince you to climb aboard?"

"Haven't figured that out yet."

"And what about my mysterious benefactor?" Remy asked. "What convinced him that I'm not the enemy?"

The dog slowly sauntered toward the cave's exit, his muscular tail swishing from side to side.

"Not sure that he is," the beast replied. "But he does believe that you're some version of Remy . . . and even a Remy that's less than a hundred percent is better than none at all."

"What do you want from me?"

The dog stopped just before the cave exit and chuckled like an engine revving its motor. "Forget all your bullshit," he said simply. "And remember what we're heading into the ruins to do . . . to find the one responsible for what happened to the world."

"Humor me. What did happen to the world?" Remy asked in all earnestness.

The dog whirled around, fur bristling, fangs bared in anger. "Are you fucking blind, too? It's dying . . . and it's only a matter of time before—"

"All right, all right," Remy said quickly. "We get to the ruins and find the one responsible. Then what? We fix things? We fix the world?"

The dog laughed again, or at least that's what Remy thought it was. There was no humor in it, only cruelty.

"No chance of that. We're done. . . . The world's done. We find the one who did this," the great beast said as he sauntered through the exit, "and then we kill the son of a bitch."

The demon dog padded down the natural cave corridor, his large eyes having no difficulty seeing in the intense darkness. There was a small chamber just to the right of a bend that dropped off precariously to a sulfurous underground stream. For a moment the dog's senses were overwhelmed by the hellish stink and part of him was reminded of another existence upon another world, so very long ago.

While another part recoiled in disgust at what it was forced to share.

"Baarabus, is that you?" an old voice called from the small chamber.

"Yeah," the dog responded as he entered.

The old man squatted, completely naked, before a bowl. He dipped a cloth into the water, then began to clean his burned and blackened body.

The dog watched the old man scrub at the loose flesh of his spindly arm, hissing in pain as the dead skin sloughed away to reveal angry pink flesh beneath. Baarabus couldn't recall exactly how many times he'd seen the old man perform this task, but he did know that it was a lot, and no matter how much skin was scoured away, he never seemed to heal.

"What can I do for you?" the man asked, dipping the stained cloth into water that had turned the color of blood-tinted mud.

"He's awake," the dog announced. The air was filled with the stink of rot and blood, and Baarabus felt his stomach gurgle with hunger. Remy wasn't the only one who hadn't eaten recently.

"And did you finish him off?"

"No," Baarabus answered, lying down on the chamber's stone floor. "But I wanted to."

"Glad to see common sense prevailed for once," the old man said, and he smiled, the charred flesh around the corners of his mouth cracking, a milky fluid bubbling up from the fissures. "Are you still convinced that he's some sort of imposter sent to thwart us?"

"I don't know what he is," Baarabus groused, resting his chin between his paws. "He has no idea what's happened to the world; it's almost as if he—"

"As if it hasn't happened to him—to his world—yet," the old man finished, his eyes twinkling in the dim light thrown by the Coleman lantern.

"I can't even wrap my brain around that idea," Baarabus said.

The old man had moved on to his chest, the bloody cloth rubbing at the layers of black that fell away to reveal new flesh beneath. New skin that would soon blacken, and the process would begin all over again.

"The Lord works in mysterious ways," the old man said, and began to laugh maniacally, his scrubbing becoming even more forceful, more violent.

"The Lord is dead," Baarabus spat. "Or have you become too senile to remember?"

"*Our* Lord is dead," the old man said, eyes wide. "Not *his*."

"This shit makes my fucking head hurt," the dog grumbled. He was quiet for a bit, watching the old man's painful procedure. "He asked about you."

The old man stopped. "What do you mean? That shouldn't be possible."

"He asked why he wasn't dead, and I said that somebody had spoken up for him."

The old-timer paused before dipping the cloth back into the filthy water. "He'll be asking more questions soon."

"Can't imagine he wouldn't."

Baarabus spied a hint of movement from a corner of the cave, a tiny rodent. His movements were a blur as he pounced upon the rodent, biting it in half before it could even realize that it was dead.

"I should think about introducing myself," the old man said dreamily as he squeezed the foul water from the cloth and went to work on his spindly legs.

"Do you think he'll remember?" the dog asked, crunching on the bones of his snack.

The old man thought for a moment. "If I'm right about where this Remy has come from, then I haven't been seen in quite some time. Maybe he'll be more understanding about what I did."

"Let's hope so," Baarabus said. "'Cause if you're wrong, and he isn't so forgiving, he'll probably try to rip your fucking head off."

The old man smiled again, the skin again splitting and weeping.

"I suppose he would at that. Maybe I'll just keep my mouth shut."

CHAPTER EIGHT

The forever man paced about the forbidden library, careful not to disturb Malatesta as he worked.

The demonically possessed sorcerer sat in the center of the crowded space, countless tendrils of ectoplasmic webbing excreted from his body connecting him to the numerous esoteric volumes on the shelves. Simeon wanted to know everything that had been collected by the Keepers, and this was the easiest way to gather that knowledge.

He ducked beneath a large cable of woven strands connected to multiple bindings, reading the titles as he passed. He could remember when many of them were written, and he had even contributed some of the information gathered on the dusty pages. It would nice to be able to reference them again, but what he was interested in most was anything that could give him perspective on this Unification business.

He glanced away from the books to watch Malatesta as he worked. The sorcerer sat rigidly in the wooden chair, his eyes rolled back in his head as all the information contained within the multiple, multiple volumes flowed down the tendrils and into his body for storage.

Momentarily distracted, Simeon's thoughts meandered back to Remy Chandler, and how the wayward angel could help him reduce the Kingdom of Heaven to ruins. Previous encounters with the Seraphim warrior had proven that the angel could be quite volatile. The forever man had only to figure out how to use that to his advantage, especially if this Unification ceremony was to be taking place.

Yes, Remy Chandler would be a most interesting piece on the game board, he mused.

"How close are we to being done?" Simeon asked Malatesta, suddenly impatient.

Malatesta twitched with exertion. "It . . . won't be . . . long . . . now," he grunted.

Simeon turned away and, stepping over the cooling corpse of Patriarch Adolfi, walked to a bank of video monitors on the wall. He was surprised to see two Keeper agents approaching the entrance to the secret chamber. "Make it snappy," he demanded of Malatesta. "We have company coming."

"Just about . . . done." Malatesta strained, beads of sweat decorating his face.

Simeon raised his hand, tracing symbols of summoning in the air. It was as good as a cell phone call. The atmosphere before him rippled like a stone being thrown into the reflection upon a still river, and a yawning passage opened wide. He could the see shapes of three demonic entities in his service waiting on the opposite side.

"Sir," Dorian said with a slight bow, motioning for their master to pass through.

The two other demons, the female Beleeze and the one called Robert, also bowed their heads to him in equal parts respect and fear.

Simeon stepped toward the pulsing orifice, then stopped at the entrance and turned back to Malatesta. "Are you coming, or should I leave you here for your fellow Keepers to find?"

Malatesta writhed in the chair, letting out an agonized moan before slowly opening his eyes. "Done," he panted.

"It's about time," Simeon retorted, watching as the sorcerer yanked free of the ectoplasmic tendrils, which had already begun to dissolve.

The sorcerer lurched toward the forever man, careful not to tread upon the corpse lying on the floor as he joined his master.

Simeon gave the Patriarch one more dispassionate glance before following Malatesta into the passage. It slammed closed behind him as he stepped out in a penthouse suite of the Las Vegas hotel he had acquired after a rap star, facing financial ruin in the wake of the massive failure of his most recent recording endeavor, had slaughtered his entire entourage.

Blood spatter still decorated the walls, and the once boring, ivory white furniture was now livened with stains of crimson.

Stains of life.

It had been part of the deal that the suite not be disturbed, and for the amount of money that Simeon's representative had offered, the sellers were more than happy to oblige. There was something about a place where life had been suddenly and unexpectedly taken that Simeon loved. He longed for the day when that would happen to him.

But until such a time, he would work on carrying out a promise that he'd made to himself a very long time ago. A promise that would see Heaven reduced to rubble and the Lord God Almighty vanquished.

"Beleeze, I'd like you to do something for me," Simeon said from where he stood before the floor-to-ceiling window that looked out onto the lights of the Vegas strip. Flecks of blood stained the glass, and Simeon reached out, scraping at the smallest bit of dried life stuff with a perfectly manicured fingernail.

"Anything, my master," the demon said quickly, standing at attention.

Simeon examined his fingernail; he could almost hear the screams of the one whose blood was beneath the nail. He brought it up to his lips, scraping the blood into his mouth with his teeth. He could taste the fear in it . . . taste the life as it drifted away.

"Find Remy Chandler and tell him I'd like to see him. Tell him we need to speak about Heaven, before something terrible happens."

Francis opened the old folding chair and sat down to study the demonic assassin propped against boxes labeled CLOTHES in black magic marker.

Madeline's clothes, Francis thought, and that just made him feel all the worse. His friend had lost his wife, and now he himself lay dying in a bed upstairs because of this infernal piece of shit on the floor in front of him.

Francis didn't know all that much about the Bone Masters, only what he had picked up by reading the cooked brains of the one who'd tried to kill his friend, but he was about to learn more.

"Open your eyes," he ordered, leaning forward with a squeak of the metal chair. "I know you're playing possum."

The demon remained still, not a sign of life evident, but Francis knew better. He reached into the pocket of his suit coat and removed the pistol he had used to shoot the assassin. It was one of the most deadly weapons in existence, and his bond with it was something special.

"I know you're still alive because I told the bullet I put in the back of your head not to kill you. I can feel that bullet lodged in your noggin, and it tells me that you're conscious and pretending not to be." Francis stroked the gun like a cat. "I wonder, if I asked that bullet to move, would you wake up then?"

The demon's eyes flew open and his mouth formed the beginning of a shriek of pain. But Francis was faster, sliding off the chair and clamping his hand firmly over the assassin's mouth.

"I don't want to hear it, and neither does anyone else in this house," he said calmly, though his words dripped with menace. "And if you even think about biting me, I'll have the bullet start doing cartwheels."

The Bone Master's eyes registered that he understood, and Francis slowly took his hand away. "Good," he nodded. "I like when folks listen to reason. Gives me hope that our little conversation here is going to be productive."

The demon watched him with unblinking, reptilian eyes as Francis sat back on the folding chair and put the gun back into the pocket of his jacket. The former Guardian angel could sense the gun's reluctance; it wanted to be used, wanted to kill this foul creature. The Pitiless pistol was something of great power, and it needed a strong hand to control it. It said quite a bit that Lucifer Morningstar had bestowed the pistol upon Francis.

He silently reassured the gun that it would only be a matter of time before it was needed again, and that seemed to satisfy the weapon, allowing Francis to focus fully on the assassin before him.

"Why don't you start by telling me a little bit about yourself."

He waited for the demon to respond but got only a blank stare, as if he'd said nothing at all.

"Okay," Francis said. "I'll give you one more chance before we take this in a different direction entirely. Who put the contract out on Remy Chandler, and what do I have to do to get it rescinded?"

The demon continued to stare blankly, and Francis was beginning to wonder if the bullet inside its skull had done more damage than he'd intended, but then there was the slightest hint of a twitch at the corner of the pale-skinned creature's mouth, and a smile began to form.

"You can do nothing," the Bone Master stated flatly. "The contract will be fulfilled. As long as there is a Bone Master in existence, the Seraphim will meet his end."

Francis already suspected as much. "Not what I wanted to hear," he said calmly. "Are you sure there's nothing? No little piece of fine print that might be able to save me and your organization a little trouble?"

"He will die, and so will anyone who tries to keep us from our task." The Bone Master continued to smile. "There is no escaping—"

Francis had heard enough. He dropped from the chair again and, in one smooth movement, had removed the special knife—the scalpel—from inside his coat and plunged the thin blade squarely into the assassin's forehead. He wasn't going to get anything more from the demon, so he might as well root around himself.

The former Guardian angel gasped as the flood of information from the undamaged brain flowed through the knife into his own mind.

What a twisted fucking piece of work, he thought as he was made privy to the demonic assassin's last few days, weeks, and months of kills. *Can't say anything bad about his work ethic; I'll give him that.*

But Francis needed more and began digging deeper. It was as if safeguards had been put in place to keep certain information safe, for as he began to withdraw even more pertinent information, the threads self-destructed before he could read them.

The assassin's brain was literally dissolving.

Fearing for his safety, the Guardian removed the blade, severing the connection. He felt a tickle beneath his nose and reached up to find a drop of blood from his nostril. Another admirable attribute— even the extraction of information could result in death. These assassins were certainly an efficient bunch but no less frustrating. Francis didn't know much more than he did before he started.

Thick blood like tar had started to leak from the Bone Master's ears, nose, and mouth, and Francis quickly found an old blanket to throw beneath the decomposing creature's head before it could stain the hardwood floor.

He was studying the corpse, trying to decide on his next move, when he sensed it. He'd heard humans refer to it as somebody stepping on one's grave, and that was pretty much the best description for it. The Pitiless pistol was in his hand with barely a thought and he spun around, searching for the source of his feelings. Finding nothing, Francis grabbed the doorknob and pulled open the door.

"Is everything all right out there?" he hollered down the hallway.

"We could use some Doritos," Squire called back.

Francis looked about the room again, but the strange feeling of potential danger was gone.

Whatever had walked on his grave had moved on.

"I don't think he's going to bring us the Doritos," Squire said, reaching for the bottle of whiskey and pouring himself another three fingers.

For a little guy, he certainly could put it away, Mulvehill thought, as he watched Squire bring the glass to his mouth and gulp most of it down.

"So, tell me about your world," Mulvehill said.

"Nothing much really to say," Squire shrugged. "Very much like this one and about a hundred others I've visited since leaving mine."

"Why'd you leave your world?"

"Fucked up," Squire said simply, finishing the whiskey in his glass. "My world was completely fucked, and so were the others."

"As fucked as we are?" Mulvehill asked, quickly reaching for his own glass.

Squire chuckled and shook his large head. "You're not even close—yet."

"Yet?"

"I'm startin' to see the signs," the goblin said more quietly now. He realized that his glass was empty again and reached for the bottle. "Must be a hole in the bottom of this fucking glass."

Mulvehill was about to broach the subject of signs when Francis appeared in the doorway.

"I have to go out," he said.

"Did you get anything out of it?" Mulvehill asked.

Francis seemed confused. "Out of what?"

"That thing you dragged back into the spare room?"

"Oh, that," Francis said. "I got what I could . . . which is why I have to go out."

"Want us to hold down the fort?" Squire asked as he placed the whiskey bottle back on the table and pulled his full tumbler closer.

"Yeah, if you can," Francis said.

"That's the question, isn't it?" Mulvehill said.

Francis looked at him, that muddled confusion presenting itself again.

"Can we protect ourselves against that?" Mulvehill motioned down the corridor. "All I've got is a Glock, and he has an axe. Do you think that's enough if we have any more problems?"

Francis seemed to think for a moment, then reached into his pocket and removed a ring of keys. "Here," he said, pulling a key from the ring and handing it to Squire. "That's the key to my weapons cabinet. You know where it is. Go find yourself some heavier artillery."

"Sweet," Squire said as he studied the key.

Francis abruptly turned and headed back down the corridor. Mulvehill leaned over in his chair to see where the fallen Guardian angel had gone, in time to see him returning with the body of the Bone Master draped over his shoulder.

"You're dripping on the floor," Squire said.

"Yeah, I know," Francis responded. "Will you clean that up for me? Appreciate it."

A jagged, vertical rip suddenly appeared in the center of the kitchen.

"I'll be back as soon as I can," Francis said, stepping through the pulsating crack to God knew where, the opening closing up behind him with a strange sucking sound.

Mulvehill turned back to Squire, who was sipping his drink and still admiring the key. "Does he have a lot of weapons?"

Squire slowly nodded. "Francis has a real strong appetite for things that can kill."

And then he smiled broadly, and Mulvehill couldn't help but think of a Halloween jack-o'-lantern.

"If I'm not mistaken, he really likes good scotch, too, and keeps it safe in his weapons cabinet. Weapons and scotch. If it weren't for Remy's being almost dead, this would be a fucking awesome day."

Simeon had been so busy of late that he hadn't had the opportunity to watch much television. Reclining upon the king-sized bed, he pointed the remote control to a wall of flat screens and turned them on.

There were twenty monitors in all, and on each was the image of a hospital room, a single bed in the center of the frame.

Simeon had no interest in commercial television, preferring instead his own special brand of reality TV. He'd had cameras secretly installed in hospital intensive care units throughout Las Vegas so that he might observe the struggles of life, and in most cases the inevitable deaths.

It was the deaths that he couldn't get enough of, living and dying vicariously through each patient. One day he hoped to have such an experience again, to know that peace and euphoria and not have it savagely yanked away with an unwanted return to life.

His eyes scanned the screens. Some were alone, while others had family rallied about them. Simeon did not recognize any of the subjects from the last time he'd observed the ICU; that crop had likely already left this world behind.

There was a flurry of movement on monitor seven, where family gathered about a frail old woman who appeared to be having convulsions. Simeon used the remote to focus the camera on the woman's face. Her eyes had rolled back to expose the whites, and her teeth were clenched in a skeletal grin. He had seen this countless times before and knew it was only a matter of time before she was gone.

He crawled to the end of the bed, as close to the image as he could get, remembering his own death convulsions as he observed another's.

"That's it," he whispered. He could practically see her life force collecting in the center of her being, preparing to leave the diseased body that had been her prison.

He studied every aspect of her features, the sweat upon her brow and lips, the yellowness of the whites of her eyes, the steady flow of bubbling saliva from the corners of her withered mouth.

She was almost there. . . . Almost . . .

Nurses and doctors rushed in from the left, swarming around the bed, pushing the family members back.

"No!" Simeon bellowed at the screen. She had been so close. He wanted to reach through the screen and grab the doctors, pulling them away so that she might be free.

The bodies were blocking his view as he paced before the screens, his entire focus devoted to the happenings on monitor seven. The doctors and nurses were working furiously, running to and from the room.

They thought that they were saving her, but they were only preventing her from moving on—from escaping her mortal confinement and entering the embrace of the ultimate source in the universe.

The stuff of creation itself.

Things finally seemed to settle down a bit in the room, and as a man with a dark mustache, wearing blue scrubs and a white lab coat, stepped to the side, Simeon saw that the woman had been placed on a ventilator.

Keeping her alive.

Keeping her prisoner in this cruel, cruel world and denying her the glory of Heaven, as the Nazarene and the Almighty had denied him.

He had half a mind to go to that very hospital and pull the plug himself. The woman's family were crying and hugging each other, thanking the doctors and nurses for all that they had done.

If they only knew what they had just denied their loved one.

Frustrated, he climbed back onto the bed and picked up the remote, turning off all the screens at once. There was no use in trying to relax now; his thoughts had turned to more nefarious things.

He felt a sudden tremble in the ether that usually heralded the return of one of his demonic lackeys to the nest. Throwing open his bedroom doors, he strode out into the sprawling living room in search of information.

"Tell me," he said, eyes locking onto Beleeze, who had been chatting with fellow demonic servants Dorian and Robert. "What did he say?"

The demon seemed nervous, which was usually a precursor to something displeasing him. Simeon did not care to be displeased—ever.

"He said nothing," Beleeze said. "Remy Chandler is near death at his Boston dwelling."

"Near death?" Simeon repeated. "How could an angel of such great fortitude be near death?"

"I found the angel surrounded by caretakers. It appears he was critically injured by an assassin . . . an assassin of the Bone Master guild."

"The Bone Masters." Simeon made a face. "A nasty bunch indeed."

"Chandler is being cared for by an angel of healing, while his friends stand watch."

"Hmm," Simeon said in agreement while gnawing on the nail of his thumb. "That's actually a good idea. The Bone Masters don't give up until their target is dead."

"One friend was questioning a Bone Master and attempts to somehow put a halt on the contract."

"A friend?" Simeon questioned, suddenly curious. "What kind of friend?"

"An angelic friend," Beleeze answered. "He had the stink of one fallen about him."

"A fallen angel. Interesting."

"And he carried a weapon the likes of which I have never seen," Beleeze added.

Simeon's curiosity was piqued even more.

"A weapon? What kind of weapon?"

"It was a pistol, but I could sense . . . I could sense that it was so much more than that."

"One of the Pitiless weapons, I'd imagine," Malatesta said, coming out of one of the bedrooms, where he'd gone to rest after returning from the Vatican.

"The Pitiless," Simeon said. "I heard rumblings that they'd been reclaimed by their master."

Malatesta seemed to think about that a moment, accessing the information that had been taken from the volumes in the Vatican library.

"They had been lost to the ages until recovered by Remy Chandler. It was said that they had found their way back to the Morningstar, but recently there have been reports—sightings of a golden pistol . . . a golden Colt .45 Peacemaker in the possession of a fallen angel assassin."

"Remy's ambitious friend, perhaps?" Simeon suggested. "And do you by any chance have this fallen angel's name?"

Malatesta again paused, his eyes blinking wildly as he searched the countless pieces of information that now took up residence inside his mind.

"His name before the fall was Fraciel," Malatesta said. "But here on Earth he goes by Francis."

With Remy Chandler out of the picture, Simeon's plan was missing a critical piece. He was amazed at how solutions to problems often presented themselves seemingly out of the blue. Almost as if some higher power were attempting to help him.

That thought made him smile, and he wondered what kind of a higher power would have any interest in the end of all things.

"I think I would like to have words with this Francis," Simeon said. "It wouldn't surprise me to find that we have some things in common."

CHAPTER NINE

Remy finally felt confident enough to stand.

The ringing in his ears had stopped, and the painful aching in his joints had quieted to a manageable roar. Using the cold, damp wall of the cave, he pushed himself into a standing position and waited for the vertigo to clear. Sure that he could stand without holding on, he did just that, losing his balance for only a second or two before it all seemed to stabilize.

There was a tightness in the flesh of his belly, and he opened his shirt to examine the puckered remains of wounds there. Who would have thought that hellhound spit would be so conducive to healing?

Concentrating so that he did not stumble, he walked the length of the chamber and out into the natural corridor. He could hear the sounds of people talking and was drawn toward the source, the passage opening up into a larger chamber where the children of Samson waited. From the shadows he watched them, young men, at least ten of them, and one woman—the one who had given him the sword to defend himself—waiting for what was to come.

Once again, he tried to remember the mission they'd shared thus far, and once again, he was met with a sucking void. Frustration welled up inside him.

Remy left the shadows in search of the hound, hoping the demon dog would have some answers, and nearly ran into the young woman. It was Leila, Samson's daughter.

"Sorry," Remy stammered, attempting to move around the dark-haired beauty, who smiled at him slyly.

"I'm surprised to see you up and about so soon," she said. "It's not easy to walk away from a beating like that."

"I'm still feeling it a bit." Remy returned the friendly smile. "But I think I'll be all right."

"Baarabus wanted us to kill you, but the Fossil stopped us. Said you were still needed."

Baarabus, he thought. *Is that what the demon hound is called?*

"The Fossil?" Remy questioned. He remembered the dog talking about somebody who thought he should live. "Who's that?"

"The old man," Leila said with a shrug. "That's who he is."

"Does he have a name . . . ?"

"The Fossil," Leila repeated. "That's all I've called him since I was a little girl."

"So he's been around for a while."

She nodded.

"Friend of your father?" he asked.

He could see the mood change in her eyes. "I'm not sure if he knew my father," Leila said. "I can barely remember him myself."

Remy couldn't help himself, the need to know urging him to pry, to toss aside the rubble of his memory and see what waited for him beneath.

"What happened to him—your dad?"

She looked at him funny, cocking her head slightly. "You should know more than any of us, I'd think."

Remy slowly shook his head. "If I knew I wouldn't ask."

"I barely remember him, but I've heard my brothers talking about this amazing day when the world was supposed to change and everything was going to be incredible."

Leila stopped, looking over to where her siblings prepared for something he had yet to understand.

"Dad was called upon and went off with some of my older brothers to be part of this amazing event," she finally began, then stopped again.

"I'm guessing that something went wrong." Remy prodded, desperate to know but dreading the information.

"And then the world as we knew it came to an end, and he and my older brothers never came back."

"And nobody knows what happened?"

"Some of them might know more," she said, looking at the other members of her family. "All I know is that we had to struggle to stay alive . . . after *it* fell from the sky."

"Heaven . . . when Heaven fell from the sky."

"Things were totally crazy after that; angels, their skin burned black, and stinking like the pits of Hell, hunting us down like wild dogs. It was as if they'd lost everything when Heaven fell, and they blamed us for it."

Remy remembered the angels they'd encountered outside the caves and tried to imagine what could have made them that way.

"But you survived," Remy said.

Leila smiled at him then. "We certainly did. We survived with the help of an angel who came walking out of the ruins with a devil dog by his side, who asked if we wanted to take down those who were responsible for doing this to the world."

Somehow, Remy knew she was talking about him, but the memory still was not there.

"And I'm guessing your answer was . . ."

"Fuck yeah," Leila said with a sexy curl of her lip. "We're going to make those fuckers pay."

Methuselah's was the place to go for the most unusual information, and they had a halfway decent bar selection.

It was opened by the Biblical figure himself, Methuselah, who'd used his amazing longevity to create an environment where the citizens of the weird could go for drinks, the latest gossip, an appetizer, and maybe even a meal. The meat loaf was pretty damn good.

The ancient establishment wasn't actually constructed in a specific place, it was built between the here and the there—the now and the then. And not just any Tom, Dick, or Harry was allowed inside; one had to be special member, in possession of a special key that would always take you to the establishment's door.

Francis used to have one of those keys, but he'd lent it to Remy. Thankfully, now that he was in the employ of the Morningstar, a special key wasn't the least bit necessary.

The Son of the Morning always had an open reservation at Methuselah's.

All Francis had to do was find an abandoned structure, pass through any of its doorways, and he would find himself where he needed to be.

The stone alleyway glistened wetly in a source of light that, no matter how hard he tried to find it, Francis could not quite locate. He approached the large rounded wooden door, gazing upward at the red neon sign that told him he was where he wanted to be.

He didn't even have to knock. The door swung inward, and the minotaur stuck its large bull-like head out to see who was there.

"How's it hanging, Phil?" Francis asked, already making his way inside the bar.

"Hey, look who it is," Methuselah's doorman—*or would it be doorbeast?*—said, patting Francis on the back as he passed by the eight-foot-tall creature of myth. "Didn't think we'd be seeing you here, considering what's going on."

Francis stopped in front of the bar and looked around the dark establishment. It was completely empty. He reached inside his suit coat pocket for his pack of smokes and tapped one out, then pulled out a stool and sat down.

"What's going on?" Francis asked, taking some matches from an ashtray on the bar and lighting up.

"Don't tell me you haven't heard?" the minotaur said, following him to the bar. "It's gone out all across the ether. . . . Unification is on the horizon."

Unification?

Francis looked at him quizzically, then shrugged, exhaling a stream of smoke. "I'm not following."

"Your boss," the minotaur said. "It's finally going to happen for him. . . . He's going to be allowed back." The beast man gave Francis a congratulatory slap on the back.

"Are you fucking kidding?" Francis asked.

"I know, right?" Phil nodded his large, horned head. "It's about freakin' time."

Francis immediately considered contacting the home office but then remembered why he had come to Methuselah's.

"It went out on the wire this morning," Phil continued. "The Heavenly Choir, broadcasting to anybody with the ability to listen. Sent some serious shock waves through the place, as you can see."

That explained the emptiness of the usually crowded establishment.

The door to the supply room came crashing open and a great stone figure emerged carrying two old crates.

"Hey, Methuselah," Phil yelled to the golem. "Look who's here."

Methuselah stopped and set down the crates. "What the hell are you doing here?" the golem asked.

When Methuselah had finally reached the end of his life span, he'd come to the realization that he really enjoyed this living stuff and never wanted to die, so he'd had his soul transferred into a stone body specifically built for him.

So far it had worked out pretty good for him.

"I was hoping to get some information," Francis said, taking a pull on his cigarette and letting the smoke stream from his nostrils.

Phil used that as his cue to return to his seat by the door.

"What can I get you?" Methuselah asked Francis.

"Scotch. The older the better."

"No cheap shit for you," the stone man said, taking a dust-covered bottle from the back of a row. With thick fingers he deftly pulled the stopper and poured some of the dark, golden liquid into a tumbler.

"Thanks," Francis said as Methuselah slid the glass within reach.

"So?" the bartender asked.

The scotch was good, really good, and went down his throat smoothly. Francis could only imagine how much this stuff cost by the glass.

"Not sure if you've heard, but Chandler's been hurt pretty bad."

The red in the golem's eyes seemed to burn a bit brighter. "No, I hadn't heard. What happened?"

"Somebody put a contract out on him," Francis explained. He took another drag from his smoke. "Ever hear of the Bone Masters?"

"I've heard of them," Methuselah said. "Surprised Chandler is still amongst the living if they've been bought."

"As of right now he's still alive, and I'd like to keep it that way."

"I hear they don't give up too easy," the golem said.

"Yeah, which is why I was hoping you could put me in touch with one of their brokers. I want to see if there might be a way to call off the contract."

Methuselah had proceeded to pry open the wooden boxes behind the bar to reveal what looked to be bottles of champagne.

"As far as I know they don't use the typical circles to make their deals, wouldn't really have any idea who to get in touch with," the stone man said as he reached inside the wooden case and extracted two of the bottles.

"I was afraid of that," Francis said, finishing his scotch. "Any suggestions?"

Methuselah shook his blocky stone head.

"Afraid I don't have anything," he said. The golem then lifted the green bottles up so that he could see. "Can I interest you in a Veuve Clicquot champagne extracted from a ship that went down in the Baltic Sea in the nineteenth century?"

"Fancy," Francis said, snuffing out the last of his cigarette in the ashtray.

"Yeah, knew I had a few cases in the basement somewhere—thought it would be appropriate for the celebration and all."

Methuselah carefully set the bottles down atop the back bar.

"Your boss must be pretty excited," the stone man said.

"I wouldn't know," Francis said. "Haven't heard a peep about this Unification business. You sure it's legit?"

"When you hear the sounds of the Heavenly Choir blaring inside your head you have the tendency to listen. Yeah, it's legit."

Methuselah reached for the scotch bottle and brought it over to fill Francis' glass again. "It's going to change things pretty dramatically, I'd imagine," he said while pouring.

"I think you're right." Francis tried to remember what a unified Heaven looked like—felt like. It was almost distracting enough to take him off course, but Remy's plight was much bigger than that.

He downed the fresh pour in one gulp and slid from the stool.

"Looks like I'm going to have to get my information elsewhere," he said, pointing to his empty glass. "Boss's tab?"

"Boss's tab," Methuselah agreed, his powerful body moving far more gracefully than it should as he returned the scotch to the shelf. "Tell him I said congratulations."

"Yeah, I'll do that," Francis said. He grabbed the packet of cigarettes from his coat pocket and plucked another. Lighting up, he headed for the door, searching his memory for anybody else who might be able to help.

"Take it easy, Phil," Francis said, pulling open the heavy wooden door, about to step out into the stone corridor that would take him home.

"Yeah, I'll do that," Phil said.

The door was closing behind him when he sensed that he was no longer alone and turned to see the imposing form of the minotaur standing there, the door partially closed behind him.

"What's up?" Francis asked him. "Did I forget something?"

The beast man seemed to be thinking, his dark brown eyes practically boring into Francis' skull.

"I overheard you with Methuselah," the minotaur said.

"Yeah," Francis responded, taking a pull on his smoke.

"Think I might know a little bit more than he did."

"About the Bone Masters?"

The bull man nodded his massive horned head. "Methuselah doesn't care for the assassination stuff, but I've been known to broker a deal every once in a while."

"And you've done this for the Bone Masters?"

"They've got a guy."

"And can you get in touch with this guy?"

"I'll see what I can do," Phil said. "But if you're planning on talking to their guy and asking him to quit, it isn't going to happen. Once they take a contract, they finish it no matter what."

"Well, it can't hurt to ask," Francis said as he puffed on his cigarette. "Besides, I can be pretty persuasive when I need to be."

His flesh seemed to be growing colder.

"I think he's getting worse," Linda said. She sat on the bed beside Remy, gripping her lover's hand.

Assiel sat on the opposite side, his eyes closed. For the last hour or so he'd looked like he was asleep.

Linda watched as his eyes slowly opened.

"You're right," the fallen angel said.

"I'm right? I'm right that he's getting worse? Shouldn't we be doing something if that's the case?" She could feel herself ramping up again even though she'd promised to keep herself in control. Losing it wasn't going to do anybody any good at all, but she could feel her grip beginning to loosen.

"I'm doing what I can to slow the process, but there's only so much that can be done given the circumstances."

"There's got to be something more we can do," she said, running her thumb along the back of Remy's clammy, pale hand. "You said his essence was missing . . . his soul. . . . How can we get that back? If we got that back, he'd be better, right?"

The angel was staring at Remy.

"It would be a start, but—"

"Then that's what we have to do," Linda said assertively. "We have to get that back. You said that you're a healer, so do something . . . anything to . . ."

The tears were back again, followed by the raging emotions of fear and grief. She pulled back on them, wrestling them under her control.

"I understand that you're upset," Assiel said. "But it isn't a simple task like applying a salve, or ingesting a pill, or drinking a potion."

She didn't want to hear how difficult it would be to do something, she just wanted him to do it . . . do anything . . . try everything, to bring her Remy back to her.

"An angel's essence is its connection to the force of life . . . the source of all things. Remy's is missing, but there appears to be a connection of some sort, an umbilical cord if you like, trailing from him to someplace else."

She thought about what he was saying.

"You're saying his soul has left his body and gone elsewhere?"

"That's exactly what I'm saying."

"Is this something that happens? Is this common? Does an angel's soul just . . . just . . . fly away sometimes?"

Assiel shook his head.

"I've never experienced such a thing before."

She looked at her lover, her heart swelling with emotion. "Leave it to him, right? I guess he's got a bit of a rep?"

"He most certainly does."

"I'm guessing that with his essence—his soul—gone, his body really can't survive, can it?"

"No, it can't. The essence is needed or the body withers away."

"How much time does he have?"

"It's difficult to say," the angel healer said. "I'm doing everything in my power to prolong his life, and—"

"Do that," Linda interrupted forcefully. "Please—please keep doing that."

The angel stared at her.

"Please," she begged him.

And the angel closed his eyes, returning to what he'd been doing before.

CHAPTER TEN

Samson's oldest son, Dante, saw the danger of it.

"You're asking us to follow a leader who doesn't exactly know where he's leading us to," the tall, haggard-looking man said, his anger and frustration obvious in his stance.

Baarabus considered the man's statement briefly. "That just about sums it up," the demon dog said, agreeing with the futility but seeing no legitimate alternative.

"That's bullshit," Dante said. He turned his back to face his brothers and sister, who stood behind him. "If I'm going to die—*we're* going to die—I'd like it to be for a purpose."

Baarabus understood, he really did, but dissension in the ranks wasn't good for anything. The demon dog considered the quickest means to an end, and readied his body to pounce. He could kill the kid in less than a heartbeat, fill his always-grumbling belly, and remove the troublemaker, all at the same time. But it didn't mean that somebody else in the family wouldn't pick up the torch right behind him.

"We're working on it," the dog growled instead, refusing to look them in the eyes.

"He promised that we were going to end this," the oldest said, as his siblings grumbled in agreement. "But now the poor son of a bitch doesn't even seem to remember who the fuck he is."

"This seems like as good of a time as any to make my entrance," said a familiar voice entering the chamber.

Baarabus watched as the old man, lovingly nicknamed the Fossil, hobbled toward them, his raw and blistered flesh glistening in the light of their lanterns.

"Only caught the tail end of what you said," the Fossil said to Samson's oldest, "and I completely understand your concerns, but . . ." He smiled, although there was nothing charming about the look—it was actually kind of disturbing, with his exposed and glistening flesh. "There's always a *but*, isn't there? But we don't have a choice." He looked at each one of the children. "We really don't."

"So you're saying we should just keep our mouths shut and follow him blindly, even though he doesn't have a fucking clue as to what he's doing?"

"I'm saying that we all need to have a little bit of patience," the old man retorted. He began to pick at specks of blackened skin clinging stubbornly to his wrist. "I believe his story, and I think we just need to wait a bit and see how it plays out."

"How much longer do you think we have?" Dante asked. "You see how bad it is out there. The clock is ticking. If we're going to punish anyone, we—"

"See, that's a question that was being asked even before everything went to shit," the old man interrupted. "We've never known how much time we actually have."

"So we just wait."

"It might take a little time, but I think we're going to be all right. The mission may be a little different now, but it will still happen."

The Fossil seemed to think about what he had just said, that awful smile slithering across his bloody face again.

"I think the powers that be"—he looked to the cave ceiling as if searching for something there—"or whatever's still out there guiding this rudderless ship, has just thrown us a bit of a curveball."

"And what's that supposed to mean?" the oldest son of Samson asked.

"Exactly," the old man said, pointing a long finger at him. "I don't know, but I want to, and I think we will figure it out in time."

The children of the Biblical strongman waited for a bit, but when there seemed to be nothing else to say, they began to disperse.

Baarabus padded across the cave chamber toward the Fossil, the smell of his raw, seeping flesh, as always, making the demon dog's stomach rumble hungrily.

"That was good," the dog said. "Might even buy us twenty-four hours or so before they come back with the same fucking questions."

"I'm well aware of that," the Fossil said.

"So?"

"So, I think it's time for me to get acquainted with our new old friend."

The old man rolled up one of his loose-fitting sleeves and began to pick at the fresh batch of scabs that had formed on his arm.

"Maybe I can help him remember."

Methuselah's had some back rooms that were rented out for private parties and sensitive business deals.

Phil escorted Francis to one such room. He told him that Methuselah knew nothing of the minotaur's little side business and wouldn't appreciate it much if he did. When Francis agreed to keep the info on the down low, Phil left, saying he'd send someone by as soon as possible.

Francis sat at a large round wooden table and looked about the room as he waited impatiently. There was a certain vibe about the place, as if the off-white walls and dark wood floors had somehow absorbed some of the nastiness that had been agreed to there, but also some of the fun times as well. It was a strange, conflicting mood that seemed to flow about the room, and Francis didn't know whether to plot somebody's murder or dance on the table with his pants around his ankles.

He didn't care to have his emotions toyed with, especially now, when they were already raw. He thought of his dying friend back at the Beacon Hill brownstone, and suddenly intense sadness blossomed into full-fledged rage.

But just as quickly as it hit, the fury was defused by the presence of another.

The cloaked figure had simply appeared in the chair across the table from him, his face hidden within the darkness of his hood.

"Oh, somebody's angry," the figure spoke, his pale, boney hands moving in circles upon the tabletop in front of him. "I like that. . . . We can work with that."

"I didn't hear you come in," Francis said, studying the visitor.

"They never do," said the man, and then he laughed.

"Your group is that good?"

"You know the answer to that, or you would never have attempted to contact us."

"Maybe this is a test."

"A test?"

Francis said nothing, only shifted in his seat to cross his legs. And then became immediately aware that they were even less alone now. Four more shapes seemed to flow out from the corners of the room.

"If this is a test, then let's get on with it," the man said, leaning back in his chair, pulling the hood away to reveal the bald head and gaunt face of an old Bone Master. "I don't like to waste time."

The pause that followed was filled with an increasing tension, the string of a longbow being slowly pulled back before the arrow releases.

"I think you guys passed with flying colors," Francis said finally, forcing a smile.

The Bone Master appeared annoyed. "Will there be any more games, or can we get down to business?"

"Business sounds good," Francis agreed.

"Very well, then." The Bone Master leaned forward again, placing his spidery white hands flat upon the table. "Who would you like us to kill?"

Again, Francis didn't answer right away. He didn't take his eyes from the Bone Master in front of him but could sense others near him, one not too far from the back of his chair.

"Now, that's a little tricky," he said slowly, running a fingertip over the grooves in the tabletop. "I believe you've already been hired to kill the person I'm interested in talking about."

The Bone Master cocked his head strangely; it reminded Francis of some great carrion bird, watching—waiting—for its prey to finally die so that it could feast.

"If we have been hired, then the one that you're interested in has already been dealt with."

"That's the thing, though: He hasn't—and I'd like to keep it that way."

Francis looked square into the dark eyes of the assassin broker. He did not attempt to hide what he was then, confirming that he, too, was a force to be reckoned with. That he, too, had done his fair share of killing.

The change in the Bone Master's expression confirmed that the former Guardian's message was received.

"Ah, I understand now," the broker said. "You come in support of the Seraphim. The one called Remiel."

"That's the one," Francis acknowledged. "I'd like you to leave him alone."

The assassin smiled—at least that's what Francis thought the movement on the demon's white, chiseled face was supposed to be.

"That isn't possible."

"And why is that?"

"A contract was made."

"And it has yet to be fulfilled."

"Yet."

"Yet," Francis repeated. "So there's time to work on a new contract."

"It doesn't work that way."

"Why not?"

"Your kind's arrogance is irksome," the Bone Master said. "I'm surprised we're not contracted to kill more."

"Ouch," Francis retorted. "Was that supposed to hurt my feelings?"

"I care nothing for feelings," the assassin said. "But you, on the other hand . . ."

"I was hoping we could come to some sort of agreement."

"An agreement has already been made," the assassin representative stated. "Between myself and the client who retained us to kill your friend."

The broker began to move his hands in slow circles on the tabletop again. "That is who he is, am I correct?" he asked, his dark eyes twinkling. "Your friend?"

It was Francis' turn to smile, but it was more like a snarl. "He is much more than that."

"Then I am sorry for your loss," the broker said. "But once a contract has been made with the Bone Masters, there is nothing that can break it."

Francis felt the familiar anger inside him, and he allowed it to surge forward. It had always served him well, keeping him alive on the battlefields of Heaven and on countless assignments as an assassin for the angelic choir, Thrones, and now Lucifer Morningstar. The anger was his friend, a tool as important as the pistol that he drew from within his coat as he stood.

"Have I mentioned that I've already killed one of your master assassins today?" Francis aimed the barrel of the golden Pitiless pistol at the Bone Master broker.

He sensed before he saw the other assassins begin to move and was already spinning to deal with the killer behind him when the Bone Master broker spoke.

"Hold."

The assassins froze, their skeleton weapons drawn.

The broker rose from his chair. "We are done."

"I thought we were just getting started," Francis said, his weapon still aimed at the ancient Bone Master.

"Then you are mistaken, fallen angel. What you want is impossible," the broker said. "All you've managed to do is wake the ire of the deadliest of assassins' guilds."

"Not the first time," Francis said. "And I doubt it will be the last."

"You've made an enemy of the Bone Masters this day," the broker continued. "If there ever comes a time when your name is brought before us for consideration, and it would not surprise me in the least if this was to occur, we will honor that contract without any expectation of payment."

"You'd do that for me?" Francis asked.

"We eagerly await its happening."

The Bone Master tugged his hood back up over his bald head, and Francis knew that the broker and his assassins would soon be gone, shifting into nothingness as easily as they had arrived.

He had to make his point before they were gone.

"I had hoped to do this easily," Francis stated, lowering his pistol. "But it looks like I'm just going to have to kill you all."

The Bone Masters did not move.

"We'll remind you what was said when it comes time to snuff out your life," the broker informed him.

"Thanks, but no thanks," Francis said, sliding the Pitiless back inside his coat. "When it's time, I'll tell you myself."

Frustrated and seething with anger, Francis left the function room, walking the length of the winding, wood-paneled corridor to the back of Methuselah's bar.

Phil the minotaur was in his seat at the door but stood as Francis approached, winding his way around the empty tables. "How'd it go?"

"Well, I didn't make any friends."

"That doesn't sound good," Phil said.

"No, it isn't."

"Told you the Bone Masters were a squirrelly bunch."

"Yeah, and I tried to be on my best behavior, too." Francis was taking a smoke from its pack when he realized that Phil was staring at him. "Yeah, I'm full of shit. I know."

"Sorry about that, Francis," Phil said, patting him on the back with a large hand while opening the door.

"Not your fault, Phil."

Francis was about to step out into the stone passage when someone called out from the bar behind him.

"Excuse me," the voice said, and Francis and Phil turned to see a lone customer sitting on a stool, facing them.

"Can I help you with something, buddy?" Phil asked.

"Not you, him." The pale-skinned man with the jet-black hair motioned with his chin. "Francis, right?"

Francis and Phil exchanged looks.

The minotaur shrugged. "I have no idea who he is."

"Do I know you?" Francis asked as he walked back to the bar.

The man smiled and shook his head. "No, we've never met," the man said. He was twisting a silver ring on the ring finger of his right hand. "But I thought I recognized you as you passed. Having some problems with the Bone Masters, are you?"

Francis studied the guy; there didn't seem to be anything about him that set off alarms. As far as Francis could sense, he was harmless.

"What if I was? What's that got to do with you?"

"Nothing, really," the man said. "It's just that I know some things about them, and I know some things about you. Maybe we can work out some sort of arrangement that would benefit the both of us?"

Francis realized then that if he left Methuselah's, he would leave with nothing, but now an opportunity had presented itself. What would it hurt to see what the guy had to offer?

"Talk," Francis said, pulling out the stool beside the guy and sitting down.

"Excellent," the man said, extending his hand. "It's a true honor to finally meet you, Francis. My name is Simeon."

And Francis took his hand.

In that strange state between being awake and asleep, Linda remembered what it had been like when her Nana had died.

She'd been thirteen years old, old enough to feel the weight and sadness of the loss, but also old enough to know that it was for the best, that the poor old woman had been suffering terribly with cancer, and now she would no longer be in pain.

She remembered how her mother had busied herself with phone call after phone call—to the funeral home, to the florist, to family members and friends. Linda had hovered just within earshot, listening as her mother was mostly strong, but hearing the tears reserved for only those closest.

Linda awoke with a start and nearly pitched forward off the bed, where she sat beside Remy. She quickly pulled herself together, catching sight of the angel Assiel still on the other side of her love, his dark hand resting upon Remy's chest.

Nothing appeared to have changed.

She stood, stretching the numbness from her legs, then leaned in closer to her man. If anything he looked worse, and she felt her mood grow heavy.

Marlowe came into the room again. The poor boy had been back and forth between upstairs and down, almost as if he believed that if he left and returned, he would come back and find his master well. If only that were the case.

"How you doing, boy?" she asked the dog as he came to stand beside her. She scratched behind his ear and rubbed his side.

She knew very well that Remy could die, and she was trying her best to prepare herself. It was one of the hardest things she had ever done, like sticking a toe into bathwater that is too hot. You immediately pull away, but when you keep going back to it, the discomfort gradually lessens, eventually becoming something bearable.

Something bearable.

She doubted that it would ever be.

But what if it did happen? What if Remy just couldn't hold on anymore? She—everyone should be prepared.

Just as her mother had informed her family about Nana, Linda knew she had to prepare Remy's friends.

She stared at Remy and Assiel, then turned to leave the room. Marlowe watched her as she went, the look in his dark eyes questioning.

"It's all right," she reassured him, keeping her voice low. "I'm going downstairs for a while. You can stay here if you want, or you can come with me. Whatever you like is okay."

She stopped at the door and heard a soft sigh from behind her. Marlowe had returned to his bed in the corner of the room. It was nice to know somebody who loved Remy as much as she did would be with him.

In the kitchen, she found Steven Mulvehill and Squire sitting at the table, a stack of weapons piled in its center; there were knives and guns, and, if she wasn't mistaken, a few grenades.

"Hey," Squire said.

Mulvehill stood, concern on his face. "Is he . . ."

"The same," Linda said. She couldn't take her eyes from the stack on the table. "What's all this?"

"Francis asked us to grab some stuff from his place, y'know, just in case."

"Are we expecting a third-world nation to attack us?" Linda asked.

"We don't know what to expect, really," Squire replied. He reached into the pile and removed a handgun, looking it over carefully before setting it back down beside him. "We just have to be prepared."

"Can we do anything?" Steven asked.

Linda barely knew this cop, but she could tell he was a good man, and he certainly cared for Remy. She hoped that when—if—this all resolved, no matter how it turned out, they'd have the opportunity to get to know each other better.

"No, no," she said, suddenly realizing she was incredibly thirsty. She went to the refrigerator, pulled out a bottle of water, and nearly drained it one long gulp. She turned and leaned against the counter. An uncomfortable silence filled the room.

"People should probably know," Linda finally blurted out.

Steven looked at her, confusion on his face.

"Remy's friends: They should know what's happened and that things might not turn out so good." The words were painful to utter, and she felt her eyes grow hot with the potential for tears again. "Sorry," she said, wiping at her eyes.

"It's all right." Steven looked at Squire, who was testing the sharpness of a ten-inch blade by shaving patches of thick hair from his arm.

The room grew silent again and Linda took another swig from her bottle of water before asking the inevitable question, "Is there anybody I should call?"

Steven seemed to give it some thought for a few moments. "He really doesn't have that many friends. He knows a lot of people, but"— he paused again—"I don't think he made many friends because of who and what he is."

"Does he have any . . . angel friends?"

"He doesn't seem to get along all that well with his own kind."

"Ashley," Squire suddenly blurted out.

Both Linda and Steven looked at him.

Squire set the blade he was still playing with down on the table. "If you're going to get in touch with anybody, it should be Ashley."

"He's right," Linda said.

"Yeah," Steven agreed. "They are pretty tight."

"Does she know what Remy is?"

"Yeah, she knows," Squire said. The goblin pushed back his chair and stood. "She should see him, just in case."

The weight of the goblin's words was crushing.

"Does anybody know how we can get in touch with her?" Linda asked.

"I know where she is," Squire said, walking toward a growing patch of shadow by the kitchen window. "We—Remy, Ash, and me— were all involved with this thing once," he said. "We've stayed in touch since."

Squire turned and ducked into the shadow as if it were a thing of substance, like pulling back a curtain and disappearing behind it.

"I'll see if I can bring her back."

Linda and Steven heard the words echo hollowly from somewhere beyond the shadow.

CHAPTER ELEVEN

Ashley was supposed to have been up at six for an eight-o'clock Early Childhood Development class, but she hadn't been able to find the energy to get it done.

Instead, she'd lain in bed, listening to the Top 40 DJs and their inane banter, and music that she couldn't stand interspersed with news, weather, and traffic. It should have been more than enough to drive her from bed, but it hadn't.

She'd thought she might be getting sick—a cold maybe, or even the flu, but physically she felt fine. There had just been something wrong about the morning, and it had lasted well into her day.

Ashley had asked her roommate if she felt it, too, but she'd just laughed and said Ashley was probably getting her period.

But that wasn't it; that wasn't it at all.

The day felt wrong.

She sat in a lawn chair in the backyard and played with her phone. There were no messages from anyone, and nothing she could find on the Internet that would give her such an intense sense of unease.

Just crazy, I guess, she thought. She figured a shower might help and was about to rouse herself from the chair when she heard her roommate call her name.

"Yeah?" Ashley responded, her skin suddenly prickling and her heart beginning to race.

"Can you come in here?"

She bolted from the chair, up the back steps, through the mudroom, and into the kitchen, where she found Melissa looking pale and more than a little befuddled.

"What is it?"

"Your friend is here," Melissa said.

"My friend? What friend?"

"The creepy one. He's in the dining room, eating cereal."

"The creepy one," Ashley repeated, already on the move into the small dining room.

Squire sat at the table, just about to shovel another spoonful of Lucky Charms into his mouth, as she burst in.

"Squire," she said. "What . . ."

The goblin wiped his milk-stained mouth with his sleeve and stood.

"We gotta go," he told her.

"Go where?"

"Boston . . . Remy's place."

"What the hell is going on?"

"It's bad, Ash," Squire said.

"What's bad? Tell me what's going on, or I'm going to fucking lose it."

"It's Remy," Squire said. "He's been hurt. . . . We don't know if he's going to make it."

"Remy," she said, her voice little more than a trembling whisper.

It all made sense to her now. This was what she had been feeling.

"Take me there, Squire," she said, walking over to the goblin. "Take me right now."

Marlowe awoke with a guttural *woof.*

The black Labrador lifted his blocky head, looked around the room, and climbed to his feet. He had heard something and thought that maybe his master—his Remy—had awakened.

But that hadn't happened. The angel who was helping Remy was still sitting on the bed beside Marlowe's unconscious friend.

Marlowe sniffed the air and padded to the bed, his nails clicking on the hardwood floor. *Woof,* he said again, then laid his chin upon the mattress and sighed. He longed for his Remy to playfully pat the mattress, inviting the dog up to join him as he had so many times before.

There was no movement—no invitation.

Stepping back slightly, the Labrador tensed his muscular back legs, then sprang gracefully up onto the bed. He waited for recrimination from the angel Assiel, but there was none; the angel didn't move, his hand still resting upon Remy's chest.

Marlowe sniffed around the bed, catching hints of a familiar smell that made him remember the woman, his Madeline, who had left the pack some time ago. He still missed his Madeline, but this scent made him very nervous.

It was not a good smell. The dog knew it as a sad smell, a bad smell that told him of sickness. Of things coming to an end.

What does this mean? the dog wondered as he sniffed around his master's still form. *Is Remy going to leave me, like Madeline did?*

Marlowe stood upon the bed, breathing in the smell of something that made the thick black hair at the back of his neck and down to his muscular tail bristle. He would not stand for this. He knew that his Remy loved him and would never leave him voluntarily. They enjoyed being a pack too much. There were still many walks to the Common to be had, many rats and squirrels still to chase, so many things that they needed to do again and then do some more.

No, he would not let his Remy leave him.

Marlowe dropped down as close as he could to his master, his furry body pressed against his Remy's side, his chin resting on Remy's naked hip so that he could look up the length of his master's body to his unconscious face.

This was where he would stay. Lending his strength to his Remy's struggle, his fight against whatever it was that had caused this smell that made Marlowe think of terrible things.

Of his Remy going away and never coming back.

His tears were scalding hot.

And lying in the darkness of the cave, Remy reached up to wipe the liquid away. The angel had no need for sleep but would often slip into a deep fugue state where he would heal and reflect on matters of importance to him, the people that he cared for, and the world. It was from one of these states that he'd awakened.

He could not remember what rumination had caused this release of emotion, but whatever it was, it had tugged greatly upon his heart.

Absently, he rubbed the moisture between his finger and thumb as he tried to recall what it was that had stirred him so.

"Lost in thought?" asked a voice from nearby in the darkness, startling him.

Adjusting his vision to see better in the gloom of the cave, Remy saw a hunched and hooded figure standing by the cave's opening.

"Don't get too lost," the hooded man continued, his voice sounding raw, as if it should hurt him to speak. "Maybe next time there won't be a place for you to end up in."

"Is that what you think happened to me?" Remy asked. "That I got lost and ended up in this body . . . in this place?"

"It's possible, but then after all I've seen in my lifetime, just about anything seems so."

Remy sat up in the gloom. "Who are you?"

The man chuckled wetly. "Bet you like asking that question rather than hearing it for a change."

"I've always known who I am."

"Strangely enough, so have I."

Remy studied the man, noticing the raw, wet flesh of his hands. "So you know me?" he finally asked.

"Let's just say I know of you."

"You must be the one who came to my defense."

"Yes. They actually wanted to kill you—thought you were part of some sort of evil Shaitan plan or some sort of nonsense."

"But you know otherwise."

"I believe I do. . . . I'm right, aren't I? You're not a Shaitan, are you?"

Remy smiled and almost laughed. It felt strange, almost as if that action might be somehow forbidden in this place. "No, I'm who you think I am."

"Good," the man said. "It's nice to be right every once in a while."

"It is," Remy agreed. "So who are you?"

"No one you'd remember. We met in passing, but I never told you my name."

"Which is?"

"I haven't used it in a very long time, and I would really rather forget it. They just call me the Fossil now."

"That's easy enough to remember."

"I like to keep things simple these days."

"Is that even possible . . . these days?"

The Fossil picked at a spot of angry flesh before answering. "There really isn't much to it now; it's all about staying alive long enough to complete the mission."

"The mission that I was supposed to lead," Remy added.

"Yes, that's the one."

"The one that I have no recollection of."

"One and the same."

"I ought to be doing something about that," Remy said.

"You're probably right." The old man gestured as he started from the cave. "Come with me."

Remy followed him up the winding stone passage, moving quickly so as to not lose sight of the Fossil, who was far more spry than the angel would have imagined. As they grew nearer the surface, Remy could smell the stink of a Heaven fallen to ruin.

Of a Heaven rotting in what remained of the sun.

The old man stopped just inside the entry to the caves, peering out at the bleak landscape. As far as the eye could see, there was only devastation.

Remy found himself drawn to it, pulled out into the open.

But a thin, bloody hand, flat against his chest, stopped his progress.

"You don't want to be seen," the Fossil said.

Remy shook off the pull of outside and squatted down in the dirt and dust, looking out from the cave entrance.

"How could I not remember something like this?" he asked, feeling waves of emotion threatening to beat him to a bloody pulp. There was sadness the likes of which he'd never experienced, mixed with nearly overwhelming anger.

"Maybe it's not your memory yet," the Fossil said. He leaned against the stone wall and slid down to the floor. "The one whose body you're wearing, this is his world."

In the muted light from the outside, Remy got a better look at the old man, his face as raw and bloody looking as his hands. As if all the skin had been scoured away in hopes that something better waited beneath.

"I have to know," Remy said, turning away and looking out over the ruins of Heaven and the world. "I have to know what led to this so I can do something, so that I can . . ."

"Fix it?" the Fossil suggested.

Remy glanced quickly at him, and then back to the ugly scene outside. "Is that even possible?"

"I guess it all depends on your definition of *fixing*," the old man said.

"How did it happen?" Remy asked with growing dread. "How did it all become so . . . broken?"

The Fossil stared out over the remains of the world and Paradise, his eyes suddenly welling with moisture, tears running over the raw, open flesh of his face.

"It was supposed to be something wonderful," he said wistfully. "The Unification of everything above, below, and what had been lost." He tore his tearing eyes away to look at Remy. "The dawn of a new Heavenly Kingdom."

Remy wasn't sure he completely understood, but if what he thought was true—it *was* something wonderful.

But the question still hung there like an ugly wound, the crack in an otherwise perfect façade.

"What happened?"

"Death . . . Death is what happened." The Fossil once again gazed out over the graveyard the earth had become. "Somebody killed Him, Remy," he said, his voice cracking with emotion.

"Who?" Remy asked, although he dreaded the response.

"The Almighty," the old man said, his voice a raw, pained whisper. "Somebody murdered God."

Francis followed Simeon from Methuselah's, to find three Demonicus demons waiting for them in the stone passage.

He reacted in an instant, reaching into his coat for protection when he felt Simeon's hand on his arm.

"That's quite all right," the man said. "They're with me."

One of the demons nodded his head as they both approached, then activated a sphere of transference around them.

Alarm bells sounded in Francis' head. *Who the hell is this guy, and when did I get to be so trusting of strangers?* He quickly answered his own questions. *Since my best friend is dying in a bed in Boston is when.*

Simeon looked at him as if sensing his unease and smiled.

The sphere of transference rose up around them all, and Francis found himself holding his breath, experiencing that strange sense of vertigo that always happened when using a magickal spell to transport from one place to the next. Then as fast as the sphere had surrounded them, it began to collapse again.

"Welcome," Simeon said, stepping out and into a room. He spread his arms for Francis to take it all in, and he did just that.

There was no doubt that they were underground, but how far down exactly he wasn't sure. What was visible of the walls of the vast chamber appeared to be combination of rough stone and dirt. Thick, knotted vines protruded from the visible surfaces, cracking the stone as they pushed outward from the earthen walls.

But all the rest, as far as the eye could see, were taken up with bookcases and tables holding stacks upon stacks of ancient tomes and objects of indistinguishable origins.

"This is where I come when I need to collect myself," Simeon said as his eyes moved wistfully about the space. "I spent many an hour here in my youth perusing the volumes of ancient arcana and things esoteric."

"Impressive," Francis said with a nod. "How far underground are we?"

"A few miles, give or take," the man answered. "The original structure above was destroyed by a great fire, and what was left collapsed into a swamp. I was shocked when I discovered that this chamber of vast knowledge had somehow been preserved."

"How long ago was that?" Francis asked.

"When I discovered that the chamber had survived?"

"That you spent many an hour here," Francis clarified.

Simeon smiled again. "Let's just leave it at a long time ago."

He turned away then and headed to a small sitting area with two leather club chairs with an antique wooden table between them, atop which sat a crystal decanter and two glasses.

"May I offer you a glass of my favorite sherry?" he asked, gesturing to the container.

"Sure—why not?" Francis said, joining him.

Simeon sat down in one of the chairs, and Francis took the other, watching as the man gestured to the demons, who still stood where they'd first entered the room. "We'd like some sherry," he said.

One of the demons approached, picked up the decanter, and carefully poured one glass and then another.

"Our guest first, Beleeze," his host said, nodding toward Francis as the demon tried to give Simeon the first glass.

Francis locked eyes with the creature and at once felt uneasy. Beleeze lifted the glass and offered it to him, his curled upper lip showing off yellowed, razor-sharp teeth. Francis took the sherry and watched as the demon leapt back as if to escape his vicinity as quickly as possible.

Simeon chuckled as the demon handed him the other drink as far from Francis as he could be.

"He's repelled by the dichotomy of what you are," he explained to Francis. "A creature of divinity, and yet fallen into great darkness. I think your kind confuses them."

He held his glass up in a salute to Francis, and they both sipped their sherry. It was good as far as sherry went.

"Well, sometimes I confuse myself," Francis said in all truthfulness. "What's your story?"

Simeon tilted his head ever so slightly.

"You're obviously human, but you're palling around with demons. What's that all about?"

"There's no palling around, I'm afraid," Simeon said, shaking his head. "They are strictly my servants."

Francis watched as the man and the demons exchanged looks. There was little love there.

"If given half the chance they would rip me open and feast upon my entrails," Simeon said, smiling again. "And that would only be if they decided to be merciful."

"Must be something pretty special that keeps them in line," Francis said, having some more of his drink.

"Special," Simeon repeated. "It is at that."

One mystery piling up atop another. Francis decided that it was time to cut to the chase and discuss what had brought them here. "So, what can you tell me about the Bone Masters?"

Simeon turned his head slowly to rest his gaze on the fallen angel. "Ah yes, the dreaded Bone Masters," he said with dramatic flourish.

"Yeah, them."

"Demonic killers with the utmost expertise," Simeon added. "To hire them is to guarantee your quarry's demise."

"Sounds like you've been hired to manage their PR," Francis said. It was his turn to smile, but it didn't last for long.

"I admire them," Simeon explained. "That's all. It's hard to find dependable help these days." He sipped the last of his sherry and then turned in his chair as he set the empty glass down upon the table. "I've actually heard the same about you, Francis."

"Me?" Francis responded with a laugh. "I doubt that I'm anywhere near the level of the Bone Masters."

"You're too modest."

"More realistic than modest," Francis said. He, too, finished his sherry and leaned over to rest the glass upon the table. "But we're not supposed to be talking about me. I need to know everything you can tell me about the Bone Masters."

Simeon leaned back in the club chair and crossed his long legs.

"Let's see; a demonic species that excels in the act of murder, psychically linked with a species of animal that is transformed into their chosen weapon upon its death. A biological weapon that fires bullets coated with one of the deadliest venoms in all existence."

"Any cure for the venom?" Francis asked, already knowing the answer.

"Not that I'm aware of," Simeon answered. "To be hit by these projectiles pretty much signs your death warrant."

"Where can these Bone Masters be found?"

"That is a secret of which they are very protective."

Francis didn't like that answer. "So you don't have a clue?"

Simeon shook his head. "No idea whatsoever."

"I thought you said . . ."

"I never said that I knew where they were, but I do have an idea of how you might find them."

"All right," Francis said. "I'll bite. How?"

"The animals," Simeon said simply. He poured another glass of sherry for himself.

"The animals," Francis repeated. "What exactly does . . . ?"

"The animals that become their murder weapons. I know the location of their habitat."

"So if I know where these creatures can be found . . ."

"Exactly," Simeon interrupted. "The Bone Masters will not be far behind."

"I like that," Francis mused. "So here's the question, then. What will this information cost me?"

Simeon played it coy, downing his second drink and smacking his lips almost comically as he let the empty glass dangle from his grasp. "It will not cost you a single cent of money."

Francis waited for the bomb to drop.

"As I mentioned earlier, your reputation precedes you," Simeon began. "And I have need for someone with your special skills."

Francis didn't have a good feeling about this, watching as Simeon began to spin the ring upon his finger.

Imagine that.

CHAPTER TWELVE

"It was to be a time unlike any other," the Fossil continued. "That which had been sundered was to come together again; Heaven was to be unified once more, and the world of man was to join this new holy union."

Images flickered in the recesses of Remy's mind, flashes of memory that were not his own. He saw the streets of his home, the streets of Boston flowing with people, their faces turned to the sky, bathed in the unearthly light that shone from the Heavens above them.

It was true. It was all true.

"We were being invited into a pretty exclusive club," the Fossil said. "We could all feel it in our very souls, believers and nonbelievers alike. God was asking us to join His kingdom—asking us to be a part of Heaven."

Remy closed his eyes, trying to tempt more from another's memory. There were flashes of the Golden City that made him gasp aloud. He was there, amongst his kind again—accepted, wanted.

"I was there," he whispered as he tried to dredge more from the deep recesses of someone else's mind. It was there, just beyond his reach.

He stretched out with mental fingers, reaching . . . reaching. . . .

The flash of memory was like a physical assault. Remy grunted, pitching forward to the dirt floor. His mouth was filled with the taste of blood, and his mind with the image of a city.

For a moment he was mistaken, believing it to be the golden capital of Heaven, but it was not. This was another city, one recently risen from the fire and the ice, shaped from the desolation of the world's original purpose.

Called Tartarus in frightened whispers, it had once been a prison for those who had betrayed the Lord God, a place of great suffering for those who had sworn their allegiance to the Son of the Morning during the Great War.

But the Morningstar had returned, taking Tartarus and the world upon which it sat and shaping it into a kingdom he could call his own. A sprawling city to rival Heaven's golden spires.

It was to be called Pandemonium.

That was what Remy saw.

"Hell's city . . ." A sharply angled metropolis that seemed to have been chiseled from polished black stone. "Pandemonium was there."

The old man smiled his sad smile, his lips cracking and starting to bleed. "Well, of course it was. As was the Garden of Eden. How else could Heaven be made whole?"

"Unification," Remy said aloud, as the images of the Golden City, the Garden, and Pandemonium beginning to merge—to come together as one—exploded in his mind. "I see it."

But then there came a sensation of dread. He could feel it building the deepest, darkest corners of this memory, a pressure intensifying, growing to critical mass before . . .

There were flashes of utter devastation; buildings composed of darkness and light crumbling toward one another, a jungle as old as reality burning, all plummeting from the sky to the earth below.

Remy recoiled, trying to push back the memories, afraid that they would most certainly be the death of him.

"Did you see?" the Fossil asked him.

"I saw the end, the death throes of Paradise."

"And the cause?"

There were images, but unformed. "Nothing yet," he said, feeling warmth upon his face and reaching up to find blood trickling from his nose.

"Certain memories can be dangerous things," the Fossil counseled.

Remy wiped his nose with the sleeve of his heavy coat.

"I can't avoid them forever."

"No, you can't."

Remy reached into his pocket to find something to stifle the flow of blood and pulled out a filthy handkerchief. As he stared at the stained piece of cloth, that niggling sense of something dancing on the periphery of his brain was there again.

Something was wrapped in the handkerchief.

"What have you got there?" the Fossil asked.

Within the crusty folds, Remy found an old key. Images flashed again inside his skull. He saw a rounded, heavy wooden door, a broken neon sign hanging above it. He could make out some of the letters— *M, T, H, S.*

"Do you know what it's for?" the Fossil asked him.

"A door," Remy replied. "A door that I need to find."

The Bone Master known to his clan as Ripper of Souls loomed above his latest assignment, watching her die.

She had once been part of a powerful coven of witches, but a greed for power had gotten the best of her and she'd stolen the coven's Book of Shadows—the source of their power—to sell to the highest bidder.

The leader of the coven had not appreciated the betrayal and had contracted the Bone Masters to deal with it.

Ripper of Souls had little difficulty in locating the thief, whose name was Amanda Blite. Her mother, who was suffering from a rare form of bone cancer, had recently moved into a very exclusive, very expensive hospital for the terminally ill. All the Bone Master had to do was stake out the hospital and wait for the inevitable visit by the caring daughter.

It was all too easy, almost as if she wanted to die.

Standing above his prey, he stroked his weapon as he watched the light of life go out of her eyes. Blite had tried to fight back, but her magickal power had little effect once the first of his tainted bullets entered her flesh.

What was that saying that humanity used to reward a valiant yet fruitless trouble? An A for effort? Yes, that was what he would give this target.

An A for effort.

The bones of his weapon vibrated beneath each of his affectionate strokes, pleased that yet another victim had fallen to its venom.

More, the weapon thought, excited for yet another kill.

The sound of something falling to the floor triggered an instantaneous reaction in the assassin. Ripper of Souls spun around, aiming the head of the animal skeleton that he held in his hands. But he did not will the weapon to fire, for it was not a threat at all.

The old woman lay on the hospital bed, reaching for the device that would sound an alarm and bring her aide. However, Ripper had already disabled it.

The dying woman locked eyes with the assassin, and he believed that if she had the ability to slay with a glance, he would most assuredly have suffered grievously.

A humorous thought crossed his mind at that very instant. What if she were to hire an assassin to slay him? By the looks of her, though, she'd never get the chance. Death was hovering very close by this one.

He was drawn to the bedside. The dying woman was little more than skin pulled tightly over bones. Her mouth moved pathetically as she tried to speak, but she was too weak to create much more than wheezing croaks.

The weapon cradled in his arm wanted to strike, but Ripper of Souls felt that it would only be a waste, and besides, no one ever got rich by being merciful.

Ripper of Souls pulled his cloak tighter about himself, preparing to leave and collect his fee, when his weapon suddenly began to vibrate.

At first he thought it was a warning, but then realized that the living gun was the first to respond to a psychic communication from the Broker.

Ripper of Souls allowed his guard to fall, feeling the tickling sensation of the telepathic call. Perhaps he was about to receive his newest job, the killer thought, feeling that sense of excitement he always did when being given the death notice on some hapless individual.

But then he realized that he and his weapon were not the only ones to receive this call—it was for all the Bone Masters. Their honor was being challenged. A quarry had managed to survive.

That could never be allowed.

Ripper of Souls felt himself aroused. To be the one that managed to prevent this potential embarrassment would be glorious.

His weapon agreed, vibrating eagerly in anticipation.

All the information he required to fulfill this existing contract filled his consciousness and that of his weapon.

An angel, he thought. He and his weapon had never killed anything of the divine before. They could barely contain their excitement.

The sound that disturbed his thrill was little more than a squeak, but it distracted him anyway.

Ripper of Souls looked toward the bed, at the dying woman, as her mouth moved again, emitting a single, barely audible word. "Murderer," she managed, the toll that the effort took upon her obvious.

The assassin could not contain himself, and he stepped closer to the bed.

"Yes," he whispered, ignoring the psychic pleas of his weapon. It so wanted to kill the woman, but Ripper decided that he would not waste a single projectile or drop of venom.

Instead, he reached out, placed a skeletal hand firmly over the woman's mouth and nose, and held it there. Her eyes grew wide with the realization that this was her time and that he would be the one to take her life.

"I *am* a murderer," he told her, watching the life drain from her eyes as he had her daughter before. "And I do so love my job."

Ashley bounded up the stairs, her heart pounding to the point that she thought it might just burst through her ribs.

"Remy," she cried as she practically leapt into the bedroom, her momentum stopped cold by the sight of him lying so very still upon the bed.

Marlowe let out an excited bark, his tail wagging furiously as he jumped from his spot next to Remy and ran to greet her.

"What's happened, boy?" she found herself asking, on the verge of crying, but she refused to let the emotion override her control. It wouldn't do her any good to lose it now.

It was then that she noticed the dark-skinned man sitting so very still at the top of the bed beside her friend, his hand pressed to Remy's heart.

"Hello?" she said. "Can you tell me what happened? . . . Can you tell me if he'll be . . ." Her voice started to crack and she stopped to take a deep breath. "Can you tell me if he'll be all right?"

When the man didn't answer, Ashley rounded the bed with Marlowe close at her side. The man appeared to be in a kind of trance, his eyes barely open—just slits, really.

"Hello?" she said again.

The man continued to remain perfectly still. Slowly, she reached a tentative hand out.

The tips of her fingers touched his shoulder.

"Can you hear me?"

Assiel walked in the darkness of the angel Remiel's psyche.

It was a turbulent place filled with equal parts darkness and light, and in all his time he had never seen another like it.

It had been his purpose to help heal those who were injured; sometimes using balms, sometimes potions, and sometimes something more drastic.

Something far more intense.

Assiel had the ability to connect with a being's inner self, that which linked him to the flow of creation.

The source of all existence.

In humanity, it was the most fabulous and wonderful of creations. A very piece of the Lord God Himself imbued in each and every one of these special life-forms.

The soul was always a source of amazement for him, but until this moment, he had been certain that only on members of the human race had this amazing gift been bestowed.

Until this moment.

The healer had never seen anything quite like this.

An angel's life essence was like a ball of fire, consistently feeding upon and being fed by the life energies of the universe, whereas the soul was a thing of absolute beauty, an intricate mechanism of branches and roots connected not only to the source of all life, but to the Almighty Himself.

What Assiel saw before him now was a thing of awesomeness. It was all that made Remy angel, blended with what looked to be the beginnings of a human soul.

It was something vibrant and alive. It was what all angels had craved since the creation of humanity.

Only the Lord God could have created such a thing as this.

But as Assiel drew closer to the pulsing energy that was shaped like a mighty tree, he found something that tweaked his curiosity. Root-like tendrils extended from the base of the tree, flowing down into the earthen substance of Remiel's psychic landscape. The tendrils seemed to be discolored, growing darker as they entered the earth.

Assiel knelt down and began to dig at the dirtlike substance. The blackening roots seemed to merge together, becoming entangled as they continued downward. Sensing that something wasn't right, the healer dug deeper into the gritty matter as he followed the braided root.

The ground beneath his knees suddenly gave way, exposing a swirling void of indescribable origin. Assiel managed to grab hold of the root at its thickest point and haul himself back up to firmer ground, even as he felt the maelstrom of nothingness beneath him attempting to pull him down.

But now he knew what was happening to Remy.

The angel's special life energies were being drained, drawn through the darkened root, down into the swirling abyss, to . . .

"Can you hear me?"

The dark-skinned man sitting beside Remy gasped and spun around to face Ashley.

"I'm sorry," Ashley said, quickly stepping back, nearly tripping over Marlowe.

The man's eyes were wide and dark, and he seemed confused, as if awakened from a very real dream.

"Who are you?" he asked.

"I'm Ashley."

"Another of the Seraphim's lovers?"

"Lovers?" Ashley repeated, horrified at the thought. "No way, I'm his friend."

The man made a face that could only have meant *whatever* and turned his attentions back to Remy.

"How is he doing? Is he going to be all right?" Ashley asked as she crept closer to the bed.

The man was examining her friend, and for the first time she noticed that Remy was completely naked, but she didn't care; there wasn't room for modesty or embarrassment now.

"I had just managed to infiltrate your lover's psyche—"

"He's not my lover," Ashley interrupted.

"And had discovered the source of his unconsciousness," he continued as though she hadn't spoken, "but your touch drew me back." The man focused his cold, dark eyes directly on Ashley.

"I'm sorry, I . . . ," Ashley stammered, suddenly terrified that she could have somehow made Remy worse.

"I had no choice," the man said, again ignoring her words. "I couldn't fight the pull of your want."

"My want? I don't understand. . . ."

"The concern for your lover," the man explained. "You wanted—*needed*—to know if he would be all right, and I was the source of that information."

"I guess," Ashley said slowly, not even bothering to correct the man this time. "So, will he be all right?"

The man returned his intense gaze to Remy. "If things continue as they are, he will leave us."

Ashley felt like she'd been punched in the stomach.

"Is everything okay, Ash?"

Ashley turned to see Linda and Steven Mulvehill in the doorway to Remy's room. "Yeah," she answered on reflex, but then changed her mind. "No, nothing's okay," she said, fighting back her emotions.

"Unless . . . ," the dark-skinned man suddenly said.

"Excuse me?" Mulvehill asked.

"If things are allowed to continue as is, Remiel will leave us—unless . . ." His voice trailed off.

"Unless what, Assiel?" Linda asked.

Assiel turned from the bed and approached them. "The strength of your affections for him," he said, reaching out to lay his hand atop Ashley's head, then Linda's.

Mulvehill tried to move away as Assiel reached for him, but the angel would not be dissuaded. He laid his hand atop the detective's head and then leaned down to do the same to Marlowe.

"Incredible," the angel physician said, the hint of a smile playing at the corners of his mouth. "It could work."

"What?" Linda demanded. "What could work?"

Assiel returned to Remy's side, ignoring Linda's questions. "Yes, it's definitely a possibility," he muttered to himself.

"I swear I'm going to scream if you don't—," Ashley started to say, but was once again interrupted by Assiel.

"You could prevent his soul energies from leaving. . . . You can help to anchor him here."

CHAPTER THIRTEEN

In the beginning, there was the black of nothingness.

But then there was the light. That first spark of brilliance—a thought of creation—sent out into the nothing by the Supreme Power that began it all.

And from that godly contemplation came the beginning of everything.

Thuc Pham sat upon a bamboo mat in a hut in the tiny North Vietnamese village of Nà Bái and watched the creation of the universe unfold.

He had done this over and over again for days, but it never got old.

He pulled the statue of the open-armed infant closer, allowing the influence of the contents stored within the vessel to radiate through his body.

Thuc smiled as he watched the universe take shape, experiencing the exultation of genesis and the euphoria that followed. He was there as a fragment of creation itself fell to the newly birthed world below, where it nestled in the belly of the earth and slept, sated by the fulfillment of its purpose.

Thuc saw all who had come before him, the holy men whose purpose it had been to protect that fragment after it had been taken from the earth. He was the last of such holy men. He had managed to save the fragment from the woman called Delilah, who had stolen it in hopes of reshaping the world in her own perverted image.

Since then, he had watched over the vessel as he and the fragment had wandered the world that it had helped to fashion so very long ago.

And eventually they'd ended up here, in the very place where it had first fallen.

Where it was to now be returned.

Hugging the container to his naked body, he wanted to remember everything about being guardian to a piece of creation itself, before letting it go.

And that was his downfall, for he had waited too long.

Their location had been found.

Francis stepped from a patch of darkness thrown by the trees of a primordial jungle just beyond the outskirts of the Vietnamese village. Simeon had insisted that that three demons accompany him to Nà Bái, but for what reason, Francis really wasn't sure.

Maybe it's a trust issue, he thought. Maybe Simeon wanted to be sure that he wouldn't abscond with the artifact that he'd agreed to acquire in exchange for information that could help Remy.

Maybe.

"Looks like that's where we're going," Francis said aloud, as he stared across a clearing at the small rustic village.

The demons remained silent, but their eyes followed his gaze.

"Do you have names?" Francis asked them. "Or would you prefer that I make something up?"

They remained silent, appearing uncomfortable with the fact that he was talking to them.

"For example," Francis continued, "the first person who comes to mind when I look at you is Buddy Ebsen."

The tall, lanky demon looked at him with a snarl of confusion.

"Yeah, doesn't make any fucking sense to me, either. I'm not even going to tell you the name that came to mind when I looked at the chick beside you."

It was the female that then stepped forward.

"I'm Dorian," she said, and then hooked a finger toward Buddy Ebsen, beside her. "This is Beleeze."

"Huh," Francis said. "And you?" he asked the last of the three.

"Robert," the demon said.

"Robert?"

"You have a problem with Robert?"

"His name used to be Tjernobog," sneered Beleeze.

"I can see why you went with *Robert,*" Francis said, turning his attention back to the village. "Okay, now that we're all BFFs, let's figure out what we're doing next."

The demons silently agreed.

"We're supposed to be looking for a metal vessel in the shape of a baby, which is in the possession of some Vietnamese guy who has been holed up in this village. Did I get everything?"

The demons stared.

"Thought so," Francis said. He reached into his suit coat pocket and pulled out a circular metal compass.

"Your boss gave this to me," he said as he flipped back the hinged golden cover. "It's a compass supposedly attuned to specific supernatural energies."

He pointed it toward the village, watching as the needle wobbled within the glass casing before pointing to the left of a Quonset hut at the edge of the clearing.

"And it looks like we need to be concentrating our attention that way."

Francis began to move into the clearing, checking to see that his demonic backup was with him. They were indeed.

And they were armed to the teeth.

"Seriously?" Francis asked them.

"Not taking any chances," Dorian said, making sure that her .45 had one in the chamber.

Beleeze held a nasty-looking hooked blade that hadn't been designed for anything but killing, while Robert held a Glock 18 machine pistol.

Maybe they knew more than they were letting on.

Francis was tempted to take out his own pistol but decided that he would wait.

They rounded the hut into what seemed to be a small community area. One by one, villagers stopped what they were doing and stared.

Francis could sense the tension building in the demonic trio behind him. "Stay cool," he warned. Then stepped forward with what he hoped was a winning smile. "Hello," he said in fluent Vietnamese. "My friends and I have traveled a long way in search of a man and the special item that he carries with him."

He paused to gauge their reactions. Lots of sideways glances and muttering voices told him that they knew who he was talking about.

"Could you point us in the right direction?" he asked. "Would really appreciate it."

The crowd remained quiet, many returning to the tasks they had been performing when he and the three demonic amigos had arrived.

"Hello?" he called out, wanting to give them another chance before they did this the hard way.

And then he saw the young boy.

He was shirtless, his sunburned skin the color of a penny. He wore a pair of red swimming trunks, tube socks, and ragged sandals, and carried a burlap sack slung over his shoulder.

"Hello there," Francis said, almost believing that they'd struck pay dirt. "Do you have any information . . ."

The boy sloughed the sack onto the ground in one fluid gesture. As he reached his hand inside the sack, a monkey leapt out and, with a shriek, ran off through the village. Then the boy's hand emerged holding an old, rusty-looking pistol. Without a moment's hesitation, he fired three quick shots, hitting Francis square in the chest and hurling him back to the ground.

The demons reacted at once, opening fire on the child before he could shoot again.

"Knock it off!" Francis yelled as he watched the child crumple to the ground. The wounds in his chest were already healing, but they were still painful as he lurched to his feet and stumbled toward the fallen boy.

"You stupid ass," he scowled.

The boy smiled a bloodstained grin. "He's ready for you now." Then he laughed a short, gurgling laugh and died.

The villagers had gathered together, and Francis saw that many carried weapons.

"Something tells me this is about to get complicated," he said, turning to his demon buddies.

"*Complicated* is for pussies," Robert said as he raised his machine pistol and sprayed the crowd with bullets.

Through the vessel, Thuc Pham felt a sudden disturbance in the ether, alerting him that trouble had arrived.

Cursing, he released the metal infant, cutting off his wondrous connection to the stuff of creation. How could he have waited so long?

The gunshots outside told him that now he was too late. A nagging voice in the back of his mind said running would only delay the inevitable, but still he attempted escape, quickly dressing and grabbing the vessel.

"Hey, I've been looking for one of those."

Thuc Pham spun around toward the unfamiliar voice from the doorway. A tall, bald-headed figure wearing dark-framed glasses and a three-piece business suit stood there, pointing a golden gun at him.

Thuc immediately felt the fragment within the vessel react to the man's presence and wondered if this was actually a man at all. In his mind, he saw flashes of a Heavenly city and the winged beings that called it home.

"You're of Heaven," Thuc said, believing for a moment that a greater power had been sent to aid them.

The man seemed momentarily taken aback, the barrel of his pistol lowering just a bit, but he quickly recovered. "That was a long time ago," he said as he raised his gun again. "Put the vessel down and step away from it."

Thuc did not understand. The fragment continued to bombard his mind with images of the Almighty's winged messengers.

The power of creation said to trust this man—this citizen of the Heavens—but his actions . . .

Thuc bent to place the vessel upon the hut's dirt floor, when there was a flurry of movement behind the man at the door.

And the demons stepped in.

Francis felt the stooges step up behind him and watched the Vietnamese man straighten with the vessel and make a run for the open window at the back of the hut.

Francis prepared to fire, but a sudden sense that he was about to do something truly wrong caused his trigger finger to relax. *What the fuck is this about?* the former Guardian angel wondered, feeling as though his brain had just been scorched by fire.

The sound of a gunshot made him jump, pulling him from his troubled thoughts. He watched the man tumble forward to the ground, atop the metal container, as Dorian pushed past him.

"Don't tell me you can't shoot a man in the back," she said with a snarl that showed off delicate, pointy teeth, reminding him of a piranha.

Her partners in crime chuckled as she loomed over the still body of the Vietnamese man.

"Be careful," Beleeze called out, and Francis got a sense that he really meant it.

She turned to look at him ever so slightly, a hint of a smile playing at the corner of her mouth, before reaching down to turn the man over. But he rolled on his own. He was holding the metal container up toward her, and it had begun to open.

Dorian had just enough time to utter a gasp of surprise as a wave of a churning energy radiated from the parting seams, enveloping her in a swirling cloud that quickly dissolved her flesh and bones. Within seconds she was gone, little more than particles of dust whirling amidst the unbridled power that continued to leak from the vessel.

"No!" Beleeze wailed. "No! No! No!"

He started toward the Vietnamese man, who now knelt with the receptacle outstretched before him, the vertical slit opening wider, sending forth even more of the corrosive energy.

Francis leapt at Beleeze, tackling him before the demon suffered Dorian's fate.

"No sense in killing yourself, too," Francis said, hauling the thrashing demon to his feet and attempting to drag him toward the door, away from the expanding cloud of destruction.

"No! I want to be with her!" Beleeze hissed, fighting the former Guardian's grip upon him.

"We might all be with her shortly," Francis said.

It was as if the room was being disassembled, broken down to its molecular structure, and scattered to the wind. Francis briefly wondered what it would be like to be uncreated as the power contained within the vessel flowed dangerously closer.

He was about to open an escape portal, but the sight of a figure in the open window behind the Vietnamese man gave him pause. He watched as the figure crawled through the window and crept up behind the man.

A fountain of blood suddenly erupted from the man's chest, followed by the point of a sword. The Vietnamese man stiffened, dropping the vessel to the floor, where it snapped closed, cutting off the radiance of the power contained within. As if in slow motion, the man slid forward, falling face-first to the floor, revealing the mystery man who had dispatched him, bloody sword still in hand.

Francis immediately recognized him; tall, blond hair, an air of authority about him—but also a stink of the demonic. He'd last seen this man with the Vatican sorcerers, the Keepers, on the Japanese island of Gunkanjima.

But what was he doing here?

The Keeper stared at Francis, his eyes filled with hate, giving the fallen angel a sense that something supremely evil was behind those dark portals.

Saying nothing, the man dropped the bloodstained sword and approached the container. He knelt down, preparing to retrieve it, but Francis still had questions to be answered.

"I wouldn't do that," he said, aiming his gun.

The man ignored the threat, carefully lifting the vessel from the floor with a defiant smile.

"It's quite all right, Francis," a familiar voice said from behind him. "Constantin works with me."

Simeon strolled in through the front entrance, his focus on the man holding the object.

"He works for the Vatican," Francis said. He still hadn't lowered his pistol.

"You remember that, do you?" Simeon asked.

"I do," Francis answered.

"I wish you didn't."

"What?"

"I wish you didn't remember him," Simeon said, twisting the ring on his right hand. "In fact, I'm telling you to forget him completely."

Francis was suddenly confused, almost positive that he'd been about to ask an important question, but now it was gone.

"What was that?" Simeon prompted.

Francis just stared as he lowered his gun.

"Excellent," Simeon said. He motioned to a man Francis did not recall seeing enter. "Now let us return home so that I can fulfill my part of the bargain." Simeon left the hut, the man carrying the vessel directly behind him.

Francis reluctantly followed, the idea that something important had been lost niggling at the back of his mind, but within seconds, that, too, was gone.

CHAPTER FOURTEEN

Baarabus slunk down the side of the mountain, snout raised to the noxious air, sifting through the numerous scents in search of danger.

The smells were there; the stink of Filthies was weak, old, the enemy having moved on.

He stopped, perched upon an outcropping of smooth, melted stone, and gazed out over the ruined landscape and beyond, a hint of what had once been rising to the surface in a miasma of memory.

The recollections came in violent flashes, moments of a past that he could no longer recall but remained there, waiting for him like images in a stranger's album of photographs.

He saw what the world had been like before. . . .

He remembered the happiness of freedom, the sounds of birds chirping in rows of trees, of running through thick summer grass, the smell of a recent thunderstorm still lingering in the air. The nearly overwhelming emotions felt as a gentle, loving hand petted his head and a voice that made him quiver with adoration told him that he was a good boy.

They were not his memories but the memories of a life lived before.

A life prevented from ending.

A life grafted to the existence of another to create . . .

What exactly am I? Baarabus pondered, bombarded with the sensory remembrances of another.

A good boy, answered a voice—a ghost—from another time, unaware of what nightmarish occurrences had created something as far from a good boy as could be.

The demon hound felt the sensation of a gentle hand upon his head, scratching behind his ears, and quickly stood, as if to pull away from the loving touch.

But it was all a memory.

A memory belonging to another.

A good boy.

Baarabus turned his powerful snout to the air again. It seemed safe enough to resume their journey.

And that sparked another thought. Though he did not care to, Baarabus had no choice but to consider the sudden, dramatic change in their leader. It was maddening, and the demon hound's true nature wanted nothing more than to surge forward and rip the angel's throat out when his guard was down.

But that wouldn't help anything, other than to release some aggravation. They'd be in an even worse situation without Remy than they were with a Remy who wasn't quite himself.

It was all so maddening.

The Fossil believed Remy's memories would awaken with time. They would just have to wait and see.

The hound began the climb back up the face of the mountain to the cave entrance. They could leave now. To hopefully continue where they had left off.

Offhandedly, the demon hound wondered whether it would be painful for this Remy to remember what his part had been in the fate of the world. What he had done.

Baarabus hoped that it would be.

It took them the better part of the morning to reach the ground below the mountains.

Remy tried to figure out exactly where he was, but nothing looked familiar anymore. They could have been on another planet, except for the occasional twisted remains of a car or a blackened street sign rising up out of the dirt and rubble.

"Hard to believe," he said, more to himself than to anybody.

"What?" the Fossil asked as he walked along beside him.

"This," Remy answered, motioning with his chin at the bleak landscape. "That Heaven was somehow responsible."

The old-timer squinted, causing the skin around his eyes, thick with scabs, to split and bleed.

"It wasn't the intention, I assure you," the Fossil said, rivulets of blood running down his cheeks like tears. "It was all supposed to come together." He locked his fingers together. "Like the pieces of a puzzle, to form a single glorious thing."

He looked at his scab-covered hands, seeing something else.

"A unified place."

The Fossil let his hands drift apart. "But it didn't happen. . . . It went wrong—horribly, horribly wrong."

"Now, that's a fucking understatement," Baarabus added.

Samson's children laughed, the sound strange in the bleakness of the environment.

"With God dead, the pieces didn't fit anymore," the Fossil went on. He made two fists and started to bang them together. "But the motion had already begun."

The wind picked up suddenly, blowing across the bleak landscape, throwing clouds of scouring grit into their faces. The land before them was flat as far as the eye could see. At one time, a city might have stood here, or an ocean, dried up after the supernatural calamity.

They walked in silence for what seemed like days, but even the passage of time wasn't what it used to be, the clouds of dust, ash, and smoke so thick in the air that this new world was always in a perpetual state of twilight.

The remains of a great city seemed to suddenly appear in the distance, rising up out of the thick clouds, like the sheet in a magic trick being pulled away to reveal the broken remnants of the metropolis beneath.

Remy squinted through the blowing grime, trying to get a bead on which city this was, but it was visual gibberish, the once striking structures of Heaven's sprawling celestial city crammed together with those of a far more human design.

Through the swirling dust it looked like something out of a very bad dream.

"For a moment you'll think you recognize something, and then you won't," the Fossil said. He had pulled up a scarf to protect most of his bloody face from the flying dirt. "That's just how it is now. Everything has changed; there's nothing familiar anymore."

The demon dog padded up alongside them. "And you're planning on simply walking in there and finding the door that fits your special key." The dog turned his large black head to fix Remy in an icy stare.

"That's the plan," Remy said, staring as the city disappeared and reappeared again in the shifting environment.

"It's fucking nuts," the dog grumbled.

"But it's all we've got," Remy said, putting his hand into the deep pocket of his heavy coat to touch the key. Like sparks of fire, there were flashes inside his head; images of a long stone corridor with a heavy wooden door at the end.

He started to walk again, not caring if the others followed or not; the key would take him where he needed to go.

Hopefully there would be answers there.

Streets once bustling with people and traffic were now buried beneath mounds of shifting dirt and rubble. Remy walked down the center of a passage, half-buried storefronts peeking out from beneath filthy drifts that hissed and changed shape as the whipping winds continued to erode and redefine the devastated landscape.

"Any of this familiar?" Baarabus called to him.

Remy stopped to see the great hound standing before the partially buried front of an apartment building. It wasn't at all familiar, but he approached for a closer look anyway.

The building appeared to be a typical brick brownstone, but another element had tried to join with it. Brick and the stuff of Heaven's Golden City melded together, two structures fighting to share a single space.

"Is this it?" Baarabus asked.

"No."

"Huh," the dog grunted. "Didn't figure we'd be that lucky."

Remy turned back to the street to see that Samson's children were fanning out, searching, although he couldn't tell them what to look for, other than a wooden door. Hopefully, he would know it when he saw it.

The sounds of somebody screaming nearby changed the subject in an instant, immediately putting them all on alert.

"Stay together," Baarabus commanded, as Remy started to move toward the desperate sound.

He trudged through the sand and dirt to the end of the street and peered around the corner. A man was staggering toward him, his exposed skin and clothing covered with blood. Behind him was a wall made of the twisted wreckage of old cars and trucks.

"Help me!" the man cried, reaching out to Remy, his eyes wide with desperation. "Please!" He fell into Remy's arms, and the angel could see that the bleeding was caused by multiple bites and scratches, as if the poor fellow had been attacked by an animal.

"I have to get away or they'll take me back."

"What's his story?" Baarabus asked, slinking up beside them.

The man lifted his head to the voice, and upon seeing the hound at once began to shriek.

"No! No! No!" he cried, tearing himself from Remy's grasp, his arms flailing as he attempted to run back from where he had come.

"Not a dog lover, I'd guess," Baarabus said.

"He said that somebody was coming to take him back," Remy said.

The man fell but continued his desperate struggle to get away, trying to crawl to his knees, glancing back at them with escalating terror.

"Leave him," the Fossil said. "I see nothing but trouble there."

Remy looked at him with squinted eyes. "He's injured," he said, then turned away, walking toward the man.

He reached down and helped the man to his feet where he'd fallen, receiving little resistance. "We'll find shelter and see if we can patch him up," Remy said to the others as he guided the moaning figure toward a cluster of buildings whose entrances seemed free enough of dirt to allow them access.

Remy dragged the nearly weightless man into one of the buildings and gently laid him down on the floor of what used to be an office directly to the right. He placed beneath the man's head a dusty cushion that had once been on the seat of an overturned chair.

Glancing toward the entry way he saw that the others had followed, looking about as they cautiously entered.

"It seems safe," Remy encouraged them as he knelt beside the practically unconscious man.

"Seems," the Fossil emphasized, removing the scarf from his face. "Things that seem normal, like that man right there, can often lead to something dangerous," he warned.

"He needs help," Remy countered. "We'll patch him up the best we can and then be on our way."

The old man scowled as Baarabus came to stand beside him.

"Guess he told you," the hound said with a chuckle, then sauntered away.

Remy began to open the man's shirt, and a young woman knelt down beside him. It was Samson's daughter, Leila, and she carried a canteen of water, some bandages, and what looked to be some almost-used-up tubes of antibiotic ointment.

"Thanks," he said as she went to work cleaning the injured man's wounds.

Leila looked at him briefly, then back to her work. "I really don't have any idea why I'm doing this. It's a waste of time—he'll probably be dead shortly anyway."

"At least we're trying to do something," Remy said.

She laughed then, shaking her head.

"What's so funny?"

"You. If anybody was still doubting that you're some other Remy, this proves it."

"I don't understand."

"The Remy that came out of the ruins wouldn't have thought twice about letting this guy die," Leila said, putting as much of the ointment on the wounds as she could spare. "Probably would have helped put him out of his misery."

Remy had no idea how to respond, trying to imagine the kind of being the other version of himself had become. "I'm not that far gone yet."

She gave him a sideways look.

"Yet."

Leila finished cleaning the man's wounds without another word, then was gone, going back to rejoin her brothers.

Remy stayed by the man's side as the group rested, closing his eyes and actually drifting off into a fugue state. But instead of the normally calming state of mind, all he could see was the world coming to an end accompanied by a symphony of screams. And above those screams, boring into his brain, were the prayers of those begging to be spared, asking their Lord God Almighty what they had done to deserve a fate so terrifying, and why He wouldn't be merciful and take them without pain.

Remy opened his eyes with a start and found himself staring directly into the open eyes of the injured man. It took him a moment to realize that the man was dead. Leila's assertion was correct. He hadn't made it.

There was a thick green trash bag nearby, and Remy reached for it, using it to cover the dead stranger's face.

"Now how do you feel?" asked the Fossil, suddenly standing before him.

"What do you mean how do I feel? How do I feel that he's dead?"

The Fossil shook his head. "How do you feel that what you did was all for nothing?"

"I don't think of it that way," Remy said, staring at the body lying so very still upon the floor.

"You should have left him there."

"Alone . . . injured, to die in the street?"

"I know it sounds harsh, but yes."

"I'm not him," Remy said.

"Yes, yes, you are. You're just not him *yet*."

Remy sneered at the old man.

"There's still a lot for you to learn."

Remy stood, eyes still on the corpse. "I suppose we'll just have to leave him here," he said.

"Where else would you put him?" the Fossil asked. "Do you feel obliged to give him a proper burial? Wake up, Remy. The whole fucking world is a cemetery."

He was about to begrudgingly accept the Fossil's words when he heard the sounds above them. At first he thought it was just the wind howling outside, but it became louder, more insistent, almost as if there was somebody—or some*thing*—moving in the ceiling above.

Baarabus heard it as well, bolting over to them, his dark eyes riveted to the stained panel ceiling.

"We've got to get outside," he started to say, but his words were drowned out as their attackers dropped down through the panels.

Angels—or what passed for them these horrific days.

They dropped down to the ground, sparse and diseased-looking wings furled to slow and silence their descent. In their hands were weapons of sputtering fire, as if the divinity they had once possessed was on the verge of running out.

"Filthies!" the children of Samson bellowed, grabbing their own weapons and charging in to join the fray.

The filthy angels continued to drop through the ceiling, a seemingly endless storm of twisted divinity. Baarabus was something to behold, reminding Remy of that character in the Warner Brothers cartoons that swirled around in its own portable tornado; it took a moment for the memory to come, but it was suddenly there. The Tasmanian Devil—the demon dog moved like the Tasmanian Devil as it dealt with its multiple attackers. Guns were fired, and screams of rage and pain filled the air.

Filthies swarmed around Remy, and he tried unsuccessfully to summon wings, only to feel a searing pain and an overwhelming sense of loss.

But there was no time to ponder these sensations. Instead, Remy tapped into the pool of anger and frustration that he had been feeling since awakening in this nightmare place.

It was good to give it somewhere to go, good to have something to lash out against.

The Filthies were upon him, their combined weight driving him to the floor. One held a bent and jagged piece of metal that glowed with the remnants of divine fire, and was attempting to shove the blade into Remy's neck. With a surge of strength, he managed to toss off one of the scrawny warriors that clung to his arm. He reached up, shoving his thumb deep into the eye socket of the wretched creature above him. The angel went rigid, and the blade dropped from its grasp as it fell away. Remy retrieved the weapon and immediately went to work, jabbing and slashing at those who attempted to take him down.

He drove the blade of his knife into the neck of a Filthy, nearly severing its head from its shoulders, and retrieved that dying angel's short sword. That was much more to Remy's liking, giving him more distance and striking power. There were flashes of memory amongst the screams, and spurts of black blood, flashes of another time when he was forced to slay those who had once been his brothers.

He remembered the war and Heaven and the lives he took, how he'd walked away when all was said and done, swearing never to return or to be that deplorable creature again.

And here he was.

The realization was like being doused with cold water, and he was suddenly paralyzed by the carnage he had wrought.

"No," he screamed at the hacked and bloody bodies that had piled up around him, trying to force back the howling rage that wanted him to continue the carnage he'd started.

That moment of hesitation was all that the Filthies needed. The tip of a burning knife slid into his flesh, the heat of its weakened Heavenly fire searing him from the inside out. Remy opened his mouth in a silent scream as he fell, his own body cushioned by those he had already struck down.

He fought to shrug off the electrifying numbness that rendered his limbs nearly useless. He could see more Filthies continuing to pour in through the ceiling, and now through the door, a tidal wave of poisoned divinity seemingly hell-bent on bringing them down. Samson's children fought well, but many had fallen beneath the Filthies' weaponry. Remy's eyes darted about the carnage, looking for Leila, but he did not see her.

A deafening roar filled the room and Remy watched as Baarabus was brought down by a net infused with the remnants of divinity draped around his body and cinched tight.

"No need for any more of the rough stuff," he heard the Fossil say and saw him raise his scab-crusted arms in surrender. The Filthies beat him over the head with the pommels of their swords until he crumpled to the floor.

Remy fought to rise to his feet and managed to get to his knees, kneeling upon the slain Filthies, swaying as his still living enemies encircled him, brandishing their weapons eagerly.

"Let's get this over with," he croaked, ready to die despite the fact that there was still so very much he did not know.

Maybe, said a part of him, *that is for the better.*

The Filthies appeared to be about to pounce on him, when there came a sudden buzz, voices of the angels at the far back of the gathering speaking in harsh whispers that spread throughout the crowd.

Then the crowd parted like the Red Sea in the old Cecil B. DeMille classic to reveal a hunched figure slowly making its way toward Remy.

"Does my eye deceive me?" asked a voice as dry and seemingly encrusted as the flesh of the Filthies. Yet there was something familiar about it.

The figure stood before Remy, and he felt his blood become like ice as he recognized the angel.

The Archangel Michael was a shell of his former glory: his perfect skin covered with puckered scars; only one of his once glorious golden wings left upon his back; his luxurious hair, at one time like spun gold, merely stubble upon a pocked and scarred skull.

Michael leaned closer, focusing his single good eye on Remy.

"Ah yes, it is a familiar face," said the archangel with a chilling smile of black and jagged teeth. "So very nice to be reunited with family."

And with a barely perceptible nod from their master, the Filthies reacted, swarming upon Remy, fists and weapons raining down upon him, driving him into a bed of corpses.

CHAPTER FIFTEEN

She felt as if they were gathered to say their good-byes, but that wasn't the case at all. At least that's what Linda kept telling herself.

"So this will save him?" she asked, pulling her gaze from the paleness of her dying lover.

The angel Assiel was standing at the foot of the bed. "There is a chance, yes," he said, but his tone didn't quite give her the boost of confidence she was looking for.

"If there's any chance at all, I say we do it," Ashley said, nervously petting Marlowe's head as he sat beside her.

"I'm still not a hundred percent on what you're asking them to do," Mulvehill said. He and the ugly little man named Squire were standing in the doorway. "Could you run it by me again?"

"Jesus," Squire said with an eye roll. "He's going to send them into Remy's psyche to anchor his life energies before they're completely drained away. Do you need me to draw a fucking diagram?"

"Y'know what? A fucking diagram might be helpful," the police detective snapped, the tension in the room beginning to show its effects.

"They are the three closest to his heart," Assiel said.

"Three?" Linda asked.

"Yes, three," the healer confirmed. "Ashley, you, and him." The angel pointed to Marlowe, whose tail had begun to wag.

"Marlowe? Are you serious?"

Assiel nodded. "The animal shares a special bond, similar but unlike the connection you two share with him. Marlowe's link will serve to reinforce each of your own."

Linda knelt before the dog and gave him a hug as he licked her face. "I always knew you were a special boy," she said. "Of course you'll be part of saving Remy."

"And us?" Squire asked. "Should we be part of this Vulcan mind-meld pajama party?"

"Unnecessary," Assiel said. "I think these three will be more than sufficient. You two will need to stand guard over us, for as long as we are connected to Remy, we will be unable to defend ourselves."

"See, that's something I can understand. We'll hold down the fort while you guys are fixing him up."

Mulvehill was staring at Remy, and Linda could see the concern in his eyes.

"I've got a good feeling about this," he said with a nod. "I think it's going to work."

"Yeah, linking up two women and a dog to the dwindling life energies of a Seraphim—what could go wrong?" Squire asked sarcastically.

Mulvehill slapped the top of the ugly little man's head. "We don't need that right now," he said with a snarl.

"Watch it, Detective," Squire said, rubbing the sparse hair of his oddly shaped head. "We aren't that close."

Linda had had enough. "What do we need to do?" she prompted Assiel, nervously rubbing her hands together.

"Get on the bed with him," Assiel ordered, motioning with his long fingers.

Linda sat next to Remy.

"Closer," the angel corrected. "I need you all as close to him as you can get."

"Like this?" Linda asked, crawling up onto the bed and lying beside her lover.

Assiel nodded. "Closer if possible." The angel looked at Ashley. "You as well—close."

Ashley moved around to the other side of the bed and lay down beside Remy. "This is a little bit uncomfortable," she said, giving Linda a quick, embarrassed look.

"It's all right, Ash," Linda said. "Get closer." She had put Remy's arm around her and was snuggling closer.

Ashley reluctantly did the same.

"Marlowe?" Assiel addressed the dog.

"C'mon, boy," Linda said, patting the area between Remy's legs.

The Labrador obliged, jumping up onto the bed and plopping himself down with a grunt between his master's legs. The dog sighed as he rested his chin on Remy's thigh.

The angel looked them over and seemed satisfied.

"I will be the means by which you are connected," he explained. "The anchor that keeps you rooted to Remiel's psyche."

The healer hopped up onto the bed and positioned himself as close to them as he could up near the wooden headboard.

"Is this going to hurt?" Ashley asked nervously. "I'm okay if it does; I just want to prepare myself."

"You will find the experience . . . jarring," the angel told them. "Each of you—each of your souls—will connect to the specific aspect of his psyche that has made you so important to him, hopefully providing Remiel with the strength to remain."

He paused to let it all sink in.

"Are we ready?"

Linda held on to Remy as tightly as she could, seeing that Ashley was doing the same. Marlowe still rested his chin upon his master's leg and was snoring loudly. Maybe the Labrador had already made the journey inside.

"Ready," Linda said.

"Me, too," Ashley confirmed.

"Then let us begin."

Assiel lifted his hand and held it out before him. Linda could not help but look, and she could have sworn that the lighter-colored flesh of the angel's palm had started to glow.

"Good luck," Mulvehill called from the doorway, while Squire remained silent.

Linda was sure that the strange little man knew more about things like this than he was letting on. But there was no turning back now.

Assiel lowered his hand to Remy's bare chest.

Linda's eyes became incredibly heavy, and as they closed, she felt the bed—the very world—disappear from beneath her.

And she began to fall.

Mulvehill watched the group on the bed, expecting something dramatic. "Is that it?"

"Yeah, I'd say so," Squire answered.

"They just look like they've gone to sleep."

"What were you expecting?"

Mulvehill shrugged. "I don't know, just thought there would be a little more to it."

"There's plenty to it already," the hobgoblin replied. "If they can't stop Remy's life force from draining away—"

"He'll die."

"Bingo."

They stood there, staring at the five forms crowded upon the bed.

"What should we do? Do you think we can leave them?" Mulvehill asked.

"Don't see why we can't."

"Will they be all right?"

"Can't answer that," Squire said. "But there's nothing we can do anyway, with us out here"—he pointed at Remy—"and all of them in there."

"Yeah," Mulvehill agreed. He continued to watch them, making sure that they were all still breathing—they were, but it didn't stop him from worrying.

"I need a drink," Squire said.

"I'm sure you do; it's been, what? Twenty minutes?"

"Are you always this big of an asshole, or are you just tense on account'a the situation?"

"I'm an asshole," Mulvehill said, following Squire as he left the room and headed for the stairs.

"Thought so."

Mulvehill stopped at the top of the stairs and looked back into the room, just in case. . . .

"Are you coming?" Squire asked, already halfway down.

Mulvehill tore his gaze from the doorway and started down.

"I could use a sandwich, too," Squire added.

"That doesn't surprise me, either. You haven't eaten in an hour."

"Has it been that long? Maybe I'll make a meal instead."

Mulvehill had stopped again, looking back up at the top of the stairs.

"What now?" Squire asked, annoyed.

"Nothing," Mulvehill said. "I think I'm just going to sit here for a little while." He lowered himself down onto the step.

Squire continued down to the hallway below. "Do you want anything?" he called over his shoulder.

"No, I'm good," Mulvehill answered.

"Suit yourself, but don't think you're going to have any of my sandwich."

But Squire's words were lost on Mulvehill as he tuned in to the bedroom above, listening carefully for any sounds that might be out of the ordinary.

Ashley wanted to scream. It all happened so fast.

One second she was on the bed, huddled up close to her dying friend, and the next . . .

Her brain was telling her that she was falling, but she couldn't see . . . anything. There was no up or down, nothing to show her what was happening, other than her every instinct screaming that she was about to die, but if that was the case . . .

When?

The falling sensation seemed to go on and on, and soon it became almost old hat, like something she was completely used to, just the way things were, plummeting forever into the darkness.

And then she wasn't.

Ashley had arrived—somewhere. As suddenly as she had disappeared from the bed, she was now standing in a field of tall golden grass.

As she tried to acclimate to her new and unfamiliar surroundings, the field of grass suddenly erupted in fire, and all around her were the screams and smells that could only herald death.

It was pure survival instinct that drove her to run. She had no idea where she was going, only knew that she had to get away.

Smoke writhed up into the sky as the golden grass burned. Ashley's gaze followed the snaking trails, and what she saw in the perfect sky caused her mind to freeze. She fell to her knees, eyes fixed on the sight above her.

The war that she thought was being fought in the golden field around her was actually taking place in the sky above. Mesmerized, she watched the winged and armored figures, brandishing weapons of burning metal, clashing in savage battle. Swords came together with a clamor so powerful that she felt it in her chest, sparks of divine fire raining down to set the fields aflame.

Ashley found her cheeks wet with a steady stream of tears as she watched the war of angels unfold, wincing as if injured herself as some of the magnificent beings were struck down, their cries as they fell the most heartbreaking sounds she had ever heard.

Winged bodies were falling like rain, landing in broken heaps, most of them dead, but some . . .

Ashley could not move, paralyzed by the sights. She wanted to close her eyes and wish herself away, but she fought the impulse, knowing somehow that this was part of helping her friend.

Of helping Remy.

An angel, one of his beautiful wings of white and speckled brown charred black with divine fire, landed in a broken heap not two feet away. She watched the figure as he lay there, his ornate armor spattered with the blood of battle. With a grunt, the figure pushed himself to his feet. His wing was still burning, and he beat the feathered appendage upon the ground in an attempt to put the fire out. But the angelic warrior did not have time to complete the task.

An ear-piercing cry filled the air, and the angel threw himself toward the ground in search of the sword he had dropped. He grabbed it up and spun toward the shrieking cry. Another angel, his features hidden by a helmet of gold and red, dropped down from above to confront him, relentless in his assault, swinging a sword that seemed to burn brighter—hotter—than all the others, driving back the injured warrior.

Ashley wanted to scream at them to stop, but she knew they would not have heard her, imagining that she was only a ghost in this strange, psychic landscape.

The battle was furious. She could see that the injured angel was tiring, his own blade's brightness diminishing the longer they fought. The injured angel feigned a slash across his opponent's midsection, but instead wiped what remained of his still burning wing across the attacker's eyes, perhaps hoping to blind him.

But his adversary was too fast, capturing the smoldering append-age in his gauntlet-covered hand and twisting violently. The angel cried out and pulled away, but that served only to rip the fragile wing from his body.

Ashley felt her heart breaking over and over again as she watched the hopeless sight.

The wounded angel pathetically tossed his sword at his enemy and turned to flee. His foe was like a machine, capturing the cold blade—a blade that at once again burned to life as he held it. In a burst of energy, the injured angel dashed away, pushing through the burning golden brush in an attempt to escape.

Ashley watched with growing horror as the angel attacker simply stood there, holding two blades now that burned white in their inten-sity, his eyes unblinking through the holes of his helmet as he stared at the fleeing angel.

For a moment, she thought that maybe the attacker would have pity on his injured foe. But then wings exploded from his back, lifting him from the ground in pursuit.

Again, she tried to look away, but found that she couldn't—she was seeing this act for a specific reason, and it was to help her friend in dire need.

The wounded angel continued to run; he did not turn around even though Ashley was certain he could hear the sound of pounding wings behind him.

Death at his back.

She rose and followed them, as if drawn, both horrified and desper-ate to experience the outcome.

The injured angel tripped over the corpse of another warrior and fell to the ground in a clamor of metal, but he did not stay there long, fighting to climb to his feet.

Ashley expected him to run again, but he must have known that it was too late, his fate inevitable.

Instead, the angel turned to face his pursuer, who now floated in the air above him, his wings pounding the air feverishly to hold him aloft. It looked as though the injured angel was about to say something, to proclaim some powerful last message, before . . .

The attacker struck with incredible speed, casting down one of the fiery swords with such force that it pierced the injured angel's battle-stained chest plate, continuing out through his back in an explosion of blood.

Ashley cried out at the savagery.

These are creatures of Heaven, she thought as tears poured from her eyes. *Servants of God Himself. What could make them so very cruel?*

The angel looked down upon the blade protruding from his chest and dropped to his knees. His surviving wing slowly unfurled and then began to close for what Ashley imagined would be the last time. The sadness in the air was palpable.

The helmeted angel stood before his fallen prey like a statue. Then he returned his sword to the scabbard at his side and reached up with both hands to remove the helmet from his head.

Ashley gasped at the sight of the cruel angelic warrior. There were differences in his appearance, traits in the eyes and the shape of his face that made him appear not quite as human, but there was no mistaking the face of her friend.

The face of Remy Chandler as he must have been at one time.

She was drawn to the angel and saw with surprise that there were tears on his face as well.

Tears for a fallen foe.

And her heart nearly broke as the fearsome warrior dropped to his knees before his dead enemy and wrapped his armored arms around him, pulling him close.

Crying for what had been done.

For what had been lost in war.

Ashley was suddenly falling again, the golden fields of Heaven dropping out from beneath her.

She was in another place now, but knew it to still be Heaven. The war had ceased, but things were forever changed.

Behind her was a city of such size that it seemed to go on forever in every direction. Somehow, she knew this was the capital of the Holy Kingdom and that it was called the Golden City.

In the distance, a lone figure walked through the city's white stone gates. There was a weariness to the figure's posture, to his plodding step, as he walked away from the grandiose city.

It was Remy, a Remy whose face was slack, devoid of emotion. Ashley knew why he looked that way—the war had taken nearly everything from him. And even though it was over, and the Morningstar vanquished, Remy and the place that he had called home had lost too much.

Ashley watched him as he passed by her, leaving the world of Heaven to find his way to Earth, where he sought to hide himself, to think, and to heal.

She had never really understood how long Remy had been around—how old her dearest friend actually was—and she marveled at the snippets of the long life he had lived, and those he had helped as he became more enamored with the most fascinating and intricate of God's creations.

And as she watched, she saw him change, going from the pitiless warrior striking down enemies even though they were his brothers to a meager shell of what God had created, to finally something more than what he was and what he had been.

The emotion filled up her eyes again as she watched a Remy with whom she was oh so familiar wearing the guise of a Boston private investigator on a very specific day on Beacon Hill.

A day when he had befriended a scared little girl who had just moved in with her family and helped her catch her cat, Spooky, who had escaped during all the activity.

She remembered the day, each and every detail, as he introduced himself to her and became her friend.

And she his.

Linda accepted that she was falling through darkness and that this was all part of the game.

This was all part of making her Remy well.

She had no idea how it long it was that she fell; it could have been minutes or it could have been days.

Even so, the transition was abrupt, and it took her a moment to process it. One moment, she'd been falling through an endless night; the next, she was sitting in a center aisle seat in a beautiful old theatre.

She remembered a theatre very much like this. When she was a little girl, her grandmother had taken her to downtown Boston to see a show; she actually looked around to see if her grandmother was with her now. She wasn't, and in fact Linda was the only one present in the former vaudeville house.

She began to wonder what she should be doing, when the velvet curtain covering the stage parted to reveal an enormous movie screen. A projector snapped on from the back of the theatre and covered the screen with a bright white light.

A show was about to begin.

Linda felt like her childhood self again, mesmerized by the luminescent screen, anxiously anticipating what she was about to see. Her mind drifted back to that special afternoon with her grandmother, remembering that the movie they saw was a rerelease of *Snow White and the Seven Dwarfs*.

This movie began with no credits, no list of stars, no title, but somehow Linda knew what it was about and already felt herself enraptured by it.

It was the story of an angel who became a man due to the love of humanity, and most especially the love of a woman.

Linda was overwhelmed by a tidal wave of emotion as she experienced the life and love that Remy Chandler had shared with wife, Madeline. It was the kind of love that everyone wished for: transformative in its intensity, yet completely mundane at times.

It was as love was supposed to be, a thing as necessary as food and air.

But it was so much more important to the angel called Remy, for it was his anchor, keeping him rooted in the world, a constant reminder of what it was to be human.

Without it, another side of him might rear its head.

Linda was dreading what was to come, wishing that she might change the narrative as it unfolded before her.

But that wasn't how the story went.

For with great love, there also came great sadness. The woman who was the angel's world became sick, withering before his eyes. And he was powerless to stop it.

All he could do was watch as the love of his life passed away, taking a large part of his humanity with her.

He began to wonder if being human was worth the pain. Maybe it would be easier to become what he had been created to be: a messenger of Heaven, a soldier of God, unburdened by the crippling emotions of love.

But as he loved Madeline with all that he was, Remy grew to realize that he also loved this world, and all its imperfections as well, and he decided—even though it would be difficult—to stay, to find a way to be human again.

The angel did just that, living in the world, taking from it all that it offered, and learning all over again the joys of the earth and its inhabitants.

And learning to love once more.

Linda could not help but smile when she saw that the angel eventually found love again—that *she* was that love.

As she stared at images projected upon the screen before her, she made a promise to the angel—the man she loved—that she would be his anchor.

That she would never let him go.

Marlowe did not care for this falling feeling, and he growled and whined and barked and yipped his disapproval, hoping that somebody—*his Remy*—would answer his cries.

Finally, he stopped falling and sat in the darkness, waiting. And then a light shone on the one place he loved almost as much as his home and Remy's bed.

The Common.

Marlowe loved the Common. The Boston Common, he'd heard it called. But the Common was what he knew it as. What Remy called it when he asked if Marlowe would like to go for his special walk.

A special walk to the Common.

And the answer was always yes. Yes! Yes! Yes! Rain or shine, it was always yes.

Marlowe eyed his special surroundings, surprised that there seemed to be no one else around—no people—no dogs—it was just the Common.

The wonderful Common.

With total freedom, the Labrador took off across the great green expanse, running as fast as his four legs would carry him, stopping only to inspect the base of the occasional tree, sniffing wildly for scents that he knew.

Squirrels. Rats. Other dogs.

He lifted his leg and urinated, letting everyone know that he had been there and that at that very moment, this tree and the area around it—the entire Common really—belonged to him.

To Marlowe.

The dog took off again, the joy in his freedom flowing through his body—his legs—making him feel as though he could run forever and ever. There was nothing that could catch him and nothing that he could not catch.

The Common was his alone.

And it was that realization that stopped him. He sat on one of the many paved paths, panting, scanning his most beloved place.

The reality of the situation surprised him with its intensity. Here he was at the Common, not having to share anything—the trees, or the grass, or any delicious trash that might have missed going into a barrel—but it wasn't right. For this to be everything that he wanted it to be, he needed his master.

He needed his Remy.

In the distance, near a fenced playground, he saw a hint of movement and at once focused his gaze. At first he believed it to be children playing, but saw instead that it was a man—a man with his dog.

Excited, Marlowe bounded across the grass, barking wildly. But they did not seem to hear or see him.

The man was tossing a green tennis ball for a puppy—a black dog, just like Marlowe—who eagerly chased the ball and brought it right back to the man.

And as Marlowe stood there, his tail wagging furiously, an understanding of what he was seeing blossomed within his simple dog mind.

This was a memory—his own memory—of when he was just a pup.

He watched his Remy, desperate for him to be real and to acknowledge him, but he knew that this Remy could not see or hear him.

This is a reminder, Marlowe thought, watching the two at play—watching as an unbreakable bond formed between him and his Remy.

Remy was his everything. There would be nothing without Remy.

His Remy defined him—his existence. His very world.

Remy was his world.

And with that realization, the memory of their time together faded like the early morning mist that sometimes floated above the Common, and in its place grew a tree. A tree unlike any Marlowe had ever seen in the Common, yet somehow—

Familiar.

As he padded closer, the Common shifted around him, changing, becoming a landscape totally alien to him, but it did not deter him.

The tree was why he was here.

From the shadows at the base of the growth, Marlowe saw two figures emerge, and he knew that this was right.

Ashley and Linda smiled when they saw him, and his tail wagged so very hard that it made his entire back end move from side to side. They embraced him, loving him with hugs and kisses that made why they had come here to this spot—to this tree—all the more important and special.

They had all come for Remy.

CHAPTER SIXTEEN

Francis stepped through the vertical slash he'd made in reality and into the back parking lot of a storage facility in Brockton, Massachusetts.

The passage hissed and crackled as if in protest, but Francis wasn't listening. Instead, he was committing to memory the crudely drawn images on a map that would eventually lead him to the Bone Master assassins.

On reflex, he looked around to make sure that his unconventional arrival hadn't been noticed, and made his way to his rented storage shed.

For payment of services rendered—*What had he done again?*—Simeon had allowed him to see the map. It wasn't all that large, drawn upon the tanned skin of an unbaptized newborn with the blood of the child's mother. Simeon mentioned that it had been made by a fifteenth-century Satanist by the name of Hotinger, who believed that he'd channeled the ghosts of a religious sect targeted by the Bone Masters at the turn of the century.

The ghosts knew where the Bone Masters' weapons originated and had supposedly passed the information on in hopes of having their murders avenged. Francis wasn't sure if the murdered order had ever gotten their revenge, and he briefly wondered if he might be doing some angry ghosts a favor.

He stopped at the door to his storage unit, removed a small pocketknife from his pants pocket, and opened the blade to slice the pad of his thumb. Blood as black as tar bubbled up from the cut, and he allowed some of it to flow into the keyhole before sticking his thumb in his mouth to stanch the bleed. There was a loud click, and the lock fell away. He caught it in his other hand and jammed it into his pocket, then lifted the corrugated metal door to enter.

The unit was much larger on the inside than it appeared, an attribute for which he'd paid a magick user handsomely when he'd realized that his weapons collection was getting a bit out of hand. He flipped the switch on the wall next to him and fluorescent lights illuminated the cavernous space, filled with rows of metal shelving. Quickly, he slammed the door closed behind him.

Inside the space, surrounded by so many of the deadly things that he loved, the fallen angel began to think more clearly, formulating a plan that he hoped would save his friend's life.

He reached into that bottomless inside pocket of his suit jacket and found his phone. He couldn't remember the number off the top of his head, and truth to tell, he had never planned on using it again, but the current situation required him to rethink his past decisions.

He scrolled through his contacts, found the number he needed, and hit the button, listening to the phone ring on the other end for what seemed like forever.

"What do you want?" a voice dripping with angry venom finally growled into the phone.

"You have every right to hang up now, and I wouldn't blame you," Francis said quickly.

"You've got some nerve calling here after what you did to her," the voice said.

Francis imagined the guy on the other end snarling, his face twisted with anger.

"You're right, I do, and I would never even think of doing it if it wasn't an emergency."

"Emergency," the voice scoffed. "I bet."

"I need her again."

"No. No way. I'm still paying the price for the last time."

"I'm sorry, but you know it couldn't have been helped; there was a situation, and things got out of hand."

The person on the other end of the phone laughed, but there wasn't any humor in it. "A situation . . . Do you know what I've had to do to get her back to running right?"

"I offered to buy her from you."

"I could never sell her—especially to you. She hasn't been the same since."

"Difficult to manage?"

"Nothing I can't handle."

"Doesn't sound like it," Francis commented. "Sounds like she's become quite the handful. I think maybe she got a taste of the wild stuff and liked it more than you care to admit."

"Don't you worry about me; she gets more than enough."

"I'm not so sure."

"I think this call is done," the voice said, but there was a hint of something hidden beneath the angry timbre. Something that told Francis that it might not be so difficult to get what he wanted.

"Are you sure?"

"About what?"

"That you want this call to end . . . that you want me to hang up and leave you with—her."

"She's been with me for years; why would I have—"

"Admit it," Francis said. "She's never been this bad."

There was a long pause. "And that's all your fault," the man finally spat. "If it weren't for you taking her on that ride—"

"She wouldn't be so hard to manage," Francis finished. "She's getting to be too much, isn't she?"

Again the man was silent, but this time, Francis could hear the rumbling of a powerful engine in the background.

"Let me take her again," Francis said, hoping to further weaken an already weak resolve. "It will do her good, and it sounds as though it might do you some good as well."

"But . . . but what if she comes back . . . worse?" the voice asked, a tremble of fear evident.

"How much worse could she get, really?" Francis asked. "But if it does happen, I promise I'll help you with her. Do we have a deal?"

"I can't fucking believe I'm even considering this," the man on the other end of the phone growled.

The sound of the engine seemed louder now.

"But you are," Francis said. "And to show what a nice guy I am, I'll pay you double what I did before. . . ."

"Double?"

"Yeah, and I'll do my best not to spoil her. Do we have a deal?"

All Francis could hear now was the sound of the engine, rumbling like the purr of some great mechanical beast.

"Well?" he prodded.

"She's been especially hungry lately. Will you . . . ?"

"Yeah, I will," Francis said. "I promise to bring her back well fed."

This seemed to satisfy the owner, and he hung up without saying good-bye. Francis put his phone away and turned back to the vast storage of his collection. There were a few things he had to pick up before going to get her.

Walking to the center of the storage, he stopped, digging through his memory for the layout of the place and attempting to remember where he'd stored one of the Plagues of Egypt.

Michael turned his head ever so slightly, focusing his one good eye on the still-unconscious Remy Chandler, who now lay on the floor before the archangel's throne.

He felt a loathing the likes of which he had not experienced since—

In the pool of darkness that collected in the empty socket of Michael's eye, the archangel saw it all again, as he always did. The end of Heaven brought about by the ceremony of Unification.

The angel shoved a skeletal finger into the empty socket, wiggling it around to disrupt the disturbing imagery for a time. He didn't want to see any more, preferring instead to focus on the body of his foe lying before him.

He'd thought this angel dead, either reduced to ash in flames that burned hotter than the sun as Heaven and Hell vied for the same moment in time and space, or crushed beneath the rubble of Heaven's golden spires as they toppled down upon humanity and the cities that they'd built.

But here he was, looking the worse for wear, but alive nonetheless. At least for now.

Michael had believed his angels had slipped even further into madness when they'd told him they had found another of their kind in the ruins of the city as they'd searched for a sinner who had escaped their clutches. They'd told him that this angel was different, his body covered in sigils of magickal power.

Fascinated, Michael had gone so far as to leave his throne made from the bones of the unworthy, his domicile, to see with his own eyes—

Eye.

Who it was that his soldiers had found out there in the wasteland.

Never could he have imagined this. If God weren't dead, he would have believed that this was a reward for what he'd gone through since the fall of everything.

The darkness within his missing eye started acting up again, and the angel violently shook his head, attempting to rattle the imagery that had once more started to play in the theatre of his mind.

Michael leaned forward and reached a trembling hand down to the slumbering Remy, pulling at the collar of his shirt to see the markings etched upon his flesh.

Sigils. Sigils of power. He had seen such markings before, inscribed upon the flesh of angels who had sided neither with the Lord God Almighty, nor the Morningstar, during the great war. He'd called them cowards, but they referred to themselves as Nomads—angels who had no real place, wandering amongst the realms of Heaven, Hell, and Earth.

Had Remy fallen in with that craven angel sect? An all-too-familiar rage welled up inside Michael at the thought of those angels and how the Almighty would have forgiven them their indiscretions as well, allowing them back into the bosom of Heaven, if Unification had happened.

But it hadn't, and the Nomads remained unforgiven as they should have. If Michael had had his way, they would have been hunted down and put to death long ago. For if there was one thing the archangel could not stomach, it was cowardice.

That was the one thing he never would have ascribed to the angel before him; insolence and naïveté, yes, but never cowardice.

The darkness in the socket of his missing eye started to fill with memory again, and this time he let it play out, watching the angel who lay prostrate before him now, as he had been when the Lord God summoned him—when the Lord God had summoned them all. How beautiful they had been; how wondrous it was supposed to be.

Michael snarled. He'd known something bad was going to happen, had felt it tingling in the very fabric of his being, but how could he tell his Creator—his Lord of Lords—that what He was doing would lead to nothing but despair?

The archangel had wanted to be wrong; he really had.

But he wasn't, and it all went to—Hell.

The angel smiled sadly as the memory played out. He saw the Lord in all His magnificence as He was about to reunify all that had once been and raise humanity to its next level.

A new Heaven to define them all.

Michael had never experienced such bliss as he had at that moment, touched by the power of He who had made it all. And a single thought had run through his mind.

Maybe I was wrong.

Michael twitched violently as if stabbed, crying out with the sudden savagery of his memory.

It always made him scream, no matter how many times he relived it.

One moment God was alive—one with everything as He brought together that which had been sundered—and the next . . .

There came a sound like something harkening back to the creation of it all, when the Almighty wished something from nothing . . . but this time it had nothing to do with the beginning . . . with life.

It was about the end of it all . . . death.

The sight of his Lord God falling dead on the steps of the Golden City brought steaming tears to Michael's eye.

The memory was as overwhelming as it always was.

He remembered crying out as he'd turned to the gathered multitude, remembered the horror-filled expressions of those who had come to participate in an event of celestial magnitude, but instead bore witness to an atrocity of cosmic proportions.

He saw them all, their faces frozen in the darkness of his memory.

Had any of them been responsible?

It was a question he believed would never be answered, for he'd thought those whose faces haunted his memories to be as dead as the God who'd created them.

Or were they?

Michael looked down upon the angel Remiel.

"Time to wake up, Remiel," the archangel said, willing what little divine fire he could muster into his hand as he grasped the angel's throat.

And the air was filled with the hiss and stink of burning flesh.

He remembered the feeling. There was nothing quite like it.

It aroused every sense; he could smell it in the air, feel it beneath his feet and through everything he touched, hear it with sounds like the planet's largest symphony tuning its instruments, and see it—

One only had to look into the sky to see it.

Remy saw through the eyes of someone else's memory, but that someone just happened to be another version of himself.

The realization caused an increasing wave of discomfort, a horrible burning sensation that threatened to draw him from the wonderful memory of how it had been when Heaven had made its presence known to the world.

He remembered how he'd left his home on Beacon Hill, going out into the streets as nearly everybody else on the Hill had done. They were all just standing there, looking up into the sky above them. It was still blue, with gorgeous, puffy white clouds that looked as though they'd been torn from bales of cotton, but there was something else.

Something else behind the sky.

Remy had known what it was, and he'd suspected that many others who gazed upon it knew as well. Perhaps they knew it by a different name: the Hereafter, Utopia, Providence, Elysium, Canaan, Zion . . .

But all were the same place.

The place in which the Creator dwelled.

Heaven.

Remy recalled people crying as they looked upon it, some dropping to their knees and praying. Others just laughed, and smiled, and hugged one another, sensing that this was a special time.

And it was. It was a time that Remy had believed he would never see.

"What is it, Remy?" asked a familiar voice from behind him.

He'd felt Marlowe's cold snout nuzzling his hand, as he'd turned to look upon the visage of . . .

Madeline, his wife. Alive.

The memory became suddenly . . . wrong, reminding him that this wasn't his memory, but the memory of another . . . him.

Although he had to admit she'd never looked more beautiful as she'd stood there upon the steps of their home, the ravages of old age and cancer not evident in any way whatsoever.

The sight of her was better than . . . better than Heaven in the sky above.

And he knew suddenly that it was because of him.

Because of something he had done.

He had broken the rules to keep her with him.

"Isn't it wonderful!" she'd exclaimed, gazing up at the Kingdom of Glory, tears in her beautiful brown eyes, clear of cataracts and the dullness of sickness.

And he'd had to say, *"Yes,"* as he looked upon his living wife. It was the most wonderful thing he had ever seen.

There was that painful burning again—like a flaming rope around his throat, distracting him for just a moment.

Until he remembered hearing above the sounds of Heaven, a siren of sorts that spoke directly to him—to all creatures of a divine nature. A siren that called to them, telling them to come, telling them they must bear witness to something of great importance.

Come to Heaven . . . for Unification is upon us.

He remembered how he'd turned to her, his lovely Madeline, to tell her that he must leave her, but promised that he would return.

"And things will never be the same," she had said wistfully as he'd petted Marlowe's head.

And she was right.

The memory—his memory—turned to fire and chaos, the cries of a dying world deafening, his own screams joining the cacophony of the end.

Through the fire he turned to see her standing where he'd left her, in front of their Pinckney Street brownstone, her body engulfed in flames, a grinning skeleton all that remained to remind him of what had been lost.

"And things will never be the same," the skeleton of his true love reminded him.

He'd held his hand out and seen that he, too, was in flames, which crawled up the length of his body to consume his human guise and expose his angelic nature to the nightmarish devastation that had changed the world.

Wings covered in fire exploded from his back, stirring the air and scattering the bones of his wife, to be lost amongst the countless dead claimed by the fall of Heaven.

Rising up above the conflagration, he looked down upon the apocalyptic sight in horror. His guise of humanity gone, the unnatural fire began its consumption of his divinity, his angelic flesh slowly eaten away, drifting ash adding to the blackness that now blotted out the sun.

And the angel Remiel began to scream.

Screaming for the loss of all he loved.

Screaming as the world below him died.

Remy opened his eyes and found himself looking up into the scarred visage of the Archangel Michael.

The archangel's hand was locked tightly about Remy's throat, and his skin was burning.

"There you are," Michael hissed, his single eye bulging with twisted glee. "I didn't think you were ever coming back to me."

Remy squirmed in the angel's grasp, but his hands were bound behind his back. "I like the new look, Michael," he wheezed as the grip grew tighter and the flames danced upon his flesh. "It suits you."

The archangel growled like an animal, hoisting Remy up from the ground and giving him a savage shake.

"You can't even begin to imagine how hard it is for me to restrain myself," Michael said. "To feel your neck snap beneath my fingers would be like a kiss from God."

For a moment Remy believed that his neck would indeed break, the pressure on his throat causing the blood to pound in his ears, but just before the vertebrae were pulverized, the archangel threw his body to the ground.

"But I must remind myself," Michael said, flexing his long, spidery fingers. "This isn't all about me."

Dots of color danced before Remy's eyes and he coughed, the taste of pennies flooding his mouth. He managed to sit up, spitting out a wad of bloody phlegm to be absorbed by the ash collected on the ground.

Looking about his surroundings, he felt that sick feeling in the pit of his stomach. The Filthies stood around him, their bodies covered in horrible black scars, and as he looked upon each of them, he saw only madness in their expressions, the spark of the divine that should have been there long ago extinguished. These were merely shells of creatures once holy, seemingly unaware that what had made them what they were had died.

But across from him, bound as he was, were two familiar beings.

"Nice to see you're still with us," the Fossil said, lying on his side, his face a mass of blood.

One of the Filthies did not approve of the old man's talking and jabbed the point of a filthy sword into his side. He cried out and then went limp, the pain driving him to unconsciousness.

Baarabus roared his displeasure, struggling against his bindings. "You fuckers are going to pay for that!" he bellowed.

The Filthies jumped upon him as well, jabbing at his muscular body with their spears and drawing blood.

"Enough!" Remy's voice echoed throughout ruins.

The Filthies stopped their torture of the hellhound and stared at him with those awful eyes, most assuredly debating whether to attack him now.

"Ah, a voice of authority," Michael said.

Remy looked toward the archangel, who was now sitting on a throne made from bones that appeared blackened by fire.

"What happened to you?" Remy found the words leaving his mouth before he could stop them.

Michael stiffened and then slid forward.

"What happened to me?" he repeated. "What happened?" The

archangel looked about at the remains of Heaven, cobbled together to remind them of what had once been and what had been lost. "One would think you were new to the world, Remiel."

Remy remained silent, staring defiantly at the creature that had once stood at the right hand of God.

"We were once a reflection of our God and the kingdom in which He lived," Michael said. He stood, grimacing as if the movement caused him pain. "But that God is gone now," he said, moving closer to Remy.

"And His kingdom?" The archangel lifted his arms, as if presenting the environment. "Take a good look, and I think you'll understand."

Remy did, and he was repulsed by what he saw. "It's sad" was all he could manage.

Michael's single wing unfurled with a whiplike snap. "Exactly!" The archangel bounded over to where Remy knelt upon the ground. "We are but shadows of our former glory."

He walked past Remy toward the Filthies. "Look at you!" he screamed. "You should be ashamed!"

The Filthies cowered before the angel's verbal assault.

Michael looked back to Remy. "But how else could they be, after surviving what they have?"

"This isn't what God intended," Remy said.

Michael turned his good eye upon the tribe.

"They're monsters," Remy told him.

Michael looked back, and Remy caught a spark in the archangel's single, bloodshot orb.

"Would you expect anything less for what we have done?" Michael asked. "It's well deserved. . . . It's what we are supposed to be for now."

"For now?"

"Don't you know, Remiel?" Michael strode back toward him. "This is our punishment. . . . We are to live in this . . . this . . . wasteland until the Lord God sees fit to forgive us our sins and . . ."

"He's dead, Michael," Remy said flatly. "Murdered. There's no one to forgive you except yourselves."

The archangel smiled; where once there were teeth that glistened whitely like stars in the sky, there were now only jagged protrusions rotting in bloody gums.

"And that is where you're wrong," he said, shaking a finger at Remy. "He's still here. . . . The Lord God is still here. . . ." The archangel looked about, his single eye widening. "And He's watching!"

"You're insane," Remy said.

"He's watching to see what we'll do with this new and twisted world, filled with the damned . . . overrun with sinners."

Remy struggled to stand, and the Filthies immediately bounded toward him, burned and blackened wings flapping pathetically.

"Hold!" Michael ordered, and they reluctantly backed away.

"Sinners?" Remy asked. "Who determined this? You?" He laughed. "There aren't any sinners left in the world, Michael. Only survivors."

Michael looked at him smugly and shook his scarred head. "You're so blind, Remiel. Those taken when things went horribly awry—they were the blessed. Those who remain . . ."

"The sinners," Remy finished, and Michael nodded. "You actually believe that, Michael?"

The archangel gradually straightened, the lone wing upon his back swishing back and forth like the tail of an agitated cat. "Why else would He have left us here? He needs to be sure we're ready . . . ready to make the tough choices now that this world is winding down to its final days."

"And once you're done, and all the sinners are gone?" Remy asked. "What then? Do you think He's coming back for you? To take you all to some new Paradise? . . . Is that what you think?"

"It's what I know," Michael said. "It's what I see inside my head. It's what keeps me from ending my own existence . . . from driving a sword up through my chin and into my skull. It is what keeps me, and in turn, my legions, sane."

Remy looked to the Filthies again, remembering what they once had been. He shook his head sadly. "I hate to be the one to break it to you, Michael, but He's gone."

Michael's deformed face became even more monstrous as Remy continued.

"This is it for us . . . for the world. We had our chance, and it ended badly. The Lord has been removed from the picture. . . . We're lost now, cast adrift. It's over, unless . . ."

Remy stopped, the pain inside his head suddenly excruciating.

There was something in there—something trying to get out. Something from another's memory that wanted to be recognized.

Michael was before him, the archangel's hand once again wrapped around Remy's throat.

"Unless what?" the angel demanded. "What do you know? Has He communicated with you? Has He shared something?"

"I have to go into the city . . . to what's left of the Golden City," Remy managed to get out.

Michael pushed him back to the ground, looking at him in utter amazement. "Why on earth would you need to do that?" He let go of Remy's throat, backing quickly away as he considered Remy's words.

"It's something I need to do," Remy gasped, catching his breath.

"Why?" Michael demanded. He held his hand out again and it began to spark, and then smolder, and then burn. "Did God tell you to go to the city?"

The picture of an elderly gentleman in a dark suit standing with a tidal wave frozen behind him suddenly flashed through Remy's mind.

"I . . . I don't know. . . . I just know what I have to do."

"As do I," Michael said. "For the true voice tells me so."

The archangel turned and stomped to his throne of bones, and just as he reached it, just as he was about to sit down, he spoke.

"The Almighty has whispered to me His wants," he proclaimed as the Filthies eagerly listened.

"Don't do this, Michael. Listen to me for once," Remy begged.

The archangel lowered himself to his throne with a grunt. "He wants you all taken to the pit."

CHAPTER SEVENTEEN

Can you hear me?

Linda flinched at the sound of Assiel's voice.

"Did you hear that?" Ashley asked.

Linda nodded. Marlowe's tail was wagging and the dog was looking around for the source, showing her that he, too, had heard the healer's voice.

"Is he here?" she wondered aloud, looking about the bizarre landscape that continued to shift and change as they stood beside the massive tree. One moment they were standing in the vastness of some great desert, the next in what looked to be a field of wheat, and then amongst rocks and ice.

I'm here, Assiel confirmed for all to hear.

"What is this place?" Linda asked, growing dizzy from the swiftly changing environment.

You are at the center of Remy's being, the angel answered. *The place where what you would call his soul dwells.*

"Why does it keep changing?" Ashley asked.

It reacts to your thoughts, to your moods. It's attempting to find something that your minds can fully comprehend—a common ground.

"How do we get it to stop changing?" Linda had to close her eyes as a wave of nausea threatened to overtake her.

Calm your minds, Assiel instructed. *Focus on a place of pure tranquility.*

"Where should it be?" Ashley asked. "I'm not sure if I've ever been to a place of pure tranquility."

It doesn't matter where it is, as long as it is a place where you were once safe and content.

Linda thought of the mountains of New Hampshire, the beaches of Cape Cod, and the rocky shores of Maine. All the places she had traveled to as a child. Places where she had felt secure and at peace.

"Cool," she heard Ashley say, and she opened her eyes.

The world around them had calmed, transforming into something akin to a peaceful glade, with the sounds of birds chirping in the trees and the amazing smell of the woods after a summer rain.

"We did good," Linda said, looking at Ashley, who nodded. "You, too," she said, bending down to ruffle Marlowe's black, velvet ears. The dog licked her face and wagged his thick, muscular tail.

"Now what, Assiel?" Linda asked.

"Bet it has something to do with this," Ashley answered instead.

Linda turned to find Ashley staring at the large tree. The thick brown bark seemed to be flaking off, and a reddish liquid leaked from underneath to drip down the trunk, pooling at its base.

"It looks like it's bleeding." Ashley reached a tentative hand out, laying it flat against the bark—and suddenly stiffened, her eyes rolling back in her head.

"Ashley!" Linda cried as Marlowe barked frantically.

She grabbed Ashley's hand, and pulled it away from the tree. Her palm was stained with the bloodred sap.

"Are you all right?" Linda asked.

For a moment, Ashley appeared confused, as if she wasn't sure where she was, but then she seemed to remember. "Oh my God!" she exclaimed, pulling her hand from Linda's grasp and staring at it.

"What is it?"

"This is him," Ashley said, pointing to the tree. "This is Remy . . . or at least it's part of him."

"Assiel said that this is his soul." Linda stepped closer to the tree and found herself raising a hand toward it.

"It'll freak you out," Ashley warned.

"Yeah, that's okay."

Linda swallowed as she laid her hands upon the rough bark. It was warm, as if flushed with the heat of blood. She felt the tree as it pulsed with life, but she also felt it weakening.

The tree was dying.

Remy's soul was dying.

Linda suddenly felt herself falling backward and realized that Ashley and Marlowe had pulled her away, severing her connection to the weeping bark.

"Oh my God," she whispered as she got her bearings back.

"I know," Ashley agreed.

They all gazed at the tree now as it continued to weep the thick, bloodlike substance, saturating the ground beneath.

"I don't think we have much time," Linda said.

You are correct, Assiel responded from the ether.

"So how do we fix this?" Ashley asked. "How do we stop him from dying?"

You must add your strengths . . . your life essences to his.

"Will that be enough?" Linda questioned.

It will sustain him.

"But for how long? That doesn't solve the problem of where his life energies are going."

No, it doesn't.

"So we're just keeping him alive with our strength until . . ."

The angel remained quiet.

"Until we run out, too, and then I'm guessing we all die," Ashley finished Linda's sentence. "I'm not sure how I feel about that."

Linda turned back to the tree, watching it continue to bleed. "I know how I feel. I feel like we can do more."

"Like what?" Ashley wanted to know. Both she and Marlowe fixed Linda in their gazes.

"Where is his energy . . . his soul, going?" Linda asked, then pointed to the darkly stained earth and answered her own question. "It's going into there."

Marlowe immediately jumped into action, bending forward and digging furiously with his front paws.

"Hey!" Ashley warned. "Do you think that's a good idea?"

Linda watched the dog and the hole that had started to form, and felt compelled to move closer. She found herself dropping to her knees beside the Labrador, and began to dig at the moist earth with both hands.

"Okay," Ashley said slowly; then she joined Linda and Marlowe, and she, too, began to dig.

They dug deeper and deeper, exposing the lower regions of the tree. Linda was the first to notice something odd.

"Wait," she said, and Ashley immediately stopped. Marlowe was lost in the moment, continuing to paw and dig.

"Marlowe, stop," Linda ordered, and the dog did, panting tiredly.

"What is it?" Ashley asked, crawling closer to the edge of the hole they'd excavated.

"Careful." Linda held out a hand to keep the young woman from getting too close. Then she squinted into the darkness of the hole. She could see the tree's roots as they intertwined about one another, extending downward into . . .

It should have been earth, but instead there was nothing but darkness.

Linda watched the sap flow down the trunk of the tree, onto the thick roots, then drip off into—nothing.

"There's nothing there," Linda said, leaning forward, reaching her hand down into the blackness of the void. The loose earth beneath her knees gave way, and she was suddenly falling forward into the hole. She felt herself begin to panic, fingers scrabbling for a hold on the roots.

But her momentum was stopped as Marlowe grabbed a mouthful of the back of her blouse. And then Ashley was there to help pull Linda back to solid ground.

"Are you all right?" the girl asked, fear in her tone.

"I'm fine. Thanks for the hand." Linda petted Marlowe's head and gave him a quick kiss before turning her attentions back to the hole they'd dug. She smiled slightly. "There's something down there in the darkness."

"And that's where Remy is."

The Harvester was proud of his job, but he wished he were killing.

That was what the Bone Masters were born to do—to kill—to be the best assassins in existence.

Unless born a Harvester.

He scowled as he gathered up his tools, tools that had been used by his father and his father's father.

It had been his lot in life to have been born into a Harvester family, and once a Harvester, always a Harvester. There was no point in railing against it.

Harvesters selected the eggs from the many nests that littered the pocket dimension, searching out the healthiest, returning them to the home world, where they would be matched with a novice Bone Master. It was an important job, and that was what the young Harvester kept telling himself, even as he imagined bonding with one of the hatchlings and eventually starting a career as an assassin for the Bone Master guild.

With a heavy sigh, he placed his special tools in the egg basket, ready to embark on his journey to the pocket dimension that had always existed alongside the Bone Master home world. It was only accessible once every five cycles, when the barrier between the worlds was thinnest.

Today would be that day.

The Harvester picked up his basket and left his dwelling. He stood outside, in the early hours of the day, and closed his eyes, listening for the familiar sound. It was a sound he'd heard in his mind since coming of age, a sound that only a Harvester could hear, the sound of a passage opening to the pocket dimension. It was high-pitched, painful in many respects. It took him a moment to focus, but there it was, off in the distance . . . not too far . . . closer than it had been in previous cycles.

He found the passage in a swampy area used to dispatch the weak and infirm of the Bone Master clan. He could see it as nobody else could: a gossamer sheet of reality that separated his world from the world of harvesting.

He approached the veil and set his basket down, removing an ancient tool used by his family for countless generations. It was told that the hooked knife had been fashioned from the fang of the first of the special animals to cross from the pocket universe. He wasn't sure whether that was true, but he did know that the blade performed a very specific function.

A job that only it could do, very much like himself.

Standing before the weakness between worlds, he raised the knife and cut into the area where the barrier was thinnest, slicing an opening from his world to the other. A blast of stinking air escaped from the tear, but he was used to the thick, acrid smell, for he'd been smelling it all of his life. The stink had clung to the clothes and skin of his father and grandfather, and he was aware that he stank of it as well.

The Harvester stepped through the passage and into a strange world of perpetual shadow. Plumes of thick green gas erupted from jagged cracks in the skin of the world. Two moons hung in the black sky, both full, like the blind eyes of some enormous god, another sign that it was time for harvest.

Walking across the dry and barren landscape, the Harvester carefully avoided the open earth and the corrosive gas that escaped from it, pulling the collar of his tunic up over his mouth and nostrils to filter the air. He remembered where he had seen nests on his previous visits, filled with eggs not then ready to be taken, but now . . .

From the corner of his eye, he caught movement and spun around.

A pregnant layer, its hairless flesh prickled with quivering bumps, pressed itself against an outcropping of rock and hissed at him. The beasts were ferocious in nature, and even more so when carrying eggs. The Harvester stepped back respectfully, communicating with his eyes that he meant the animal no harm, encouraging it to go its way and allow him to go his.

The beast turned its swollen body and lumbered off toward another formation of rocks in the distance.

Next cycle, I'll take its eggs back with me, he thought as he watched it disappear into the shadows thrown by the rocks.

A mountain of rock rose up from the scarred surface in the distance, and he made his way toward it. That promising nest had been located just inside a cave, and . . .

Something else caught the Harvester's attention, and he slowed just a little bit as he grew closer to the cave.

Eggs . . . There were eggs scattered on the ground, their thick leathery skin torn, leaking fluids into the thirsty dryness of the ground.

How can this be? he wondered, starting to run now. The beasts of this world had no natural predators; in fact, everything here seemed to exist only to allow these creatures to flourish. Even the toxic gas that escaped from the planet's bowels was loaded with minerals that acted as nutrients for the gestating eggs.

What could have done this horrible thing?

The Harvester stopped before the first of the ruptured egg sacs. The pale, spindly animal that had once been inside it lay not far away. But as the Harvester grew closer to the corpse, he took notice of something even more disturbing—the creature's head appeared to have been twisted completely around on its neck.

"I'm surprised at how fragile these things are," said a voice, so loud in the silence of the world that the Harvester cried out, dropping his basket.

He looked up to see a human—at least he appeared to be so—step from the cave and approach him holding another of the eggs.

"I would have thought that something that was to become a demon assassin's ultimate weapon would be a little more"—the man then threw the egg sac to the ground, where it burst open, its liquid contents spraying across the dirt—"durable."

The Harvester gasped, making a move toward the ruptured egg, and the important life that had started to painfully emerge from within.

"Leave it," the man warned, and there was a menace in his voice that froze the Harvester in place.

The animal had partially emerged from within its broken egg sac, struggling to free itself as it opened its mouth and wailed—a wail that was cut violently short as the man crushed the animal's skull beneath the heel of his shoe.

The Harvester screamed at the horrific sight. It was his purpose to harvest and protect the young life-forms. To see them so cruelly slain caused something inside him to snap.

A killer's nature to emerge.

The Harvester dove for his basket, reaching for the hooked blade. He grabbed it and lunged at the man, aiming for his pale throat.

But the man moved with incredible speed, capturing the Harvester's wrist and twisting so violently that the bones snapped with a sound like the crack of whip. The Harvester cried out in agony, dropping his sacred weapon as he fell to knees. He cradled his broken wrist and glared up at his attacker.

"I have no idea who you are or why you are here, but—," the Harvester began.

"So glad you've asked," the man interrupted, stepping ominously closer. "I need to get to the Bone Master home world, and I'd like you to take me." He smiled then, a predator's smile.

"I will never betray my sacred trust," the Harvester said defiantly, still cradling his broken wrist as he shook his head. "I will never take you there."

The man loomed above him. "I don't need you to take me there. I already have a ride."

A deafening sound reverberated from within the confines of the cave, and the Harvester gasped as two glowing orbs ignited in the darkness—the eyes of some unknown beast. The animal emerged, and the Harvester saw that it wasn't an animal at all but a wheeled vehicle that moved with a life of its own.

"This is Leona," the man said, addressing the vehicle, its inner workings revving louder as it bounced slightly—excitedly—on its four wheels. "She was hungry, so I told her to have a look around."

The Harvester did not understand the man's meaning at first, but then noticed the lifeblood dripping from the front end of the machine, pieces of egg sac hanging in tatters as if from some sort of mechanical mouth.

"No," he whispered in disbelief.

"Yeah," the man said matter-of-factly, glancing at the roaring machine with a smile. "Who'da thunk she'd like eggs so much?"

"No!" the Harvester screamed this time, managing to get to his feet and propel himself toward the cave and the vehicle blocking its entrance.

The man lashed out with his leg, tripping the Harvester, and he fell to the ground directly in front of the rumbling—growling—machine. Its front end opened wide to reveal jagged teeth of metal, the smell of burning oil and rot roiling out.

"Like I was saying," the man said, reaching down and hauling the Harvester up from the ground. "I really don't need you to take me to the home world."

He grabbed the Harvester's uninjured wrist and forced his hand closer to the opening in the front of the vehicle—to the jagged mouth.

"I just need directions."

The Filthies dragged a struggling Remy across the open ground toward the pit. He dug his boots into the dusty earth, but it did little good as they reached the edge and tossed him in.

Hands still bound behind his back, he landed on his side, the air punched from his lungs with the impact, specks of exploding color dancing before his eyes.

Slowly he recovered, and as his vision cleared, he found himself looking into the face of the dead, torn and bloody, frozen in an expression of absolute horror. Remy struggled to his knees, seeing even more grisly remains scattered about the floor of the large pit that was probably once a swimming pool.

The cries of his people caused him to turn, and he watched as three of Samson's children—the muscular and bearded Anthony; the oldest of Samson's brood, Dante; and the young woman whom he'd befriended, Leila—fell in. They landed with as much grace as they were able, lying in the bloodstained dirt collecting themselves.

"Welcome to our pit," Michael said from above.

Remy glanced up to see the archangel looking down at them. The others of Samson's brood were positioned at the edge, ready to be tossed down at a moment's notice.

"Oh yes, we almost forgot." Michael glanced to his side, motioning for his people to act.

Eight Filthies appeared at the edge of the pit, struggling with the writhing Baarabus. They pushed the demon dog over the side, where he fell with a yelp, nearly landing atop Leila, who was the last to recover.

"As I was saying, welcome to our pit," Michael repeated. "We find this a much more entertaining way to deal with sinners. . . . Keeps the morale up."

Remy pushed himself to his feet. Ahead of him, carved out of the walls of the pool, were three barred cells, and inside the cells were things, pacing back and forth and watching them.

Hungrily.

"You bastard," Remy said with a snarl, gazing up at Michael.

"I'm sorry, Remy," the archangel said. "If you survive this tribulation, then you will be that much closer to salvation and the new Heaven that is to follow."

Remy heard the sound of squealing gears, and the rusted gates in front of the cells slowly lifted.

"Shit," he heard Anthony hiss, and he couldn't have agreed more.

Six Hellions, the demon dogs that roamed the wastelands of Hell, emerged, sniffing at the air. They were mangy looking, their bodies covered with oozing sores, their eyes wild with madness brought on by suffering.

Madness—it seemed to be a recurring theme in this world, Remy observed.

"You gotta be fucking kidding me," Baarabus said, gnawing at the ropes that still bound his feet. Even though the large dog was at least part Hellion, Remy doubted it would be shown any mercy.

"How are you doing with those ropes?" Remy asked the beast.

"Going as fast as I can," the dog grumbled.

"Work faster," Dante ordered. He'd backed over to a section of wall and was frantically rubbing the ropes binding his wrists against its broken and jagged surface.

"This is going to be a slaughter even if we get our hands free," Anthony stated, his eyes locked on the horrific vision of the Hellions as they stalked from their cages.

"That's what I'm going to miss the most about you, Anthony, after the hellhounds eat your ass," Leila said. "Your overflowing optimism."

Remy noticed a jagged piece of bone sticking up from the dirt and dropped to his knees, angling down to the ground to recover it. All the while he kept his eyes on the beasts, who watched them hungrily.

"Everyone is being so cautious," Michael called down, his voice raised above the cheers of the Filthies. "The beasts must sense that their latest prey are of a special nature." The archangel paused for the moment. "But it won't matter once the first drop of blood is spilled."

Remy worked frantically with the edge of bone, trying to maneuver it in such a way as to cut through the bindings but not his flesh.

"Almost got it," Baarabus called out, pulling at the ropes around his front paws.

"I'm free!" Dante announced, pulling his hands out from behind him. Blood oozed from where his wrists and arms had been torn upon the jagged tile wall—and it was like the ringing of a dinner bell.

All six of the Hellions charged, each attempting to beat out the others. Three savagely attacked one another, but the other three made a beeline for the bleeding Dante.

Remy, whose hands were still bound, leapt at one of the dogs as it passed, smashing into it side and knocking it off its feet. The Hellion struggled on the ground, and Remy moved, driving the heel of his boot down onto the dog's neck once, and then again, feeling something collapse beneath it. The Hell dog thrashed upon the ground, coughing up wads of thick, clotted blood as Remy scurried away from its death throes.

Baarabus freed himself with a piercing howl and leapt into the fray, plowing into the other two animals before they could reach Dante. One of the Hellions immediately attacked, powerful jaws snapping at Baarabus.

The remaining Hellion would not be distracted, launching itself at Dante. The oldest son of Samson stood his ground, swinging his fist and punching the attacking Hell beast. The punch was good, sending bits of broken teeth arcing into the air, but it wasn't enough to stop the demon dog's momentum.

The Hellion crashed into Dante like a runaway truck, slamming him backward into the wall of the pit.

The Filthies cheered as the remaining children of Samson gasped.

Enraged by pain, the Hellion did not hesitate, burrowing its snout into Dante's belly, ripping away his shirt and the skin beneath, exposing his inner workings to the world.

"No!" cried Remy in horror, his screams mingling with those of Dante's brother and sister down in the pit.

Anthony, still bound, charged at the ravening beast, kicking the Hellion as hard as he could. "C'mon, you son of a bitch. . . . Come on!"

The blows were powerful, and the demon dog stopped its gorging to spin at its aggressor, snapping at him with broken teeth.

Remy watched as Leila ran to her brother's aid, just as the three Hellions that had been fighting amongst themselves charged over to join the fray.

Baarabus roared, still in the midst of his own battle, blood spurting into the air as he and the Hellion rolled upon the ground, their jaws snapping like triggered bear traps.

Remy realized that it was all up to him, but what could he do? Once again he struggled with his bonds, but they held fast, drawing tighter around his wrists as he bled. Remy was desperate as he sought some sort of answer; they would all be dead in a matter of minutes if he didn't find a solution.

The beast he had felled thrashed upon the ground as it died, and Remy saw a possible answer in its snapping maw.

Remy dove toward the dying animal, spinning himself around and falling backward toward its vengeful mouth.

He just needed a solution—anything at all would suffice. It didn't really have to be all that good or smart.

The Hellion bit at Remy's hand furiously, a high-pitched, gurgling whine of anger escaping the dying beast as it attempted to do as much damage as it was possible of doing before it expired.

Remy cried out as its jaws came down on his hands. He screamed in a mixture of rage and pain, jamming his hands and wrists farther into its maw, choking the Hell animal, as he attempted to rub his bindings against the creature's teeth.

It might have been stupid and cost him some pain and blood, but it worked.

It worked.

Remy pulled his lacerated and bleeding hands from the monster's mouth, painfully flexing his fingers. Some of the bones were broken—for now—he knew that they would heal, given time.

But now he had friends to help.

Hands free, Remy charged across the dirt, screaming as loudly as he could at the four Hellions that were now circling Anthony and Leila. Remy knew that he didn't have a moment to lose. His eyes scanned the ground for something, anything, that he might use to distract them.

A severed head was the best he could do at the moment. He reached down at a run and scooped it up. He continued to scream as he ran at them, throwing the head with all his force, striking one of the Hellions in the side of its face.

All the beasts reacted to the intrusion, fixing their eyes upon Remy, who did not slow as he came at them. The Hellions appeared thrown by his aggression, backing up as he continued at them unabated. One became braver than the others, charging to meet Remy's advance. Remy stopped abruptly, reaching out to grab hold of the Hellion's head in his hands and drive both thumbs into its eye sockets, rupturing the moist orbs within its skull with gratifying pops.

The sightless Hellion lashed out, jaws snapping at the air as it ran off in the opposite direction, driven to the brink of madness by the intensity of its injuries. One of the remaining four temporarily out of the way, Remy stalked toward the others, which now crouched low to the ground, realizing that this adversary would not be as easy as past prey had been. He saw that Leila and Anthony had managed to get to the other side of the pit and continued to work on their bonds. They were safe for the moment.

"Who's next?" Remy growled, trying to keep their attention. "C'mon, you sons of bitches, I'm waiting." Then he reacted purely on instinct, remembering himself as a soldier of Heaven, not the ragged being he had become, reaching down within himself, to where the divine fire resided—the Heavenly power of the Seraphim—and attempting to draw it to the surface.

The pain was excruciating, unlike anything that he'd ever experienced before. The fire—the power of God that roiled at the core of his being—was no longer as he remembered.

It was changed, different. There was a darkness to it now, an anger that threatened to destroy him as it surged up excitedly from the lower depths of his person.

A madness.

It was the power that had defined him as Seraphim, and it had been driven insane by what had happened to this world. Remy fell to the ground; it was as if his legs had been cut out from beneath him.

He heard his name called from somewhere seemingly miles away, but did not—could not—answer. The angry power was filling him up, threatening to drown him—consume him—for it wanted very much to be free.

And wanted to be in control.

Leila watched as Remy fell. One moment he was standing up to the Hellions, a badass beyond words, and the next he was taking a nap in the dirt.

"Hurry up!" she screamed to her brother, who, having finally freed his own hands, was working on her ropes.

"Remy!" she cried out as her hands were set free. "Get the fuck up!"

But she could only watch in growing horror as the three Hellions circled his twitching form on the ground.

Easy prey.

The blood of his Hellion adversary filled his mouth in gushing gouts that burned like fire. Baarabus allowed the blood to flow onto his face and down his throat as he chewed and swallowed the large bite of flesh that he had torn from his enemy's throat.

"How's that feel?" Baarabous growled, spitting a bloody wad into the dying Hellion's face. "Yeah, I thought so."

The Hellion's legs gave way beneath the demonic animal, and it collapsed to the ground in a twitching heap, a deep pool of crimson spreading out from beneath its head.

Baarabus looked up to see the three remaining Hellions move in for the kill on an apparently unconscious Remy, as Leila and Anthony looked on in horror. He leapt over the corpse of his foe, kicking up clouds of dust and dirt as he bounded toward the angel called Remy Chandler.

My Remy, said a soft, loving voice from somewhere inside his mind.

"Fuck you," the demon dog grumbled, savoring the taste of his enemy's blood, still inside his mouth. "Fuck you. Fuck you. Fuck you."

The Fossil watched from the edge of the pit, not quite sure what he was about to see. At first it looked to be a total slaughter, the Hellions taking down his comrades with little difficulty. But then things changed; his friends were not about to lie down and become food for the rabid Hell beasts.

"Are you watching?" the archangel asked, a twisted smile on his ugly, scarred features. "This is God's justice. . . . This is how His love shall be shown to those chosen for the new Heaven."

Not taking his eyes from the action below, the Fossil's only response was a scowl. Everything was in movement, and his addled brain was struggling to process it.

Remy had fallen. The Fossil had no idea why. It didn't look good for the angel, even though the others had managed to free themselves, and Baarabus was hauling ass across the pit to save him.

"Watch," Michael commanded.

The Filthies were silent in anticipation of what was to come. The Fossil, and others of his troop, watched as well, none certain what they would see.

For one never could be in the strange world they now lived in.

"Remy, get the fuck up!"

He heard Leila's voice off in the distance and wanted to holler right back, *Can't you see I'm busy dying?*

The power awakened inside of him was overwhelming. It flowed through his body, wanting to take control. It was angry at him— angry for keeping it locked up, restrained, for so very long.

It wanted to be master now, and he was dying for it.

It was happy to be awake—happy to have finally been unleashed, even though it was killing its host.

The power was wild, irrational, unhindered by thoughts of repercussions. Remy tried to calm it, to wrestle it back under his control, but it was far stronger than he was.

It wanted to be free, to destroy the pain that had driven it insane.

For the Creator was dead, and all the world would pay.

Remy sensed an opportunity. *What if I were to help you?* he suggested to the sentient force. *What if I were to deliver those who did this terrible thing to God?*

The corrupted power of Heaven made a noise that sounded like a chuckle, but it did not refuse him.

Give yourself to me, and I—we—shall make all who were responsible for the death of the Almighty pay for their crimes.

The divine force of the Seraphim was tempted by Remy's offer and withdrew ever so slightly. *And when will I have this . . . retribution?* it impatiently asked.

You shall have it in time, Remy promised. *But first you must give yourself over to me. You must let me guide you.*

The power hesitated briefly but quickly relented.

Take me, it said.

Give me the deaths of the guilty, and I will be yours to wield.

He didn't want it to end like this, winding up in the belly of some godforsaken piece of shit from the wastelands of Hell, so he did what he had to do.

Remy accepted the offer from the power within.

You will have your death, he told the rage of the Seraphim, and the power responded in kind. He felt a wave of strength wash over him, an adrenal surge the likes of which he'd never experienced before: one moment nearly comatose, the next fully awake and ready to deal.

The bravest of the Hellions made its move, darting in for a quick and crippling bite.

Remy saw it as it was happening, as if in slow motion. He moved just a fraction, and the demon dog's jaws closed around empty air. The beast yelped as its teeth ground painfully together, but it immediately spun around for another try.

Remy was going to move again, but this time something angry within told him to hold his ground. The Hellion was like a tidal wave of violence, its stink of fire and brimstone repulsive. It leapt into the air, its front legs spread, claws distended, ready to pull him into a killing embrace.

There came a sudden icy chill in one of his hands, a chill that quickly turned to burning. As the Hellion's body fell toward him, he stepped forward, driving his fist into the descending chest, punching through the flesh to where the beast's foul heart beat wildly. Remy took hold of the throbbing muscle and tore it from the Hellion's body, stepping quickly aside as the demon dog fell, dead before it struck the floor of the pit.

Another of the Hellions lunged at Remy from behind. He could hear it, could smell its fetid excitement, and he spun on the beast, its sibling's bleeding heart still clutched in one hand. Remy jammed the muscular organ into the Hellion's mouth. It landed upon him, slashing with its claws. The angel managed to squirm from beneath the beast and leapt upon its back, throwing his arms around its neck and squeezing with all his might.

It continued to fight, thrashing and bucking beneath him, but the power within Remy wouldn't give up. There came a loud snap, and the demon animal's legs splayed out beneath it. The Hellion writhed and twitched as Remy climbed from its back, and, feeling a twinge of mercy, he bent down and punched the paralyzed creature's skull, sending splinters of bone into its brain and ending its life.

Remy felt the power of the Seraphim roiling with pleasure but not yet sated, and he looked around for the next kill. He saw the last of the healthy beasts making a hasty retreat from him, bounding toward where Anthony and Leila now waited, ready to fight.

The power of the Seraphim was on a roll, hungry for more foes to be vanquished. Remy dove after the running animal, grabbing hold of its short, nubby tail. At first he wasn't exactly sure what he would do with the beast, now that he'd halted its progress, but as it turned toward him, jaws open wide to bite, Remy felt a surge of intense pain explode outward from the center of his body, flowing down the length of his arm. The hand still holding the Hellion's tail ignited in flame, the divine fire quickly spreading from him to the tail of the Hellion.

It was like watching a fuse ignite.

The divine fire was hungry as it consumed the shrieking hellhound. The dog died in agony, spinning in circles and rolling upon the dusty ground of the pit in an attempt to put out the fire.

But it would not be extinguished until its hunger was sated.

Leaving only a pile of blackened ash roughly in the shape of the consumed Hellion, the fire flowed back to Remy's hand. Sensing that there was still one more enemy to deal with, Remy looked around the pit.

The blinded Hellion cowered near its cell, nervously sniffing the air and picking up the scent of death from its murdered brethren. In its injured state, it did not seek out Remy, self-preservation making it stay cautiously away. Remy felt a smile that he could not control creep onto his face as he started to walk toward the injured animal.

But Baarabus was suddenly there, leaping upon the blinded Hellion and tearing out its throat in an instant. "Can't let you have all the fun," he said, his large face stained crimson with blood.

Remy was furious, for the living fire was cheated of its prey and demanded that it be satisfied.

Demanded that a replacement be made.

And before he could even question his action, Remy extended his hands, allowing the flames that now welled up from his core to explode from his body.

The sigils tattooed upon Remy's body throbbed painfully as if somehow attempting to halt the flow of divine energies that he now emitted, but they were overwhelmed by the ferocity.

Remy cried out in pain as the force flowed from the tips of his fingers, gouts of divine fire igniting the corpse of the felled Hellion, while Baarabus leapt back from the hungry flames.

The dog was shocked by Remy's action and looked upon him with surprise.

"What the fuck?" he asked.

Remy's hand raised again, the flow of corrupted energy about to come forth once more. He was caught up in the moment, no longer in control of his actions. It was the power that was in the driver's seat now, and all he could do was sit back and let the inevitable happen.

The power needed more death, and Baarabus would have to do.

"Remy, what are you doing?" a familiar voice asked close by. A hand grabbed him roughly by the shoulder and spun him around.

Remy snarled as he looked into Leila's concerned face. He raised his hand, feeling the fire about to flow, not picky about whom it killed. It was the girl's horrified expression that broke the power's hold over him.

But it wasn't enough to keep the flow of divine energy at bay. He held the power back for as long as he was able, spinning around to direct the force at the ogling Filthies on the ledge above. He screamed as the fire flowed out from his outstretched hand and watched in horror as the power pounced upon those angels unlucky enough to be in its path. They screamed as the holy flames fed.

"Remy, what the fuck is going on?" Leila asked him as he gathered his resolve, attempting with all his might to pull back upon the angry force within him.

"No time," he said breathlessly, fighting the power that wanted desperately to be free again, to hurt and murder.

To burn.

Baarabus came at him angrily, his dark fur bristling like the spines of a porcupine.

"You better have a good excuse for trying to kill me," he said in a roar.

"Can't talk about that now," Remy said, managing to dampen the ferocity of the power. "Think we've got other concerns."

They turned their attention to the opening of the pit to see Michael's enraged features as he glared down upon them. This wasn't what Michael had expected at all, certain that the Hellions would have done exactly what he'd wished for.

"We've proven our worth," Remy called up. He was feeling weak as he fought to hold the power of the Seraphim at bay. He knew if he was to release it again, nobody around them would be left alive.

"Let us out of the pit."

Michael actually appeared surprised by the suggestion.

"That was only the first trial, I'm afraid," the archangel said. "You've many more to go before you are deemed worthy to live in His new and perfect Paradise."

The remaining Filthies were all staring at their master, eager for him to tell them what they should be doing.

"Go down there and kill them," he commanded.

And the Filthies cried out with a perverse joy, tensing to do as their master commanded, when there came a most terrible sound.

It was the earsplitting blare of a horn.

And even from within the pit, Remy could see the terror that filled their eyes.

CHAPTER EIGHTEEN

The Archangel Michael sat before a roaring fire in the great stone fireplace and crossed his legs. He glanced at his hand resting on his thigh, at the long, delicate fingers, and saw that the tremble persisted.

"Satquiel," he called out, clenching the hand into a fist as he gazed into the fire. "Has there been any word?"

He sensed his second in command beside the leather chair in which he sat.

"No, Commander," the angel said. "We've received nothing."

Michael felt a small sense of relief with the news. He focused on the orange-and-yellow flames, seeing the Golden City within the fire, imagining that would be its fate if the ritual of Unification were to take place.

When the Almighty had told him of His plans, Michael had been rattled to his very core, and he feared the Lord God Almighty would sense his displeasure and punish him for his lack of faith.

But how could he have faith after the experiences of the Great War?

He shifted uneasily in his chair.

"Are you all right, my lord?" Satquiel asked nervously, still beside the archangel's chair.

Michael pulled his eyes from the fire to look at Satquiel. "I'm fine," he said, the lie feeling like poison upon his lips. "Leave me to my thoughts; disturb me only if something of great import arises."

"Very good, sir," Satquiel said, then departed with a bow, leaving Michael alone in the stone chamber of the monastery.

An angel of Heaven was impervious to the elements, but Michael—since receiving God's message—had felt nothing but cold. An icy ball had formed in the center of his chest, radiating a chilling sensation of supreme dread. He did not wish his subordinates to see him this way, but Michael knew that they suspected something was not right between him and Heaven's edict.

The burning logs collapsed upon themselves with a whiplike crack, sending sparks to sputter out in front of the stone hearth.

So here he sat, waiting for the final word from the Kingdom of Heaven that would signal Unification.

And the return of the Son of the Morning to his former status.

Just the thought of Lucifer welcomed back into the folds of Heaven and God's embrace . . .

Michael trembled, feeling his entire body vibrate. He wondered if that was somehow the work of the Almighty, his Heavenly Father attempting to show him the consequences of his doubt. But then, he doubted the Lord God would be so subtle, recalling the conspicuousness of the Great Flood, and Sodom and Gomorrah. No, these feelings were Michael's own.

And he feared they would be his downfall.

As the archangel stared into the dwindling flames, he suddenly sensed that he was no longer alone but in the presence of awesome power.

"Hello?" he called out as he slowly turned in his chair.

Another angel stood stiff and expressionless in the center of the great stone chamber.

"Greetings, Retriever," Michael said, rising from his seat to face the imposing being.

The Retrievers were created by the Almighty to find and return to Him anything He believed lost. This one wore streamlined armor of shiny black; even the great wings furled upon its back were covered with the glistening reflective coating. The face that peered out from the confines of a helmet wore the bluish white of glacial snow, its eyes equally as cold and unfeeling.

"To what do I owe this visitation?" Michael asked, moving gracefully toward the angel.

The Retriever stared intently at him, giving Michael the uncomfortable feeling that it was able to look right into him, seeing things the archangel would rather remained hidden.

"A time of greatness is almost upon us," the Retriever finally announced, its voice like the blast of a ship's horn.

Michael cringed inwardly, trying not to show the Retriever his displeasure. "It is." He nearly choked on the words.

"The worlds must be made ready for the ritual," the Retriever added.

"Of course they must," Michael reluctantly agreed.

"You will oversee the preparations of one such world." The Retriever pointed a long, sharpened finger at the archangel.

"Me?" Michael responded with surprise. "Surely there are others better suited. . . ."

"You will oversee its preparedness," the angel repeated more forcefully, its voice so loud and booming that the ancient mortar holding in place the stones of the wall began to crumble and rain to the floor.

Michael bowed his head, accepting his burden. "Of course."

He lifted his gaze to see that the Retriever was reaching to its side, the black armor near its hand shimmering as if suddenly liquid. The angel reached into a pocket in the aqueous metal and pulled out an object, holding it out to Michael.

"This is your first duty."

Michael studied the object in the angel's gauntleted hand before reaching to accept it. It was a blackened piece of branch, a twig really. The archangel could not discern the meaning of the simple object until his flesh came in contact with it, and then he knew what it was.

And where it was from.

It was a branch from the Tree of Knowledge. Images exploded in his mind. He saw the Garden of Eden as it was conceived, blossoming into a part of Heaven that would bring about what the Lord God perceived to be His greatest achievement but, in all actuality, was His biggest disappointment.

Michael rubbed his thumb along the bumpy shaft of the stick, bearing witness to the birth of humanity and its downfall, the first step in Eden's being sundered from the Kingdom of Heaven. Then he saw the Garden as it was now, detached from Heaven, drifting from one reality to the next.

Homeless.

"Eden," Michael said aloud, his gaze focusing on Heaven's emissary.

"You will go to it," the Retriever ordered. "And you will secure it in preparation for what awaits it."

The archangel wanted to say no in the worst way, to refuse to take part in what would most assuredly be an epic catastrophe.

"I will do what is asked of me," he said instead.

The Retriever stood there, watching him with eyes that told him nothing but at the same time seemed to bore into Michael's very being.

"Will you?"

Michael was taken aback. Did this Retriever somehow suspect that he did not agree with their Master? Had God cautioned him on the archangel's faithfulness?

"I will," Michael answered, his gaze unwavering.

The black-clad messenger continued to stare, and Michael felt the first strands of his resolve begin to unravel, just as a faceplate of liquid fell over the Retriever's face, hiding his pale features from further view.

"See that you do," the Retriever warned as he spread wide his impressive wings. Then, without so much as a flutter, he was gone, as if he had never been there.

But he had been, and what he had left behind filled the archangel with a growing sense of unease.

Unification was going to happen.

And he was going to have to be part of it.

His anger suddenly exploded from him, and Michael threw the branch from the Tree of Knowledge at the grand fireplace and into the flames. The fire roared like an angry animal, tongues of flame erupting from the hearth to set his chair aflame and try to claim him as well.

The door to the room flew open and Satquiel rushed in. "Is everything all right, Michael?"

The archangel did not take his eyes from the fireplace. "We have received our orders," he said without feeling.

The branch was resting, untouched, in the center of the fireplace. It had started to bloom: small olive-colored buds on its once black and withered surface.

Satquiel stepped in front of Michael and retrieved the branch. "Eden," he whispered as he came in contact.

"Yes," Michael agreed, keeping his disdain in check. "We must prepare for its homecoming."

And what could be God's biggest folly.

Clouds of exhaust that stank of sulfur and death billowed from Leona's dual exhaust pipes as her engine revved with excitement.

"All right, let's try this again," Francis said. He held the collar of the Harvester's leather tunic, forcing the demon toward Leona's grill, where strands of leathery shell still hung. "You're going to give me the location of the Bone Master home world, or I'm going to feed you to my car."

He could sense the Harvester's fear as the car growled, its back wheels spinning wildly, kicking up clouds of dust.

"I am ready to meet my fate," the Harvester said with great resolve, his back stiffening.

"Do you think I'm joking?" Francis asked, pushing the man closer to a horrible death.

Leona's front grill bent and writhed, showing off the inside of a cavernous mouth lined with teeth like multiple saw blades.

"It won't be pleasant, I can assure you," Francis said.

The Harvester remained defiant, and Francis decided to show him that he meant business. Tightening his grip on the back of the demon's collar, Francis thrust him forward, pushing his head into the open maw of the car just long enough to help the demon understand how horrible his death would be.

The Harvester screamed as Francis yanked him back and shoved him to the ground.

Leona leapt forward, ready to help herself, but Francis intervened. "Not yet, girl."

The car obeyed, but Francis could tell she wasn't the least bit happy. Her engine was idling loudly, and she bounced on her shocks in anger.

"But if our friend here doesn't talk soon . . ."

"I'm not going to talk," the Harvester said defiantly. "For generations my family has served the Bone Masters, and I am not about to abandon their trust. Feed me to the vehicle, and I hope it chokes on my bones!"

Leona surged forward, her open mouth less than an inch from the demon's terrified face.

Francis put his hand between Leona's grill and the Harvester's face. "Back it up, would you, girl?" he asked.

She revved angrily, refusing to move.

"Please," he encouraged her nicely.

Abruptly, she did just that, her back wheels screeching on the hard surface of the pocket world as she reversed.

"That's a good girl," he soothed before turning his attention back to the Harvester. He was running out of time and was considering killing the demon and using his scalpel to extract the information, but something told him he'd be best served by leaving the demon alive. But another idea niggled at the back of his mind.

He squatted down before the Harvester. "Your family has served the Bone Masters for generations, is that right?" he asked.

The Harvester remained silent, refusing to even look at Francis.

"So for hundreds of years, your entire family has collected these eggs," Francis continued anyway. He gestured to the cave behind him. "Collecting these eggs in your little baskets and bringing them back to the home world."

Francis fell silent for a few moments, and the only sound to be heard upon the world was Leona's engine purring in anticipation. Finally, the Harvester looked at him.

"I've had an interesting thought," Francis told him, smiling and raising his eyebrows. "This is the only world where these special critters exist, am I right?"

The Harvester did not answer, but the look in his dark, beady eyes said volumes.

"All over this tiny, special world are eggs designated for young Bone Master assassins to be. Now, here's a scary thought." Francis looked out over the landscape. "What would happen if there weren't any eggs?"

He locked eyes with the demon.

"What if somebody had, say, planted explosives inside all the caves—explosives that could be detonated with just the push of a button."

The Harvester's eyes were so large now that they looked as though they might pop from their sockets. Francis reached into his pocket and pulled out a silver object, allowing his thumb to dance along the top of it.

"What about that? I'm sure the Bone Masters would be pretty annoyed if something like that were to happen, never mind the spirits of your forefathers."

"Please . . . ," the demon begged. "Do no harm to the eggs . . . please."

Francis slipped the object back into his coat pocket and studied the demon. The Harvester seemed to grow smaller, his defiant posture deflating.

"Then take me to your home world." Francis waited, knowing that his ruse had worked.

The Harvester looked up at him then, defeat in his horrible demon eyes. "I will take you."

Francis rose to his feet, his knees cracking noisily as he did.

"Outstanding," he said with a smile. "I knew you'd see it my way."

Above the pit, the Filthies were screaming.

Remy looked up, trying to see what was happening, but could only make out furious movements of panic and a sound that he recognized as the release of magickal energies.

"What the fuck is going on up there?" Baarabus growled.

Remy didn't have a clue but was desperate to find out. He ran to the wall of the pit, searching for handholds. He decided he would try to climb out.

Looking around at the litter-strewn floor of the pit, he found another, thicker piece of bone, likely a thighbone, and snapped off its end. He then went to the wall and started to dig handholds to begin his ascent.

Leila and Anthony waited below for him to get a good start before they began to follow.

"Hope you're not expecting me to get out the same way," the demon dog called up to him.

"We'll get you out as soon as we reach topside," Remy said, digging the jagged end of bone into the crumbling grout and broken tile, gouging out a place for his fingers.

The screams above were louder, more frantic, and Remy experienced an odd sensation inside him. Even though he'd gotten the fiery power under control, it was as if something on the outside was calling it out, tempting it to the surface once more.

There was a scream above his head, and Remy instinctively pressed himself against the wall as a winged body fell past him to the floor of the pit. He followed its fall, noticing that its body appeared to be cocooned in a shroud of crackling black energy.

The Filthy writhed and croaked, enwrapped in the strange darkness, finally lying still.

"You sure you want to go up there?" Baarabus called out as he sniffed at the angel's corpse.

"I'll let you know as soon as I get there." Remy quickened his pace.

He'd noticed that it had grown more quiet, only the occasional sound of magickal release to break up the silence. Remy had no idea what he was in for, or what he would find when he got to the top, but that just seemed to be par for the course in this strange world he found himself trapped in.

Getting closer to the lip of the pit, he carefully reached up, feeling around for a proper handhold. He felt a boney hand wrap around his wrist and begin to assist him in climbing up over the edge.

"I've got you," the Fossil said, free from his bonds.

Remy was glad to see that the old-timer was all right, and he climbed up over the side, then turned back to help Leila and Anthony.

"We still have to get Baarabus out of there," Remy said, turning to face the Fossil, whose exposed flesh had accumulated even more dark scabs in the short time since Remy had seen him last.

"No problem," he answered, signaling to several other of Samson's children, who immediately grabbed some rope and tossed it into the pit to help the demon dog up.

It was then that Remy noticed them in the background, standing perfectly still, waiting to be acknowledged. There were ten in all, cloaked in fabric that seemed to be cut from the darkness of the night sky, patterns of star constellations twinkling on their hooded capes and robes.

He knew these beings, these angelic warriors that had refused to pick a side during the Great War between God and Lucifer. They were known as the Cowards by the soldiers of Heaven, but all others called them Nomads.

"What are they doing here?" Remy asked, moving around the Fossil to face the line of cloaked angels.

"They said they're here for you," the Fossil answered.

"For me?" Remy asked, walking toward the Nomads.

As he approached, they bowed their heads, and something began to gnaw at the edges of his mind—something that did not belong to him but to the other.

Something that struggled to be remembered.

"Hello, Remiel," one of the Nomads said, stepping from the line. "It's good to see you again."

"Have we met?" Remy asked him.

"I told Azza about your little problem," the Fossil said, coming to stand beside him. "That you're not him but some other version from an alternate reality."

Remy looked back to the hooded figure.

"You're who you need to be," the angel Azza said, unfazed by the absurdity of the information.

"I'm guessing that we have you to thank for driving away Michael and his Filthies," Remy said.

"Only temporarily, I fear," the Nomad said. "They'll return shortly. I suggest we start our journey as soon as possible."

"Our journey?" Remy questioned.

Azza smiled, turning to look at the others of his ilk. They, too, were grinning from within the darkness of their hoods.

"Of course," he said. "Why else would you have summoned us?"

"I didn't. . . ."

"You released the power," Azza said, reaching out to place the tips of his fingers upon Remy's chest. "These markings upon your flesh had been put there to alert us when this would be so."

Remy watched as Azza returned to stand with his brethren.

"A power you swore would never be called upon again until it was time," Azza finished.

"Time?" Remy questioned, for some reason fearing the response.

"Time," the Nomad leader said with a slow, knowing nod. "Time to bring about the end of something old . . ."

Azza paused and looked about the village of the Filthies before turning his attention back to Remy.

"And the beginning of something new."

CHAPTER NINETEEN

Leila tossed the thick, knotted rope over the side of the pit to Baarabus.

"Hold it with your mouth, and we'll pull you up," she told him.

Baarabus took hold of the rope in his cavernous mouth and bit down.

"Are you ready?" the daughter of Samson asked him.

He looked up at her and acknowledged her question with a nod.

"Let's go!" he heard her cry out to her siblings, and the rope suddenly grew taut, and he began the process of scaling the pit wall.

"Heave!" Leila called out as they attempted to haul his weight.

Baarabus was helping them as much as he was able, the claws of his front and back paws sinking into the broken tile and concrete of the pit wall as he climbed.

Halfway to the top, the great dog wondered what he would find when he got there. A tingle of apprehension raced down the length of his spine, causing the hackles of hair along his back to rise like spines. He recalled the Filthy that had fallen from the sky, and the magick that had encased and killed it.

There was something about the way the magickal force charged the air, the way it smelled; it stirred something deep in the back of the animal's memories, drawing it from the blackness.

Making him want to release the rope and fall back down into the pit, away from what potentially awaited him above.

But he didn't, surging toward the object of his apprehension instead, climbing up the side of the pit all the faster.

He used the powerful muscles in his back legs to spring up over the edge, spitting the rope from his mouth as he scanned the area before him for a sign of what had chased away the Filthies and filled him with such foreboding.

His gaze fell upon Remy, the Fossil, and a robed and hooded figure. It was the sight of that stranger, and others similarly adorned, that brought the fear to the surface like pus from an infected wound.

"Hey, Baarabus," Leila asked, suddenly beside him. She placed a tender hand upon his large blocky head. "You all right?"

"Don't touch me!" the dog roared, snapping at the offending hand.

The young woman recoiled with horror, jumping back as the dog again turned his attention to the strangers speaking with Remy.

His Remy.

The memories surged to the surface, recollections thought buried so very deep that they would never be considered again.

Memories of another time, before . . . when the animal was something else, something loyal, innocent, and pure of heart.

Marlowe watched as his world crumbled around him.

Something bad was happening, something that made his ears hurt and the house in which he lived tremble and shake, raining plaster and glass onto him and his Madeline.

His Madeline.

He wanted to protect her, to get her away from the bad happenings, but they were all around them.

Marlowe barked excitedly as the air became filled with the choking smoke and dust. His Madeline was trying to make it toward him, to follow the sound of his voice, but the ceiling above her head started to crumble, collapsing down upon her.

Without hesitation he charged forward, over the rubble and through the dust, searching for the woman. Marlowe could not help himself, whimpering and barking pathetically as he scoured the area now covered in the broken pieces of his home.

The building continued to shake, creating sounds that foreshadowed even more terrible happenings. There were other noises as well—sounds from outside that terrified him so badly that he wanted to pee inside. But he tried his best to ignore his fears, to be the good dog—the best dog—that his Remy and his Madeline always said that he was.

And right now he had to find his Madeline and take her from this breaking place.

Marlowe sniffed and listened. He heard a moan nearby, and then caught a whiff of blood, which made him cry out. He followed the coppery scent, pressing his nose against the dust-covered floor, pushing aside the rubble to find his most cherished prize.

He found her under a section of wall that had tumbled inward. She moaned beneath the rubble, her hand extended out from underneath the wall and window frame. He could see that her hand had been cut, and blood oozed from the multiple wounds. He approached gingerly so as not to scare her, placing his snout into her open fingers to let her know that he was there. She responded, her fingertips weakly scratching at his nose. He was so happy that she was still moving; excitedly, he licked at the wounds to stop them from bleeding further.

"Marlowe," he heard her say softly from beneath the rubble. She started to move, to try to wriggle out from beneath the wreckage that had fallen atop her. He tried to help her, furiously digging around the rubble with his front paws.

"Hold on, boy," she said to him, grunting with exertion as she tried to shuck off the covering of shattered wood and plaster that had pinned her to the floor.

Madeline cried out, and the smell of blood grew stronger in the room. She had managed to partially free herself; her head, shoulders, and arms stuck out from under the cover of rubble.

Marlowe went to her, licking her dusty face as his tail wagged excitedly. He was so scared, so very, very scared.

"That's a good boy," she said, reaching up to pat him. He continued to lick at her, the taste of plaster, blood, and tears salty in his mouth. The tastes just made him all the sadder, all the more scared. He did not know what to do, but knew that he must do something. Standing upon

the pieces of broken ceiling and wall, he tentatively reached out with this mouth, gently grabbed the shoulder of her shirt with his teeth, and began to pull. If she could not move herself, then he would move her—drag her from beneath the wreckage of the room if need be.

His Madeline moaned once more, and the smell of her blood was stronger, wafting out from beneath the filthy cover atop her. He tried with all his strength, being a very strong dog—his Remy had told him this often when they played tug-of-war with his favorite rope toy— but the clothing clutched between his teeth began to give way, to tear, and his Madeline was still pinned beneath.

"I can't," he heard her say, moving closer to her face so that he could listen to her. He looked down into her eyes and she spoke the words again to him. *"I can't."*

He did not understand them at first as she lay there, slowly shaking her head, but then she tried again to free herself, and he realized that she could not. Even with his help, she was trapped.

Marlowe did not want to give up, sniffing around the rubble, trying to find a way to free his Madeline. But the more he sniffed, the more blood he smelled, and he came to the sad realization that his Madeline was hurt quite badly.

Frustration and fear got the better of him, and he found himself leaping back from where she lay and barking wildly. He was telling her that she could not give up, that she had to fight. She could not lie there beneath the stone, and the wood, and the broken glass. She needed to get free, and he would help her get from the building, and then they would find their Remy, and he . . .

"I can't get free," she said again to him, her voice soft and filled with resignation. She was trying to get him to understand, but he couldn't— he wouldn't.

She had to get free; she had to get free and follow him so that they could find their Remy.

The noises from outside were louder now. Marlowe cowered, looking all around, fighting the urge to run and hide. But he could not leave her. Instead, he moved closer to his Madeline, lying down atop the broken pieces of his home.

"You are such a good, good boy," she said to him, reaching out a blood-covered hand to stroke the side of his face.

No, no, he wasn't a good boy, he wanted to tell her. A good boy would get her free. A good boy would help her from this broken house.

"You can leave me if you like," she told him. *"I'll be fine—promise."*

Marlowe stayed right where he was, moving his body a little bit closer to her, laying his face beside her head, where it lay on a pillow of broken plaster.

"Go. I'll be fine. I don't think the old wall will be standing much longer, and . . ."

She started to cough then, hard coughs—scary coughs that shook her body even though she was pressed beneath the broken wall. Her movement made more things fall, pieces of the house crashing down, but he stayed where he was.

There was blood on her mouth now, on her lips, and the smell made him very nervous. Gently, he extended his snout, lapping away the blood that now stained her face.

Marlowe was scared, more scared than he had ever been. He wanted to run away, but where would he go? And he could not leave his Madeline.

He was shaking now, and he moved that much closer to the woman who was his life.

"That's all right, good boy," she said, her voice so soft now that it was practically a whisper. *"I'm here. . . . I've got you."* He felt her hands weakly upon him, stroking his fur and trying to calm him.

She was everything to him, she and his Remy.

Where was his Remy? the dog wondered. Why wasn't he here to help them? He almost sprang up then—to go and find his Remy and bring him back so that he could save their Madeline and . . .

Marlowe lifted his head and looked at her lying there. His Madeline was hurt, and he could not—would not—leave her.

He nuzzled closer to her and listened to her breathing.

Marlowe wanted to tell her that everything was going to be all right, like she did for him on the nights when the thunder boomed or firecrackers exploded, and he hoped that just being there, pressed up close to her, would let her know that he loved her.

He could tell—dogs just knew such things—that she was about to leave him. Her body had grown cold, her breathing—he had to listen very hard over the scary sounds outside, to know that she was still breathing.

Marlowe pressed his face to hers, wanting her to know that she wasn't alone.

"It was supposed to be so wonderful," she said.

He lifted his head to look at her, to listen. Her eyes had grown wide, and she was staring up to the ceiling, which wasn't there anymore. The ceiling was gone, and she—they—were looking at the sky.

Marlowe could not understand what it was that he was seeing. Where was the blue? The clouds? The birds that darted across his field of vision?

The sky was wrong, filled with fire.

As something tried to take its place.

"I wonder what happened," his Madeline said.

The noises outside grew even louder, which caused his house to shake even more, the sounds of other walls, other windows, breaking, crumbling, falling inside.

He was scared . . . scared for his Madeline and scared for himself.

"Come here," he heard her say to him, and he felt her arm go around his trembling body and draw him closer. *"I've got you,"* she said.

She held him, and loved him as much as he loved her.

And the world that they shared came crumbling down around them.

I wonder what went wrong.

"Marlowe, no!"

The words left Remy's mouth before he had the chance to check them.

There came a roar and a flurry of movement, and Remy turned to see the great demon dog newly emerged from the pit, charging across the ground with murder in his fiery eyes.

The dog came to a sudden halt before him, his burning gaze now fixed upon him instead of on the Nomad. He was breathing heavily, his hackles raised along his back and tail.

"I told you," he roared between labored breaths. "Never to call"—thick spit flew from his enraged mouth—"me that!"

And before Remy could react, before he could say something that might calm the beast down, Baarabus lashed out, swatting Remy aside.

It was like getting hit in the face with a shovel. Remy's feet left the ground, and he sailed about three feet before gravity reclaimed him, pulling him hard to the earth. He managed to keep his eyes open and saw the demon dog stalk toward the Nomads.

"Baarabus, wait!" Remy called out. "They're part of the plan!"

But the dog seemed not to hear him, padding menacingly closer, growling like the rumble of a Sherman tank engine.

Remy knew that he had the power to stop him. All he had to do was reach inside and call upon the divine, but the thought of rousing that insane power again made him desperate for other options. He got to his feet and caught sight of the net the Filthies had used earlier to confine the demon dog. Remy ran for it, scooping it up and tossing its weighted end toward Baarabus just as the beast was about to pounce on the unmoving Nomads.

The net draped across the animal's hunched shoulders, doing little to stop the demon dog as he sprang. The Nomads didn't move, as if they were waiting for Baarabus to land on them, to bite and rend them limb from limb.

But that wasn't it at all.

Azza casually lifted a hand, his robes falling way to reveal white flesh tattooed with sigils very much like the ones that now adorned Remy's own body. Tendrils of black, ethereal energy flowed from the tips of the Nomad's fingers, snagging the attacking hellhound in a net of dark magick. This was the magick that he had sensed, that had torn the Filthies from the sky.

Baarabus hung in the ebony webbing, biting at the tangible shadow, ripping and tearing with tooth and claw, but it did him little good, for the other Nomads joined their magicks to that of their leader.

"Now, is that any way to treat those who saved your life?" Azza asked, moving his hand in such a way that the struggling Baarabus floated closer.

"You should have let me die!" the dog roared, thrashing within the net, but finally fixing his burning gaze on Remy. "*You* should have let me die!"

"We did only what was asked of us," Azza consoled. "A request made in an emotional moment."

Remy watched Baarabus continue to struggle against the magick holding him, his movements growing weaker as his strength began to ebb.

"What are they going to do to him?" Leila asked, suddenly by Remy's side. "You've got to do something."

Remy knew that he should, but what exactly, he did not know.

"Azza," he said, moving closer.

"Yes, Remiel," the Nomad leader said, his hand still extended, veins of dark magick flowing toward the floating dog.

"Let him go."

The angel continued to stare at Baarabus.

"I'm not sure that would be wise," the Nomad answered.

"Please," Remy begged. "Let him go. . . . It's not you he's mad at; it's me."

Azza and the Nomads remained silent as Remy moved even closer.

"Release him. If he's going to hurt anyone, it should be me." Remy reached out to lay his hand upon the sheath of darkness that covered the animal's powerful frame.

"Don't touch me," Baarabus growled, struggling to shake off his bonds, but it was really only for show.

"They only did what I asked them to do," Remy said, not really remembering but knowing that the words were right. "Something happened—something awful—and I did what . . ."

Baarabus looked at him in such a way that Remy could have sworn his heart had just been run through with the blade of a sword.

"Something awful did happen, and you chose to make it worse."

There were disturbing flashes of memory, not enough to piece together the entire story but enough to tell Remy that it was indeed something terrible.

"I . . . I'm sorry," he told the beast. "I'm truly sorry. . . ."

"Do you even know what you did?" Baarabus interrupted.

Remy said nothing.

Baarabus made a noise of supreme disgust. "How can I rip your guts out if you don't even know what you did?" the dog grumbled. "Waste of my fucking time." He turned his attention back to the Nomads. "Let me loose. You have nothing to worry about with me."

The Nomads hesitated, then Azza drew back on the dark energy, and the others followed suit.

Baarabus dropped to the ground. He shook wildly, eyeing them all before turning and walking away.

"I need to be alone for a while," he said, and Remy watched him pad toward the ruins of the Filthies' habitat.

Remy wanted to say more but knew that no matter what he said, it would likely never be enough.

CHAPTER TWENTY

The Broker eyed the iPhone 6 resting on the top of the pitted workstation with a kind of revulsion best suited for spiderlike insects and venomous snakes.

He knew that he couldn't avoid it any longer and reached out with long, spindly fingers to snatch up the Earth technology, prodding it to life. The Broker would have preferred the older methods of communicating with an advanced form of telepathy, but as the years passed, he'd found that unique talent less and less amongst the newest assassins. The old ways were slowly fading away.

There was no choice but to embrace technology and utilize it to the best of their abilities.

He studied the device, recalling what he would need to do in order to transmit a message—text a message—to all his assassins in the field. Carefully he stroked the appropriate buttons on the face of the device, calling up the keyboard, and began the process of writing his message.

It was a simple message, one that told all his killers that a specific assignment had eclipsed all others and that the honor and reputation of the Bone Master guild was being challenged.

The angel, Remy Chandler, was still alive, the job already having claimed the lives of three assassins. That would not do—not in the least.

And that other divine creature, the fallen angel who had requested a meeting. The nerve of that being to think he could buy out an existing contract. The Broker was sure there were other guilds out there that might entertain the idea of backing off for the right price, but never the Bone Masters. Once a contract was initiated, it was fulfilled no matter the price. That was how it had been for millennia and how it would be for countless more.

Which made the fact that the Seraphim was still alive all the more galling.

The Broker finished his message and, satisfied that it was clear, hit SEND, sending it on its way over the ether. Setting the phone down again, he walked across the office to a table where a bottle of wine—a gift from a satisfied customer—awaited his consumption. He studied the unlabeled bottle, attempting to remember the specifics of the assignment. The Broker recalled that it had been an Earth case, something to do with a jealous husband and suspicions of infidelity. Not one of the more exciting jobs, but one that continued to fill the guild's coffers and provide him with the occasional drink of fine wine.

The Broker popped the cork and brought his nostril slits to the open bottle. It smelled delicious, and as he was certain that the troublesome Seraphim assignment would soon be brought to a close, he decided that he'd imbibe in a precelebratory sampling. But as he lifted the bottle to his mouth, a loud banging at the door startled him. Wine spilled from the lip of the bottle, staining the front of his robes.

The Broker hissed as he set the bottle down, wiping away wine that dribbled down his chin. Then he stalked across the room and down a short staircase to throw open the circular wooden door.

A man lay just beyond the entryway, and the Broker could see that he was injured.

"What is this?" the Broker demanded. "Who are you?"

The man moaned in response, his body trembling as he curled into a tighter ball.

The Broker nudged the body with his foot. "Who are you?" he asked again.

"Please forgive me," the man pleaded, his voice trembling.

"Forgive you? Forgive you for what?"

The man uncurled and lifted his battered face to the Broker. "I didn't want to do this . . . but he threatened the eggs."

It took a moment for the Broker to recognize the man as a Harvester, and from one of the oldest and most prestigious families.

"What are you talking about? Who threatened the eggs?"

The Harvester seemed to grow faint, his head lolling to his chest. With an angry sigh, the Broker reached down and hauled him to his feet. He slung the Harvester's arm over his own shoulder and dragged him through the door and up the stairs to the office, where he unceremoniously dumped him into a chair.

"Wake up," the Broker ordered, slapping the Harvester's bruised and bloody face. "Somebody threatened the eggs—who would dare such a thing?"

The Harvester listed to the side of the chair, still not fully conscious.

The Broker left him, going to the table where he'd left the wine. "Here," he said, returning to the Harvester and thrusting the bottle at him. "Take a swig of this; it'll help clear your mind."

The Harvester took the bottle and brought it to his mouth, taking a long sip.

"Better?" the Broker asked, taking back the bottle.

The Harvester nodded, his eyes growing more clear.

"Explain yourself, then," the Broker commanded.

"It has been my family's duty . . . my sacred duty to safeguard the eggs, and I could not bear to see them destroyed."

"The eggs? Somebody was going to destroy the eggs?"

The Harvester nodded furiously. "Unless I told him . . ." And he stopped.

The Broker felt a cold trickle of fear race down his spine. "Unless you told who . . . what?" he prompted impatiently.

"I'm so sorry," the Harvester said, burying his face in his hands. "I couldn't think of any other way."

The Broker lashed out, swatting the Harvester with the back of his hand, the force of the blow knocking the man from his chair. "Tell me!"

The Harvester stayed on the floor, a trembling hand wiping at the blood that bubbled up from his swollen and split lip. "He wanted to come to the home world," he cried.

"What?" the Broker shrieked. No one, other than a member of the Bone Master race, was allowed to bear witness to their world, and its location had remained a secret for countless millennia. "You didn't!"

The Harvester cowered on the floor. "I had no choice. . . . I couldn't let him destroy the eggs!"

"Who?" The Broker reached down and hauled the Harvester to his feet by the front of his tunic. "Who made you commit this atrocity?"

The Harvester would not meet the Broker's angry gaze, lowering his eyes in shame and fear. "He did not tell me his name. He appeared human—but I don't think he was."

As if on cue, a shrill sound, like the beeping of a horn, sounded from outside.

Immediately, the Harvester began to panic, struggling in the Broker's grasp. "Oh no, no, no! He's here!"

Letting go of the Harvester, the Broker stormed to the room's only window. Outside, in the center of the assassins' compound, was that fallen angel leaning against the hood of a shiny black automobile.

The Broker was furious. The audacity of this angel. He pushed open the window and was immediately accosted with the smell of automobile fumes and something else that stank of cooking meat.

"You do realize that you'll never leave this place alive," the Broker said.

"See, here's the difference between you and me," the fallen angel said, crossing his arms as if he hadn't a care in the world. "Bang, you start right off with the threats. How is there anything constructive in that?" He shook his head. "Why don't you come down here and we can talk about what's brought me all this way to your doorstep."

"I believe we've already had this discussion," the Broker said.

The fallen angel smiled, and the Broker suddenly felt an overwhelming sense of dread.

"No," the angel said. "We haven't had *this* conversation."

And the smile grew wider and far more feral.

Francis did not make threats lightly. He would never have gone to this much trouble if he hadn't meant business.

He watched the demon in the window as he leaned against Leona's hood. The car thrummed with life, excited by the prospect of being fed.

"Why don't you come down here?" Francis called up to the Broker. "And we'll talk this through like reasonable beings."

At first the Broker did not move, but then he closed the window and disappeared from view.

Is he actually going to be reasonable? Francis wondered. He'd never known a demonic entity to be even remotely so, but one never could tell.

There was a sudden blast of gunfire, and bullets raked across Leona's driver's-side doors.

So much for being reasonable.

The car roared to life, her wheels spinning wildly, kicking up clouds of dust and burning rubber. It was the perfect screen as Francis drew the Pitiless pistol and went to work. Making his way around Leona's body, he watched for muzzle flashes, took aim, and fired, satisfied with the muffled cries.

Multiple figures emerged from the smoke, clutching machete-like blades, screaming as they ran at him. Francis hesitated momentarily at the sight of his attackers—they were little more than demon children, which explained why they were resorting to guns and bladed weaponry.

Behind him, Leona's engine revved, her headlights glowing bright.

Why the hell not? he thought.

"Go ahead," Francis said aloud. "Eat your fill."

He watched in awe as the car surged forward, attacking the swarming crowd of young demons. It was like a nightmare version of Animal Planet, a living car attacking its flesh-and-blood prey. Francis had never seen anything like it, yet as gruesome as it was, he couldn't take his eyes away.

Leona was insatiable, wheels spinning for traction as she chased after the youths, who attempted to escape her wrathful hunger. There were explosions in the distance, followed by fire; the screams of the unlucky drifted in the fetid air of this demon world.

Francis suddenly sensed someone behind him. "So, are you ready to talk?" he asked, spinning around, the Pitiless at the ready.

The Broker faced him, aiming his own weapon made from the bones of a special animal.

And they fired as one.

*   *   *

The Pitiless' bullet coursed through the air, first striking the venomous tooth as it made its way toward Francis, pulverizing it to so much powder before continuing on to its true destination.

The Broker was just about to fire a second shot when the Pitiless' bullet then struck the weapon of bone, causing it to explode in his hands. Bone fragments shot into the air, slivers burying themselves in the pallid flesh of the Broker's face and hands. The Broker cried out in pain, not only from his physical wounds, but from the traumatic severing of the psychic bond he'd shared with his weapon.

Francis watched as the Broker lowered himself down into a crouch, moaning pitifully as he did, only to spring at him in attack. A knife appeared in the Broker's hand, slicing toward Francis' throat. The fallen Guardian angel felt the tip of the blade glide across the side of his neck, parting the flesh and causing it to weep.

"And here I was thinking we were going to be gentlemen," Francis said, pulling back from the blade as the Broker tried to bring it around again for another taste of his neck. Francis brought himself up under the Broker's arm, taking it beneath the elbow and bending it in the opposing direction until there was a muffled snap of cartilage and ligament. Again the Broker wailed, but did not stop his attack. As the blade dropped from his now-useless hand, he caught it in the other, bringing the knife toward Francis' ribs in an upward thrust.

"You are a sneaky bastard, aren't you?" Francis said, managing to prevent the point from finding its target. Pulling the assassin off balance and dragging him closer, Francis brought his forehead down into the Broker's face, pulverizing one of the demon's cheekbones.

The Broker went temporarily limp, stumbling back. His broken left arm flopped uselessly by his side, but he still managed to hold on to the knife in his other hand.

"Are we going to talk now?"

But the Broker still wasn't ready to give up. Blinking away the blood that now dribbled from the gash above his pronounced brow, he lunged at Francis again.

"This is about suicide, isn't it?" Francis asked as he easily evaded the stabbing gesture, taking hold of that arm as well and breaking it like a twig. The screaming was intense, the Broker's two arms now flapping pathetically at his sides. "You want me to hurt you . . . to kill you so you won't have to answer the question."

The Broker fell to his knees but tried to stand.

"I'm not going to kill you until you answer me," Francis said. "Will you cancel the contract on Remy Chandler now?"

The Broker fell down, crying out as he tried to catch himself with his broken limbs. He rolled upon the ground onto his back, looking up at the fallen angel.

And he began to laugh.

"I really don't see much to be laughing about," Francis told him as he stepped closer, bringing his foot down upon the center of the Broker's closest arm.

The Broker screeched.

"Will you cancel the contract?" Francis asked again.

The demon looked up at him from the ground with unwavering, defiant eyes.

"You have no understanding of what we are, do you?" he asked.

Francis glared back.

"We are the Bone Masters, one of the most aggressive clans of demon assassins that ever existed. We do not shy away from any assignment—nobody is too big or too small to die at our hands, and we have never not fulfilled a contract."

"First time for everything," Francis said in all seriousness, aggravated beyond words but not surprised where this was going.

"No," the Broker said with a wet-sounding chuckle. "With the Bone Masters, there is not."

"So what are you saying?"

The Broker looked up at him incredulously. "Are you that dim-witted, angel? Your friend is going to die no matter what you do to me." He smiled again, his jagged yellow teeth stained with his own blood. "That's just the way it is."

"Unless all the Bone Masters sent to do the job are stopped."

"They would have to be killed."

"Yeah, figured as much," Francis said. He turned toward the sound of a rumbling engine as it came closer. Leona pulled up alongside him, the stench of death wafting off her in waves. Her windshield was covered in a thick coating of gore, pieces of mangled bodies dangling from the front of her grill.

"An impossible task, angel," the Broker said.

"Maybe," Francis answered, going to the car. "But, like my former Lord and Master, I'm a pretty big fan of miracles." He went around to the back of the car. "Open the trunk, Leona."

The trunk lid flipped open and he leaned inside, finding what he was looking for and carefully hauled it out.

Francis brought the ornate metal canister around so that the Broker could see, gently setting it down upon the ground between his feet.

The Broker strained to rise up in a sitting position, wincing in pain as a result of his two broken arms.

"And what is this, angel?" the Broker asked. "Perhaps some form of payment to buy away the contract on your friend's life?"

"It's death," Francis said matter-of-factly.

The Broker looked at him, and Francis was sure that the demon really didn't quite understand how far this whole business had gone and how far it was still to go.

"Inside this canister is the distillation of God's wrath."

"He is not my God," the demon spat defiantly.

"No matter whose God He is, this canister holds but a sample of the anger that He heaped upon the Pharaoh of Egypt for not releasing the Israelites from slavery."

Francis lovingly stroked the ornate, copper-colored canister.

"Maybe you saw the movie? One of Chuck Heston's finest." The angel paused, ruminating. "That and *The Omega Man*—and the one with the monkeys, of course."

"What are you babbling about?" the demon asked. "You tell me you have a container that contains the power of your God, and I ask you, so what? It changes nothing in the scheme of things."

"But it does," Francis said.

"What does it change, angel? The Bone Masters will continue to be the deadliest of assassins, and your friend is going to die." The demon smiled nastily. "You see? Canister or not, nothing changes."

Leona's engine purred strangely, almost sounding like a chuckle—at least, that's what it sounded like to Francis.

"With this, everything changes," Francis said, lifting the canister of God's wrath up from the ground about an inch and then setting it back down.

"This is your end," Francis said icily, waiting a moment for what he was saying to sink in. "I never wanted it to get this bad, but no matter how I tried to figure it, you were right. No matter how many assassins were taken off the game board, as long as Remy was still alive there would be Bone Masters coming for him."

"Maybe even the simple-minded eventually come to understand the futility of fighting back against the Bone—"

"So I decided to change everything," Francis said, interrupting the demon. "To clear the game board completely."

The Broker still wasn't quite getting it, but he was onto the fact that something serious was about to go down.

"Sure, I understood that there was probably nothing that I could do about the assassins already on the job, especially if you had zero intention of calling them in—I got that."

Francis looked away from the demon, at his dwelling, and at the barracks behind it. He then looked in other directions at the dwellings there as well.

"But then I started to think of the Bone Masters and what absolute pains in the ass they've been to me since this whole business happened. Nothing but a perpetual thorn in my side, and a continued thorn in the side of my friend Remy if he should survive the current contract."

"Go on, angel. I'm starting to lose interest."

Francis smiled again, that cold, awful grin.

"So I decided to do something drastic. I decided that I would remove that thorn from my ass and from the asses of anybody else out there that might some day have a run-in with you Bone Master douches."

Francis slowly squatted down, taking the top of the canister in hand and beginning to twist.

"What are you doing?" the Broker asked. Was that a hint of panic he was now hearing in the demon's voice?

Should have been.

"Isn't it obvious?" Francis answered. There was a resounding crack as the seal was broken, and the lid slowly began to unscrew.

The Broker started to push away, as the bluish gray–colored mist began to escape from beneath the lid, seemingly heavier than air, slithering down from the canister to the ground.

"I'm going to kill you all," Francis then explained, continuing to twist the lid. "I'm going to kill everything in this world—the young and the old; all future Bone Masters in training will never get to ply their trade, I'm sorry to say."

"You're mad!" the demon exclaimed.

"I'm mad, all right," Francis said, removing the lid and tossing it aside, where it clattered to the street. "I'm pissed the fuck off at the fact that I have to do something so drastic, but you left me little choice."

He stood up, leaving the canister where it he had placed it. The contents continued to crawl out from inside, where they had been kept—*imprisoned*—since they were last used against Pharaoh.

"Never thought I'd ever actually be that desperate to open it," Francis said, shaking his head as he watched God's wrath continue to emerge. "But desperate times and all that shit."

The Broker had managed to push himself up against the wall with his legs and was fighting to stand. "You can't do this!"

"But I am," Francis said. The Wrath of God had fully emerged now, filling the air and spreading off in various directions. "In the old days it took the form of plagues: water into blood, locusts, death of the firstborn, boils, frogs . . . Honey Boo Boo."

The angel laughed then. "That last one was a joke, but you never can tell."

The air was suddenly filled with the screams of an awakening populace.

The Broker looked terrified, pressed against the wall of his abode.

"It works fast," Francis said, the cries spreading and growing louder by the second. "I doubt it'll take long." He looked at the Broker. "It'll take you last as a favor to me."

He then moved toward the waiting car, opening the door to get into the driver's seat.

"Wait!" the Broker yelled.

Francis paused, one foot in the car.

"We can talk. . . . Perhaps something could be done to lift the contract on the Seraphim—please."

Francis slowly shook his head.

"Not all the *please*s in the universe could get me to put this genie back in the bottle, and besides, I couldn't even if I wanted to. Once it's released, it has to do its business; it could never be controlled."

There was the shattering of glass above them and a demon fell through the broken window to land upon the street, obviously dead before he struck the ground. It was the Harvester that had told Francis what he needed to know, his face swollen horribly, thick blood like tar leaking from his mouth, nose, and eyes.

"Huh, I was wondering where he went."

The Broker pushed off the wall with some obvious discomfort.

"Kill me," the demon demanded. "I will lift the contract, and then allow you to kill me—just spare my people."

Francis stared and then shook his head sadly.

"Now, why couldn't you have been this reasonable before you pissed me off?" he said, climbing into the vehicle and slamming the door closed.

The Broker threw himself against the car, kicking and flailing with his useless arms as the world and all living things upon it were murdered by the Wrath of God.

Francis ignored the desperate actions of the Broker, reached over to turn on the radio, and tuned the channel to an oldies station, cranking up the Beach Boys to drown out the cries of the dying.

CHAPTER TWENTY-ONE

T hey continued to dig at the base of the tree, careful so as not to disturb the crumbling ground around its base.

"We're getting there," Linda said breathlessly. She wiped the back of her hand across her sweating brow as she eyed the darkness within the hole.

A darkness that seemed to call to her.

"And why exactly are we digging around the abyss?" Ashley asked, pulling a handful of earth toward her.

Marlowe had gone to the other side of the tree and was digging and sniffing, sniffing and digging.

"I'm beginning to think you want the hole big enough for us to climb into," Ashley complained.

Linda shook her head. "No," she said flatly. "We're not going in." She saw a place where the hole could be widened and went to the edge, reaching in to pull clumps of dirt away.

"That's good," Ashley responded. "Because I'm not sure what . . ."

"I am," Linda interrupted, busily working at the hole. She could feel Ashley staring at her.

"You're going into the hole?" the girl asked incredulously. "You're going down into that abyss?"

"He's down there, Ash," Linda said. "I can feel him down there."

"Down there," Ashley repeated. "We don't even know where 'down there' is . . . or what it is, for that matter."

"Yeah, but we're here for a reason, and I think me going down that hole is part of it."

Linda was staring again into the blackness of what Ashley called "the abyss." It was as good a name as any. She could feel its pull on her, something akin to that gentle tug on the hand when the water of a full sink went down the drain. Only this was a tug upon something much deeper.

This was a tug upon her soul.

"No." Ashley seemed flustered. "I don't think that's a good idea; in fact, I think it's horrible. We have to stay together." She looked around. "Wherever 'here' even is. If I lose somebody to talk to . . ."

Marlowe appeared from around the tree.

"Sorry, baby, but you're not much of a conversationalist." Ashley apologized to the Labrador. "I don't know what I'd do here alone."

"You'll help to keep him alive," Linda stated simply.

Ashley looked as if she was going to cry, and her shoulders slumped. "And how am I supposed to do that?"

"You and him," Linda said, pointing to Marlowe. "You and he are going to lend your strength to Remy—to this tree." She was about to touch it but decided against it, not wanting to weaken herself before . . .

Before she began what she was intending to do.

"Are you sure?" Ashley said, her tone telling Linda that she hoped the woman wasn't.

But Linda was sure. She could feel it. Deep down in that darkness, her Remy was there. And she had to bring him back to where he belonged.

"Yeah, I really am."

"Shit." Ashley turned away from her.

"You can do this, Ash," Linda encouraged. "This is why we're here; we're his strength. We're the reason why he's still around."

Ashley turned back, her arms folded across her chest. "Fine, I guess I have to trust you."

Linda smiled slightly. "Even though you barely know me?"

"I know," Ashley agreed. "You're practically a stranger, and here I am, wherever the frig I am, waiting for you to go down a hole to find my best friend in the whole world."

Marlowe barked.

"Exactly, Marlowe," Ashley said. "Totally fucked up."

"A stranger?" Linda questioned. "After this, we'll be BFFs for life."

"After this," Ashley repeated. "First we have to survive whatever this is, *then* we do movie nights."

Linda laughed, but her eyes were again drawn to the yawning blackness before her.

"So how are we going to do this?" Ashley asked.

"I'm going in," Linda said.

"Yeah, I know you're going in," Ashley responded with exasperation. "But how do we get you out? How do we even know when you're ready to get out?"

Linda hadn't thought that far and didn't answer right away. Then she shook her head. "I don't know. I guess I should tie something around me."

"Yeah, like what?" Ashley asked.

Again Linda said nothing.

"We're in a field with a tree, nothing much else around—maybe we could rip up strips of our clothes, or—"

"Look," Linda interrupted, pointing to something in the distance that hadn't been there before. In fact, the entire landscape had suddenly changed dramatically.

"Are those swings?" Ashley asked. "Hey, it looks like we're in the Common now."

"Yeah, I think we are. Did you do that?" Linda asked.

Ashley shook her head. "Not at all."

Then Linda noticed Marlowe staring off into the distance, his tail wagging excitedly, and she began to put two and two together. "You did this, didn't you, boy?" she said, squatting close to the Labrador and lifting his snout to look into his eyes.

He licked her face and continued to wiggle.

"But why the Common?" Ashley asked.

Linda gazed off at the playground, at the swings gently moving on their chains in the breeze.

Swings.

On chains.

Chains.

"Chains," Linda said.

"What?"

Linda pointed to the empty playground in the distance. "The swings are hung with chains. We wrap the chains around me."

Ashley stared at the playground for a bit, then looked at the dog by her side. "Chains. Good job, boy."

The bullet jacket had been fashioned from the melted-down gauntlet of Joan of Arc.

Simeon had always known the metal glove of the divinely touched warrior woman would come to use someday.

And now it had.

The iron of the multipieced gauntlet had been imbued with powerful energies, energies that continued to linger long after Joan's execution. Energies that were capable of containing those within the infant effigy retrieved from Vietnam.

"How are we doing?" Simeon asked from across the room.

The possessed magick user Malatesta sat on a stool, hunched over a table, working on the bullet jacket. "As well as we were doing the last time you asked."

Simeon peered around the wall of protective supernatural shielding that they'd erected. The power that they were working with was something extraordinary, and to not take precautions was to risk absolute disaster. After all, they were attempting to contain a piece of creation itself.

"Will it be enough?"

"Will what be enough?" the sorcerer asked, a hint of the demonic leaking through.

"The casing . . . Will the casing be enough to hold it?"

Simeon had wondered this since they'd first brought the fragment back. It would have been preferable to use the metal of the infant receptacle, but he still needed that to contain the power until they were ready.

And that's where metal blessed with the divinity of Joan of Arc came in.

"I'm enhancing it with some spells of my own, but it should be sufficient," Malatesta explained.

"And you're sure that it will be—"

"Yes, I'm sure," the sorcerer snapped. "And if it isn't, we won't have anything to worry about because our atoms will be scattered to the wind."

"There's no reason to get testy," Simeon said.

"This is why you needed me, isn't it?"

"I don't understand."

"For this procedure," Malatesta said. "You needed a sorcerer with exceptional aptitude."

"Incorrect," Simeon countered. "I needed a sorcerer with far more than exceptional aptitude. I needed somebody with a taste for darkness who would have no problem spitting in the eye of the Creator."

He watched Malatesta's reaction. The former Keeper agent of the Vatican trembled briefly—violently—as if somebody had just electrocuted him. Simeon knew that the holy man had again attempted to assert control over the demon Larva that had possessed him since childhood.

But to no avail.

"Then it's a good thing you found me," Malatesta said, his voice sounding more demon than human.

There was a flash of supernatural power, followed by the smell of burning ozone, and Malatesta pushed back his chair, admiring the ornate bullet casing he had fabricated. "Isn't she lovely?"

Simeon reached for it, but the sorcerer pulled it away.

"There is only one," the former holy man taunted. "Screw it up, and there won't be any more."

Simeon silently extended his hand, the expression on his face brooking no argument. And without another moment's hesitation, Malatesta gently placed the .45 casing into the palm of his master's hand.

Simeon studied the shell, feeling the magick fused to the molecular structure of the metal. He smiled as he turned it around in his hand. "Yes, this should do nicely." He imagined its purpose fulfilled and felt a surge of pleasure very close to ecstasy.

"We finish it," he said curtly, crimping down the intensity of his pleasure, preferring to feel nothing until what had become his purpose was fulfilled. He handed the shell back to Malatesta.

"And now the tricky part," the possessed man said, a twinkle of evil dancing in his eye.

"And now the tricky part," Simeon repeated, watching as the man crossed the underground chamber and approached a table where the metal container, filled with the power of creation, waited.

Waited to be shaped into something of amazing power.

Something that would lay a God low.

Steven Mulvehill moved carefully, not wanting to make his back hurt any more than it already did.

"I'm going to be a fucking cripple if I sit here for much longer."

He and Squire sat on the wooden steps, halfway up to the bedroom where two very brave women and a dog were attempting to save his best friend's life.

Squire munched on some oyster crackers from a package he'd miraculously produced from his pants pocket.

"How do you even have those?" Mulvehill asked.

Squire gazed up at him midcracker. "Have what?"

"Those. The crackers."

Squire popped one into his large mouth and began to chew. "I think I had chowder recently."

"And you saved the crackers?"

The goblin thought for a moment. "No, I probably ate them. I love these things in chowder."

"So we're back to the beginning, then."

Squire looked at him as he dug another round cracker from the cellophane bag and shrugged.

Exasperated, Mulvehill changed the subject, craning his neck to see the doorway to the bedroom. "How do you think they're doing?"

"How the fuck do I know?" Squire answered, with a mouthful of crackers.

"I would think you would know is all."

"And why is that?"

"I don't know, because you're, like . . . part of this shit?"

"Part of what shit?" Squire finished the crackers, noisily crinkling the cellophane package and sticking it in the front pocket of his shirt.

"This," Mulvehill said, making a sweeping gesture with his hands. "All this bizarre shit."

"This bizarre shit's got nothing to do with me."

"Yeah, but you're part of it. . . . You know what I mean."

Squire scoffed, shaking his large head. "You're all the fucking same, whether it's this reality or another."

"So what, I've hurt your feelings now?"

"Let's just say I've been made a little prickly by humanity always pointing fingers at something that doesn't fit with their idea of the normal. If it isn't normal, it must be the problem. If I had a dollar—"

"Or an oyster cracker," Mulvehill interrupted.

"Fuck you," Squire spat. "If I had a dollar for every time I'd been pointed out as being the problem, just after I'd saved humanity from some world-ending, supernatural event, I'd be living the life of fucking Riley."

There was a beat of silence before . . .

"Who is fucking Riley anyway?" Mulvehill asked.

Squire glared, and then his grotesque features softened. "I haven't a clue, but I bet he'd appreciate somebody like me being around to save him from the fucking end of the world."

"I appreciate you," Mulvehill said, shifting his position again. "But my back doesn't appreciate these steps."

"Then we should go down to the kitchen," Squire said. "I'm getting hungry anyway."

Mulvehill looked at him. "You just had crackers."

"Yeah, I just had crackers. Crackers. They're like eating big pieces of dust. I need something a little more substantial."

"I wouldn't feel right going in there," Mulvehill said. He again looked up the stairs to the open bedroom door.

"They haven't made a peep since they went under."

"I know, but what if they need us?"

"They're not gonna need us," Squire said. "Where they are, we couldn't get to them even if we wanted to."

"I feel like staying here is the least I can do."

"We all have our jobs," Squire explained. "Their job is to go into Remy's soulscape. Ours is watching the fort, which is exactly what we're doing."

"I still think I should stay here—just in case."

Squire sighed as he stood. "Suit yourself, but I'm heading down to the kitchen to whip up something to eat before I pass out from starvation."

"You do that," Mulvehill said. "I was going to say that you were looking a little malnourished."

"Yeah, keep it up. You have no idea about a goblin's metabolism," Squire said as he started down the steps. "You want me to bring you anything?"

"No, I'm good."

"Suit yourself."

His eyes still on the open doorway, Mulvehill listened to the sounds of Squire as he reached the next floor below, continued down the short hallway, walked across the living room, and . . .

Steven wasn't quite sure what he heard from the tone of voice that wafted up from below.

"Mulvehill, you might want to get the fuck down here . . . now!"

The goblin sounded like he might be upset. More upset than there wasn't any pasta in the cupboards, or that they were out of spicy brown mustard.

No, this sounded more trouble-filled than that.

Mulvehill made sure that he had his gun as he sprang down the stairs, the pain in his back all but forgotten.

CHAPTER TWENTY-TWO

Remy and the others followed Azza and the Nomads deeper into the ruins of the city.

It was like looking at a patchwork quilt, nothing really matching but still forming something altogether—

New.

They passed a section of unearthly structures that appeared to be carved from the blackest obsidian: probably buildings from the recreated Hell. And those alien superstructures swiftly gave way to the ruins of a coffee shop, then a popular chain drugstore.

Remy turned, looking past the children of Samson for Baarabus. He hadn't seen the great dog since their conversation with the Nomads.

"I wouldn't worry about him," a voice said from his other side.

Remy glanced over to see the Fossil, his face scab free and moist with bloody raw flesh. For the briefest of moments there was a flash of recognition, but it was fleeting, evading Remy's grasp as it disappeared as quickly as it had come.

"I haven't seen him since we left the Filthies' encampment."

"Yeah, he was pretty upset, but he'll get over it," the Fossil said.

Remy turned back to watch the Nomads as they navigated the ruins, staying close to the shadows in case somebody—or something—might be watching.

"I feel like I have a lot to apologize for," Remy said. "But at the same time, I haven't a clue as to what I did."

The old-timer chuckled, and Remy looked at him inquisitively.

"Sorry," he said, wiping away some blood that was trickling over his brow. "But when you were down in that pit and tapped into your divine power . . . ," the old man began.

Remy looked at him with uncertainty. "There's something wrong with it."

"Yeah, there is," the Fossil said. "And judging by the way you looked, it was obvious you had no idea."

They had progressed into an area where huge trees, right out of an evil Disney forest, had started to grow, pushing up through the streets, skeleton-finger branches intertwining to form a kind of canopy above their heads.

The Nomad leader stopped. "We're close now."

Remy stepped closer to the Nomads. "Where exactly are we going?" he asked. "You said you were going to get us away from the Filthies and further our journey, but you never said to where."

Azza seemed amused, but any attempt at an explanation was interrupted by the sounds of a battle from somewhere behind them. Nomads and Samson's children alike turned as one toward the noise, tensed and ready to face whatever danger was approaching. Grunts and growls gave way to screaming and then sudden silence—until something moved in the shadows, something large and powerful.

Remy realized what it was—*who* it was—before Baarabus sauntered out of the darkness, the neck of a Filthy clutched in his mouth, dragging the body with him. The demon dog dropped the mangled body at Remy's feet.

"Found this guy spying on you and decided to surprise him."

"Surprise," Remy said aloud, looking down at the twisted angel's corpse. This one had strange circular markings on its forehead and cheeks.

"It's a scout," Azza said. "Michael and the Filthies are probably not too far away. When this one doesn't report back . . ."

"They'll be on our tails," Remy finished.

"Yes," Azza responded.

"Then we should probably get going." Remy looked at the group, and they all nodded their agreement. Even Baarabus.

"And where is it that we're going?" Remy asked again.

"To find a door," the Nomad said, turning away and leading them beneath the branches of the skeletal trees. "A door to fit your key."

They'd been walking for hours when Remy began to see the fatigue in Samson's children: the way they walked, the dullness that had appeared in their eyes. They may have been super strong, but they were still human, and humans needed to rest.

He'd convinced Azza to stop for a while, and they'd found a place to set up camp under the remains of a stone bridge. Remy guessed that at one time a river or stream had run beneath it, but now there was just dirt and rock. He also found it strange how the groups had segregated themselves—the Nomads clumped together on one side of the camp, Samson's children on the other side. Even the old man sat off by himself, tending to the scabs that grew like moss upon his body.

Remy caught Leila's eye, and she quickly looked away, which immediately drew him to her.

"Are you guys all right?" he asked as he approached her. They were eating some provisions that looked like tree bark, boiling some water that they'd found in an overturned light fixture. Remy had no recollection of any recent rain, but then again, he'd been himself for only a short while.

"We're good," she answered, eyes darting to her brothers, who watched her from their fire. They didn't appear all that thrilled that Remy was talking to one of them. "Just not very happy with you at the moment."

"With me? What did I do now?"

"It's what you didn't do," she corrected. "They think you didn't do enough to save Dante."

"I had no idea what I was doing in that pit," Remy confessed. "They're probably right."

"They've seen what you can do," she told him. "It was like you were holding back."

"Maybe I was. I had no idea what happened to the power of the Seraphim inside me."

Leila seemed confused at first, but then remembered. "Right, you're not you."

"I did what I could," Remy said. "If it wasn't enough . . ."

"They'll get over it," she interrupted. "Isn't like this is the first time we've lost a brother."

Remy could feel the others' icy glares on him. "You should get back to them." He turned to leave.

"You might want to figure it all out," Leila called after him.

He turned to face her.

"Figure it out?"

"You know, what we're supposed to do when we get there, wherever *there* is." And without waiting for a reply, she returned to her brothers' fire.

Remy watched her for a few minutes, thinking about her words, then walked toward the Nomads where they sat together, gazing up into the Heavens, or at least whatever remained up there.

"What can we do for you, Remiel?" Azza asked without turning around.

"I need you to tell me what I don't know."

"But you do know," the Nomad leader said. He stood and slowly turned, the others following suit. "It will take some time, but the knowledge is there, waiting to be used."

"I think it would be nice if I could use it now."

"After the failure of Unification," Azza began, "we believed that the end of our kind—that the end of all things—was inevitable." He stared at Remy with eyes that were suddenly alive with power.

Remy felt the sigils on his body begin to tingle and burn, and he ripped open his shirt to see them raised like welts on his flesh. "What are you doing?"

The Nomads opened their robes then, exposing similar tattoos on their own pale flesh.

"We are sharing," Azza said. "Showing you that the answers are there, that you need only to be patient—the true plan will be revealed."

Darkness welled up from their bodies, forming a cloud of writhing black that drifted above Remy's head.

"You were that answer for us, Remiel."

The cloud fell, engulfing Remy's face. He tried to scream, but his cries were absorbed by the shroud of shadow.

"You were the answer to the end . . . as well as the beginning."

The Nomads wanted him to remember, their strange magicks urging him toward what was too devastating to recall.

Remy's thoughts were filled with the end, and the closer he got to them, the more pain—the more terror—he felt.

All he knew was that the worst possible thing had happened.

He was tempted to go there, again and again, like a curious tongue probing at an open sore in one's cheek, the pain so intense that he could not fully explore the magnitude of the wound.

Remy drew back from the memory, only to find another level of catastrophe waiting underneath. He was trapped, his body crushed beneath the weight of ruins, the pain beyond the highest magnitude.

Is this it? he had wondered as he'd lain paralyzed in the darkness. *Is this how it ends?*

The darkness was warm and comforting as it tried to pull him down, telling him that yes, this was how it should be. That this was the end of him, and all things.

Flashes cut through the darkness, sparks, like pieces of flint rubbed together. Inside the sparks, Remy saw the love of his life, Madeline. The cancer had almost taken her, but Remy had made a deal with Death itself—the angel Israfil—to keep her with him. He saw his beloved Marlowe, the purest beast he had ever known. The level of love he felt for the animal who had taught him so much about appreciating life was like a force unto itself. And then there were flashes of the world that he'd come to love and call home, and the people who lived in it; his friends, clients, and even those he had yet to meet.

They were all there in the cool, comforting darkness—and they told him that he couldn't give up on everything he'd learned to love so much.

Remy used those sparks to reach out to his own inner fire, to rouse the power of the Seraphim within him. The power was very slow to respond, and he had to coax it forward, and when it did finally arrive, it was but a shadow of its former self. It was wild, unfocused.

Insane.

It was all he could do to control it. And Remy suddenly realized that he was afraid of it, afraid of what the divine power had become—afraid of what it could do.

He roared like a wild beast as the unbridled power radiated from his body, turning to rubble tons of rock that had fallen upon him. He spread his wings and surged upward, bursting through to the surface with something very much akin to a birth cry.

But upon witnessing his surroundings, he saw that birth—*life*—had nothing to do with what he was experiencing. The world was in ruins, the cries of the living—*dying*—a deafening cacophony.

This was . . . this was Unification gone horribly wrong.

Remy wanted to cry out—to scream his question into the ether. What had happened to cause such a thing?

Again his brain attempted to take him there, and again he refused to see—it was too much to bear.

The darkness invited him back down into the comforting rubble of the world, but he remembered those who depended on him, those he'd always protected from things such as this. With wings afire, he launched himself into the smoke-filled air, soaring through a sky choked with the ashen remains of civilization.

And as far as the angel could see, there was nothing but death—this was the fate of the world.

Tears blinded him as he choked on the dusty remains of those who once thrived upon this planet. The emotion was like an arrow to his chest, and he dropped from the sky, crashing onto a car roof, the windows exploding outward in a shower of prismatic glass shards. He wanted to stay there upon the twisted metal roof, to curl into a ball and let the darkness take him. . . .

But he needed to find the ones he loved.

He did not even question that they wouldn't be all right as he rolled off of the crushed vehicle and began to run. The streets were clogged with burning pieces of Paradise, the golden spires of Heaven fractured, raining down upon the world and crushing cities beneath their immensity.

Remy had no idea how long he wandered the twisted landscape. It could have been minutes or days—sometimes it felt like it was forever.

Time really didn't seem to matter much in this new reality. Sometimes he flew, sometimes he walked, sometimes he crawled, but he never gave up the search for his home, for his loved ones.

The brownstone seemed to appear out of nothing, rising up from the smoke, damaged beyond repair but mostly standing—almost as if he'd finally built up enough strength to will it into existence. What he saw gave him hope. Remy spread his wings and flew in through a hole he found in the wall leading to his living room. His heart sank as he saw the extent of the damage, the floor having collapsed to the basement below.

He remembered calling out their names—Madeline! Marlowe!—but the only response was the death moans of a dying world. The darkness began to call to Remy once more, and he considered ending his life by flying into space, and then to the heart of the sun.

But then there came another sound.

It was barely perceptible, and he strained to hear over the worldwide cries and prayers of those who still lived.

It was a whine . . . an animal's whine.

Marlowe! he screamed as he began to tear at the layers of flooring that had fallen into the basement, tossing them aside with a display of superhuman strength. His wings pounded the air, blowing away lesser pieces of debris.

It was the body of his wife—his Madeline—that he found first. She had been dead for some time, her skull crushed beneath a pile of bricks.

Her face . . . her beautiful face.

Kneeling in the rubble, he forced himself to remember her as she had been, retrieving every single moment they had shared during their wonderful existence together. He pulled her limp and broken body into his arms and held her close. Silently he apologized for not having been there when the world ended, and begged for her forgiveness, so very sad that this time, there was nothing he could do to bring her back.

So lost in grief was he that he had forgotten about that first soft, pathetic cry.

Until he heard it again.

Gently setting down the body of the woman he had loved with

every fiber of his being, Remy began to look for the source of the sound, hoping for a glimmer of joy amongst this sheer misery.

The angel cried out as he lifted a section of wall to find Marlowe. The dog still lived, but only barely. Remy knelt beside the animal, the human emotions that he had crafted over the years in full bloom. Marlowe opened his eyes and looked at Remy and, as injured as he was, still wanted to know if his Madeline was all right.

"She's fine," Remy lied, as he gently stroked his head.

The dog was trembling, not from cold but from internal injury, and Remy knew that it wouldn't be long before . . .

He couldn't stand the thought. To have already lost his wife and now to be losing his best friend was more than the angel could bear, and he felt his psyche begin to crumble. The dog moaned, and Remy reached down to pull the broken animal into his arms. He could feel Marlowe's life force waning. He bowed his head, placing his brow against the dog's cheek. He wanted to feel everything he could before it was gone.

Marlowe was suddenly awake again, fighting to hold on to what life he still had. *"Why?"* he asked. *"Why you not here?"*

Remy wanted to explain, but the words would not come, for he was ashamed. He should have been there. He should have been with the ones he loved most at a time like this. All he could do was silently look into the poor animal's eyes as Marlowe's life force gradually ebbed way.

"Stay with me," he commanded his friend, his emotion gradually turning to fury. *"Did you hear me, beast? I told you to stay!"*

But the last of Marlowe's life energies dwindled like the smoke from an extinguished candle. And just as they were about to be gone altogether, the Seraphim called out for help.

That was when they came, rising up out of the shadows of the basement; the Nomads had been listening.

Remy knew them at once.

"Is it true?" one asked as he stepped forward, his voice filled with wonder.

Remy could feel himself slipping, the divine fire at his core raging to be set free. He wasn't sure of the question, but . . .

"Yes," he replied anyway, the weight of his response crippling.

The Nomads looked up from the shattered basement, up through the floor, to the levels above.

"It is true," the leader said.

"It is true," repeated the others as one.

The leader stepped closer and placed a hand on Remy's shoulder. *"You said that you would do anything."*

The spark of Marlowe's life was nearly extinguished, and Remy did not have the strength to live without him. *"I would,"* he agreed, pulling the dog closer, hoping that would somehow give Marlowe a bit more time—a bit more life.

"We can save him, and you." The leader's touch was cold, a numbness radiating from his hand down Remy's shoulder, into his chest.

"I don't want to be saved." Remy buried his face in the black fur of his dog.

"Yes," the Nomad leader agreed. *"But we do. . . . We will be part of the ending and this new beginning."*

Remy looked up at the hooded angel standing beside him. The leader's face was pale, the darkness around it filled with twinkling stars so beautiful, and yet so very cold.

"I don't understand."

The Nomad smiled. *"You will,"* he said. *"But first you must tell us yes, that you truly do want our help. . . ."*

"Yes," Remy said before the leader was even finished. *"Yes."*

"And second, you must prepare."

Remy held his dog tighter, willing the animal to hang on for just a moment longer. *"Prepare?"* he asked.

"You must be ready," the Nomad leader answered, slowly nodding his hooded head. *"For there will be sacrifice."*

The memories that followed were a bombardment to his senses, a deluge of moments that made him cry out.

Remy saw what he had done—the deal he had made in exchange for . . .

The caul of shadow that had covered his head was freezing to the touch, blistering the flesh of his fingertips as he tore the icy membrane from his face. But it still wasn't enough. It took all that he had not to rip out his own eyes, to stop the flow of imagery. The memories.

How could I have been so cruel? So damnably selfish?

Each recollection was like the thrust of a knife, the guilt he was feeling worse than anything the Nomads had done to him.

Remy saw what he had sacrificed, the golden wings cut away from his back with a dagger forged from a darkness that had existed before the Almighty's blinding light. He did not cry out as they hacked at the flesh, bone, and feathers, collecting the blood that spilled from the wounds.

They would use the blood to mark him as they were marked, the sigils providing him with the means to control the growing madness of the Seraphim before its fire could consume him.

And when the transformation was complete, when the fire had been suppressed, a cold darkness filled him. He was one of them, but he was also something more.

Remy begged for the visions to stop, but they rushed in to fill the empty places in his memory as if desperate to be known—to be recalled.

The Nomads had taken Marlowe and placed him within a crystalline coffin. Remy remembered breaking into that crystal case.

"I'm going to save you," he told his best friend, but the dog begged him not to, as if he sensed the change in Remy.

Please let me die.

And Remy told him, *"No."*

The angel knelt upon the ground and cried, remembering what he had done to his beloved dog. "I'm so sorry," he sobbed, recalling it all in every loathsome detail, not strong enough to hold back the memory.

Marlowe's body had been severely injured, but his life force—his soul—was still strong. The Nomads had called forth a Hellion—a survivor of the most twisted Hellscapes—and its powerful body would house the soul of Remy's most loyal friend.

And even though his best friend had begged him not to, Remy helped the Nomads transfer Marlowe's soul from the dog's broken body into the body of the hellhound.

Marlowe's soul had fought, struggling to escape the dark magicks that were attempting to contain it. Remy tried to reassure it, telling the animal's soul that everything would be all right.

In retrospect, even then, he knew it was a lie.

For the Hellion had an essence of its own and refused to be usurped by this other soul. The two life energies battled within the confines of the Hellbeast's body before both succumbed, becoming something else that was equal parts Marlowe and Hellion.

A Unification of another kind.

It wasn't what Remy had planned for his friend, but it was what he had to live with.

What they both had to live with.

"What did I do?" Remy remembered the tormented question as his dog had awakened transformed by the magick of the Nomads.

"You should have let me go," the dog had growled from the body of a monster. *"You should have let me die."*

Remy could hear the hurt, feel the misery as it exuded from his best friend, but it didn't change the simple fact of the matter.

"I couldn't lose you, too."

It was the look in the dog's blazing eyes then that finally made Remy realize the depth of his error. It was a look that said he *had* lost his best friend.

And a little more of Remy Chandler had died.

Remy surged up from these newly awakened memories feeling as filthy and wretched as the world he now inhabited, but there was little opportunity for him to wallow in self-loathing, for they were under attack.

Remy jumped to his feet and suddenly realized that he had been moved. "Where?" he began, looking around at the darkened city streets. "How did I get here?"

Azza was looking in the direction of the sounds of a skirmish. The children of Samson were already heading to confront the threat.

"You've been out for a bit," the Nomad leader said as he motioned for the other Nomads to go and help the others.

"How long?"

"Does it matter now?"

Remy felt a flash of anger, but he let it go and instead began to follow the Nomads.

"No," Azza said, grabbing his arm. "That battle isn't for you. You're to go that way." He let go of Remy's arm and pointed toward a street shrouded in darkness.

"But the Filthies . . . ," Remy began.

The Nomad leader shook his head. "You must go that way . . . to the door."

Instinctively, Remy reached into his pants pocket and found the metal key. It was warm, far warmer than it should have been.

"Go," Azza commanded. Then he abruptly turned and walked away in the direction of the battle.

"This door," Remy called after him.

Azza turned.

"What will I find behind it?"

"The answers you seek. The solution to the problem . . . to the end and the beginning."

A part of Remy wanted to chase the Nomad into battle, to join with his friends in the defeat of the Filthies that had tracked them from their encampment.

He wasn't sure he could stand any more knowledge.

But there was a pull upon the key. He could feel the tug on the tarnished metal, leading him into the shadows of the city block behind him.

Remy allowed himself to be drawn down the street, over the busted concrete, past the shattered windows of storefronts and the bizarre and twisted architecture of Heaven and Hell melded together. It was like a fever dream become reality.

The drag upon the key continued, until Remy found himself standing before a partially collapsed building, the structure leaning precariously to one side, the top floor having collapsed inward. Its front door sat crooked in its frame, three steps up. The pull on the key increased, and Remy took it from his pocket. Carefully, he climbed the broken steps and inserted the key in the lock.

There was a white flash: a simple, static shock? Perhaps. Or maybe something more.

Remy pushed open the door and stepped inside, closing the door behind him. Instead of the lobby of the nearly collapsed brownstone, he found himself staring down the length of a long stone corridor, at the end of which was a heavy wooden door.

He knew this place. The name was on the tip of his tongue.

As he drew closer, he saw the broken neon sign, hanging askew over the door.

M TH S AH'S

Methuselah's. He had found Methuselah's.

And then the heavy wooden door at the end of the stone corridor slowly creaked open, urging him to come forward.

Urging him to enter.

CHAPTER TWENTY-THREE

Francis loved Roy Orbison.

The former Guardian angel sat in Leona's front seat, eyes closed, humming along to the tune of "Only the Lonely."

He'd been sitting there with the car running for close to an hour, waiting for everything to die before trying to put the genie back in the bottle.

Or God's wrath back in its canister.

The fallen angel opened his eyes and glanced out the window. The Broker lay just outside the passenger door on his back, eyes wide with the realization of the terror that he had caused.

Francis opened the car door and stepped out. He looked down at the demon and felt something that could only have been a twinge of guilt. "Look at what you made me do," he hissed, kicking the demon's corpse. "We couldn't have played nice? No, that would have been too fucking easy."

He imagined all those that lived in the Bone Master encampment, the young training to be the clan's latest assassins. They were all dead now, dying horribly because their spokesperson wouldn't bend the rules.

"Was it worth it?" he asked the corpse at his feet. He gazed away from the body of the Broker, looking out over the compound, listening to the eerie silence of what the Wrath had wrought. Through a heavy, blue-tinged mist he could see the bodies of those who'd tried to escape their fate, struck down by the anger of God. A by-product of the Wrath, the mist swirled about the air, even though the air was deathly still. It was looking for more life, desperate to do more of what it was created to do.

But all good things must come to an end, even for the Wrath of God.

Francis walked over to the canister that had held the Wrath and picked it up. Gazing into the darkness of the container, he prepared himself for what he knew wouldn't be easy.

Inside the pocket of his suit jacket he found the wrinkled piece of paper where he'd written down the invocation that would call the Wrath back to its vessel. He studied the writing for a moment.

"Let's get this show on the road," he muttered, clearing his throat before calling out to God's anger in the language created specifically to control it.

Francis continued to read the words, watching as the bluish gray fog grew thicker, whirling around him as if angry. He held out the open vessel as he reached the halfway point of the invocation. The fog flowed toward the opening, then veered off defiantly.

Great, he thought, speaking the words louder and more forcefully.

It was like watching a bass at the end of a hook fighting not to be pulled into the boat. Francis continued to read, remembering the guy he had gotten the canister from stressing how important it was to read the spell to draw the Wrath back with the utmost confidence, explaining that the death force was like an unruly dog, easily sensing weakness and challenging the one who sought to bind it.

For a brief moment he wished that he had a newspaper to whack it on the snout. Instead, he kept reading, sterner, harder—he'd show this plague of anger who was boss. The Wrath continued to fight him.

And just when he thought that he had it contained, it deviated away from the opening, what had already gone inside spilling out and flowing down to the street level. Francis watched with interest as the Wrath flowed into the dead Broker's body, entering through the demon's every orifice.

Great, Francis thought. *How the fuck do I get it out of there?* He didn't have time for this shit.

He moved closer to the corpse. It had become swollen now, filled up with the Wrath of God.

"I know you're in there," Francis said to it. "Why don't we make this easy and you come out and get back into your canister?"

He prodded the corpse with the toe of his shoe.

The demon's body gurgled grotesquely and seemed to expand, almost as if the Broker were still alive and breathing.

And then the corpse began to move.

"That's different," Francis said, stepping back from the corpse, which had started to flop around on the ground like a fish tossed up onto a dock.

The Broker's mouth started to move, and an awful croak flowed out from its recesses.

"Un . . . under . . . understand?" the Wrath of God strained to ask.

"Do I understand you? Yes, yes, I do," Francis said. "What I don't understand is what the fuck you're doing." He held out the vessel. "Quit fooling around and get back in here."

"Things . . . ch . . . changing," the Wrath stammered.

"Yeah, the times they are a-changing, I get it. Back in the can."

"No! The . . . the great forgiveness is . . . is about . . . is going to occur . . . Unification . . ."

Francis recalled what he had heard at Methuselah's but had never bought that it would ever occur. However, if anybody—or thing—would know of such things, it would be something that still held a connection to the Creator.

"Seriously?" Francis asked. "God is going to forgive . . ."

"Everything . . . changes," the force of rage stated. "Peace . . . and love . . . in . . . in the cosmos . . . No hate . . . no rage . . ."

"No Wrath," Francis added. "So you're afraid that if you go back in the container, you'll never get out again."

"Confined for eternity . . . never being free . . . again."

The Wrath was getting better with communicating, getting a handle on manipulating the vocal cords of the demon corpse. Francis didn't like that, not wanting it to get too damn comfortable, so comfortable that it might not want to leave.

"Y'know what, I just don't buy it," Francis said. "Sure, the Morningstar is welcomed back to Heaven with open arms, but I can't imagine that there isn't something out there that just wants to piss in the great cosmic punch bowl. There's an awful lot of darkness in the cosmos, and I'm sure there are things hiding in it that don't like the idea of everything being all sunny, warm, and cuddly."

The corpse looked at him with huge hopeful eyes, the blue mist leaking out from its tear ducts to float in the air about its head like a thought bubble.

"Seriously, I can't think of a time when something like you wouldn't be needed . . . or somebody like me, for that matter."

Francis thought about a universe where he wouldn't be required to kill and imagined that it would be pretty damn boring.

"No, I think we're good even if this Unification business ends up happening."

The corpse of the Broker studied his features, perhaps searching for a hint of dishonesty, or maybe it was just looking a little more deeply at the one who had set it free.

"We are . . . alike," the Wrath told him.

Francis didn't like to hear it, but he knew that what the anger entity was saying wasn't too far off.

"Yeah, we are at that," he said.

The Wrath went quiet then and seemed to be thinking about its next move. Francis decided that it might be worth a try to see if he could get the Wrath to do what he wanted.

"So what do you say?" Francis asked it. "One force of death and destruction to another. Will you get back inside your canister?"

Again the corpse stared, but then it opened its mouth all the wider and the thick mist began to flow outward. Francis didn't even have to continue with the spell of invocation; the Wrath went back inside its container willingly, trusting him that it would be called upon again. Placing the lid upon the vessel and making sure that it was sealed, Francis had no doubt that it would be.

He hadn't been lying to the Wrath when he said that he couldn't imagine a universe where death and destruction weren't as much a part as life and creation.

Placing the canister beneath his arm, he took one good last look around, then climbed into Leona, telling the car that it was time to go home.

The car responded sluggishly, sated and drowsy from all that it had eaten. He'd promised her, as well as her owner, that she would eat well, and he'd most certainly done his part. Leona turned control over to him, and he put her in drive. Hitting the gas, he drove through the open courtyard area of the compound, paying little attention as he rolled over the bodies of those stricken by the Wrath.

"Anytime you're ready, girl," he told the car, massaging her dashboard.

Her engine purred loudly as she worked her magick, tearing through dimensional barriers like spiderwebs and ending up back home where they'd started. She pulled into the driveway and into the large garage, its doors open wide, welcoming her back.

Francis was gathering up his belongings when his cell phone rang. Fearing that it had something to do with Remy, he answered without checking the caller ID, feeling cold fingers of dread in his chest when he realized who was on the other end of the line.

"What can I do for you?" he asked. "Yes, your information was most certainly correct. Thank you."

He listened to the silky voice as it told him there was something to do.

"I'll be right there," Francis said, instantly forgetting everything else.

Having no choice but to obey.

These days Steven Mulvehill felt as though he was trapped in some bizarre kind of nightmare, only it was real, and no matter how many times he pinched himself there was no waking up.

He came down the stairs with his gun in hand, finger on the trigger. He felt it almost immediately upon reaching the fourth step from the bottom, almost a complete change in atmosphere.

He remembered the old days, when just being a cop was enough to create the kind of stress that kept him awake for far too many hours. Some therapy had actually helped him with those anxieties.

But that was before Remy Chandler had entered his life. Now all bets were off and the nightmares were actually walking the streets, and sometimes they were even waiting for him when he got home from work. Yeah, thanks a bunch, Remy Chandler.

The air downstairs had become deathly still, stagnant. He saw Squire in the doorway to the kitchen. The goblin was just standing there, staring ahead at something that Mulvehill could not yet see.

"Squire," he called out. "What's the story?"

"Get over here," Squire ordered, not moving.

Mulvehill braced himself.

So much had changed since Remy had first revealed his true nature. The angel of Heaven had pulled back the curtain and shown him what things were really like. Mulvehill guessed he should have felt special, but instead, he was just terrified. And the terror had become part of the new normal.

He saddled up alongside Squire, his gun ready, and what he saw chilled him to the core.

One of those killers, demons, whatever the fuck they were, stood in the kitchen, perfectly still, like a statue.

"What's it doing?" Mulvehill asked, his voice rife with tension.

"I don't know," the goblin replied. "It's been like that since I found it."

They stood there watching, feeling their tensions increasing—a balloon of anxiety slowly inflating, growing larger and larger until . . .

"Well, we just can't stand here staring at it," Mulvehill hissed, moving past Squire and into the kitchen.

"What the fuck are you doing?" Squire cried.

"What does it look like? It's waiting for something."

He felt like he was moving across a minefield as he slowly grew closer, stopping a mere six feet away.

The demon continued to stand there, its dark gaze staring ahead. Mulvehill wasn't exactly sure what it could see, but he made a show of putting his gun away, then lifted both hands to show that they were empty.

"What do you want?" he asked, even though he knew exactly what the killer was looking for, and it was upstairs in a coma.

The demon assassin's head turned ever so slightly to look at him. "Finally, someone who understands the etiquette of the parley." The demon's hands appeared from beneath its robes, causing Mulvehill to jump back and reach for his gun.

But the demon showed that his hands were empty as well, and then chuckled. "Simply a talk to understand the situation."

"A talk," Mulvehill repeated. He glanced back at Squire, who was tightly gripping his axe. "A talk," he said again to the goblin, motioning for him to lower his weapon. Begrudgingly, the goblin did what was asked of him.

"Talk, then," Mulvehill ordered the demon.

It bowed its bald head and began to speak. "A contract is still open. The quarry is in this dwelling. A contract is *always* fulfilled."

It was no surprise to Mulvehill why the assassin was there, and he remained silent.

"You," the demon pointed a long finger first at Mulvehill, then at Squire. "And you . . ." His eyes went to the ceiling, as if he could see through the ceiling to the rooms above. "And any others who are with the quarry . . ."

The demon's eyes dropped down again to fix upon Mulvehill. "You are not our targets," the assassin said, slowly shaking his head, "but you obstruct our actions."

Mulvehill remained silent.

"All of you may leave this dwelling safely and let us complete our contract."

Us—the word struck Mulvehill. His eyes darted to the windows in the kitchen, catching traces of moving shadow that told him the assassin in the kitchen wasn't the only one who had dropped by.

"Let us complete the contract, and our dealings will be done."

The Bone Master fell silent then, his spidery hands once again disappearing beneath his robes.

"Are you finished?" Mulvehill asked. "Is it my turn to . . . parley?"

The demon smiled, bowing his head again.

Mulvehill stepped closer, never breaking eye contact with the demonic killer. "You can't have him, and we will do anything to keep him with us."

They continued to stare at each other, until finally the demon spoke. "Are you finished?" he asked.

"I am."

"Very brave," the assassin complimented. "But very stupid."

"Yeah, I've heard that before," Mulvehill said.

The tension inside the kitchen continued to expand, that balloon of anxiety so big now that it was only a matter of seconds before it burst.

"We are done here," the demon stated.

"We are," Mulvehill agreed.

The balloon grew bigger . . .

He and the demon continued to stare at one another.

And bigger . . .

Mulvehill's hand began to twitch, eager to snatch the gun from the waistband of his pants.

And bigger.

Was that movement beneath the layers of cloth?

And bigger.

The Bone Master suddenly stepped back, moving sideways into a passage of shadow, and was gone.

Mulvehill turned to Squire, who raised his axe.

"Remember the Alamo," the goblin said as shadows shifted all around them.

Mulvehill drew his own weapon without a word.

And the balloon finally burst, sounding very much like a shot from his gun.

Ashley gave the chain a solid tug to make sure it would hold.

"Are you sure about this?" she asked as Linda started to wrap the end of the chain around her waist.

"As sure as I'm going to be," she answered, then looked toward the tree again and appeared troubled.

"It looks sicker, doesn't it?" Ashley said, as she followed Linda's gaze.

Marlowe whined from where he lay at the base of the tree. He gave it a sniff, his tail going between his legs.

"Yeah, it does," Linda agreed. "Which makes what I'm about to do all the more important." She walked to the edge of the hole and looked down.

"How far down do you think it goes?" Ashley asked.

"Hopefully no deeper than the length of this chain." Linda checked the chain around her waist. "I guess this is it, then."

Ashley tightened her hold on the length of chain in her hands and braced herself against a large root. "Unless we can come up with a better plan."

"Something's telling me this is where I've got to go," Linda said.

"And something is telling me that this could turn out to be a very bad idea," Ashley countered.

"We'll never know unless we try," Linda said. And then she went to Ashley, wrapping the girl in her arms in a hug.

Ashley was a bit taken aback by this sudden show of affection, but she hugged Linda back just as tightly. It was at that moment she knew Remy had made a really good choice.

"Everything is going to be fine," Linda whispered, finally releasing her.

"Is something telling you that, too?" Ashley asked.

"Exactly." Linda smiled.

Marlowe got up and came over to lend his support.

"You be a good boy and protect Ashley, all right?" Linda told the dog.

He barked once and wagged his tail.

"There's a good dog," Linda said, petting his head before returning to the hole. She turned and backed up slightly, the heels of her shoes at the very edge. "You ready?"

Ashley planted her feet and gripped the chain with both hands. "Ready," she confirmed.

Linda slowly lowered herself over the edge. "You got me?"

"Got you," Ashley grunted. She watched as Linda's head disappeared over the edge, and she let out some more chain. "Are you good?"

"Good," Linda answered.

Marlowe ran to the edge of the hole and stretched his neck to peer over the side.

Ashley let out more chain, feeling the beginnings of blisters on her fingers. "Still good?" she called out, trying to ignore the pain.

"Still good," Linda called back.

"And signs of the bottom?"

"Nothing yet."

"Can you see anything?" Ashley asked, struggling to plant her feet more firmly as she began to slide forward.

"No, it's too dark," Linda hollered. She sounded farther away now.

The blisters on Ashley's hands were getting worse, and it was harder to hold on to the chain. Her biceps starting to burn painfully.

"Are you all right?" she called out, waiting for a response that never came.

"Linda!" Ashley cried.

The chain went suddenly slack, and Ashley tumbled backward, her head bouncing off the ground so hard that she actually saw stars.

"Oh shit," she exclaimed, trying to shake it off. Marlowe was there at her side at once, sniffing and licking at her face. "Ohshitohshitohshit . . ."

Ashley struggled to her knees, crawling to the hole, not even thinking to be careful as she peered over the edge.

"Linda! Are you all right? Linda!"

But the only reply was an eerie silence from inky blackness below.

Simeon stared at the golden bullet on the desktop before him.

He'd been doing this for days, imagining the effects of such a projectile as it was shot into a nearly omnipotent deity. A bullet of creation, explosively entering the body of the Creator.

A smile crept across Simeon's face as he imagined all of reality collapsing in upon itself, everything that was—everything that would be—coming to an end.

The forever man closed his eyes, imagining how peaceful and quiet it would be. . . .

But then he considered another scenario where the bullet was fired, the Almighty struck, and nothing at all happened. The end result of all of Simeon's hard work, producing only an angry God who punished him in some new and horrible way.

Simeon scoffed at the idea that there was something more horrible than the existence he already had.

Picking up the bullet, he held it to eye level, attempting to infuse the shell with a bit of his personality and his intense desire to cause as much pain as was caused to him. He rubbed his finger along the warm metal jacket, focusing all the anger and misery he'd endured through the countless lifetimes he'd walked the planet since the Son of God dragged him back from the peace of death.

"I'd be careful with that," said the sorcerer Malatesta.

Simeon was surprised to see the man up and about. After he'd worked his powerful magicks in creating the projectile, he'd practically collapsed into a coma.

"You're awake." Simeon's eyes were still fixed on the bullet he held.

"I am," he said, coming to stand beside the forever man.

Simeon managed to rip his eyes from the glorious object to look at the sorcerer. He looked healthier than he had, a pinkness to his complexion that hadn't been there before. "Rested?"

"I am," Malatesta said. "You shouldn't be playing with that." He gestured toward the bullet, looking increasingly nervous.

Simeon smiled and gently set it down on the desk. "I don't think I have anything to worry about. . . ."

The blast of magickal force struck him square in the chest, lifting him from his chair and sending him soaring across the room. Simeon struck the stone wall with such force that he felt his spine snap. The pain was excruciating, but it helped to keep him focused.

"Rested enough to wrest control away from the demon that has made me an accomplice to this heinous act," Malatesta declared as he carefully took the bullet from the desk. "Actually, I should probably thank you. The act of creating this atrocity weakened the demonic parasite enough for me to overpower it."

He slipped the bullet into the front pocket of his shirt. "I can't allow you to carry out your plan. It goes against everything I believe in."

The sorcerer held out his hands and began to utter an ancient incantation. An eerie glow began to form at the tips of his fingers.

"Demons, come to me!" Simeon managed to cry as he turned the ring of Solomon on his left hand.

Malatesta doubled over as if struck in the stomach. "No," he gasped. The magick was leaking from his hands, and he attempted to aim the blast at the forever man, but it went awry, instead striking the floor in front of the sorcerer in an explosion of rock.

The door to the sanctuary flew open, and Simeon's two demon servants spilled into the room.

"Stop him," Simeon shrieked, his spine having mended enough that he was able to push himself up painfully.

The demon Robert was the first to reach the magick user, pouncing upon Malatesta, wrapping his arm about his throat, and trying to pull him to the floor.

"Been wanting to take you down since you first showed up," the demon hissed. One of his hands morphed into a claw, which he raked across the magick user's side.

Malatesta reacted with a grunt of pain and drove an elbow into Robert's monstrous mouth, causing a rainfall of teeth upon the floor. Before the demon recovered, the sorcerer hurled a spell that launched the demon upward, pinning him to the ceiling.

Beleeze then dove to cut the sorcerer from groin to chest with a nasty blade clutched in his hand.

Was that a moment of hesitation? Simeon wondered as he watched Malatesta and Beleeze struggle. He'd had his concerns about the demon since returning from Vietnam.

Beleeze slashed with his blade, driving the sorcerer back but also giving the magick user time to recite an incantation and . . .

Simeon's suspicions were verified as Beleeze briefly locked eyes with him before lowering his blade and facing the sorcerer.

"I'm ready to leave now," Simeon heard the demon say as Malatesta unleashed a blast of pure magickal force that disintegrated Beleeze's torso to little more than a fine mist.

Simeon had feeling in his legs again, and, with the help of the stone wall, pulled himself up to his feet. The demon Robert took the moment of distraction to rip himself down, leaving a large portion of his flesh still dangling and dripping from the ceiling above like bloody party streamers.

Malatesta threw up his hand, a ball of hissing energy, hurtling toward Robert. The demon managed to evade being hit by the sphere of power, but it struck a nearby wall, the force of the blast catching Robert off guard as he prepared to charge his foe. Robert struck a table, crashing to the floor in a heap of broken wood and office supplies. Malatesta took full advantage, launching another sphere that picked up the demon, the office supplies, and the broken pieces of table and spun them around in such a way that the flesh that remained upon the demon's body was ripped away and tossed around the room. Little more than a bloody skeleton was finally released when it was all through, splintering as it struck, the ground pelted by pieces of shattered furniture and paper clips.

Simeon watched as a blood-spattered Malatesta turned toward him. What a sight he was, and how powerful he must have felt to have come this far. A true feat of strength and perseverance.

Sadly, it would all be for naught.

Malatesta tensed, ready to lord his vast magickal talents over Simeon, when the forever man decided that he'd had just about enough.

The magick that Simeon wielded was incredibly old and lethal, radiating outward from his body with a spell that he needed only to think of.

Malatesta attempted to raise a shield of protection, but the Vatican magick user was just not strong enough to deal with magick of this nature.

Simeon's ancient magick hit him like a wave, washing over his flesh, unmaking what had already been made, and then reassembling, inside out.

Malatesta's scream was horrific to hear as he dropped to exposed knees of bone, muscle tendon, and sinew, internal workings jarred by the fall tearing loose of their connective tissue to spatter upon the floor.

It was amazing that the sorcerer was even still alive.

Simeon approached the man who had now fallen to his side, writhing on the stone floor in a puddle of blood and other foul liquids better served on the inside of a body.

"Did you seriously believe that you could best me?" Simeon asked, looking down at the Vatican sorcerer as he struggled to die. "That your pathetic magicks could somehow match mine? Magicks that I've had thousands of years to collect and practice? I'm surprised at you, Constantin."

Simeon squatted down, careful not to get any of the bodily fluids that had been splashed about on his slacks. He studied Malatesta's chest area, seeing flesh, and the clothing that had adorned it before the spell, now crammed inside the exposed rib cage. Aiming for the shirt pocket, Simeon reached between the bones, digging with his fingers into the muscle, fat, and skin until he felt the dampened cloth of the sorcerer's shirt and at last found his prize.

"There you are," Simeon said with a grin, extracting the bullet through the body of the still-living magick user.

Malatesta shuddered in the throes of death. Simeon was surprised that he was still holding on, imagining that it had something to do with the Larva demon that still possessed him.

Pocketing the bullet, Simeon searched for something to wipe his hand on. Finding nothing at hand, he resorted to wiping the foul fluids on the leg of his slacks, feeling his ire rise with the fact that now he'd be forced to change his clothes.

For a moment he actually considered being merciful and assisting Malatesta with the act of dying, but now . . .

Simeon watched the sorcerer twitch and writhe, imagining the excruciating pain. There were sounds that might have been speech coming from the man. He could actually see the vocal cords trembling as they attempted to convey some sort of audible message.

The angel Satquiel's sudden appearance actually startled Simeon. The angel soldier stood before the bloody remains of the Vatican magick user, a look of sympathy upon his statuesque features.

"What are you doing here?" Simeon asked, righting his overturned chair and sitting down.

"You told me to come when I'd learned something new . . . something about Unification."

The angel knelt down and stroked the exposed bloody skull of the dying sorcerer. "This creature's suffering is great."

"Yes, I suppose it is," Simeon agreed. "What do you have for me?"

"Preparations are being made," the angel said. "Michael has already been dispatched."

"Where?" Simeon asked. There was gore beneath his fingernails, and he was using a paper clip that he'd found on the floor to clean them.

"This man's suffering," the angel said instead. "May I?"

Simeon stopped digging and looked up. "If you must."

Satquiel extended his hand and a dagger of fire appeared. He pierced the man's skull, ending his life, as well as that of the demonic parasite possessing him.

"Are we through yet?" Simeon asked impatiently.

Satquiel disposed of his blade and stood.

"Where?" Simeon asked again.

The angel reached inside the pocket of his suit jacket and produced a piece of branch, holding it out to the forever man.

Simeon took the branch and brought it to his nose, sniffing it deeply.

"The Garden," he said, almost euphoric with the overwhelming scent of the place.

"Take me there."

CHAPTER TWENTY-FOUR

Remy stood beneath the buzzing neon sign, staring at the open door and the darkness beckoning him to enter.

He reached out and gave the heavy door a push. It creaked loudly as it swung farther inward, stale air wafting out to greet him like an eager puppy.

And Remy stepped into the cool darkness of Methuselah's.

The first thing he noticed was the missing doorman. But as his eyes adjusted to the deep gloom, he found Phil in a chair not far from the entrance. The minotaur sat in the heavy wooden seat, mighty horned head slumped forward on his chest as if dozing, but Remy knew dead when he saw it.

Sadly, he wondered what could have felled the mighty mythological beast, then noticed the streaks of white and gray in the hair that covered the minotaur's body. He had a suspicion that maybe the passage of time might have played a role in the doorman's demise.

Remy moved into the room and stood beside the bar. Lights slowly came to life, as if awakening to his presence. The lights illuminated the barroom floor, and he noticed that all the tables had been pushed back against the walls to open up the floor space. At first he wasn't sure what he was seeing there, the shapes lying on the floor looking like discarded bags of laundry, but on second inspection he believed that they were actually bodies.

What the hell happened in this place? Remy wondered to himself as a string of Christmas lights hung along the top of the bar turned on, causing him to spin toward it.

Remy gasped at the sight of the large stone body—a golem—hunched over the bar, as lifeless as Phil and the sheet-covered bodies strewn about the barroom floor. The golem was Methuselah, the Biblical figure whose human form had grown so frail while alive for thousands of years that he had his life force transferred into the body of a stone giant so that he might continue to live. He was also the owner of the drinking establishment.

Remy touched the cold stone of the golem's head, which was resting on the bar top.

"What happened?" Remy asked aloud. "Why am I here?"

He was removing his hand when there was a sudden spark, an arc of static electricity from the tips of his fingers to the golem's head. Remy yanked back his hand, now tingling and numb from the shock, and gave it a frantic shake. And then Methuselah's head began to move, slowly lifting from where it rested, eyes buried deep within their stone sockets blazing to life as if fires within the stone man's skull had suddenly been stoked with coal.

"Remy," the golem said in recognition.

"Methuselah," Remy answered.

"You're back."

"Yeah, looks like I am."

"It's been a long time," Methuselah commented. "Didn't think you'd make it."

The lights had grown increasingly brighter inside the bar, and Remy could see more of his surroundings. From what he could recall, the establishment had never been more than moderately clean, but now, in the light, he saw that it was covered in inches of dust, with so many spiderwebs that you'd think that the place was somehow being held together with strands of arachnid silk.

"Didn't know I was supposed to come here," Remy said, being honest.

The stone man studied him with glowing eyes.

"Okay," Methuselah said, then turned away, going to the dusty shelf behind him. "Looks like you could use a drink."

The bottle was covered in layers of grime, nearly masking the brown liquid that sloshed around inside. Methuselah found a dusty glass and held it out.

"Mind some dust?" he asked.

Remy shrugged. "The booze should clean it out all right."

"You haven't changed that much," the golem said with a chuckle that sounded like two pieces of stone being rubbed together.

He poured the liquid to the rim and placed the glass deftly in front of Remy without spilling a drop. "Drink up."

Remy picked up the tumbler and brought it to his mouth, quickly tossing it back. It tasted a little funky because of the dust, but other than that, it was a fine drink of scotch.

"Why am I here?" he asked.

Methuselah retrieved the glass and filled it again.

"You don't remember?"

"Let's just say I'm not the man I used to be."

The golem studied him again, tilting his head from one side, to the other. "Care to explain?"

"I'll keep it simple, but it won't sound any less crazy," Remy said as he reached for his second glass of whiskey.

"Try me," Methuselah urged.

"I'm not the same Remy that you knew," he said, keeping the momentum going before the barkeep could tell him that he was full of shit. "I'm a different Remy, from another reality. I'm not sure yet why I'm here, but I'm working on it." He downed the whiskey, strength for what he was sure would follow.

"Yeah, there's something missing in the eyes," Methuselah said, studying him. "You're not as far gone as the other, but after what he went through . . ." The golem trailed off, sliding the filthy bottle over to Remy.

"You don't seem at all fazed by my story."

Methuselah shrugged. "In a place like this you see it all, and besides, Gerta hinted about something like this after you left. . . . Well, after the other you left."

"Gerta?"

The golem looked over to the floor of the bar, at the covered bodies there. "Don't tell me—you don't remember them, either."

Remy saw that the shapes beneath the sheets were beginning to move. The first to emerge was a strange-looking creature, its skin incredibly pale, its body thin. He knew at once that it was a child and that it was alive only because of him.

Images exploded in his mind, and he had to hold on to the edge of the bar so he would not lose his balance. Remy saw a vast underground chamber beneath a great mountain, and inside that subterranean room was a craft of some kind, the wood of its hull ossified by the passage of time.

It was a ship—no, an ark.

"I . . . saved them," Remy said, remembering the creatures that had been excluded from Noah's great ship when the deluge came. They were the Chimerian . . . the orphans . . . Noah's orphans.

"You did at that," Methuselah said. "And you saved them again after the fall of Heaven."

Two more of the orphans emerged from beneath their covers, rubbing their eyes with clawed hands. And Remy was surprised to see normal-looking children poking their heads out as well, eyes used to the total darkness, now squinting in the light.

"Is it time to wake up?" asked one of the kids, yawning and rubbing sleep from his eyes.

"Who are they?" Remy asked. "Am I responsible for them as well?"

"You are," the golem answered. "You're responsible for saving all of them."

A child, no older than six, crawled out from beneath her sheet and walked over to where he stood.

"Hello, Gerta," Methuselah said.

Remy stared at the beautiful child in the Hello Kitty T-shirt and pink sweatpants, her hair a mass of pale blonde curls, her eyes the lightest shade of blue he'd ever seen. There was something about this child—something that made her as different as the Chimerian children.

The little girl leaned against the bar and stared up at him.

"So you're Gerta," Remy said, extending his hand.

She continued to look at him, ignoring his hand, the stars in her eyes twinkling strangely.

"You're another him," she said.

Remy was taken aback. "What do you mean?"

"You're another him. Another Remy."

She looked at Methuselah and smiled at the stone golem behind the bar. "Didn't I tell you that another Remy might come?"

"You did," Methuselah confirmed. "Although I wasn't quite sure what you meant at the time."

She laughed, a twinkling sound, and then looked back at Remy.

"You knew that I was coming?"

Gerta nodded vigorously. "I saw you in one of the windows."

"Windows?"

The child seemed to become bored with the conversation and hung from the bar's edge, dangling like some sort of monkey.

"Gerta's gift is the ability to see into other realities—windows, she calls them. And since you're one of her favorites . . ."

Remy couldn't help but smile at her before turning his gaze to the other children. Suddenly, he knew that they were all gifted, with abilities that scared the archangels. His brain began to hurt with the realization as two realities—both of which he knew to be real— struggled to be only one.

The other children were the offspring of angels and Nephilim women . . . children who shouldn't have been able to exist but did. In both memories, the archangels tracked them all down and believed they were slaughtered. In one reality, one of the children had used his special gift to make the angels believe they had succeeded when they had not.

But in another, harsher reality, most of the children were indeed murdered, the only ones to survive being the ones that he himself was able to hide from the murderous angel soldiers.

He'd brought them here. . . .

"I brought them here for a reason," Remy said, staring at the special children.

"You most certainly did," Methuselah said. From behind the bar he produced a bag of Cheez Doodles and presented them to Gerta. "Here ya go, sweetheart," he said as she took the gift from him with a smile. "Probably a little stale, but how could you notice? Go share them with your brothers and sisters."

Gerta ran off, proudly waving the treat above her head.

"You've come back for a reason, too," the golem said to Remy.

The angel tore his gaze from the children and focused on Methuselah. "Why am I here?"

"I can show you." Methuselah moved around from behind the bar. "Hey, Phil," he called to the minotaur. "Hold the fort while I take Remy out back, will ya? Don't let the little shits burn the place down."

"But he's dead," Remy said as he followed the stone man. "Isn't he?"

"Yeah," the stone man said without missing a step. "But that doesn't mean he can't lend a hand."

The Archangel Michael flew through the darkness of interdimensional space, peeling back layer after layer of one universe—one reality—after another as he searched for the missing piece.

The piece that would make Heaven complete—the Garden of Eden.

He held the piece from the tree out before him, feeling the pull upon the branch, a small cadre of soldiers close behind him.

The Garden had been separated from Heaven during the Great War to prevent Lucifer from using it in his attempt to overthrow God. It was said that Eden would never stay in one place again—restless— until it was allowed to rejoin its home, to reconnect with the Kingdom of Heaven.

That time had finally come, and it was up to Michael to ensure that all was safe for its inevitable return during Unification.

Michael followed the pull of the branch, flapping his wings in the cold darkness of interdimensional space, passing lifeless worlds and stars in the throes of birth. With eyes that could pick out the specifics of a grain of sand, the archangel scanned the nearly endless cosmos for a sign other than the tug upon the stick that he held.

And there he saw it.

Although not easily impressed, Michael had to admit that the sight of the Garden floating in the nothingness of space was something to behold. Another of the Lord God's most wondrous creations; an enormous island of green floating amongst the stars.

It had been quite a long time since he'd last set eyes upon the paradise the Lord God had made for His human creations. He smirked, remembering how humanity had so disappointed the Creator, with Lucifer Morningstar proving how easy it was for the newly minted life-forms to disobey.

The archangel drifted down to touch upon the land outside the closed heavy metal gates. Cautiously, he approached them and peered through the bars at the overgrown jungle beyond.

It has been too long since someone last tended this garden, he thought.

His cadre waited patiently behind him, their eyes darting here and there. They knew the stories of this place, how it had been corrupted by the Morningstar.

"Shall we go inside?" Michael asked.

The soldiers did not answer him but stood at attention, ready to do his bidding.

Michael approached the gate, sensing a divine power radiating from the lock. At the same time, he felt a tremendous pull from the twig of the Tree of Knowledge. He touched the stick to the lock, and a sudden surge passed through him.

A surge that told him he was welcome in the Garden of Eden.

The gates shuddered and then parted with a rusted shriek, the Garden beckoning them to enter.

But as soon as Michael passed through the stone columns of the gate, he felt the wrongness through the bottom of his shoes, something that tingled and writhed, as if the ground he walked upon was some-how . . . corrupted. He was about to turn and warn his soldiers, when the earth around them violently shook and then exploded upward in a shower of dirt and rock as something forced its way out from beneath the ground.

The vines moved as if they had minds of their own, like the limbs of some great plant beast hidden under the ground. His soldiers were seized at once, the vegetation so thick and aggressive that even as one vine was severed, four more surged from the ground to enter the fray.

Michael's sword of fire was in his hand in an instant, cutting at the tentacles of vegetation that sprang at him from every angle.

This was why he had been sent to the Garden, he thought as he hacked away at the writhing vines that attempted to ensnare him. This was what he had been sent to prepare. From the corner of his eye, he watched as his angels fought, their bodies igniting with divine fire in order to burn the plants away, but instead the vines wept thick gouts of sweet-smelling fluids that actually dampened the fires of Heaven.

This is madness, Michael thought, still wildly swinging his burning sword at targets that relentlessly came at him. He leapt into the air, spreading his wings in an attempt to climb above the tendrils, but the vegetation was too fast, ensnaring his ankle, holding him back. His sword bit into the skin of the vine as it seemed to grow thicker, entwining around his leg. Furiously he beat his wings, but the vegetation held fast. It wasn't long before he was being drawn back down to the Garden, where even more of the writhing vines waited to grab him.

The thick tendrils of green dragged the archangel to his knees, and he was about to call upon the fire of God that resided within him, when something stopped him cold. Two figures were walking toward him—*no,* they were being carried on a thick wave of rustling vegetation. The surge of what looked like ivy stopped directly in front of the archangel.

"Sorry about that," the male figure said. He was thin, his clothes filthy. There appeared to be vines covering his body, some having burrowed beneath his flesh like veins. "Sometimes the place gets ahead of us."

The female figure laughed. She appeared to be as thin and dirty as the man. Her skin was a duskier hue, but she, too, was covered in vines. "The place gots a mind of its own," she said. "It ain't gonna do shit unless it wants to."

"Too true," the man said. He raised a closed fist and slowly opened his fingers.

Immediately the vines released Michael. He summoned a sword of fire and raised it toward the pair. "Release my soldiers," he commanded, barely able to hold back his righteous anger.

"Oh yeah, sure," the woman said. She, too, raised her fist, then slowly opened her fingers, and the soldiers were free.

"I should cut you two down and reduce this corrupted place to ash," Michael sneered.

"I don't think that's why the Lord God sent you here, do you?" the woman asked. "Though sometimes, I don't think He can keep track of all the plates He's got spinnin'."

"Please, let us explain," the man offered.

Michael glared at them for a moment, then slowly let his sword drop. "Then do so quickly, before my patience runs out."

"I'm Jon, and this is—"

"Izzy," the woman interrupted.

"We are the Gardeners," Jon finished. "The last of the original bloodline."

"Adam and Eve," Izzy explained. "The first man and woman."

"I know who they were," Michael snapped.

"We had to stop you from getting any farther," Izzy continued as if he hadn't spoken. "We couldn't risk you waking them up."

Michael cocked his head. "Waking up who?"

Jon and Izzy shared a furtive glance before looking back to Michael.

"What do you know about the Shaitan?" Jon asked.

Methuselah led Remy back to the kitchen.

The angel could see that it hadn't been used in quite some time, a similar layer of dust and grease coating all the metal surfaces.

"First you give me drinks and now a meal?"

Methuselah stopped, grunted, and then proceeded to the back of the kitchen, where he stopped in front of the large metal walk-in freezer.

Remy heard a noise behind him and turned to see Gerta standing there.

"Are you going to visit your friends?" she asked in a little-girl voice that immediately made him want to protect her.

Remy looked back to Methuselah, who had his hand upon the handle of the freezer, ready to open it. "Am I?" he asked, suddenly feeling anxious.

"Yeah." The golem pulled open the thick, insulated door. "Yeah, you are."

Clouds of chilling mist wafted out, enticing Remy to come closer, but he didn't want to move. Then he felt the small warm hand touch his.

"C'mon," Gerta said. "I'll take you."

Together, the two walked across the kitchen. Methuselah stepped back, crossing his arms over his massive stone chest and bowing his head.

Gerta released Remy's hand and placed hers at the small of his back, gently urging him inside the freezer. "Go on. I'll be right here."

Remy steeled himself and stepped into the freezing-cold place. A layer of icy fog drifted over the floor, but he could see the covered shapes lying there. His heart lurched as he gazed at them. He turned to see that Gerta was standing just inside the freezer, the looming form of Methuselah behind her in the doorway.

"Go on and say hi," the little girl urged him, her kindhearted smile giving him the strength to go forward.

Remy slowly lowered himself to the floor. He did not feel the cold radiating from the tile beneath his knees as he reached out with a trembling hand to the top of the sheet beside him.

The covering was cold beneath his fingers and crackled nearly deafeningly in the silence of the freezer. He drew the sheet down and felt a shudder of shock and surprise as he looked upon the still, pale face of Steven Mulvehill.

"Oh" was all he could say. Then he gently touched the man's face, the skin cold and hard beneath the warmth of his fingertips. "Look at you," Remy whispered. "I'm sure you'd give me a raft of shit for making you lie here so long, and I'm truly sorry for that."

There were flashes of memory that were not his, of Remy and the demon hound Baarabus digging through the rubble of a collapsed building to find his friend.

"I'm also sorry that I wasn't there to help you."

He sensed Gerta and looked to see her kneeling beside him.

"He was your friend, wasn't he?" she asked.

"Yeah, he was."

"I bet he was a really good friend, too."

"He was."

She looked at him, all wide-eyed and innocent. "He'll always be your friend, as long as you remember him."

"I could never forget him," Remy said.

Gerta gently pulled the sheet back over Steven's face. There was something awfully sad about that, but then everything about this moment was drenched in sorrow.

Then she reached over to pull the sheet down from the shrouded body beside Mulvehill. Remy's hand shot out, grabbing hold of the child's wrist, stopping her.

"What's the matter?" she asked.

"I . . . I don't know who . . ."

"You won't until you look."

She pulled the sheet down, and Remy's heart broke all over again.

"She's pretty," Gerta said.

"Yes," Remy said, gazing with tear-filled eyes at Ashley. There was heavy frost on one of her eyebrows, and Remy wiped it away, knowing that she would have hated to have something like that there.

"She was your friend, too?" Gerta asked.

"She was more than that," Remy said, unable to take his eyes from the young woman he'd watched grow up on Beacon Hill. "When I was with her, I could imagine what it was like to have a daughter."

Baarabus had been the one to find her, and had lain down beside her corpse, not letting the angel near her. It had been quite some time before the dog had finally allowed Remy to retrieve her body.

The little girl looked off in another direction, toward a wheeled cart in the corner that normally would have held food.

"She loves you very much," Gerta told him.

"I hope that she did," Remy answered her.

Gerta touched his arm, making him look at her.

"She *does*," the child stressed the last word, insinuating that somehow Ashley might still . . .

Gerta reached across him to cover Ashley's face.

"You still have a lot to do," the child said. She took his arm, trying to pull him to his feet.

There were still two more shapes beneath sheets, and he had a feeling deep in his gut that he knew who they were.

"I have to finish," he told the child, who still held his arm.

She stared with intensity, wanting to spare him the sadness to come.

"Are you sure?"

"I'm sure," he reassured her.

He knew that this would be the hardest for him, but if he didn't do it, the journey he was currently on would never be complete.

Gerta let go of his arm but still stood by him. "I'll stand here, just in case you need me."

He managed a smile—it wasn't much, but it was all he could muster—as he turned his attention to the larger of the remaining sheet-covered forms. It felt like it took forever for him to reach down and pull the sheet away from the battered face of his wife.

Madeline.

Remy experienced a powerful jolt again as two conflicting memories struggled for supremacy. He saw his beautiful wife in life, but also in death.

But it wasn't this death he saw. No, he saw her death in a Boston nursing home, taken by cancer after a valiant fight for her life.

Two memories, two deaths—one just as painful as the other.

Remy felt his strength begin to wane, but before he lost it completely, he reached for the final sheet and revealed the corpse of Marlowe.

This was it for him, the physical representation of his humanity laid out on the cold tile floor of a walk-in freezer.

Now he knew why the Remy he had replaced had been so cruel. His humanity had been crushed. There was no longer a place for kindness, love, and warmth.

No place for the weakness of humanity.

Remy knelt amongst the dead—*his* dead—and pondered the question of what to do next. He waited for something, perhaps the incredible pain as the humanity inside this version of himself, the humanity that he still felt crying out in sadness, withered and died, leaving only the emotionless messenger behind.

"Are you through?" the little girl asked.

He was. He covered his wife's face for what he knew to be the last time, and covered his dog, expecting to feel it all come crashing down, transforming him into the cruel being that he had replaced.

But it didn't happen. For something still burned inside him. Surrounded by darkness, a tiny flame still flickered. He didn't know what it was—maybe hope?

But it was enough.

CHAPTER TWENTY-FIVE

Linda was lost in a sea of darkness.

It threatened to swallow her whole, to snuff out her light and make her a part of its infinite black, but she fought to remain.

A sudden gust of turbulence had spun her in such a way that the chain around her waist had unwrapped, allowing the currents of shadow to take her. The darkness wanted her to become part of its whole and pulled her deeper into its all-encompassing embrace.

What hope did she have?

That was all she had, she realized, and allowed herself to move with the currents.

Allowing herself to be carried . . .

To where? Where would she end up?

Having no sense of up or down, she was dragged along, never losing sight of the reason she was there, of the man that she loved with all her heart and soul.

Remy.

She would not allow the darkness to claim her; she would continue to be the light in this vast, black ocean. He needed her, for without her efforts, without the efforts of Ashley and Marlowe, he would be lost. The darkness would take him for its own.

And she would do everything—*anything*—to have her Remy back.

* * *

Ashley paced in front of the hole.

Her mind was racing.

What should I do? I have to do something. What if she's hurt down there and I'm up here and . . .

She dropped to her knees at the edge again, leaning as far forward as she dared. "Linda! Can you hear me? Make a noise . . . any noise that you can!"

But there was nothing from the darkness below, not even an echo.

Ashley grabbed the chain. She had to go down there. What choice did she have?

Marlowe stood nearby, watching her nervously.

"I've got to do this, pal," she told him, as much to convince herself as him. "She's down there someplace."

The dog continued to eye her, following her every movement.

"But what about you?" she asked with uncertainty. "If I go down there and something happens to me . . ."

Ashley was torn, but she had to do something. Grabbing up the chain, she moved toward the tree and was stopped cold by what she saw.

The tree . . . There was something wrong with it.

She could see that the bark was darkening, sloughing off. More of the dark, bloodlike liquid was draining from the new bare spots.

The tree was dying.

Marlowe was beside her now, and he had started to whine.

"I know, boy," she said. "Something's wrong. . . . Something's really, really wrong."

She dropped the chain and stepped closer to the tree. The bark was making a strange crackling sound as it seemed to wither before her eyes, then fall to the ground. The skin beneath the bark was pale and dry.

Sick.

As more of the tree's underskin became exposed, she felt it: a strange pull upon her, something compelling her to lay her hands upon it. She was leery, remembering what had happened earlier when she and Linda had laid hands on the tree.

But maybe that was what was supposed to happen. Maybe the tree, which was representative of Remy's soul, needed her to touch it.

Maybe she was what was needed to help keep Remy's soul from being drained away.

She feared for Linda but also knew that something had to be done to help the tree. She turned her head to look at the hole they had dug, sending a silent apology into the darkness, for she knew what she had to do.

Marlowe had also sidled closer to the tree, and Ashley was about to warn him away when she realized what he was doing.

The dog laid down at the base of the tree, pressing his hip against an exposed area of the tree's underskin. He sighed with the contact, lowering his face between his paws and closing his eyes.

"You're such a good boy," Ashley praised, and then she, too, reached out.

To keep the tree, and Remy's soul, alive.

Assiel felt his own energies on the wane, but he knew that he must continue to hold on to Ashley, Linda, and Marlowe, or they might very well share Remy's fate.

Part of him was attempting to keep the spiritual aspects of the three connected to the realm in which Remy's soul existed, while the other part of him struggled to keep their soul essences anchored to the physical world, where their bodies waited for them.

He knew they were having difficulty, and he wished that he could do more to assist them, but it was taking all of his strength and concentration to maintain the balance and keep his hold on the two worlds. He had already carefully reached out, compelling Ashley and the canine to join their soul energies to the tree, for without their assistance, Remy's own essence would have withered away.

Assiel was holding his own, his focus intense, when he heard the sounds: explosions of violence that drew him back to the physical world.

The house was under attack.

Squire was pissed off. The Bone Master fuckers had stolen his shtick. They were using shadows as their means of travel, just like he did, and he didn't care for that one little bit.

And there were lots of shadows in Remy's kitchen, the only light in the center of the ceiling throwing just enough illumination to create some pretty nifty passages.

"Light," Squire barked to Mulvehill, as they moved toward the kitchen table, where the weapons retrieved from Francis' apartment were waiting.

"What?" Mulvehill asked, continuing to fire his gun into the shadows.

"Light," Squire repeated. He was shoving weapons and ammunition into his pockets. "We need more light! It'll cut down on the shadows, make it harder for them to move around."

The homicide cop darted across the kitchen as bone bullets spat out from pockets of shadow around the room. He raced by the stove, pushing a button on the hood to illuminate more of the kitchen.

There were screams from some of the shadows.

"Take that, you fucking bastards," Squire growled, firing three shots from an automatic pistol into the dwindling patch of shadow.

"That seemed to help a little," Mulvehill commented as he moved alongside Squire. They flipped over the kitchen table to use as a shield.

"Yeah, some," Squire said, still not pleased with the situation.

They kept their heads low as bone projectiles hit the wood.

Squire carefully peeked over the edge of the table. A Bone Master was squeezing through one of the shadows, and the hobgoblin fired a shot directly into the assassin's face. The killer dropped to the floor, half his body still inside the passage. "That should keep that opening clogged for a bit."

"Not long enough." Mulvehill was peering around the side of the table as he slipped another clip into his gun. Squire looked as well and saw that the dead assassin was being dragged back into the shadows.

Bone projectiles were flying again, striking the tabletop.

"We're not gonna hold this kitchen for much longer," Squire said, firing at movement from another area of shadow.

"Why do you say that?" Mulvehill asked. "We've got guns and plenty of ammunition."

"Yeah, but these guys ain't your typical thugs."

There was shot from a shadow, and the light above the stove went dark.

Mulvehill looked at Squire.

"Shit," Squire said.

There came another shot, and this time the glass casing over the ceiling light shattered, exposing the four bulbs.

"Shit, shit, shit!" Squire began gathering up the weapons and ammunition that he'd placed at his feet, shoving them in the heavy duffel bag they'd brought with them from Francis' building.

Mulvehill was desperately firing into the shadows, but two of the four lightbulbs exploded.

Squire slapped his arm as he jumped to his feet. "We've got to go!"

Mulvehill emptied his clip just as the last two bulbs were extinguished, plunging the kitchen into darkness.

"Move!" Squire shouted, grabbing Mulvehill's arm.

And the two raced into the living room as Bone Master assassins swarmed behind them.

CHAPTER TWENTY-SIX

Remy slowly rose to his feet, his eyes fixed on the covered corpses that represented his humanity. This was the last he could stand of this nightmarish world that had become his twisted new reality.

"Is this it?" he asked, still staring at the dead. "Is this why I was supposed to come here?"

He turned toward Gerta and Methuselah, still standing in the doorway to the freezer.

"I think it's time," the little girl said, turning her innocent gaze up to the stone man.

"Are you sure?" Methuselah asked. "If what he said is true, this isn't even the Remy who left it here."

"No," she said, looking back to the angel. "It isn't . . . but it's the one who's supposed to take it back."

"Take it back?" Remy repeated, moving toward them. "What am I taking back?"

The golem hesitated.

"Go ahead," Gerta said.

Methuselah silently turned and walked away, only to return a few moments later holding something wrapped in a towel.

"Here," the golem said, holding the package out to Remy. "You asked me to watch over this until you came back."

Remy took the package and immediately felt it. The Seraphim fire that whirled insanely at his core suddenly surged through his body in panic, filling his every muscle, feeding him with the strength he would need to defend himself.

But against what?

"Do you know what it is?" Gerta asked, looking up at him with eyes like the windows to some great cathedral of the soul.

Remy couldn't find the words, the experience of holding the mysterious package like nothing he could remember.

"I want to put it down, to throw it away, but I . . . I don't want to," he finally gasped.

"Open it," the little girl said excitedly, as if it were a special birthday gift.

Remy's hands were actually shaking as he began to carefully unwrap the towel. He saw a flash of gold, and his heart skipped a beat. He pulled his hand away for a moment, then gently lifted the last of the wrappings.

The golden pistol lay nestled in a bedding of towel, and it seemed to speak to him in the gentle voice of a long-lost lover.

So good to see you again, Remiel. It has been too long.

The golden pistol was called Pitiless because of its incredible affinity for death; there wasn't another weapon in all of existence as deadly. Forged from the very life force of Lucifer Morningstar, this was a weapon to fear, a weapon that Remy had last seen in the possession of his friend, former Guardian angel Fraciel.

Francis.

It was the first time that Remy had thought of his fallen friend, and the realization that his was not one of the bodies in the freezer made the question surge to the surface of his mind.

Where was Francis, and why was Remy now in possession of the Pitiless pistol?

Pick me up, and I'll show you, the Pitiless whispered.

Remy stared at the weapon, the warmth of the gun radiating through the towel. It was like he was holding a living thing, and in a way, he was.

This had been Lucifer's way of hiding his power after losing the war against God: disguising it as weaponry, multiple pieces scattered to the world of man, waiting for the day when they would be found by his followers and his full strength would return to him.

And that power was returned, as the Morningstar ruled Hell once again. But the pistol remained as it was created, almost as if it had a special purpose.

A purpose it had yet to fulfill.

"This doesn't belong to me," Remy said, looking from Gerta to Methuselah. "How . . . ?"

"After everything went to shit—"

The little girl looked sternly at the golem.

"Excuse me," Methuselah apologized. "After everything went bad, you showed up with it, handed it over to me, and said that there might be a time when you would come back for it. You said I was to hold on to it for you until then."

"But why would I have this?"

Gerta's voice was calm yet commanding as she spoke to him. "Maybe you should listen to it." She motioned to the Pitiless with her chin. "It might know something that you don't."

He knew that she was right, but the idea of holding the weapon, of letting it worm its way into his head . . .

Remy looked down at the weapon, feeling it pulse powerfully in his hand. He had to know how the Pitiless came to be in his possession, and the only way he could learn this was right there at his fingertips.

He just had to be brave enough—strong enough—to find out.

Remy reached for the gun, his hand wrapping around the grip, and the floor of reality dropped out from beneath him.

The Pitiless transported him to another place . . . another time . . . another moment.

Just before the end.

Before the fall of Heaven.

The images came at Remy fast and furious, combined with the overwhelming emotions of the time.

It was a moment of absolute glory—Heaven about to be reunited with its missing pieces, and the Earth about to be made part of God's empire.

Remy was jubilant as he stood amongst a gathering of Heaven's representatives—the angelic as well as humans touched by the divinity of God.

The Golden City hovered before them, the Almighty represented as a glowing sphere of the purest light, rays of His holy omnipotence radiating outward, calling for the lost regions to return.

For Heaven to be unified once more.

Remy could feel the anticipation in the air as the Garden of Eden and the territorial mass that had become known as Hell slowly returned to the places they had inhabited before the Great War.

But a sudden dark tremble, a vibration through the ether, warned him that something was amiss. All eyes were upon the Lord of Lords, but Remy turned his on those gathered to witness the wonder. Instincts honed by the profession he had mastered in the world of man were on full alert. Something was wrong.

Remy wandered through the gathering, scanning the crowd. He saw the Archangel Michael and his soldiers, their expressions surprisingly grim as they perched upon the shores of Eden. There were those who had fallen amidst the gathering as well, their sins about to be forgiven, their penance completed as the Morningstar was welcomed back into the family of Heaven.

But the odd feeling continued to worsen as Remy moved through the crowds, watching their euphoric expressions as Eden and Hell gradually returned to their rightful places.

Remy's eyes were drawn to his Lord God, and he experienced a joy unlike any other as he looked upon the glowing sphere.

Then the configuration of Heaven began to shift and change as what had been excised returned with the divine cacophony of the celestial choir.

The regions were realigning. Remy could see dark towers that could only have been erected in Hell, rising up alongside the spires of the Golden City.

And from one of the towers a shape appeared, clad in armor that seemed to be forged from the heart of the morning sun. The figure leapt from the spire, wings of solid black springing from his shoulders as he glided down to gently land before the sphere of God.

Lucifer Morningstar stood before his God and did what Remy had never believed possible. The Son of the Morning knelt before God and bowed his head in acquiescence.

It was truly about to happen.

Remy stared in awe at the scene before him, the strange sensation that something was wrong temporarily forgotten.

The music of the Heavenly choir intensified, vibrating inside his skull as Heaven expanded, returning to the glory of what it had once been when the universe was young.

A tendril of light reached out from the sphere, the Lord God embracing his fallen son, and everything was well again in the cosmos.

Everything and everybody were connected.

It was all the Kingdom of Heaven.

And at that moment of cosmic bliss, something went terribly awry.

Searing flashes of terrible imagery exploded before Remy's eyes.

A stab of gold from the corner of his eye.

Francis in the crowd, the Pitiless clutched in his hand.

His friend as he looked at Remy with eyes as dark as the longest night.

The Pitiless roared.

God screamed.

And the Heavens fell.

Remy cried out as it all came to a fiery end, falling to his knees inside the freezer.

Methuselah was clutching Gerta to his great stone body, the little girl looking afraid. "Was it bad?" she asked in a tiny, scared voice.

Remy nodded. "It was, but I saw . . ."

"What did you see?" Methuselah prompted.

Remy stood up, the Pitiless pistol still clutched in his hand. "I saw what was supposed to be the most wonderful thing . . . and how easily it was all taken away."

"Did you see who was responsible?" the stone man asked.

Remy looked at him, at the burning light emanating from his deep and shadowy eye sockets.

"The recollection is a little fuzzy, but . . ."

"Who?" Methuselah persisted.

"I think . . ."

"Who?"

"Francis," Remy answered. "I think it was Francis. And he used this very weapon to . . ."

"Are you sure?"

The images flashed before his eyes again: Francis holding the Pitiless, the look that the former Guardian angel gave him before . . .

"Yes," Remy said sadly. "It was him."

The golem pulled the child closer. "And what do you intend to do now?" he asked.

Remy stared at the golden weapon in his hand, knowing that it still had a part to play. That it was part of the end, and also the beginning.

"I have to go back," he said. "I have to go to the ruins of the Golden City. I have to . . . to finish what was started."

Remy turned back to the covered bodies of his friends. He was tempted to look at each again, but instead, he silently bid them farewell, stepping from the freezer and closing the door firmly behind him.

Methuselah and the child followed him from the kitchen to the front of the bar. The children had all awakened, and they watched him silently. He realized that he was still clutching the Pitiless in his hand, and he quickly slipped it inside his coat so as not to scare the kids.

There were more flashes of memory, mini explosions along the surface of his brain. He saw himself finding the children, saving them from the wreckage of the world, promising them that they would be part of something new.

"One for the road?" Methuselah asked. He had returned to his place behind the bar and was holding up the dusty bottle of scotch.

But as tempting as the offer was, Remy knew that it was time for him to go. "Next time," he replied.

"Will there even be a next time?" the golem asked.

Remy looked at the kids again, feeling the weight of the Pitiless inside his coat. "Yes, there will be a next time," he said to answer Methuselah's question as well as reassure the children of their future.

"We'll drink then," Methuselah said, returning the dusty bottle to its place on the shelf behind the bar.

Remy was about to make his way to the exit when Gerta dashed forward and wrapped her arms around his waist.

"Don't be sad," she said, hugging him tightly.

He hugged her back, a part of him wishing that he could stay right there.

"I'll try not to be," he told her.

He turned then and headed toward the door.

"And don't be afraid," Gerta called after him.

"I won't," Remy promised over his shoulder as he pulled open the heavy wood door.

His eyes brushed the still form of Phil the minotaur, covered in the passage of time. *The Hell you won't be,* he imagined the doorman saying in his gruff, no-nonsense tone, and he knew the mythical beast to be right.

He stepped from the bar into the damp stone alley that would take him back to a dying world.

A world that he had to somehow fix.

CHAPTER TWENTY-SEVEN

Satquiel's wings opened in the Garden of Eden, and Simeon emerged from the cover of feathers into a world of lush, tropical green.

He breathed deeply of the air, so fresh and clean that it caused his lungs to ache. Scanning the jungle before him, he saw a place overflowing with growth, pregnant with life and the promise of a new beginning.

Truly the Paradise it had been created to be.

Almost as if compelled, Simeon dropped to the ground, feeling the moisture of the fertile earth soaking through the knees of his slacks. He plunged his hands into the rich black soil, letting it sift between his fingers.

For a moment he felt as though he had found a home, a place where he could forget the atrocities that had been committed against him, a place where it was possible to forget a God that had taken so much.

But there was something in the dirt.

A corruption of perfection, a cancer hidden beneath layers of chaste dirt, rock, and vegetation. A reminder that faultlessness did not exist and that the transgressions perpetrated against him were not so easily wiped away.

Simeon let the tainted earth fall back to the ground. "There is a sickness here," he said aloud.

Behind him, Satquiel chuckled. "Of that you are mistaken. Life here is in its purest state, fresh from the mind of the Creator Himself."

Simeon stood, scrutinizing his surroundings. He had been so overwhelmed by the supposed perfection of it all that he hadn't noticed it at first. "Rot," he said to Satquiel, motioning toward the lush vegetation. "Look at the leaves, the stems, the very flowers."

Indeed, there were brown spots on many of the growths, some having already turned to black. On a nearby vine, a fat pod had grown, and Simeon reached out, plucking it from the vine. He turned toward the angel, holding it out.

"Pregnant with life," the angel said, a superior smile on his face.

Simeon squeezed the pod between his forefinger and thumb, and a thick, foul-smelling ooze flowed out and over his hand. "'Pregnant with rot' is more like it."

Satquiel seemed surprised, taking the pod from him and examining it carefully.

But Simeon was already on the move, noticing that the path of decay seemed to be more distinct in one particular direction. He pushed his way through the thick underbrush, keeping his eyes on the blemishes and stains of rot, finally ending up on the edge of a grove of sorts, a tree with bark of an unusual golden color at its center.

"Isn't that lovely," Simeon said, as he stared at the impressive growth.

There was movement behind him, and he turned to see that Satquiel had joined him but had dropped to one knee as he stared at the tree before them.

For a moment Simeon didn't understand, but, looking back to the tree, it was obvious. "The Tree of Knowledge," the forever man whispered.

He stepped from the overgrowth, toward the tree—and was immediately stopped as a hand like steel took hold of his arm.

"It is forbidden," Satquiel said with a threatening snarl, his eyes leaking tiny sparks of fire.

Simeon glared at the angel. "You forget who is in control here," he said, turning Solomon's ring on his right hand.

Satquiel released his hold with a hiss.

"Very little is forbidden to me," he reminded the angel as he turned his attentions back to the tree. "It would be wise for you to remember that."

He focused on the fruit hanging from the branches of the tree, imagining what it must have been like for the first daughter, Eve. But the fruit appeared to be suffering as the Garden itself did, swollen with rot, the skin splitting in places to release a viscous juice that rained to the ground.

As he stepped closer to the tree, he caught sight of something moving just beneath the tainted earth that surrounded it. At first he thought it a trick of his eyes, but closer inspection proved there was indeed something there. Call it some sort of sixth sense, honed over the countless millennia he had spent in a dangerous world, but Simeon knew that it would not be wise to tread upon that ground.

He reached down and picked up a small, smooth stone, tossing it onto the dirt at the base of the tree. Something that looked like multiple worms shot up from below and dragged the stone down.

Simeon's heart quickened with excitement.

Is it possible I've discovered the source of the Garden's illness?

"Satquiel," Simeon called, keeping his eyes on the churning patches of earth.

"Yes?"

"Do you have any idea what *that* is?"

"I don't," the archangel replied.

"Hmm," Simeon commented, reaching up to stroke his chin. "I would like to know."

"What would you have me do?"

"Go there," Simeon said, pointing to the mound of black earth. "Walk upon the ground. I'm curious."

He could see that Satquiel was trying to defy him, fighting against the power of Solomon's ring, but it was all for naught. The magick within the ring was too strong.

The archangel haltingly made his way past Simeon, and as soon as his foot landed on the loose earth beneath the Tree of Knowledge, it triggered the most explosive of reactions. It was as if some sort of trap had been sprung, the ground encircling the angel erupting as things the likes of which Simeon had never seen broke the surface, grabbing hold of the powerful angel and dragging him down.

Simeon stepped carefully back.

The thin, white-skinned creatures, their flesh adorned with strange, tattoolike markings, were brutal in their assault, clawed hands ripping bleeding furrows in the angel's exposed flesh. Satquiel cried out, and a sword of flame appeared in his hand. He hacked at the creatures, but for every creature he cut down, four more seemed to take its place.

The angel's wings flapped powerfully, kicking up clouds of dust and dirt. The creatures grabbed at the flailing appendages, spidery fingers breaking with their pounding intensity. But eventually the wings were slowed enough that the grappling hands took hold. Handfuls of feathers were torn away, pulled down beneath the ground before the eager hands returned for more.

Satquiel's body burned with the fires of Heaven, but it didn't seem enough. The creatures continued to reach for the soldier of Heaven, ripping at his flesh, dragging him down.

Closer to the churning earth of a poisoned Eden.

Satquiel's eyes locked on Simeon's, and the forever man saw the panic there. A part of him wanted to help, but another, stronger part was fascinated, preferring instead to watch how this would all turn out.

The archangel lost his sword, the burning blade tugged below the surface with a sizzling hiss. His wings were torn apart, little more than useless pieces of trembling cartilage and bone. Both arms disappeared as Satquiel continued his descent beneath the churning dirt. Soon only his head and shoulders remained aboveground, but still he continued to struggle. The creatures hungrily tore at his face, the once statuesque features now ragged and stained with blood.

"Help . . . me," Satquiel managed as a clawed hand tore away a portion of his cheek.

Simeon did not answer. He simply stood and watched as the archangel's head gradually sank beneath the writhing ground at the base of the Tree of Knowledge.

Mind racing, the forever man searched his memory for a hint of what these creatures might be, but he found nothing that he could recall. He continued to watch the earth, which had returned to a state of calm, only to be startled as it began to roil again, a large section of blighted soil moving toward him like a wave about to break upon the shore.

Simeon scrambled to his feet as the ground close to him started to churn, the hungry faces of the unknown beasts baring their razor-sharp teeth, rising out of the dirt as skeletal arms reached for him.

Simeon attempted to flee, but the beasts were faster than he was, digging away at the Garden's floor, causing it to give way beneath his steps. The forever man fell to his knees and began to crawl, but the monsters grabbed at his legs, their claws puncturing his flesh, which healed almost immediately, only to be punctured again in their attempts to hold him.

Simeon had flipped over onto his back and was being dragged back toward the grove as he began to recite a spell of protection. His hands had begun to glow with an ethereal light, and he was about to unleash his unholy power upon the things in the ground, when . . .

From across the grove on the opposite side, he saw them.

"In the nick of time," the forever man muttered happily.

And Simeon began to smile.

The Archangel Michael's mind burned with the knowledge provided by the Gardeners of Eden. Foul creatures called the Shaitan, precursors to the creation of angels, hidden in the ground beneath the Tree of Knowledge.

Outrageous.

He had known that the Garden had been severed from the Kingdom of Heaven during the Great War, but he'd never known the true reason it had been cast adrift. The Shaitan were that reason, for these shape-shifting creatures were extremely dangerous and had only the destruction of Heaven on their foul minds.

Michael and his soldiers had listened to the Gardeners' words carefully before heading toward the Tree of Knowledge to deal with the infestation.

The Gardeners had explained that Eden was dying, poisoned from the inside by the malignant life-forms created by the Lord God's top designer, Malachi. The Shaitan had been rejected by God, but Malachi had ignored their Lord's wishes and had allowed the abominations to live.

Now it was up to Michael and his archangels to finally purge Eden of these foul creations before Eden was rejoined with the Kingdom of Heaven.

And that was when the commander of the archangels had the most loathsome of thoughts, considering the idea of leaving Eden just as he'd found it and letting the ceremony of Unification turn to chaos as these foul Shaitan creatures swarmed the Kingdom of Heaven. That would most certainly show the Creator the wrongness of this entire affair.

It was certainly tempting and would show his disdain, but he was a loyal servant of the Heavenly Father and dared not bring shame to his position as commander of the archangel forces.

The Gardeners moved upon a wave of soil, the thick obstructions of vines and overgrown trees moving aside to allow them passage. Suddenly they stopped, the mound of living soil that they manipulated for travel collapsing to the ground.

"What is wrong?" Michael asked, raising a hand so that his soldiers would stop.

Picking themselves up from where they'd fallen, Jon and Izzy slowly turned to face him.

"We're getting closer to the Tree," Jon said.

"Gets harder to do our thing the closer we get to the Shaitan," Izzy added.

Michael could see that the beings looked sick; their bodies, which seemed as much plant as flesh, appeared affected by something.

"Where is the Tree?" Michael asked them, craning his neck to see through the thick jungle before them.

"Through there," Jon said, pointing with a finger entwined with blossoming vines.

Michael pushed past the strange pair and, summoning a sword of flame, began to cut a swath to their destination. He heard the pair cry out as he hacked into the wall of thick roots that blocked his way. The archangel and his soldiers turned toward them.

"Do we cause you pain?" he asked.

Izzy nodded. "Yeah, you do," she said. "Give us a second to collect ourselves, and then we'll—"

"We're sorry," the angel said, but not really meaning it. Michael's only concern was reaching the Tree and the threat buried beneath. He and his soldiers had not the time to be worrying about the health of Eden's wardens. He and the other archangels continued to cut their way through the thick wall of vegetation, ignoring the cries of the Gardeners behind them.

The closer they got to the Tree, the denser the plant life became, and that just annoyed Michael all the more. He called upon the divine fires that burned within him, allowing his body to radiate the heat of a star as he continued to hack his way through the wall of vegetation. The other archangels followed his lead, and soon they pushed through to an open grove, where their eyes fell upon their prize.

And something totally unexpected.

There was the tree, in all its glory, but there was also a man—a human, under attack from what could only be the Shaitan. The foul creatures moved through the dirt around the tree like sharks in water and were dragging the human into their filthy environment.

Michael had no idea who the human was, or why he was there, but his enemy was before him, so any other mystery would have to wait.

He turned toward his warriors. "For the glory of Heaven and the Lord God, kill them," he ordered. "Leave nothing of their kind alive."

There was nothing an archangel wanted to hear more than an order to perform an act of violence in the name of their Creator. It was an excuse to tap into areas often suppressed for great lengths of time.

But when allowed to run free, it was a sight to behold.

Michael watched as his archangels swarmed the grove, their powerful wings lifting them up in mighty leaps as they descended upon their prey. Swords, knives, and spears of flame fell upon the creatures in the dirt. It should have been a one-sided bloodbath, but the Shaitan fought furiously, using their dirt habitat to hide themselves and surprise their attackers.

From the corner of his eye, Michael caught movement and turned to find the human standing there, his clothing in tatters. Michael took his eyes from the battle briefly to fully gaze upon the man.

Yes, indeed, he was human, but there was something more to him.

He would have expected sheer terror from the man, but his incredibly calm demeanor left the Archangel Michael with a nagging question.

"Who are you, and what are you doing here?"

The human smiled, nervously playing with a piece of jewelry—a ring—upon one of his fingers.

"Me?" the human said. "You can call me *master*."

And for some reason, that sounded perfectly acceptable to the leader of the archangels.

The look of an angel being commanded by one who wore the ring of Solomon never got old. It was a look of complete surprise quickly followed by total obedience.

It was a wonderful thing.

Simeon looked out over the grove, at the archangel soldiers in combat with the creatures that dwelled in the dirt below the Tree of Knowledge.

"What are they?" he asked, captivated by the monsters' intensity, by their savagery.

Michael told him of the Shaitan and how they'd come to be. He told him that they shouldn't exist at all, but an angel of the highest order had taken it upon himself to allow them to live, hiding them away in the Garden—beneath the dirt at the base of the Tree.

Simeon found that most fascinating and began to see how the creatures—the Shaitan—might actually fit into his plans.

"I would like you to get their attention," Simeon commanded Michael.

The angel looked at him with questioning eyes.

"Go ahead," Simeon urged, waving him on. "Get them to stop."

Michael spread his wings to their impressive span, flying toward the battleground.

"Hold!" the angel bellowed, his voice like the blaring of a horn.

The archangels responded at once, looking toward their commander. The creatures, sensing that something was happening, retreated deeper beneath the soil of Eden.

Michael hovered above the Tree, directing his soldiers to the edge of the grove where Simeon stood.

"Hello," Simeon said as he turned his ring on his finger. The angels were confused, looking to their commander for an explanation.

"Excuse me," Simeon called out. "I'd like you all to look over here."

The angels did what was asked of them.

"Excellent," Simeon said. "What a lovely bunch you are. Would you all come toward me, please, away from the tree? Thank you so much."

The angels did what was asked, Michael swooping down from above to land amongst them.

Simeon pushed past the collected group, walking across the dirt, where he stopped and stamped his foot upon the ground. "It's all right," he called out. "They're under my control now."

It took a moment, but then the black earth began to churn, and the strange beings began to surface.

"Excellent," Simeon said, watching as they crawled up from the ground, eyeing him with suspicion. "Do you see?" he asked them. "Do you see what I have done?"

One of the creatures rose to his full height, the markings upon his body shifting and moving in an almost hypnotic rhythm.

"Are you the leader?" Simeon asked the creature.

It looked at him with eyes like polished black stones, eyes that told the forever man nothing.

"Let's say that you are," Simeon said. "Can you understand me?"

The creature continued to stare.

"I believe you can." Simeon looked around at the Shaitan that had emerged from below the dirt. There were far more of them than he had originally imagined. The gears inside his head began to turn all the faster, and he found his smile growing wide enough to split his face.

"The Lord God has wronged you," he said, "by decreeing that you and yours are not fit to exist." He looked at them as well as at the legion of archangels that stood awaiting his further commands. "I, too, bear a grudge against Him," Simeon proclaimed with a nod. "And would love to see Him cut down and His Golden City razed."

The Shaitan looked at one another, a silent language passing between them. Simeon could tell that they were excited by his words, for the black patterns upon their fish-belly white flesh had begun to shift and change and flow over their musculature.

"Will you join me?" he asked them. He directed their attention to the gathered archangels. "Will you join us in striking a blow to Heaven and God?"

There was a sudden noise from behind them, and almost as one, they all turned toward the sound. Two figures had emerged from the thicket of the Garden, strange beings that appeared to be made of an odd mixture of flesh and plant life.

Will the wonders of this place never cease? Simeon wondered.

"You there!" one of the pair cried. "What are you doing?"

They moved stiffly as if suffering some ailment.

"Michael, what's going on?" the female of the pair asked the leader of the archangels.

Simeon chuckled. "Yes, Michael. What is going on?"

Michael flexed his wings as he strode toward them.

"I . . . ," the archangel stammered.

The Shaitan seemed afraid of the pair, threatening to dive back down under the earth.

"No worries," Simeon assured them, raising his hands. He then walked over to where Michael stood with the newcomers to their gathering.

"And who might you two be?" Simeon asked them.

"We might be asking you the same thing," the black woman said with attitude.

"We're the Gardeners of Eden," the male said. "And what you're doing here—with them . . ." He pointed to the Shaitan. "It's extremely dangerous."

"I'm well aware of what I'm doing, thank you," Simeon said. "Aren't I, Michael?"

The archangel leader nodded. "You are."

The pair exchanged a troubled gaze.

"What did you do to him?" the female asked.

Simeon could see that she'd lowered her hands to her side, her fingers starting to tremble. The ground began to shift and move, raising the pair up on a wave of soil.

Simeon stepped back and away. "I've taken control of the situation," he said to them. "Michael." He turned to the archangel. "I'd like you to kill them."

The Gardeners reacted at once, erecting a wall of vegetation and dirt to protect themselves from the angel, who lunged at them.

Simeon looked to the other angels, and motioned for them to go to their leader's assistance. "If you wouldn't mind."

They flew in a swarm, their swords crackling with fire.

The Gardeners were moving deeper into the Garden. They'd almost made it when Michael dropped upon them, his sword of fire cutting them down. The other archangels joined him, hacking at the strange beings, who struggled to stay alive for far longer than Simeon would have imagined.

But eventually they were quiet, their bodies hacked to pieces.

"You might want to burn them," Simeon called out.

And the angels summoned their divine fire, torching the remains of the Gardeners.

Satisfied that they had been dealt with, Simeon turned back to the Shaitan, who still stood in the grove, watching with curious eyes.

"So," Simeon said to them. "Raise your hands if you want to attack Heaven."

CHAPTER TWENTY-EIGHT

The sounds of gunfire drew Assiel back to the conscious world, away from Remy Chandler and the three friends who were attempting to keep him alive.

He hated to leave them alone in the strange place created by the Seraphim and their conjoined minds, but he knew they were in danger from the waking world.

The angel healer returned to consciousness, still sitting upon the bed with the others. He checked them carefully, a hand hovering over their still bodies, feeling the pulses of their life forces tickling his palm.

The muffled gun blasts in quick succession startled him, and he looked toward the doorway. He could hear voices from below, followed by more gunshots.

Before getting off of the bed, Assiel looked down at Remy's still form, making note of the paleness of his flesh. He let his hand hover over the Seraphim and did not like what he felt. Remy's life force was continuing to wane, despite the efforts of his friends. He looked again at the unconscious forms of Ashley, Linda, and the dog, Marlowe, and considered waking them—dragging them from Remy's psyche.

Is there even a chance that they might keep the Seraphim alive? he wondered. *There is always a chance,* he answered his own question.

Assiel climbed off the bed and walked across the room to where he'd left his bag.

The commotion in the rooms below seemed to be getting louder.

He reached into his bag and pulled out twin daggers he'd had made to rigid specifications, earthly craftsmanship attempting to duplicate weapons he'd possessed in Heaven. The man who had made the blades had come close, but he was only human, and they proved to be yet another reminder of how much Assiel had lost during the Great War.

There was more gunfire from down below and Assiel left the room, a knife in each hand.

No, they were not blades forged in the divine fires of Heaven, but they would serve the purpose they were intended for.

Ashley immediately felt the angel's loss.

Hands pressed to the trunk of the tree that represented Remy's soul, she quickly looked around for signs of a disturbance.

"Did you feel that?" she asked Marlowe.

The Lab lay at the base of the tree, his hip pressed to the flaking bark. He looked at her with dark, soulful eyes and wagged his tail.

"Something feels different," she said.

She guessed that it had do with something back in the real world, but there wasn't any way for her to check it out. Instead, she returned her focus to the tree, and what she and Marlowe were doing to keep it from completely crumbling away. They seemed to be doing an adequate job, for there were fewer new areas of slough and the draining sap seemed to have slowed.

She couldn't help but be worried, though, reaching out to Assiel with her mind but getting nothing in response. The angel had been silent for quite some time, and she couldn't help but think about what might be going on back home, in Remy's bedroom.

"I don't know what we should be doing," she said.

Marlowe was looking up at her attentively.

"Something doesn't feel right out there," she said, gazing out over the playground, and the Common beyond.

Marlowe made a soft, sad whining sound.

"I know Remy needs us, but . . ." She ran her hands over the tree bark, breaking away the loose pieces and letting them fall to the ground. "But are we really even helping him?"

The dog whined pathetically.

"Who's to say that we're doing anything," she said, feeling herself growing more anxious, beginning to doubt.

Ashley looked toward the hole. It looked as though it had gotten bigger. There still wasn't any sign from Linda.

"Part of me wants to try to go back," she said. "Maybe back there we might actually be doing something." The darkness of the hole pulled at her, drawing her emotions to the surface. "But that would mean leaving Linda here alone."

Marlowe's tale wagged, thumping upon the ground.

"What if she came back and we were gone?" she asked herself, and Marlowe. "No, we have to stay," she said firmly. "We have to stay and do what we came for."

She pressed the palms of her hands more firmly to the dry bark, willing her strength into the tree. "We have to keep it alive."

Marlowe was looking at her again expectantly.

"We have to keep Remy alive."

Mulvehill imagined that Remy would be pretty pissed about the couch.

They'd retreated from the kitchen into the living room as the Bone Masters' numbers increased. Bullets and poisoned teeth were flying at that point, and he and Squire had flipped over the couch to use as cover.

"We should probably keep a list," Mulvehill said, ejecting the clip from a World War II–era Colt .45 and slipping in another.

"A list?" Squire questioned, springing up over the back of the couch to spray the kitchen with automatic gunfire from a MAC-10 machine pistol.

"Yeah, of all the shit we've taken . . ."

It was his turn now, and he sprang up from behind the grayish blue couch and eyed the doorway. There were far more of the pale-skinned assassins than he would have thought. Mulvehill fired. He missed twice but managed to get a head and two gut shots before dropping back down for cover.

". . . broken, or shit, just generally abused."

Squire was getting ready to pop up again. "So, this list." He considered. "Would it be our responsibility to replace the items on it?"

The goblin jumped up, aimed, and let out a scream as a Bone Master lunged over the furniture, a curved dagger of yellowed bone in its hand.

"Son of a bitch!" Squire screamed. He squeezed off multiple blasts from the machine pistol, but they missed, chewing up the hardwood floor and a lamp table in the corner of the living room.

"Watch the kitchen!" Mulvehill yelled as he threw himself on top of the assassin, trying to pin its flailing body to the floor.

The Bone Master was smaller, younger, but no less dangerous than its brethren. It shrieked as it tried to climb to its feet, slashing the air with the dagger. Mulvehill landed atop its scrawny arm, pinning it to the floor.

"They're making a move!" Squire shouted, spraying the kitchen area with bullets.

"Busy now!" Mulvehill grunted as the struggling killer tried to free its arm, clawing at Mulvehill's face with jagged fingernails. Mulvehill shook his head violently, trying to avoid the hand, applying as much weight as he could upon the killer's arm, waiting for the satisfying—

Crack!

The assassin cried out with a mixture of rage and pain. It thrashed wildly, trying to retrieve its weapon with the other hand, but Mulvehill did not give him the chance. Rolling atop the assassin, he pressed the muzzle of the gun into the killer's stomach and fired two shots where its heart should have been. And he must have been right, for the pale-skinned killer went suddenly still.

He stared into the face of the demon. *How many does this make today?*

"Help?" Squire squawked, firing his machine pistol until it was empty.

Mulvehill tore his eyes from the cooling corpse and popped up over the couch. The doorway was crammed with targets, and he began to fire. The bodies were piling up, and he and Squire were using them as cover, many shots striking those who were already dead.

His clip nearly empty, he ducked back down and reached into his pocket for another.

"I'm almost out," Squire said, snapping his own clip into the stalk of the machine pistol. "This is it."

"What else do we have?" Mulvehill asked, chambering a round and rising up to fire in one fluid movement.

Squire fumbled through the duffel. "Let's just hope what we've got left for bullets will outnumber the assassins," he said. "Going to do some quick recon and be right back."

The goblin crawled across the floor to a nearby patch of shadow, disappearing within as if he'd just waded into a small pond. It gave Mulvehill the creeps, which in and of itself was pretty damn funny. Five years ago, he would have been screaming his fool head off and running to the psych unit at Mass General.

He peeked over the top of the couch, trying to see into the kitchen. It was dark in there now, the Bone Masters probably using the cover of shadow to prepare for their next assault. There was a sudden burst of commotion somewhere inside the room—an explosion of screams and gunfire that illuminated the smoky darkness of the kitchen. Mulvehill could see bodies falling in the staccato flashes of machine-gun blasts and began firing himself, picking off as many of the Bone Masters as he could.

Squire's head suddenly surged up from the pool of shadow he'd disappeared into, and Mulvehill reflexively swung in that direction, aiming his gun.

"Easy, there, Tex," the goblin said, hauling his squat body up from the darkness. "This is empty, by the way." He tossed the machine pistol down and rummaged through duffel bag for something else.

"Any idea how many are left?" Mulvehill asked.

"Too many," the goblin replied grimly. "Multiple passages of shadow, all leading into the kitchen. I managed to stop up one of them, but there are too many more."

"I don't know how much longer we can hole up here," Mulvehill said in all seriousness.

"Yeah," Squire agreed, finding a pistol and loading the chamber with stray bullets from the floor.

Mulvehill was getting ready to use up the last of his clip when he heard a voice from behind him. He and Squire turned as one, aiming their weapons at the striking sight of Assiel.

"It appears that things have grown most dire," the angel said.

"You might want to get down," Squire suggested. "They're firing poisoned teeth, and we already know how you angel guys do with the teeth."

Mulvehill noticed the twin knives. "What's up with the knives?" he asked the angel.

Assiel looked at the blades, moving them in such a way that they glinted in the feeble light. "I thought I would assist you."

Squire chuckled. "What are you gonna do, take their temperature?"

The angel fixed the goblin in a frightening stare. "Just because I'm a healer doesn't mean that I don't know how to fight," he said as he slowly rose to his full height. "Remember, I did fight in the Great War."

The angel looked out over their cover to the kitchen beyond. "You two might consider heading for cover upstairs."

"What about you?" Mulvehill asked.

"Me?" Assiel asked. "I'm going to the kitchen." Then he leapt over the couch and ran toward the room.

And as Mulvehill and Squire moved to the stairs, the screams of dying Bone Masters mingled with an angel physician's cry of battle.

CHAPTER TWENTY-NINE

The Filthies found the Nomads and Samson's children not long after Remy disappeared behind the door.

They came at the group from the shadows of the city, fluttering upon broken and stunted wings, clutching crude weapons of iron adorned with mere tufts of fire in their pathetic hands.

Azza reached down deep within himself to find the pity. Here were the once divine beings that had ostracized his Nomad brethren and him, called them cowards for not choosing sides during the Great War. Now those who had rejected them suffered the rigors of the future that the Nomads had foreseen, beings of purity and light reduced to twisted perversions of their once divine selves.

The Nomads and Samson's children stood together as the Filthies drew nearer.

"Shouldn't we be leaving now?" the one called the Fossil suggested.

"There will be no more running," Azza replied, staring into the darkness of the ruined city, remembering.

The Nomads had been invited to the Unification of Heaven and Hell, the welcoming of the Morningstar back into the holy fold. They had not accepted Heaven's invitation, choosing instead to watch from the cities of man.

And as they had awaited the great change, Azza could not help but wonder if this was the end of their brotherhood. With everything unified, a wholeness brought to what was once in disarray, the Nomads would no longer be necessary.

They, too, would be welcomed back to the fold.

They, too, would be unified.

Azza had to admit that something deep inside of him welcomed the change, for he, too, remembered how it had once been, before the war.

The Filthies swarmed, but they did not attack, stopping yards away, shrieking and shaking their weapons.

"So are they going to fight, or what?" the child Leila asked, clenching and unclenching her fists, ready to charge. Her brothers were ready as well, just waiting for the call to battle.

Azza did not answer. Silently he watched as the gathering of Filthies parted in the middle, allowing their Lord and Master to come forth.

The past moving toward inevitable change.

"Where is he?" Michael asked, his scars all the more prominent as he stood there. "Where is the Seraphim Remiel?"

When Heaven fell, it was no surprise.

The Nomads had known that something would occur, but not exactly what. They had been awaiting change, and there it was in all its devastating glory.

And as Heaven and Hell collided, falling in upon themselves and raining down upon the world of man, the Nomads did as they always had. They watched, and they waited.

Searching for a sign that told them what change would be the last.

And from the wreckage of the world, they saw him emerge—Remiel, an agent of change himself. Was it not the Seraphim warrior that had abandoned Heaven after the Great War, choosing instead to live amongst humanity? And wasn't it Remiel who had inadvertently helped Lucifer Morningstar return to his former glory, leading to Unification and the horrors that followed?

Yes, Remiel—this Remy Chandler—in him the Nomads found what was to be the last agent of change.

Azza considered Michael's question for a moment before answering. "He's gone for now."

"Gone?" Michael questioned. "Gone where?"

Azza recalled the broken creature that had crawled from the wreckage of Unification, a shadow of the glory that had once been. He had lost everything, the façade of humanity that he had worn so proudly, his glorious divinity—his connection to the Lord God, which had always been his right, the fire that was in all the Creator's winged children, driven to madness by the loss. He remembered how they had approached the Seraphim and offered him a chance to join with them.

And the Seraphim had agreed, for he'd had much to atone for.

That there must come an end, before there can be a beginning.

"There are things that must be put in order before . . . ," Azza started to explain, but was interrupted by the wailing creak of rusty hinges from somewhere behind him.

"Before what?" Michael demanded impatiently.

Azza and all the others turned away from Michael to look upon the figure of Remy standing just outside the open door. He held in his hand a pistol that glistened as if reflecting the full glory of the noonday sun, but the sun had not shone in this sky for so very long.

"Before he brings it all to an end," Azza finished, but he doubted that Michael was listening.

"So, what did I miss?" Remy asked.

The Archangel Michael cried out, and the Filthies swarmed, with murder in their soulless eyes.

Just seeing Remiel standing there with his cocksure insolence was enough to fill Michael with a rage that could scour the world.

Deep down Michael had always blamed Remiel for what had transpired, the Seraphim soldier's defection from Heaven, the catalyst for what Heaven and the world had become.

If it hadn't been for Remiel—for Remy Chandler—Lucifer Morningstar would have remained a prisoner in his own mind, never to remember who he had once been, never to rise and pose the kind of threat that would cause the Almighty to consider his forgiveness.

Unification never to be attempted.

Remy Chandler.

Michael had felt in the very fiber of his being that something was not right, that the Almighty's decision had not been thought out, but who was going to argue with the Creator of all things?

All he could do was what he was told, and watch as it all played out, hoping that his blessed Creator was right . . . that he would be wrong . . . and a new and glorious phase, on a par with creation itself, was about to begin.

Michael still could not remember exactly what had happened. He saw it all in jagged fragments, terrible flashes that left deep and painful scars upon the flesh of his memory. One moment the Lord of Lords thrived, drawing the pieces of a dismembered Heaven together, and then there were the shrieks of war—an attack upon the most sacred of ceremonies. Foul winged beasts filled the air.

He remembered the glint of something golden, the flash of a weapon—a pistol molded from the very essence of the Morningstar. He could not see who wielded it, but God fell as a result of it, with Heaven right behind, and the world of man shattered below.

Michael had believed for the briefest of moments that that was the end, but then he convinced himself that it was a test, that somehow God still lived and was testing those who had survived the failings of Unification.

Those who managed to thrive in this new and twisted wasteland would be ushered into a new Heaven. That was how it *had* to be.

For why else was he here?

With the sight of Remiel, Michael's anger flared, and he decided to do what should have been done a long time ago. There was no room for one such as Remiel in God's new Heaven.

But then he saw what the Seraphim was holding—a golden gun.

And suddenly, Michael believed he knew the answer to the mystery that had haunted him since Heaven's fall.

The Filthies came at them in a wave of shrieking ferocity, and Samson's children charged ahead to their attack head-on, screaming at the top of their lungs.

Remy raised the Pitiless pistol to fire but hesitated as Azza and his Nomad brothers stood in front of him.

"We will handle them," Azza said, as crackling black energy began leaking from their bodies.

Tendrils of jagged, living darkness leapt from their bodies to ensnare the Filthies as they dropped down from the air upon them. A savage roar temporarily silenced the sounds of battle, and Remy looked over to see Baarabus leaping catlike from a perch on a nearby building's ledge, to pounce upon multiple Filthies, dragging them from the sky to the rubble-strewn streets below.

Remy stood at the center of the maelstrom, the God-killing pistol still clutched in his hand, and through the madness he saw Michael.

The archangel stood in the distance, a battle between them. Once he had been one of the most handsome and stalwart of God's creations, but now he was a twisted thing that served only to remind everyone of what they had lost.

A time that had been murdered.

But it also served to remind Remy of the seemingly impossible burden he had accepted—to somehow right this world.

Their eyes locked from across the bloody expanse, and Remy saw a hate that was like a living thing. He was drawn to it, pulled across the combat-filled city street toward the twisted mockery of what had once been a thing of awesome beauty.

The Filthies tried to stop him, but Remy was on a mission, firing the Pitiless pistol and dispatching his attackers with robotic efficiency as he methodically made his way toward their leader. Michael did not flee, damning Remy with his one good eye, the hate leaking from his body like lethal radiation from a reactor breach. But Remy would not be deterred.

A thick gathering of Filthies collected on either side of their master, desperate to protect him. But Remy moved closer, the Pitiless pistol buzzing happily in his hand, glad that it was again serving its purpose.

The Filithies looked to be about to attack when the archangel spoke.

"Join the others," he ordered. "Die in my name elsewhere," he added, waving away his protectors.

The Filthies hesitated, staring at their leader in disbelief, but then reluctantly carried out its bidding, hopping and flying off to fight alongside the others of their ilk.

"Is this what you wanted?" Michael asked Remy, the poison of his hate all the more intense.

"I could ask you the very same question," Remy replied.

"You could," Michael said, turning his white and damaged eye toward him. "But I wonder if we want the same."

"I can't imagine that we're too far off."

Michael considered that for a moment. "I want the nightmare to end. I want all of this to fade away like the mists over the fields of grass just outside the Golden City. Do you remember the fields, Remiel?"

Remy could see them, a vision of the past just behind his eyes. "I do. But I also remember them stained with the blood of our brothers."

It was as if Michael had been slapped, a sneer appearing upon his wan features.

"You remember a time long gone, brother," Remy continued. "Those idyllic fields, that memory of perfection . . . The War changed all that."

"It did," Michael agreed. "But we fought to get them back . . . to make it how it once had been."

"And no matter how much we fought, how much blood was spilled, it was never the same."

A rage seemed to descend upon the archangel, the scars on his pale skin growing more pronounced. "He was to blame for that," he spat. "The perfect child . . . the Son of the Morning. He was always His favorite, no matter how much pain he caused."

There was some truth to the words, but Remy saw no point in stoking Michael's simmering fury.

"And look," Michael continued his rant. "Look at what has happened. . . . Look at what Lucifer has caused."

"God wanted things to be whole again," Remy said. "Like you wanted the perfection of the fields outside the Golden City. He wanted it to be that way again, and Unification was to give us that."

Michael's face twisted as if he'd been given poison. "Unification killed us all."

"But it wasn't supposed to. Something . . . someone . . ."

There were images in Remy's mind again, flashes of recollection that had no place—no meaning. He saw a man, a pale-skinned man with hair as black as ravens' feathers.

And on each hand he wore a ring.

"Yes, someone was responsible," Michael said, dragging Remy from the strange vision.

Michael was eyeing the weapon in Remy's hand, and he slowly raised it, as if to show him.

"Godkiller," Michael said.

Remy did not understand.

"Godkiller," the archangel said again. "All weapons of power should have a name, and that should be its name."

"Fitting," Remy said, suddenly no longer thinking of it as Pitiless.

"Is that how you're going to do it?" Michael asked.

"Do what?"

"Fix things," Michael replied with a condescending sneer. "Isn't that what the great Remy Chandler does? Makes things right again?"

"I'm going to try," Remy said after a moment's contemplation.

"Will you give me back my fields of gold, Remiel?" Michael asked.

Remy looked at him, remembering what he had once been, and did not answer.

"I had it in my mind that I was going to kill you," Michael said. "That with you dead, things could move on, that a new Heaven would be given to us—the survivors . . . the faithful."

"And now?"

Michael looked at him, the hate no longer radiating from his eyes—there was something else coming from them now.

Was it pity?

"It's not up to me," the archangel said. He looked past Remy and tossed back his head, emitting a horrible, groaning cry.

The Filthies ceased their fighting and gathered round Michael once more.

"Do you think He could forgive you?" Michael asked Remy as he turned away.

"For failing Him?" Remy was confused.

Michael's shoulders shook as if he was laughing. Without a reply, he continued to walk into the corpse of the city, his surviving legions at his side.

CHAPTER THIRTY

Every time he found himself in the middle of shit like this, Squire promised himself it would be the last time.

At the foot of the stairs leading up to Remy's bedroom, he turned to see that Mulvehill had stopped to fire his weapon, managing to take out pale-skinned demonic assassins that had made it past the badass angel who was in the kitchen cleaning their fucking clocks.

Squire's gaze lingered on the cop a bit too long. He was a complete stranger half a day ago, but now . . .

That fucking friend thing always got him. He got attached way too easily; it had been that way with all the others, too. So what if he wasn't from this world? In this reality, it had provided him with more of a home than he'd had for many a year.

Seeing his own world crumble . . . watching his friends die even as they fought valiantly to turn the tide of darkness: It had almost finished him off. It had become survival of the fittest, and he'd hit the Shadow Paths, trying to lose himself in the dimension of shadows that existed amongst the multitude of realities. Honestly, he'd believed he would live out his lifetime alone, existing in the shadows, but no matter how hard he tried to resist, the various realities—variations of the world he'd loved and lost—always seemed to draw him back.

And there was always heartbreak, and more swearing that he'd never do it again.

And, of course, here he was again.

Squire aimed his pistol, squinted down the end of the barrel, and fired. A demon went down with a head shot, but there were more behind him, and not enough bullets to truly matter.

"C'mon," Mulvehill said as he reached the hobgoblin, grabbing his arm and pulling him up the stairs.

Now would be the time to bail, Squire thought, seeing only ugliness and more sadness to cope with if he were to stick around. There were plenty of shadows to use for escape. Dive right in and leave the sorrow behind—that way he wouldn't have to see what happened; it would remain a mystery, like missing the season finale of a favorite show.

It sucked, but sometimes it was better not knowing.

"What the fuck are you waiting for?" Mulvehill shouted, noticing his hesitation.

Squire really liked this reality, liked Remy Chandler and all the craziness that seemed to circle him. And this Mulvehill guy: Even though they'd just met, there was something about the guy he hadn't felt since . . .

Pangs of sadness pulsed through him as he again remembered those he had called friends—family, really.

Did he really want to go through that again?

A Bone Master was suddenly in front of him, a more conventional weapon, one that fired bullets instead of poisoned teeth, aimed at his face. He knew he could stop it, but . . .

Squire suddenly felt himself violently shoved aside, a body driving the demon to the living room floor. It took him a second to realize what had happened, and he watched as Mulvehill laid into the Bone Master, burying the blade of a medieval battle-axe in the demon's face before it could even get a shot off.

"What, did you doze off?" Mulvehill asked, his breathing coming in short gasps.

Squire looked at the guy and saw in him the kind of friendship that usually took years to cultivate, a bond that many would never even come close to having. Imagine how strong it could be if he stuck around and they managed to survive all this.

It would be fucking epic.

"I was thinking about trying to get into the kitchen," Squire told his friend. "I think I saw a box of Cheez-Its in one of the cabinets. I'm fucking starving."

"Jesus," Mulvehill exclaimed as the two headed up the stairs. "Cheez-Its? Now? I'll buy you a fucking case of Cheez-Its if we make it out of this alive."

Squire smiled at the thought of the future with his friend.

"I'll take you up on that," he said as they made their way to the bedroom at the top of the stairs.

The darkness had become her existence.

In the embrace of the black, she had lived what felt like many lifetimes; the pulse, ebb, and flow of the inky shadows had become everything to her.

That and the memory of her love for Remy.

Linda folded herself around the flame of recollection, the flickering light of love her constant companion in the ocean of darkness.

She was content in this place of liquid shadow, as long as she had her love—her Remy.

It was when the fire seemed to be dwindling—dying—that she lost that sense of contentment and became increasingly concerned. The fire could not go out; she would do everything—anything—to keep it . . . *Remy* . . . alive and with her.

Her emotions caused the waters of black to become more turbulent. No longer was she pulled along in a gentle flow. Now multiple currents tried to drag her in opposing directions.

Linda drew the fire to her, protecting it. She recalled things that she hadn't thought of in . . . *years*? How long had she been here, part of the vast ocean of shadow? How long had she been away from her true home?

Home.

Images flashed before her mind's eye, new sparks of fire causing the flame of her love for Remy to grow stronger. She remembered more clearly why she was there, and the friends that she had left behind.

It was all about Remy. She was trying to save him . . . to bring him back to her and to those who loved him so.

And the fire grew, warming her inside and out, even as the currents of shadow tried to pull her apart, to scatter her pieces about this dark and terrible place.

But the protected flame kept her whole.

Her memories of Remy, and why she was there in this place, kept her whole.

Try as they might, the currents of shadow could not tear her apart, and she found herself actually fighting against the pull, swimming in the oily black as she clutched the fire to her breast.

And from somewhere in the distance, Linda heard a muffled sound like the roar of thunder, or . . .

The crashing of waves upon a beach.

She moved toward the sounds. And as she swam, flowing through the oily black, she found the world to which she had grown so accustomed becoming lighter, brighter. Linda moved toward the light, clutching the fire of her love closer to her with one hand while reaching up with the other.

She would escape this ocean if she could.

Linda drifted upward, a world of lighter tones above in stark juxtaposition to the universe that rushed below her.

It was like she had been struck in the face by the sun, an explosion of light as she broke the surface of the sea, gasping for breath. She had broken through to another world, but even in this one she saw the threat of darkness.

In the sky above, the sun shone, but barely; thick black clouds rolled about its glowing immensity, attempting to enshroud it, to suffocate its warmth and light. Linda started for the shore, pulling herself along with one arm and powerful kicks of her feet, while still holding on to the flame of her love.

She could hear the waves crashing upon the shore and kicked her legs all the harder, desperate to be anywhere but in the water. Finally, she was close enough that she could allow herself to be carried in upon a wave, her tired body tossed upon the sandy shore as if rejected by the sea of darkness.

Linda lay there, collecting herself, until she could once again feel the pull of the ocean on her legs. She sat up and looked at the fire in her hand. It still burned, but softer in its intensity. Legs trembling, she forced herself to her feet, not sure if they would even be strong enough to support her after all that time adrift in the sea of shadow. But the question was quickly forgotten when she saw that she wasn't alone.

An old man and a woman watched her as she haltingly made her way from the surf toward them.

"Hello, Linda," the old man said, his voice immediately filling her with a sense of serenity.

The woman beside him smiled, and Linda immediately recognized her from the photographs in Remy's brownstone. She could feel the fire suddenly burn brighter—warmer—in her hand.

The kindly old man reached for her, to guide her closer. "We're so glad you're finally here."

"Remy needs you more now than ever before," added the woman.

Madeline.

Remy's wife.

Lazarus nearly burst into tears as he watched an age spot blossom on the back of his hand.

Silently he thanked the Lord God for what He was doing but realized there was much he still had to do before accepting His ultimate reward.

Sitting in the small café, NPR droning in the background, Lazarus sipped a cappuccino and waited. He had taken a chair at a table across from the front window, where he could observe the comings and goings on Mass. Ave. He wasn't exactly sure what he was waiting for, but the Lord God had been very specific about where he should be.

And he didn't want to disappoint God, especially after all He'd done for him. Lazarus again recalled the stupidity of his actions, how he'd attempted to make a deal with a group of rogue angels who had wanted to bring about the Apocalypse and end the world of man. He hadn't been thinking clearly then, driven to near madness with the desire to finally die. And that was what the rogues had promised him—betray God, humanity, and his friends, and he would at last be allowed to die. He was ashamed that he'd even considered such an offer, but at least—thank *God*—someone had stepped forward to stop the rogues and prevent the Horsemen from calling down the Apocalypse.

Remy Chandler, Lazarus thought. His friend, or at least they had been friends before Lazarus had betrayed him.

A sudden blast of static distracted him, and he glanced at the front counter to see the young man who had waited on him fiddling with the stereo system.

"Sorry about that," the young man said as public radio was replaced with music.

Lazarus nodded and turned his attentions back to the street outside, where he caught movement on the steps of a brownstone directly across from the coffee shop. There was a man climbing the steps to the front door. There didn't seem to be anything particularly special about the man, but for some reason, Lazarus could not look away. He watched the man ring the buzzer on the side of the doorway, wait a few moments, and then push open the door to disappear inside the building.

And then Lazarus noticed the song that was playing on the radio, and things started to make a strange sort of sense. Mick Jagger was singing, *"Please allow me to introduce myself / I'm a man of wealth and taste. . . ."*

Lazarus chuckled, raising the last of his cappuccino to his mouth and finishing it off. Then he wiped the foam from his lips and stood.

"Thanks, come again," the young man said, as Lazarus headed for the door.

"No, thank *you.*" Lazarus smiled, leaving the coffee shop, closing the door on the strains of the Rolling Stones' "Sympathy for the Devil."

He crossed the street and stopped in front of the brownstone; like many old Boston buildings, it seemed to house a small business on the first floor and apartments above.

A UPS truck pulled up behind him with a chill-inducing screech of brakes, and Lazarus immediately climbed the steps to the front door of the building. The delivery driver, carrying a small package, joined him a few moments later, and Lazarus stepped aside politely, allowing him access to the buzzers.

"Yes?" answered a voice.

"UPS delivery," the man said.

"Come on up," said the cheerful voice, and the door buzzed loudly, the driver pushing open the door into the lobby.

Lazarus followed, all the while giving off a level of confidence that said he belonged. He lingered on the first floor while the driver headed up the stairs. From what he could see, the level belonged entirely to a small men's clothing and tailor shop, and he perused a window display of some new shirt-and–silk tie combinations. Sauntering over to the door, he peered inside. It was quiet, and he wasn't even sure if the establishment was open yet, when an older gentleman with a tape measure around his neck suddenly appeared from the back and approached. Lazarus quickly turned and began to walk away.

"The person you're looking for is inside," he heard the man call from behind him.

Lazarus slowly turned.

"He's inside," the man said, holding the door open and gesturing to the back of the store. "Right this way." He left the door open and headed for the back of the store again, as if he expected Lazarus would follow.

Cautiously, Lazarus entered the store, carefully closing the door behind him. The man had already disappeared into the back, but Lazarus could hear voices in conversation and found himself drawn to them.

In the back of the small store, a series of three mirrors had been set up in front of a raised pedestal. On the pedestal stood the man Lazarus had seen enter the brownstone, his image reflected three times, from three positions, as the tailor prepared to take his measurements.

"Are you looking for me?" the man asked.

Lazarus wasn't sure what he had been expecting from the man, but he was certain that it was something more . . . menacing. "I am," he replied.

The man lifted his arms while keeping his eyes upon Lazarus' reflection in the mirror directly in front of him. "So, what is it I can do for you, Lazarus?"

Lazarus was a bit taken aback. "You know who I am?"

"I do. I also know who you've been working for of late."

Lazarus did not respond to that.

After the Apocalypse had been averted, he'd found himself washed out to sea, suffering death and resurrection multiple times before finally being pulled from the grip of the Atlantic Ocean by a fishing boat off of Newfoundland. Feeling truly lost, he'd attempted to drown himself in alcohol, but one night while asleep in a freezing alley in Nova Scotia, he was awakened by an old man who was so much more than that.

An old man who promised forgiveness and final death if Lazarus was to serve Him faithfully.

How do you say no to God?

"I'm guessing you have a message for me?" the man prompted.

"I do, but . . ." Lazarus' eyes darted to the tailor, who had wrapped his tape measure around the man's throat to measure his neck size.

"You're worried about Donahan here." The man smiled, and for a moment Lazarus wasn't sure that he'd ever seen anyone quite so— beautiful.

"Well," Lazarus stammered.

"You needn't worry," the man reassured him. "Donahan was one of my soldiers during the war. He's been doing penance here on Earth for the last fifty years or so; isn't that right, Don?"

The fallen angel smiled thinly, continuing to take the man's measurements.

"And in his time here, he's become quite the tailor. I wouldn't think of going to anyone else for a suit." And then he must have noticed the look on Lazarus' face. "What is it?" he asked.

"Excuse me?"

"That look. When I mentioned never going to anyone else for a suit, you made a face."

"Did I?"

"You did. Why?"

"Perhaps . . ."

"Perhaps?"

"Perhaps because I wouldn't imagine that somebody like you . . ."

"Somebody like me," the man said, and smiled radiantly.

"I couldn't imagine someone like you needing a suit."

"Why wouldn't I need a suit?"

Lazarus shrugged. "Do they even wear suits in . . . ?"

"Do they wear suits in Hell?"

"Well, yes."

The man chuckled as the tailor moved down to his legs. "Of course we wear suits in Hell, especially when our armor is at the cleaners."

Lazarus found himself actually chuckling, feeling far more at ease with this being than he would ever have imagined.

"Besides, I have to look sharp for Unification," he added. "So what is it that you've come to tell me?" the man asked, changing the subject.

"*He* sent me to tell you that things are in flux," Lazarus began.

"In flux?"

"Yes, there are some things that might . . ."

"Will Unification still occur?" the man interrupted, a dark seriousness coming over his handsome features.

"Yes, but there could be things that might affect the ceremony."

"What kind of things?"

"*He* didn't say."

"So you can't be more specific?"

Lazarus shook his head. "If I could, I would, but you know what I do. . . ." He stopped, regretting the words as soon as they left his mouth.

"Go on," the man prompted.

"I don't think it has to do with anything, but . . ."

"Go on," the man ordered.

"Remy Chandler," Lazarus said quickly. "The Seraphim that left the Golden City after . . ."

"I know who he is." The way the words were spoken implied much.

"He's currently in a bit of trouble—demonic assassins attempting to collect on a contract."

"What does that have to do with Unification . . . with me?"

"I'm not sure that it does," Lazarus said. "But I know that Remy had something to do with your return to power, and . . ."

"I find your concern for the Seraphim of interest," the man suddenly said, his tone far darker than it had been. "Didn't you betray the angel—the world, actually—when you actively participated in the summoning of the Four Horsemen of the Apocalypse a few years back?"

Lazarus felt like he'd been kicked in the stomach, his most chilling indiscretion laid out before him by the master of indiscretions.

"He was a good friend before my lack of judgment got the better of me," Lazarus said. "I was hoping . . ."

"Hoping what?" the man asked sharply. "That I might step in and somehow alleviate your guilty conscience?"

"No, that wasn't why I mentioned it at all," Lazarus attempted to explain. "It's just that—"

"Is that it, Lazarus?" The man cut him off. "Is that all that you have for me from Him?"

Lazarus slowly nodded. "Yeah, that's it."

"Thank you," the man said dismissively. "I'll be sure to keep in mind what you've said once the ceremony begins."

Lazarus stood there a moment longer, wanting to say something more but realizing that it probably wasn't the best of ideas. So without another word, he turned and walked out of the building.

Making his way down the stairs, he felt surprisingly lighter. He had delivered the Lord's message to the Morningstar, and hopefully planted a seed as well.

For Remy and his friends needed as much help as they could get.

"Blue or black?" Donahan asked.

Lucifer had been lost in thought, recalling a time when he'd believed himself to be somebody else and not the Son of the Morning.

"Excuse me?" he questioned, realizing that he'd been spoken to.

"Blue or black?" the angel tailor repeated.

Lucifer's reflection stared back, confused.

"Your suit," Donahan explained. "Do you want blue or black?"

"Oh, certainly," Lucifer answered. "Let's go with the black."

"Very good." Donahan finished the measurements. "You were rather hard on the messenger, weren't you, Lucifer?"

"Do you think?" he asked, stepping down off the pedestal.

"Things seemed to get a little tense when he mentioned the Seraphim."

"Remy Chandler," Lucifer said. If it hadn't been for him . . .

"His name seemed to strike a nerve. Why is that?"

The tailor had moved over to a small desk and was jotting down the various measurements from memory.

It had been Remy Chandler who had inadvertently returned the Morningstar to the Hell prison of Tartarus, where Lucifer's memory of who he was—what he was—was eventually restored.

"I have no idea," Lucifer lied. "I'm barely familiar with the angel."

Donahan looked up from his scribbles. "Seriously? I got a sense that the two of you . . ."

"The messenger was mistaken." Then Lucifer cut to the chase. "When will the suit be ready?"

Donahan considered whether to continue with his course of questioning and decided instead to drop it.

It was a very smart idea.

"How does tomorrow sound?" the tailor asked.

"Tomorrow?" Lucifer questioned. "Slowing down in your old age, are we?"

The old fallen angel shrugged.

"I suppose that's fine," Lucifer said. "I'll send someone to pick it up."

Donahan went back to his notepad. "Very good, sir."

Lucifer walked to the front of the store, stopping before a display of ties as though he were considering the various styles, colors, and patterns, but in fact his mind was preoccupied with other things.

Distractions.

A distraction named Remy Chandler.

CHAPTER THIRTY-ONE

The closer they drew to the Garden, the thicker the vegetation became.

The ruins of the city were becoming more choked with leafy vines, many of the structures nearly invisible in the overgrowth. Remy imagined a time not too far in the future when the city would be completely hidden, claimed by the outward-spreading Garden of Eden, and decided it wouldn't be such a bad thing. Thriving life was far more preferable to decaying ruins.

"Can't imagine it will be much farther," said a voice from behind.

Remy turned to see the Fossil hurrying to catch up with him, ahead of the weary-looking children of Samson.

"How are they doing back there?" Remy asked of the children.

"They're tired," the Fossil said. "Tired and sad."

Remy turned and made eye contact with Leila. He could see the sadness behind their intensity. "It isn't easy to lose family," he said, speaking from experience. The image of the freezer floor at Methuselah's appeared within his mind, and he quickly pushed it away.

"No," the Fossil said. "But they knew this trip wouldn't be an easy one."

"I haven't seen Baarabus since . . . ," Remy began, looking around for signs of the demonic dog.

"He's around," the Fossil said. "Where else does he have to go?"

"He hates me for making him into what he is," Remy said.

"You're right, but there isn't much that can be done about it now. You did what you did, and he's the end result, good or bad."

"I shouldn't have done it."

The Fossil looked at him and smiled crookedly, his face a mass of painful-looking sores. "Actually, *you* didn't."

"It was still me."

"But it wasn't," the Fossil corrected. "That decision was made by a Remy Chandler changed by the most horrific situation."

"Who's to say that I wouldn't have done the exact same thing?"

"Who's to say?" the Fossil agreed with a shrug. "But *you*—the Remy who is here with us now—didn't make that decision, weren't changed by the horrors of what you saw."

Remy stared at the man, the meaning of his words beginning to permeate.

"You're a different Remy," the Fossil continued. "And maybe your solution to the problem of this world will be different, too."

"Is that why you're all still here?" Remy asked, gazing at the path ahead of them. He could just make out the heavily robed Nomads as they led the way through the weed-choked rubble. "Because there's still a chance that I can somehow salvage something from this wreck of a world?"

"It's because you've saved us by giving us a purpose."

"This is a purpose?" Remy scoffed.

"It's something. It's movement toward what could be a new beginning."

"That's what the Nomads keep talking about: an ending for something new to begin," Remy said.

"It's that new beginning that keeps us going," the Fossil said. "And besides, it's better than sitting around just waiting to die."

The Pitiless pistol, the Godkiller, pulsed at Remy's waist, and he felt compelled to pull it free. "Somehow this is the answer," he said, admiring the powerful weapon that glistened like gold even though there was very little light. "My other self hid this away until he was ready."

"But are *you* ready?" the Fossil asked.

"I think I am. At least I think I will be when the time arrives."

Remy remembered some of the flashes of memory he'd seen upon taking up the gun. He saw the dark-skinned man with the rings, his identity and role a complete and utter mystery, but somehow Remy knew he was important.

"What's your part in all this, old-timer?" Remy asked the Fossil, wondering if there could be a connection between the man with the rings and the scab-covered Fossil.

The Fossil nervously began to pick at a thick layer of scab on the side of his nose. "Let's just say I have a healthy amount of guilt over what happened, as do all who survived, I think. I'd like to help make things right," he answered.

Remy noticed that Azza had emerged from a particularly overgrown area and was standing, waiting.

"What's up?" he asked as they reached the Nomad leader.

"We have arrived," the angel said. He turned and gestured down a passage cut through the thick overgrowth of vines. "Through there you will find the entrance. The entrance to the Garden of Eden."

Remy and the others followed Azza through the passage, emerging into what looked like a verdant jungle. The growths were wild, unkempt, and nothing that had been seen on Earth before.

It was like stepping onto another planet.

Azza and his brethren stood before one of two vine-covered pillars, the heavy metal gates that once hung between them lying haphazardly upon the ground, twisted and bent.

"Here it has fallen," Azza said, his Nomad brothers bowing their heads in reverence.

Remy looked at the Garden beyond the broken gates. The jungle within appeared even wilder than it had been the last time he'd seen it.

"You say that Heaven—the Golden City—is somewhere inside?"

Azza followed Remy's gaze through the open passage. "A part of Unification was successful," he explained. "The Garden was welcomed back home to the glory of Heaven, but then . . ."

"It all came falling down," Remy finished, squinting his eyes, trying to see through the dense foliage, hoping to catch a glimpse of the city beyond.

"Through these twisted gates you will find what you have traveled so far in search of," Azza said.

"The reason why I'm here," Remy said quietly.

He looked away from the passage to the others. "Well, let's get going." He started toward the opening but noticed that the Nomads held back.

"Aren't you coming?"

"This is where our journey together ends," Azza said, folding his hands within his robe.

"Seriously?" Remy asked. "You've come this far, and now you want to call it quits?"

"Our purpose was to assist you in getting here," the leader said. "The rest is entirely in your hands."

Remy didn't know what to say. He had been counting on the Nomads and their supernatural might to help them with whatever they would be facing in the jungles of Eden and beyond.

Instead, they began to back away slowly.

The Fossil came to stand beside Remy then, laying a bloody and scab-encrusted hand upon his arm. "You won't get rid of us that easily," he said.

Leila and the remaining children of Samson came to join him as well.

"We've come this far," she said. "Might as well see it through to the very end. And who knows, maybe it'll be a happy one."

"Maybe it will," Remy conceded, and actually managed the faintest of smiles.

He gave the Nomads one more look, sensing it would be the last he'd see of these angels. "To endings and new beginnings," he called out.

Then he turned with a wave, walking through the stone pillars, he and his small band of followers, into Eden.

The Garden appeared sick.

For all the green, there was just as much dead and rotting growth, and Remy remembered the illness that was infecting it the last time he'd been here.

"Looks as though this place is as fucked up as everything else," Leila said.

"Rotten at the core," the Fossil said, causing Remy to look at him questionably. Maybe the old-timer knew more than he was letting on.

He was about to probe a bit when he heard somebody let out a yelp.

Remy glanced over to see one of Samson's children being attacked by a tangle of vines, the dark green vegetation moving serpentlike to enwrap the young man in a constricting hold.

"What the fuck is this?" the man exclaimed, pulling an arm free with a powerful tug, only to have even more vines slither over to grab him again.

Leila went to her brother's aid, pulling the tendrils away, but she, too, became an object of the Garden's attack. The more they fought, the more the Garden reacted, thicker roots and vines exploding up out of the dirt to ensnare them.

"What should we do?" the Fossil asked. Vines gripped him so tightly that they had torn away scabs on his arms, causing him to bleed profusely upon the vegetation.

Remy stood perfectly still, remembering what this was.

Remembering what this was all about.

"Don't fight it," he ordered, and they looked at him as if he was insane. "If you don't fight, it won't think that you're a threat. Trust me on this."

"Trust you?" Leila asked as a thick piece of vine wrapped tighter about her throat.

Remy silently allowed the vines to wrap around his legs, waist, and arms. Begrudgingly, the others stopped their struggles, and eventually, although they were completely immobilized, the Garden stopped its assault.

"Now what?" Leila asked.

"It shouldn't be long now," Remy said.

As if on cue, the ground in front of him started to churn, to boil, thick black dirt being pushed up from somewhere below by some unknown and growing force.

"Tell me you know what this is," the Fossil said.

"Yeah," Remy answered. "I do."

It was like watching a tree grow in time-lapse photography. First the sprout, and then the shaft of what would eventually become the tree. As it grew, Remy watched it take on more aspects of a human form. In its face, he could see a combination of two other familiar faces.

"Jon . . . Izzy, is that you?" Remy asked, feeling the vines covering his body beginning to grow tighter.

The monolith of wood towered above them now, swaying on tree trunk legs.

"The cancer . . . ," the tree creature croaked in a voice that sounded like two speaking as one. "It grows too strong!"

"It's me," Remy said, trying to capture the Gardener's attention. "It's Remy Chandler. Do you remember me?"

The Gardener swayed, looking about the jungle with panicked eyes. "I fight to contain it, but it has become too strong."

"Jon! Izzy! Are you there?"

The tree creature finally seemed to notice him below its powerful mass.

"It's Remy," he said again. "I'm here to help."

The Gardener's face at first registered elation, then twisted in a sudden rage. "There can be no help. . . . God is dead . . . and soon I will be as well . . . and the cancer will go out into the world."

And with those words, the Gardener raised its fist, preparing to strike. Remy struggled within the grasp of the vines, tearing himself free as the fist, thick as a redwood, came down where he'd been mere moments before.

The Gardener, realizing that it had missed, reached for Remy with its other hand. Remy took hold of the Gardener's yearning fingers, amazed at how fragile they were, the wood crumbling as he twisted away in their grasp.

Samson's children had managed to free themselves as well and rushed to help him. He watched as Leila charged the tree creature, throwing herself at the backs of its legs. There was a tremendous snap as she struck, and the Gardener bellowed in surprise and pain as it began to topple, one of its thick legs snapped nearly in two.

Samson's children pounced upon the creature, pinning its thrashing body to the ground. Remy pushed past them to stand above it, looking down into its pained features.

"Jon . . . Izzy," he said, bearing down upon the creature, forcing it to look at him. "It's me . . . Remy. . . . We mean you no harm."

The Gardener seemed to focus on him. "Remy?" it asked, and he saw a spark of recognition in the creature's eyes.

"Yes, it's me. What's happening here? What's wrong?"

"The sickness—they set it free . . . allowed it to grow, change. . . ."

"The Shaitan?" he asked. "Are you talking about the Shaitan?"

The tree creature's eyes widened, awash with madness.

"The Shaitan change . . . they evolve. . . ."

"Evolve? What . . . ?"

"They evolve to better fit this horrible world."

The Gardener then fell eerily silent, its body growing still. Remy looked to the others.

"What was it talking about?" Leila asked. "What are Shaitan?"

"Mistakes," the Fossil stated. "Things that should never have existed."

Again Remy was surprised by the amount of knowledge the old-timer seemed to have, and once again, he was distracted before he could pursue it.

Screams sounded from the dense jungle, and the vegetation shook as pale-skinned creatures, their bodies covered in black sigils, exploded from the jungle.

"Those are the Shaitan," Remy announced, readying himself for attack. The children did as well, picking up rocks and tree limbs from the ground to defend themselves.

But the horrible things sprang into the air, skirting around them as they disappeared again into the jungle behind the group.

"What's up with that?" Leila asked.

"I don't know," Remy said, suddenly having a very bad feeling.

What exploded from the jungle next in pursuit of the fleeing Shaitan was something else altogether. It was most definitely Shaitan, but this one was at least thirty feet tall, and from the size of its bulbous stomach, the tightly stretched skin showing off the outline of thousands of eggs, quite pregnant.

Suddenly, Remy understood the words of the Gardener.

The Shaitan were evolving.

Changing to better fit a horrible world.

More Shaitan fled from the jungle in shrieking panic, capturing the attention of what Remy could only think of as the Queen.

The giant eagerly snatched up two of the screaming creatures and without a moment's hesitation shoved one into her enormous maw, swallowing it down with a grotesque-sounding gulp.

"For the good of the spawn," she bellowed, burping noisily before tossing back the other. "My babies will be better than this place," she cried as she chewed. "Masters of a world that the wretched God abandoned."

The Queen's belly pulsed and writhed. She brought huge hands to her naked front, massaging the pale, lumpy skin. "From the best of us, you will be made even better. The next spawn of our kind even stronger than the last."

And then she noticed Remy and the children of Samson.

They had dived for cover when she'd first appeared, but her keen eyes picked them out from their jungle surroundings.

"What do we have here?" she asked with the most horrific of smiles. The ancient sigils that adorned her flesh began to move, flowing across her white skin as if they had a life of their own.

She moved far more quickly than Remy would have thought possible, charging at them, kicking up clouds of dirt and rock as she tore through the vegetation after them. They all did the best they could to avoid her clutches, but someone was bound to be caught, and Leila happened to be the one. The girl screamed and kicked, struggling in the monster's grasp, as Remy and her brothers attacked. They punched and kicked at the giant's legs, but it seemed to have little effect, for the Queen just swatted them away like insects.

Desperately, Remy pulled the Godkiller from his waistline, aiming the weapon at the loathsome giant. A screeching Leila was just about to be dropped into the Queen's cavernous maw when the monster froze, sniffing at the air.

Remy stood there, pistol aimed. It would be a head shot for sure—if only he could fire. Something prevented him from squeezing the trigger—a memory, a recollection that came at him like a runaway train.

"An angel of Heaven," the Queen cried excitedly, tossing Leila away like a piece of trash. "What magick its flesh and bones and divine fire will provide my unborn!"

The Queen reached for him, but Remy still did not fire the God-killer.

For he was remembering another time when he'd held the gun and had shot to kill.

CHAPTER THIRTY-TWO

It was time to check their weapons again.

Mulvehill squatted down in the doorway to Remy's bedroom and fished through his pockets, trying to find more clips for his gun.

"I think this is it," he said, continuing to fumble, hoping against hope that he might feel a small pocket of heaviness somewhere and find more bullets where he least expected.

No dice.

"Yeah, I've got about four shots left, tops," Squire said, searching the duffel bag and his own pockets, finding some stray bullets and something that might have once been food. The goblin popped it into his mouth and began to chew.

"Did you just eat something you found in your pocket?" Mulvehill asked with disgust.

"Yeah."

"Was it even food?"

"Might've been at one time," Squire answered. "Think it could've been a peanut or a really old piece of lint. I'm really not sure."

Mulvehill laughed, even though there really wasn't anything all that funny going on. Squire joined in, his cackle intensifying as if he'd heard the funniest joke of all time.

There was an explosion of something from downstairs that shook the brownstone.

"Oh shit," Squire said, a look of shock on his ugly face. And then he started to laugh insanely again. Mulvehill tried not to look at him but did anyway and began to chuckle along with him.

"You know you're totally fucked up, right?" Mulvehill asked, readying his gun for what would surely be another wave of violence.

"Yeah," Squire answered, stifling his laughter.

"Listen, if this is it, I want to say . . . ," Mulvehill began, but didn't get the chance to finish.

"Save it," Squire interrupted, snapping the barrel of his pistol back into the gun. "I'm not a big fan of last words."

They were both standing in the hallway now, just outside the bedroom doorway, peering down the stairs. A fine smoke had started to drift up from the living room below.

"So, what do you think we should do?"

"Well, one of us should probably stay up here and protect Remy and the others."

"Sounds about right," Mulvehill agreed. The sounds of battle were growing louder, having obviously moved into the living room from the kitchen. "You want to stay up here while I . . ."

"No."

"Well, I don't want to stay up here, either," Mulvehill said. "How about whoever has the most bullets . . ."

"You have the most bullets; we already fucking know that," Squire said. "All right, whoever has the most bullets stays here." And the hobgoblin bolted down the stairs.

"No fucking way," Mulvehill called out behind him as he started down the stairs as well. "If you get killed right now, I'm going to be royally pissed."

A powerful, blood-covered figure appeared in the living room doorway below them, and Squire fired. Assiel moved his head aside and the bullet embedded itself in the wall behind him.

"Oh shit." Squire gasped.

The angel glared but was quickly distracted by the Bone Master assassins that threw themselves at him. With a birdlike shriek, he drove them back again with his slashing blades.

"Get up to the room!" he yelled to Mulvehill and Squire.

"We can help," Mulvehill said, moving forward, his gun ready.

"No!" the angel commanded. "Go to the room and barricade yourselves inside. Awaken Remy's friends if you can."

Assiel was wild with his blades, slashing and stabbing crazily, but Mulvehill knew that it was only a matter of time before . . .

Multiple shots were fired and he saw the angel's skin erupt, blood spewing from the entry wounds.

"What about Remy?" Mulvehill cried as he and Squire began to retreat.

"It's too late for him! You must try to save those who can be helped."

Assiel heard the human and the hobgoblin race up the stairs again. He chanced a final look over his shoulder and saw them standing in the doorway.

"No worries," the angel tried to reassure them. "At least this time I die on the side of the righteous."

And with those words, his allies slammed closed the door, and the angelic healer turned his full attention to his foes.

The Bone Masters had massed in the living area, watching him with cold killers' eyes, smiles on some of their twisted faces. He knew what they were waiting for; he could feel the effects starting to overcome his body.

The very poison that had rendered the Seraphim Remiel so close to death now coursed through his own body. And he knew not how much longer he had before he would succumb to its deadly effects.

Assiel had always wondered when and how his death would come, knowing only that it was inevitable. He'd always been shocked that he hadn't died in the Great War. The Lord God Almighty had been merciful to him afterward, allowing him penance upon the world of man. The angel had indeed recognized the error in his judgment, even more so after coming to understand humanity and their special place in the heart of God.

And now he knew.

The angel stumbled into the nearby wall. That seemed to make his killers all the more excited, slowly moving toward him en masse, their weapons clutched in their filthy hands. It wouldn't be long now, this he knew. There was a burning numbness in his limbs and joints, making his appendages feel as though they weighed tons.

His vision was beginning to fail, but he could see their numbers as they spread out through the house. There were still too many of them, even though he and the others had taken down quite a few.

He needed to cull the herd, so to speak, and he needed to do it quickly, before he was unable to move. Gripping his twin blades all the tighter, he pushed himself away from the wall and advanced toward his foes.

The Bone Masters stared at him, and he knew they were wondering if this old fallen angel still had any fight left in him.

Assiel smiled and tossed back his head, letting go a shrieking cry of war before leaping at his foes. Did he still have any fight left in him?

Oh yes, he most certainly did.

Ashley guessed that she must have been dozing.

She seemed to be having one of those strange dreams, the kind that seemed so real that the dreamer had no idea she'd fallen asleep. In the dream it was July, and she was sitting in Remy's tiny backyard, Marlowe snoring noisily at their feet. They were talking about the future.

"Four more years of school," she'd told him.

The angel was reclined in a folding beach chair, a Sam Adams Summer Ale clutched in one hand, listening to her intently as she laid out her plans for the future.

It was what she did every night before bed, to help her fall asleep. She planned.

"And after the four years?" he asked, bringing the bottle to his lips.

She preferred Mike's Hard Lemonade to beer, and drank from her bottle before answering his question. "Well, then I'll get my teacher's certificate, and then I'll get a job."

"In the Boston school system?"

"If I can. Sure." It sounded good to her.

"And what if there aren't any jobs?" he asked.

"Then I'll get a job someplace else."

"You'd move from the area—out of state, even?"

She'd already thought about that very thing. "Sure I'd move, if I have to."

Remy made a face and drank some more beer.

"What?" she asked him.

"Moving out of state," he said, making that face again. "What would your parents think?"

She thought for a moment. "I don't know. I don't think they'd care all that much. Remember, I'm an adult now . . . and by then I'll be practically elderly."

"True." Remy nodded slowly.

She had some more of her lemonade. "Will you come visit me at the nursing home?" she asked with a chuckle.

His whole expression changed.

And then she remembered Madeline, and how she had passed away in a nursing home.

"Oh, Remy, I'm sorry!" Ashley exclaimed.

He smiled at her, but there was sadness in it now, no matter how hard he tried to disguise it. "That's all right," he said. "Just feeling a little sensitive these days."

"It must be hard," she said.

"What's hard?"

"To watch time pass by, unaffected, while everything else . . . everybody else . . ." She stopped, realizing she was heading into that dangerously sad place again. *Good one, Ashley,* she thought. He'd already said he was feeling sensitive, and she had to go poking at the wound.

"You have no idea," he said, and she saw a look in his eyes that she'd never seen before, a glimpse of something that suggested he was far sadder than he'd ever let on, that maybe he couldn't take it anymore.

"Are you ever going to leave, Remy?" she asked suddenly.

"The Boston area?" He forced a smile, but it was clear he knew what she'd meant.

"Would you ever go back . . . to where you came from?"

He'd started to peel the label from his beer bottle. She was going to press him for an answer, but she could see that he was still thinking.

Then after what felt like hours, which were probably only seconds— uncomfortable seconds, but seconds nonetheless—he answered.

"This is my home now," he said. "I couldn't imagine returning to . . . that."

And that made her smile.

"Good," she said, finishing up her lemonade. Marlowe lifted his blocky head from the grass and gave her a look. She left her chair and settled on the ground next to him.

"Don't tell me you'd be sad if I left," Remy said. He'd seemed to have shucked off his serious side and was smirking. "You who's going off to school and will probably move out of state—out of the country, even—over the next four years."

She was rubbing Marlowe's nearly hairless tummy, the dog having rolled onto his back for her to be able to reach all the good parts. She was suddenly feeling very serious, imagining what it would be like—what her world would be like without Remy.

"Don't you dare ever leave me, Remy Chandler," she said.

And he smiled at her, a smile that told her he never would, and she had felt safe in that knowledge until—

Something felt wrong with the tree.

Ashley slipped from the dream to . . . *where*? Where was she?

She was in a panic, eyes darting around until she was able to collect enough of her thoughts to remember. She was in that place . . . the place somehow connected to Remy's life force, and she, and Marlowe, and Linda . . .

"Linda," she said aloud.

She looked around, remembering that Linda had left them, gone down into the hole that had opened up at the base of the tree, and . . .

Marlowe was standing away from the tree, looking off at something in the distance.

"What is it, boy?" she asked. She pulled her hands away from the trunk of the tree, where they had been pressed. They were wet, covered in a thick, black substance, like liquid darkness.

The dog was looking out over the Common, the hackles on his thick neck raised, and as she looked as well she could see why.

The Common was dissolving. At first she thought it was some sort of fog, drifting over the landscape, obscuring her view, but then she realized that wasn't the case at all. The Common appeared to be breaking apart and floating away.

"That can't be good," she said, and Marlowe began to whine.

"No," Ashley ordered, furiously petting his head, eyes still on the horror in the distance. "No crying. There will be no crying of any kind, or I will most certainly be crying as well, okay?"

She spun to look at the tree and felt as though she might throw up.

The tree was melting, rivulets of black liquid running down the trunk to the base, saturating the ground and making the hole where Linda had gone seem larger.

The world—Remy's world—was slowly breaking down. Panic threatened to grip her, but she tried to keep it controlled.

Until she noticed something from the corner of her eye and glanced at her hand. It, too, had begun to dissipate.

"Shit! Shit! Shit!" Ashley raced to the enlarging hole and dropped to her knees, Marlowe right beside her.

"Linda!" she screamed into the darkness.

Marlowe barked madly, his barks echoing in the bottomless black.

"Linda! Something's wrong! Remy's world—it's breaking up, Linda! It's breaking up!"

She looked up and saw that it was getting worse, the world—the Common around her fading away to—

Nothing.

"Please, Linda—you have to come back. . . ."

Ashley was crying now.

"Please! . . . I don't know what to do!"

CHAPTER THIRTY-THREE

The Queen saw her opportunity and struck.

The angel of Heaven stood there, his weapon pointed, but he did not fire. She was sure it was because of the sight of her, her awesome visage inspiring sheer, paralyzing terror and hopelessness.

How could anyone—anything—stand against her?

The angel struggled briefly as she ripped him from the ground, though not as much as she would have imagined, but she did not give him another opportunity to strike, instead forcing him into her mouth. She had to unhinge her jaw to make him fit, shoving him down past her flapping tongue and into her throat, the powerful muscles of her esophagus gripping the weakly flailing body as it began its descent into her stomach.

The Queen swallowed and then swallowed again, forcing her still-living prey farther and farther down into her body.

She could already feel the power of his divinity, the bubbling juices of her stomach eagerly splashing upward to digest the angel's body, excited by the prospect of what these divine nutrients would do for her unborn brood.

Since God's death and the fall of Heaven, it had been her sole purpose to create a spawn—a new Shaitan—for a new world. She had been born in the fires of ruin, rising up to wipe away the old and make way for the next stage in the Shaitan evolution.

What a world they would make, the Queen thought, imagining her babies as they tore from their leathery casings and took possession of the world. With the Creator finally gone, it would not be long before they became gods.

It would be glorious.

The Queen felt hungry once again and quickly scanned the jungle for more prey to sustain her. The survivors of the old Shaitan were around—she could smell their foulness in the air—but there were other scents as well.

Human scents, but not entirely.

There was something exotic about these humans, and she believed that it, too, might be something to benefit her children.

"Come out, humans!" she cooed, moving toward the thick patches of jungle. "It will do you no good to hide from me!" With giant hands she parted huge sections of vegetation, searching. "Don't make me angry," she warned. "Or I'll eat your limbs, one at a time, and save your heads for last."

She was already drooling as her dark eyes scanned the bushes for signs of movement. There was a rustle of brush behind her, and the Queen turned in time to see a hint of movement, the shadow of something trying not to be noticed.

"Where oh where might you be?" she asked aloud, pretending she hadn't seen the movement, while meandering intentionally toward the shadowy shape concealed behind the thick underbrush.

She started in another direction, then suddenly dove back at the thick bed of leafy greens and the shape that crouched behind them. Her malicious laugh was cut short, clogged in her terrible throat as she looked upon the unexpected.

Instead of the exotic human morsel that was to fill her belly, there was a beast, black furred and rippled with muscle. It bared its teeth at her, back legs tensing, preparing to pounce.

The Queen barely had time to scream as the demon hound sprang, knocking her backward to the ground, burying its muzzle in the flesh of her belly. She fought valiantly, but the beast's claws and teeth were sharp, and it clung to her, ripping at her magnificence, feeding upon her flesh.

Feeding upon the spawn that were to inherit the world.

Remy was dying in the belly of the Queen, even as his mind reeled from the onslaught of memory too shocking to comprehend.

Unification was in full swing, and everything was right in the universe, everything falling into place in perfect synchronization. He had never known such joy, such happiness before.

But then the feelings began, an assault upon his senses, that grating sound of static from a speaker during the most beautiful of symphonies, that slight taste of bitterness in the most delicious soufflé, the faintest hint of decay within the most beautiful of flower arrangements, the sight of that withered and blackened growth finally found in the center of all that beauty.

He looked around at the gathering of divine creatures—those who had been touched by the power of the Lord—and saw that they were all as he wanted to be, part of the sacred ceremony.

Why couldn't he be as they were? At one with the process—unified.

As the digestive fluids inside the Shaitan monster were burning him, eating at his clothes and the flesh of his body, so was his mind being broken down.

Evil.

It was as if somebody had pushed the fast-forward button on a video player, and his memories jumped ahead. Chaos was erupting in Heaven.

From such beauty, wonder, and awe, there was now only sheer terror. Unification was in turmoil—total disarray.

A writhing, shrieking black cloud exploded up from the green of the Garden, a swarm of life that should never have been given the chance to exist.

Shaitan.

The proto-angels filled the air with their rage and hate, attacking the most holy ceremony.

Was that what happened? Was it these foul creations that brought it all down? Remy tried to hold on to the tattered memories as they burned within his brain.

He curled himself tighter within the belly of the Shaitan Queen, the juices of the creature's stomach consuming him.

It was chaos, what had once been nigh perfect, now pandemonium. Remy tried to find some serenity within the discord.

And he found it in the eyes of God.

The being who was the Creator of it all stood within the confluence of chaos, a calmness in the eye of the storm.

The old man, the one who had warned Remy of the coming of war.

Was this the war He'd spoken of?

Remy's and God's eyes met, and in that moment . . .

Inside the stomach of the Shaitan Queen, Remy was close to dying. The acidic liquids he floated within were completing their purpose, using him to feed the unborn Shaitan, to make them strong.

Strong.

Remy tried to hold it together, to be as calm as God was, but something was wrong—something far worse than what he'd felt, heard, smelled, and seen.

He ripped his gaze from the eyes of God and looked upon the bedlam, finding the one for whom he searched.

His friend and confidant—the fallen angel Fraciel.

Francis.

And in the hand of his friend, he held the gun.

It wouldn't be long before the corrosive juices finished him, and Remy desperately wanted to let go, for he feared the memory that was to come. If he could only hold it back for just a moment longer, it would be gone—*he* would be gone.

Francis was gone now, and the unrest around Remy slowed. He was the center now; he was the one in control.

Remy's eyes again met God's, and strangely he saw in the gaze of his Creator that everything was as it was supposed to be.

This was as it was supposed to be.

But what is this? Remy wondered as Unification failed around him. *What. Is. This?*

The gun . . . the gun was still clutched in his hand, a hand now nothing more than bone with bits of bloody skin floating from the joints. And even though he no longer had eyes to see, Remy knew that he held the weapon—the gun that was called Godkiller.

He held the gun as he had held it before, when . . .

This was the gun forged from the power and rage of the Morningstar, an ultimate weapon to be used for the most dire of tasks. It was in his hand now, and he aimed down the length of the golden barrel at his target.

He aimed at the calm in the center of the storm.

The kindly old gentleman in the finely tailored blue suit.

God.

And Remy fired the gun, committing the atrocity that caused it all to come crashing down.

He had done it.

Remy had done it.

He'd killed the Lord God Almighty.

It couldn't be right. . . . It had to be wrong, but there it was, the memory becoming all the more clear as he replayed it—over and over again inside the theatre of his mind. He had taken the Pitiless pistol from Francis and renamed it with his actions.

Godkiller.

He and the weapon were God's killers.

The revelation was more than he could tolerate, and he felt himself shutting down, retreating so deeply into himself that the end of his existence was only moments away.

Within the belly of the Queen, Remy surrendered. He would not fight it; he would allow it to happen.

He did not deserve his life.

And then the liquids that could have eaten away the horror and shame of what he'd remembered grew suddenly turbulent, rushing to escape the fleshy containment of the Queen's body, rushing outward, carrying his stricken form with it in a wave of foul-smelling internal fluids. It was like being born, only this time he carried with him something far more loathsome than the curse of original sin.

Remy wasn't sure how long he lay there in the drying spew, wishing that he no longer existed.

But he still lived, and as much as it pained him to do so, he opened his eyes to see that he was still in Eden. Rising up, he saw the body of the Shaitan Queen dead upon the ground, her bulbous belly torn open to spill the eggs of what was to be the next step in evil's evolution. The eggs had already begun to rot.

Remy stared at the giant corpse and at the grim expression of pain and perhaps fear that adorned her frozen facial features, wondering what could have caused this.

He heard the growling sound from somewhere behind him and spun around, noticing for the first time that the Godkiller was still clutched in his hand. Remy aimed the pistol at the black mass that slunk toward him, lowering it to his side as he realized what—*who*—it was that approached.

"Baarabus," Remy said, watching in horror as the great demon dog collapsed to the ground at his feet. Dropping the Godkiller, he went to the animal, falling down to his knees and taking the giant dog's head into his lap.

"There you are," Remy said, eyeing the dog's body and seeing that his injuries were quite substantial. "I thought you left town."

"Hmm," the dog grunted, coughing up thick black blood. "Who knew what trouble you'd get yourself into?"

"You're hurt," Remy said, running his hands along the demon dog's body.

"Yeah, that bitch didn't go down without a fight."

Remy's eyes left the dog's broken body to see the bodies of some of Samson's children lying still upon the ground. "I didn't want this," he said with a shake of his head, the weight of what he now knew bearing down upon him.

"It's not about what you want," the dog said. "It's about what has to be."

"I don't know this Remy. I never did. Thought it would just come to me naturally . . . that it would be obvious."

"Nothing's obvious about this," Baarabus said. He coughed again and his body trembled in pain.

Remy held him all the tighter. "It's all right," he said, bending down closer to the dog's head. "I've got you."

"You've got to finish this," the dog said, his voice much softer now.

"I'm not sure I can now," Remy said, the horrible images of what he had done suddenly appearing in his mind.

"Knowing what you know now, do you have a choice?"

Remy gazed off into the jungle and what he knew existed beyond it. "No."

"That'a boy," Baarabus said.

They sat there like that for quite some time, Remy remembering the times that he and his friend had lain upon the couch, the dog pressed lovingly against him, reveling in the companionship that they shared. He wondered if Baarabus even remembered those times.

"Don't you think you should be going?" the dog asked.

"I want to be here with you," Remy said, stroking the dog's thick black fur.

"No," the dog suddenly barked, lifting his head and snapping his razor-sharp teeth. "I want you to go." Then his head slowly dropped back to Remy's leg. "I don't want you to be here when I . . ."

Remy pulled the large dog's body closer to him.

"You don't have to worry," Remy told him. "I've learned my lesson."

The dog chuckled and then painfully coughed.

"What's so funny?" Remy asked.

"I know," Baarabus said, his voice little more than a whisper.

"You know what?"

"Why you did it."

Remy put his face down to the thick fur of the demon dog's neck, taking the smell of him into his lungs.

"Why? Why did I . . ."

"It hurts so fucking bad . . . ," Baarabus said, his body shuddering. Remy held him tighter.

". . . It hurts so fucking bad to say good-bye."

And with those last, whispering words, the great demon dog called Baarabus fought no more, giving up the life he had struggled so hard to hold on to.

Finding some semblance of the peace he sought in death.

Remy held the dog until his body grew cold. Then, gently, he laid Baarabus' head down upon the ground and rose to his feet, saying good-bye to the animal and thanking him for being such a good friend.

He went to the bodies of Samson's children, kneeling down and thanking them as well for traveling with him and fighting beside him. He found Leila's body within the bushes, propped up against the base of a tree, and felt those familiar pangs of sadness he'd always felt so strongly when he'd lost those whom he'd cared for.

Remy gasped as Leila opened her eyes.

"Give me a sec," she said. "Just got to rest a bit, and then I'll . . ."

But he knew she wasn't going anywhere.

"You just stay here," he told her.

"Are you ditching me?" she asked.

"Yeah, I am," he said. "Where I'm going . . ." He gazed off into the jungle of Eden. "Where I'm going I have to go alone."

"Everybody staying back?" she asked, as if unaware of her brothers' fates.

"Yeah, everybody is staying back," he assured her. "This is where I thank you for all that you've done."

"That's all right," Leila said. She seemed to be having a difficult time keeping her eyes open. "Wasn't doing shit anyway . . . just hangin' out waiting for the world to end."

"You rest now," he told her, and leaned in to kiss her forehead. "I'll take things from here."

She closed her eyes and Remy left her beneath the tree. He stopped and bent down to pick up the Godkiller from the ground, feeling a thrum of power vibrate through his arm, telling him that it was ready.

"All right, then," he said aloud, and stepped into the jungle in search of his destiny.

Linda stood at the edge of the roaring surf. She could have sworn there had been an old man standing with the woman, but now she seemed to be alone, smiling sadly and hugging herself against the harsh wind blowing in from the sea.

She approached the woman and stood beside her. "You're his wife," Linda said. "You're Madeline."

"I'm an echo of something very important to him," the woman said, her eyes never leaving the approaching storm on the horizon.

"Do you know where he is?" Linda asked.

"Out there." Madeline nodded toward the ocean. "At the center of the storm."

Linda looked as well, white flashes of lightning temporarily leaving the memory of jagged bolts on the surface of her eyes.

"I need to get to him," she said. "I need to bring him back."

Madeline looked away from the storm and at Linda.

"Can you help me?" Linda asked, desperation in her voice. "Please."

Remy's wife stared at her intensely, and then her features softened, and she smiled as her image began to fade.

"No!" Linda cried, reaching to grab hold of the woman, as if she could somehow make the phantasm stay.

But she was gone, leaving Linda alone.

"Please," Linda wailed over the moans of the wind. "I need help . . . please!"

The storm seemed to be growing larger, rolling across the sky toward land, bolts of lightning and crashes of thunder causing the very air to tremble. Linda looked into the swiftly moving clouds and searched for the center, where her lover's dead wife had told her he would be.

"Remy," she whispered, suddenly exhausted beyond words and falling to her knees.

"Come back to me."

CHAPTER THIRTY-FOUR

Remy knew that he was getting close.

Jagged pieces of stone hovered in the air before him, defying the gravity of the world.

Pieces of Heaven—of the Golden City—as solid as the faith of a true believer but lighter than the air itself. He reached out to one of the stones as it spun gracefully in the air before him, and flicked it away, watching as it rolled through the humid jungle air, colliding with another, larger piece of rock that drifted through a curtain of leafy vines.

He wondered what awaited him beyond the veil of vegetation as he moved toward it and pushed the tendrils aside. It was like an asteroid field, the air filled with stones of steadily increasing size. Remy advanced, moving the stones, disrupting their gentle orbit, creating a chain reaction of weightless rubble careening by his face.

A wall of much larger pieces of yellow stone hung before him, rubbing together as they floated, making Remy think of an enormous set of teeth, grinding nervously. He stood before the wall, steeling himself for what he would find on its other side. Then, with a deep breath, he reached out and pushed at the center of the weightless rubble. The obstruction broke apart, the pieces spinning off in opposite directions.

And what he saw filled him with an odd combination of awe and incredible sadness.

The process of Unification frozen before him.

Remy's heart skipped a beat as his eyes fell upon the Kingdom of Heaven—the Golden City—at the center of it all.

Frozen in the midst of becoming something else.

Unified.

It was like looking at a single frame of a film, a power act, frozen as it occurred. Remy carefully moved through the scene, using the floating stones as steps.

And the closer he got to the city, the more carnage he observed. Bodies of angels clogged the air; all of the Heavenly hosts were represented there, frozen as they were when the horror had occurred.

He stood upon a drifting platform of rock and took it all in, the lush Garden of Eden flowing in to rejoin the mass of Heaven and the City of Gold, towering spires of reflective black stone—the structures of Hell—reaching out fingerlike to take hold of the truce that was being offered, to step from the shadows into the light and be one.

His mind became engorged with the imagery, powerful memories that hadn't been there moments before.

It was the Shaitan who had been the heralds of disaster.

Remy opened his eyes to the reality before him, seeing some of the pale-skinned abominations frozen in the midst of attack as they swarmed from the Garden, their actions stopped by an act far more horrible.

The shame he felt was crushing as he leapt from one floating piece of rock to another.

He remembered the screams, the cries of shock at the audacity of it all.

And as the gathered masses had screamed, he'd acted.

The memories were far clearer—sharper now. As the Shaitan had swarmed, and the Heavenly hosts were distracted, Remy had reached into a pocket for something that was waiting there, something that pulsed with the power of potential, something that could either create or destroy.

In his mind he saw it, and as he looked upon it, he knew its purpose.

To murder.

Remy remembered the feeling of the bullet in his hand, the warmth of the metal casing. The recollection terrified him, but for the life of him, he still could not understand why he had even considered performing the act that brought about the dusk of humanity, and the fall of the Kingdom of . . .

A vision, razor-sharp, sliced its way into his tumultuous remembrances. *He* was there, the stranger with the pale skin and oily black hair. And he was smiling as he gifted Remy the bullet.

Remy swayed upon the floating platform of rock, reeling as if the memories were a physical assault upon him. Who was this mysterious man who hid beneath the folds of his memories?

Pulling himself together, Remy looked across a broad expanse of space to the broken stairs that would take him up to the front of the Golden City, where God had been when he'd . . .

Behind the lids of his eyes, he saw himself tear the Pitiless pistol from Francis' grasp, the look of utter shock upon the fallen Guardian angel's face as Remy fired the gun into him. Remy's fingers tingled and then burned as they remembered opening the gun's chamber and placing the special bullet inside.

Remy leapt from the platform of stone, landing on the shattered stairs. He followed them with his eyes as they ascended into the hall of Heaven, from where the Creator had once surveyed His kingdom.

Slowly, he climbed those stairs, dreading what he would find at the top.

And with each footfall, images exploded inside his mind, forcing him to recall what this other version of himself had done.

He heard the chamber of the Pitiless pistol snap shut with a click so sharp it could be heard over the screams and cries of the Shaitan attack.

And then he climbed these very same steps, raising the weapon, taking aim, and . . .

Remy reached the top of the stairs and gazed upon a sight that froze him in place like those caught in the release of power when the Lord God was felled by an assassin's bullet.

It was a sight that defined it all, the physical representation of what this most holy process—this Unification—was all about. The Almighty, resplendent in robes of purest light, His holy visage appearing as the old man Remy had seen in his dreams, speaking of a coming conflict. He stared at Him as He floated in the air above the floor, petrified in the moment of His demise, and briefly wondered if God appeared this way to everyone, or if the image of the Creator differed for any and all who looked upon Him.

And flying to His aid on wings as black as night was Lucifer Morningstar, the look frozen upon his flawless features reflective of the utter horror of being on the cusp of forgiveness and having that blessing savagely ripped away.

Remy approached the scene and felt a kind of resistance in the ether around him, almost as if the surroundings somehow knew that he was the one.

That he was responsible, and sought to push him away.

Then he heard the gunshot, a sound so loud that it swallowed all other sounds, a sound that demanded one's attention, a sound that said, *Listen to me, for this is the end of it all.*

And that sound finally stole away his strength. Remy dropped to his knees before the moment frozen in infamy.

"I'm so sorry," he said, his eyes welling with scalding tears. He pulled the Godkiller from where he'd tucked it into the waist of his pants at the small of his back. "But I'm here now. . . . I've traveled so very far to make things right. . . . You just have to let me know . . . what I need to do to fix this. . . . Please . . ."

And then there came a voice.

"Do you think they can hear you? . . . That *He* can hear you? Oh, I certainly do hope so."

Remy turned his head to see a man—*the man* from his visions . . . from the memories that cascaded into his skull. He stood upon a piece of floating stone, a once fine suit dust-covered and torn, his skin deathly pale, and his hair as black as the night.

"Who?" Remy began, but . . .

The man raised a finger to his lips. "Silence," he commanded, and the angel was compelled to be so. "I'll be doing the talking."

Remy noticed a ring upon the man's finger that seemed to pulse with an ungodly power.

"You want to start with *who*, but really, it should be *why*," the man said, stepping onto another floating stone, closer to Remy.

Remy wanted to speak, to demand answers from the mysterious figure, but found himself unable to.

"Why would anyone want to ruin something as potentially magnificent as this?" The man spread his arms, taking in the whole incredible, petrified moment. "It's quite simple, really."

The man stood before Remy now, but his focus was on God.

"He took something unbelievably special from me, and so I took from Him." He looked back to Remy. "See? Simple."

Remy wanted to speak, but the words would not come—were not allowed to come.

The man studied him, seeing how Remy strained against his commands.

"Go ahead," he said finally, giving the ring on the finger of his right hand a twist. "You may speak."

The words spilled from Remy's mouth. "The Lord God stole from you? And you decided that ending the world would be an appropriate response?" he asked incredulously.

The man thought for a moment, looking briefly back to the moment of God's death. "In hindsight, I guess it did get a little out of hand." He shrugged. "But I swore that . . ."

"You swore?" Remy interrupted. "Are you out of your fucking mind?"

The man smiled sadly. "After all this time, I'd probably have to say yes."

A fiery rage surged up inside Remy and he felt his body tense, ready to spring.

"You'll stay right there," the man ordered, and again Remy's eyes fell to the ring upon his finger.

He felt as though his feet had been cemented into place. "That ring," he said, his eyes locked upon the silver piece.

"This old thing?" the man said, raising his hand. "I've got two of them." He raised his other hand so Remy could see the pair. "The rings of Solomon—one controls the angelic, and the other, the demonic. I could not have achieved this greatness if it weren't for them." He laughed proudly. "Created by Solomon and Heaven itself to maintain balance between good and evil, but instead they helped me to achieve my most cherished desire."

"Who are you?" Remy asked with a snarl, the crazed Seraphim within him threatening to explode from his body.

"I was nobody," the man said. "A nobody named Simeon, until the

Lord God Almighty stole away my chance at bliss . . . ripping the euphoria of being one with the universe—with God and Heaven— from my grasp and sentencing me to an everlasting eternity of misery and pain."

Simeon glared at him with an intensity that Remy could feel, and finally, the angel understood the extent of this man's madness and rage.

"Then I became something more . . . something terrible." He paused as if remembering where he'd come from and where he had ended up. "Someone who made it his purpose to take away God's joy, to tear down everything that He had built."

Simeon looked around at his surroundings and then back to Remy.

"And I couldn't have done it without you."

Remy seethed, fighting against the magick of Solomon's ring, but it was to no avail.

"At first you were a nuisance, sticking your angelic nose into things that really didn't concern you, but eventually I began to see where you might be a benefit instead of a hindrance." He smiled at Remy. "You became my secret weapon, Remy Chandler."

"How could I not have known?" Remy asked, more to himself than to Simeon, shaking his head in disgust. "How could I not have known that someone like you existed?"

Simeon laughed again, holding up his hand and wriggling his fingers. "Because I didn't want you to," he said.

Remy's body vibrated with fury. "So, what now? You've accomplished your heart's greatest desire; where do you go from here?"

Simeon began to pace. "An interesting question," he said. "And one I've asked myself repeatedly." He stopped before the frozen visages of God and the Morningstar. "When is it enough?"

He turned his head to look at Remy.

"They're not quite dead," he explained. "The bullet you fired could only do so much damage." He smiled again and then chuckled. "He is God, after all."

"He's still alive," Remy whispered, staring at the image of his Creator. And suddenly, he knew why he had traveled so far.

"Still alive and, most important, still suffering."

Remy could barely comprehend the madness that was coming from the man's mouth.

"That's right," Simeon said. "As far as I'm concerned, He just hasn't suffered enough."

Remy began to scream, his rage roiling up from within. "How dare you! To think that your petty issues are somehow worth the price of all this."

"They are, and more," Simeon spat. "But I'm not surprised that someone like yourself is incapable of understanding the level of offense . . . of betrayal. He was my God, and I loved Him with all my heart and soul, and He was supposed to love me, but instead He cursed me to an eternal life where the promise of euphoria in the bosom of His love was dangled in front of me like a carrot."

Simeon was nearly hysterical. He lunged toward Remy, his face mere inches from Remy's own. "I can make you understand," he said, his eyes wild and insane.

Remy had no idea what was to follow as Simeon stepped back.

"I'll teach you the pain of betrayal."

He walked to the edge of the stairs and looked out over the broken ruins of Heaven.

"He's here, Francis," Simeon called out. "The one who took away your forgiveness. Come to me, Francis." He played with his ring. "Let me give you your prize."

Remy could hear the sound of something approaching, crying and mewling like some sort of wretched beast. He didn't want to believe. . . . He didn't want to see.

Simeon turned to stare at Remy, that smug smile upon his face. "He's coming, Remy. And I'm sure he has much he'd like to say to you."

A ragged and bloody hand appeared over the side of the city's base. Remy didn't want to watch, but he had no choice. The Guardian angel Fraciel, fallen from Heaven during the Great War, a fallen angel that Remy knew as a friend, hauled himself up and stood, tattered and bloody, before them, madness burning in his eyes.

"There, Francis," Simeon said as he played with the ring of Solomon. "There is the one who murdered your God. Show him how you feel."

Francis bared his teeth in a snarl of animalistic fury and charged.

"What did you do?!" he screamed, lunging at Remy, knocking them both back and over the side of the floating island that the Golden City had become.

"What did you do?!"

Francis' mind was filled with acid; acid and broken glass and spiders and explosions—lots and lots of explosions.

It had been like that since . . .

Since Remy had done the unthinkable.

He saw it again inside his head. God was going to make it all right; God was going to forgive them all their trespasses. He was going to make Heaven whole again. . . . He was going to make him, Francis—*Fraciel*—whole again.

Francis couldn't have imagined anything more wonderful. He hadn't been the greatest of angels, nor the worst, in all seriousness, but he knew that he had done wrong and understood that he must pay for his sins.

And pay he had, over and over again, but when the Morningstar returned, and Hell began to change under Lucifer's restored might, Francis had been abandoned, left to sink or swim in the shifting landscape of Hell.

He thought he was going to die then and had pretty much accepted his fate—*Que sera, sera*, as Doris Day once sang. It was okay.

But then he'd been saved by the very one who had betrayed the Lord God and who had originally led Fraciel down the path to banishment.

Lucifer Morningstar had saved his life, and for that Francis had no choice but to serve him. And serve him he had, all the while hoping and believing that it might lead to something—

Eventful.

And it had at that—the Lord God saying to the one who was once His favorite, *You shall be forgiven and your kingdom will be joined to mine.*

And here was the kicker . . . the most glorious of kickers: The Creator had also planned to forgive all who had once fought with the Son of the Morning.

All would be forgiven and things would return to the way they used to—*were supposed to*—be.

The Almighty called it Unification, and Francis said, *I'm there.*

And he was, as were all the angels of Heaven as well as all those who wished to be absolved of their sins. It was the most monumental of occasions, and Francis remembered what it was like to truly be a part of something far larger than he.

But as the Kingdom of Heaven was about to be restored, and all those who had fallen so far from the path were to be forgiven, something happened. Something that put acid in his brain, then added glass and, for good measure, a heaping portion of spiders. And that was all before the explosions began.

Remy . . . his dearest friend in all the world . . . Remy had done the unthinkable. It still didn't seem true, but it was—the spiders told him so.

When all was about to become right again, Remy had taken Francis' weapon, the gun given to him by Lucifer Morningstar, and had used it on him—shooting him square in the chest and nearly ending his existence. Francis liked to think that Remy had shot him that way on purpose, not wanting to harm his closest of friends.

But it was what the Seraphim had done next that caused the acid to bubble and the spiders to scream.

Remy had used the Pitiless to murder God.

And that was that.

There were no two ways about it.

Simeon was right; Francis had no choice.

He had to kill Remy.

It was only fair.

They bounced onto a floating piece of the Golden City, rolling across its cracked and brittle surface before tumbling over the side and crashing to the ground below.

All the while Francis was screaming, a mournful wail that filled Remy with great sadness.

"Why did you do it? Why? Why? Why?"

Remy wanted to answer, tried to answer, but the blows raining down upon his head made it difficult to respond intelligibly. Instead, he planted a foot against his friend's stomach and kicked, hurling the former Guardian angel away.

"Francis, you have to listen to me," Remy said, jumping to his feet, preparing for what was to come next.

"No, I don't," Francis said, looking around the rubble-strewn ground and finding something that brought a twisted smile to his face. A sword.

The blade was black and tarnished as if left in a fire too long, but

Francis raised it high above his head as he leapt toward his nemesis. Remy grabbed a piece of stone that was floating by and used it as a shield to meet the sword's descent. It shattered the stone but gave Remy enough time to leap out of the way before it could cleave his skull in two.

"Always thought you were the good one," Francis continued to shriek, swinging the blade again. "The one we could all aspire to be like!"

The blade whispered as it passed over Remy's head, setting Francis off balance and giving Remy an opportunity to smash a jagged rock into the side of the fallen angel's head.

"Please, listen," Remy begged as his friend dropped to his knees with the blow. "You have to trust me! I wasn't in control! Please! It's so fucking complicated!"

Francis quickly recovered, tackling Remy and bringing him down in a heap beneath him. "It doesn't change the fact that it was you who took it all away!"

He wrapped his hands around Remy's throat, pulling him up and then slamming him down, again and again. Remy tried to break the grip, but the fingers locked on his flesh dug in so deep they were like a part of him.

"You killed them all!" Francis wailed. "You murdered everyone . . . everything!"

Remy tried to tap into the fire that raged deep inside him, but he couldn't, for the savagery of Francis' attack was relentless.

And the sweet, sweet voice of oblivion called to him from not so far away. Remy considered the offer of her embrace, her promise to take him away from all the pain that he had caused.

All he had do was take her hand.

Simeon hadn't been that amused in ages.

From atop the stairs leading into the Golden City, he watched the two angels fight.

"That's it, Francis," he encouraged. "Show the murderer how much pain he's caused."

Simeon had always suspected that Remy Chandler would find his way back here, to the scene of the crime, so to speak. There was a part of him that wondered why he hadn't just ordered the Seraphim to slay himself. He really didn't have an answer, but the additional amusement did bring him some joy.

Francis continued to pummel his friend, the fight really seeming to be one-sided. It wouldn't be long, Simeon guessed, before the former Guardian angel slew his friend.

Finally tired of the fight below, he turned back to the petrified visages of Lucifer and God.

"I see what You did," he said, directing his words to God. "Somehow You managed to reach out to Your warrior angel and call him here." Simeon strolled closer, his eyes never leaving the one he hated most of all. "I'm not sure if that's even possible, but it makes a good story, doesn't it? The last vestige of the Lord God Almighty calling upon the one who struck Him down. Calling upon him to somehow right the wrong, to pull victory from the fire."

Simeon laughed. "There will be no victory from this fire," the forever man said with an enthusiastic shake of his head. "Your attacker . . . your pathetic pawn . . . will meet his fate at the hands of his friend, and things will return to the new normal.

"You know the new normal, don't you?" Simeon smiled. "It's what I've put into place . . . as Your reality slowly fades away and dies."

The forever man stopped, digging his hands into his pockets as he considered his next bit of musing.

"I wonder," he said. "When it's all gone . . . when it all winds down, will You cease to be? Will it all blink out like someone turning the lights off? Will I cease to be, for that matter?" He couldn't help but smile again. "I'm excited to see what happens."

He'd started to pace again, when his foot struck against something that skittered across the rubble-strewn ground, glittering seductively.

"What do we have here?" Simeon asked, bending down to pick up the weapon that Remy had dropped. "Ah, would you look at this—the murder weapon, so to speak."

He chuckled, presenting the gun to God and Lucifer.

"Your lackey brought this," Simeon said to Him. "And why is that? Was this supposed to help You? Was he supposed to finish what he started?"

"You mean what *you* started," said a voice from nearby.

Simeon spun toward the sound, the gun instinctively pointed at the man who stood there, his skin covered in weeping wounds and scabs.

"Who the fuck are you?" Simeon demanded.

The bloody man smiled.

"Wouldn't want to spoil the surprise," he said as he lunged.

CHAPTER THIRTY-FIVE

Remy wasn't alone in the embrace of darkness.

He'd at last succumbed to the paltry promise of unconsciousness but was startled to see that he wasn't alone in the cool world of shadow.

"Hello?" Remy called to the indistinguishable shape hunkered down across from him.

"I was curious if you'd ever get here," said a voice, strangely familiar. It almost sounded like . . .

The shape became more defined as it rose and crossed the darkness toward him. The figure raised its hand, and it began to glow faintly, chasing away the shadows.

Remy stared at the man across from him, for a moment believing that he was staring into a mirror.

"What's happening?" Remy asked, as much to himself as to his doppelganger.

"Where should we begin?" his double responded. "You're being murdered by your insane best friend, and that's just for starters."

"You're me—the other me," Remy said, staring at himself.

"Yeah, I'm the one who got evicted from my body so you could come in."

"Evicted?"

"Yeah. I was probably going to die anyway, but instead I ended up here—waiting for you."

"You're the one who murdered God."

Remy's other self became very quiet, as if thinking about that statement.

"It's not easy to live with that knowledge," he finally said.

It was Remy's turn for silence.

"It's like a cancer inside you, the darkness growing until it consumes just about everything you ever were. The fire of the divine corrupted into something else." He touched his chest, his fingers moving beneath his shirt, opening it to reveal the dark sigils tattooed on his chest. "After a while, it takes some doing to keep it locked away, and eventually . . ."

"You can't," Remy answered for him, feeling the madness of the Seraphim writhing inside of him, feeding upon the misery of the world he'd become trapped in.

His other self looked at him knowingly. "Eventually, it just gets to be too much; the loss . . . the weight is too great." He paused, his words seeming to have a physical effect upon him. This version of himself, somehow smaller.

"It breaks you . . . and then you fall."

Remy wasn't sure how to respond, to look at himself and see himself—broken.

"But that's where you come in," his double said. "With you there's still a chance. As much as we're the same, we're not—it's the little differences that separate us. You haven't done what I did in my lifetime. . . . You're still whole—a little cracked, a bit bent, but you're still whole. With you, there's still a chance to fix things."

From somewhere in the darkness Remy heard the sound of pounding surf and moaning winds. It reminded him of a place very important to him, a place of reflection and healing.

Remy.

Remy thought he heard his name called on a distant wind and began to move deeper into the darkness in the direction of the sounds.

But a hand gripped his arm, stopping him.

"Not yet," the other Remy said. "There's still work to be done."

Remy strained his ears to hear more, but the darkness had grown sadly silent. "I have to go back," he said, trying to pull away.

"Better you than me," his other self said.

"If I do this," Remy said, "if I'm able to fix things . . . will I get to go back to where I'm supposed to be?"

The other Remy had turned and was walking back into the shadows. He stopped, as if considering the question, then continued on without answering.

Perhaps he did not know the answer.

But then again, maybe he did.

The Fossil's true name danced on the tip of his tongue.

He wanted to make the forever man understand that he was not as unique as he believed.

But Simeon was too busy trying to kill him.

Good luck with that, the Fossil thought as Simeon smashed him in the face with the butt of the golden gun. He went down hard, the scabs that already covered most of his body ripping away and causing the blood to flow.

"What a horrible-looking thing you are," Simeon said, looking down at him. "Are you one of Chandler's friends? His backup, perhaps? My, the pickings certainly were slim."

The Fossil pushed himself up, his face awash with flowing blood. "Well, after all these years, you managed to get being a smug son of a bitch down pretty good," he said, enjoying the surprised expression on his opponent's face.

"I asked you a question, worm," Simeon sneered. "Who are you and why are you here?"

"I'm somebody who should have done something about you a long time ago," the Fossil said as he wiped blood from his eyes. The wound was already scabbing over, and he was able to see and appreciate Simeon's annoyed expression.

"Do I know you?" Simeon asked, pacing before the bloody old man. "I'm sure I would have remembered someone in such grievous condition, but then again, I have been busy."

The Fossil collected himself. "We've never met, as far as I know," he said. "But we do share quite a bit in common."

Simeon stopped, smiling a nasty, predatory grin. He still held the pistol and tapped the butt against the side of his leg. "Do we now?" He leaned menacingly closer. "Pray tell."

Just a little bit closer, the Fossil thought. "We've both been around long enough to make mistakes," he said aloud. "A lot of mistakes."

Simeon studied him intently, tilting his head to one side ever so slightly.

"I spent the majority of my time trying to figure out my place in the world. Why the hell was I still here?" The Fossil shifted so he was a bit closer to Simeon.

Almost there.

"I kept making the same mistakes again and again. It got bad for me for a while. In fact, I actually believed that contributing to the end of the world by bringing about the Apocalypse would take away my pain."

The Fossil smiled as Simeon's eyes widened.

"Sound familiar?"

Simeon quickly stepped away, pulling back the hammer and aiming the pistol at the Fossil. "Tell me who you are or . . ."

Now or never, the Fossil thought. Then he lunged at Simeon, wrapping his scab-crusted hands around the man's throat.

"I will tell you who I am," the Fossil said, squeezing with all his might.

Simeon struggled wildly, his arms flailing as he tried to aim and fire the pistol.

"And you will come to understand the meaning of this moment."

Simeon managed to fire the pistol, filling the place of Unification with the sound of thunder, but he missed the Fossil, who continued to squeeze the life from the forever man's throat.

Frantically, Simeon tried to break the Fossil's grip. He thrashed and flailed, and pulled his attacker across the broken stage of the Golden City. And still the Fossil stuck.

The back of Simeon's foot connected with a piece of stone that floated three inches from the ground, tripping him up, causing him to fall backward with the Fossil atop him. The gun skittered from his grasp, out of reach.

Simeon was desperate now, reaching up with clawed hands to rip at the man's face. But the Fossil knew pain, and this was no worse than anything he'd endured since the fall of Heaven.

Simeon's struggles were growing weaker, and the Fossil leaned into his grip for last of the act.

For the murder of Simeon.

The Fossil lowered his face to within inches of Simeon's, being sure to look directly into the man's bulging, oxygen-deprived eyes. The realization should have been dawning on him that this time it would be different.

That this time he would not be coming back.

"Who?" Simeon managed, a pathetic squeak, filled with fear as the reality of the situation settled in.

"Lazarus," the Fossil said, letting the name sink in. "I am Lazarus."

Simeon made a last feeble attempt to overpower him, but it was all for naught. He should have known that he would be powerless against another like him.

That it would take a forever man to kill a forever man.

Remy let go of oblivion's hand and rushed swiftly to the surface of consciousness just as his head was slammed once more against the ground.

He opened his eyes, looking up into the madness-etched face of his friend.

"Enough," Remy ordered.

The former Guardian appeared surprised that the angel was suddenly conscious—still alive.

And Remy took that opportunity to act. He allowed that horrible, burning madness to bubble to the surface and flow from his hands. Blasts of fire hit Francis directly in the chest, lifting up and propelling him back through the air.

Francis bounced off a floating piece of Paradise and fell to the ground with a grunt.

Remy rose to his feet, the power that he fought to restrain seeking further release. How easy it would have been to set it free, to allow it to flow from his body and out into the accursed world.

What's a little more fire and insanity? he thought as the miasma of fire formed a writhing corona around his head.

Francis lay still for only a moment, then sprang up, ready to continue their bout.

Right then, Remy was more than happy to oblige, but a body dropped from above, landing with a sickening, wet thud between them.

Remy stared in shock at the body of the man called Simeon, eyes wide in death, his tongue thick, black, and protruding from his mouth.

"It's done," announced a voice from above.

Both Remy and Francis looked up to see the blood-covered Fossil peering down at them.

"It's time that you finish what you came here to do," he added, looking squarely at Remy.

Remy looked away from the Fossil to Francis. The former Guardian seemed confused now that Simeon's hold was broken.

"I'm going to fix this," Remy told him.

Francis glared, but for a moment Remy saw the madness dissipate and the old intensity of his friend return. "Why should I believe you?"

"Because I'm your friend, and I'm asking you to."

Francis looked away. "Sorry I tried to kill you," he mumbled. "I wasn't myself."

"A lot of that going around," Remy said, turning away from his friend and beginning his ascent to God.

The Fossil stood before the frozen moment of Unification, his robes soaked with blood.

"Are you all right?" Remy asked.

"I haven't been all right for a very long time," he said, swaying slightly. He turned to look at Remy. "But I think that might be about to change."

"You killed him." Remy looked out over the edge of the ruins to where Simeon's body lay. The forever man still looked shocked that he wasn't alive anymore.

"I did," the Fossil said. "And I think that might've been the reason why I'm still around." The blood was really flowing from his wounds now, actually forming little puddles where he stood.

Remy focused upon the man. "You look worse than usual."

"Yeah, I think this might be it."

"Are you going to tell me?" Remy asked. "Before you . . ."

"Die?" The Fossil smiled widely. "I can almost believe it'll happen now."

"Tell me."

"Lazarus," the Fossil told him. "I'm Lazarus."

Remy studied the bloody man, trying to find something that he might recognize, but it remained hidden beneath the blood and scabs. "I don't see it, but all right."

Lazarus chuckled. "So are you as pissed off at me as the other Remy was?"

It was far away in his thoughts, almost as if he were remembering a dream from a very long time ago, but Remy recalled the Lazarus from his own reality—how his obsession with death had led him to befriend some bad-apple angels who wanted to see the Four Horsemen bring about the end of the world. Remy had managed to stop the Horsemen and the bad angels, but Lazarus had been washed away in the deluge of the conflict and hadn't been seen or heard from since.

"Yeah, I think I am," Remy said.

"Well, hopefully that makes up for it," Lazarus said, pointing at Simeon's corpse.

"It's a good start." Remy shrugged.

They both laughed, the sound of their humor tapering off as Remy found himself staring again at the body of God, Lucifer in flight coming to his aid.

"He brought you here to make this right," Lazarus said. "He brought us all here."

"But what do I do now?" Remy asked, walking toward God as he hung in the air, in the midst of death. "Simeon said that You were still alive . . . still suffering. . . . Give me a sign. Show me how to make this right."

There was a hole in the Creator's forehead, and Remy found his gaze transfixed on the bloodless opening for some grotesque reason.

Then he saw the light.

At first he thought it might have been a trick of his eyes, what little light there was in the ruins of the Golden City playing with his vision, making him see things that weren't there.

But there it was again.

Remy moved closer, his eyes never leaving the black hole in the Almighty's forehead.

"Is this it?" Remy asked Him.

From the darkness within the hole, Remy saw flickers of light, reminding him of lightning flashes over the waters of Cape Cod on a hot summer's night. For a moment he was transported there, smelling the ocean, the air charged with a coming storm.

"What is that?" Lazarus asked as he, too, stepped closer.

"It's a sign," Remy said.

He stepped up on a piece of stone so he could stare directly into the circular opening, studying the flashes of white light as they seemed to intensify. And suddenly, he was compelled to do the unthinkable.

Remy reached out, raising his fingers toward the hole. The flashes grew brighter as his hand grew closer, and he pulled back, unsure if he should follow through.

But he did, reaching into the hole—the skull—of the Lord God Almighty. Remy's eyes widened as the skin and bone around his fingers grew more malleable.

He felt it before he saw it, his finger and thumb closing around something that caused an incredible warmth to flow through his body and fill his mind with thoughts of things to come.

Carefully, Remy withdrew his prize.

"What is it?" Lazarus asked.

Remy stared at the object as it flashed and pulsed with a power that he recognized as the inspiration for creation itself.

"The future," he said.

He stepped down from the stone upon which he stood, mesmerized by the slug as it gradually morphed back into a bullet.

He sensed Lazarus' approach and managed to tear his eyes from the object he held.

"I think you're going to need this," Lazarus said, holding out the Godkiller.

"I think you're right."

Remy took the gun from the man's bloody hands.

Lazarus stepped slowly back, then sat upon a piece of floating stone. "Go ahead," he said to Remy. "Load it up."

Remy flipped open the cylinder, staring into the chambers. Then he slipped the bullet into one of the black holes. The weapon thrummed in his hand as if it had somehow gained a pulse—a heartbeat. He looked to Lazarus, who was slumped upon the rock.

"It won't be long now," Lazarus said, slurring his words.

And Remy could feel that he was right. It was time for him to do what he'd been brought to this hellish reflection of his own reality to do.

He was going to fix things. He was going to make things right.

Looking out over the edge of the Golden City, he saw Francis standing below, looking sadly up at him. Waiting.

Waiting, as this very world was waiting.

Remy raised the gun, and Francis gave a barely perceptible nod of acceptance.

The Seraphim turned away and gazed upon the Lord God as he hung frozen in time and space. He took a deep breath, walking toward the moment, remembering how it had all played out, Simeon's commands rattling around inside his head, the ring of Solomon compelling him to do exactly as he was told.

Now he awaited another command. Standing before God, he waited, pistol in hand. He was about to ask his Creator what was expected of him now, when his eyes were again pulled to the circular black hole in the center of the Almighty's head. He couldn't tear his gaze away, his stare becoming more and more intense—the hole seeming to grow larger the harder he concentrated upon it.

Soon all that he saw was the hole.

There was nothing but the lonely darkness.

And that was when he knew what he had to do, raising the gun that had once been called Pitiless, before it was a Godkiller.

Pitiless to all who fell to its bite . . . pitiless now to the void before it.

Remy aimed the weapon into the dark and placed his finger upon the trigger.

"Let there be light," he said as he squeezed and fired.

Murdering the darkness with light and what would follow.

And there was light.

CHAPTER THIRTY-SIX

The world was ending.

At least, that was how it seemed at the moment.

Ashley held tightly to the trembling Marlowe, trying to be strong for him.

This strange place somehow connected to Remy was coming apart. Did that mean Remy was gone?

Where there had once been a sprawling park and a playground, there was now only gray static, and it was quickly finding its way toward where they waited, pushing them closer to the hole, which also continued to grow larger.

Soon there would be no place for them to go.

Ashley looked to the sky above them and, instead of blue, she saw only the salt-and-pepper snow of static.

"If you can hear me, Assiel, it might be a good time for you to reach out," she said, hugging Marlowe all the tighter.

Marlowe seemed to be getting more nervous, struggling in her grasp.

"It's all right," she tried to soothe him.

But the dog shook off her arms, pushing her backward onto what remained of the grassy area.

"Marlowe, no!" Ashley yelled as she scrambled to her feet.

The dog had positioned himself at the lip of the spreading black hole and had begun to bark crazily, as if calling to their friend.

"Marlowe," she called again, crawling across the grass toward him. "Come here, boy."

He looked up, but his attention seemed to be captured by something behind her. He began to growl, and instinctively she turned around to see the wall of crackling white sweeping toward them.

Moving far faster than it had before.

Marlowe darted between the static and Ashley, barking and snarling wildly as it moved inexorably toward them.

Such a brave boy, Ashley thought just before the wave covered them both.

The world was ending.

Linda stood on the beach in the midst of the raging storm.

The dark waters churned and boiled as hurricane-force winds whipped. She watched in horror as waterspouts formed in the air above the angry waters and jagged bolts of lightning stabbed from the heavens, as if attempting to agitate the storm to an even greater fury.

She'd never experienced anything like it and doubted very much that she ever would again, for there was no doubt in her mind that this was the end.

Her end.

There was an instinctual part of her that was urging her to run, to seek cover and survive, but she knew there was nowhere in this world that she would be safe. This world was ending, slowly coming apart at the seams, and to hide from the reality of the situation was pointless.

Instead, she stood there cold and frightened, drenched by the crashing waves and torrential downpours, watching the world coming to an end and wondering what it all meant.

Is he all right? Is Remy still alive, or is this a sign that . . .

Lightning flashed, brightening the darkness of the sky, and though she had raised her hands to shield her eyes from the searing white light, she thought she saw something in the turbulent skies above the raging waters.

She thought she saw a man, hovering in the eye of the storm.

A man that she knew . . . and loved with all her heart and soul.

Linda found herself wading into the dark waters, the pull of the shifting currents taking hold of her eagerly and dragging her away from the protection of the shore.

She struggled to keep her head above the water, to see past the shifting, boiling cloud formations, to see if she could catch a glimpse of him.

To see her Remy again.

The world was ending, and he was responsible.

Remy Chandler floated in the eye of the cataclysm, at the center of a cosmic storm.

He was the end . . .

And the beginning.

The Alpha and the Omega.

It was up to him to pick up the pieces, to shape the new, to wield the stuff of creation. To make a better world from what had come before.

For all intents and purposes, he was God, and the forces of creation bent to his beck and call.

He would reshape this universe in his own image; he would be a part of all that was and will be. He would be in the sky above, and the earth below, in each and every drop of rain that fell and every single grain of sand that was trod upon. He would be in the sun and the moon and all the stars that shone down upon the multitude of worlds that he would form.

He would be part of everything, and everything would be part of him.

And gradually, little by little, the being that was once called Remy Chandler . . . Remiel . . . Seraphim . . . angel of Heaven began to go away.

To forget what he had been.

To become something far greater, until . . .

There was a voice . . . little more than a whisper.

"Remy."

But there was a power behind it as it made its way out into the universe, floating upon the cosmic winds, drifting up into the maelstrom of creation, to fall upon the ear of the one who was the Creator.

"Remy."

He almost did not recognize the name being called, so far was he from what he once had been, but the voice . . . the voice . . .

"Remy."

The pieces of his identity slowly, gradually fell back into place.

A being of Heaven . . . an angel in the Heavenly host Seraphim . . . Remiel . . .

"Remy."

He turned his gaze to a facet of a world in transition, drawn to the sound of a voice with a power as great as the one that now coursed through his body.

In that voice was the power to heal and to transform, to take something once cold and heartless and make it—

Human.

In the world before, that power had belonged to a force of nature called Madeline, whose voice had been silenced by death. But that same power would not—could not—die.

Fighting to remain who he had been, Remy focused his attention on a particular portion of reality in the midst of transition. It was from that area of the maelstrom that he'd heard his name called, brought back from the brink by the power returned.

The power born again in the form of another.

"Linda," he said from the center of it all.

Searching for his love from within the eye of creation.

Linda had never believed that she would be around to see the end of the world, never imagined being a part of it.

She had swum out into the turbulent waters as far as she could go, trying to keep her eyes on the spot in the sky where she'd thought she'd seen something.

Seen him.

But it was all chaos now, with the lightning and the thunder and a wind that raked across the water with its claws of air, driving the ocean into spasms of agony.

A small speck upon the vastness, Linda refused to let the elements have her, even though the wind tried to snatch her up from the water, and the great, angry sea tried to swallow her up. She remained afloat, eyes rooted to the spot where she thought the sky would be, and thought about the man she loved and how she had tried so very hard to save him.

And then it was time for it all to end.

There was no difference between the ocean below and the sky above. It had all turned to chaos. Yet still she managed to hold on to her thoughts, refusing to acknowledge the terror that now gripped her as the end of her existence drew near.

She thought of Remy, and how if he had been there he would have taken her in his arms and told her . . .

"Everything is going to be all right."

She heard him say it, and a smile came to her lips even at the end of her reality. She was brave enough to open her eyes to catch a glimpse of the final death throes of a world, and in her delirium she thought the impossible, that Remy was there, a calmness at the center of the storm.

And then she felt the strength of his arms as he drew her to him, and the beating of his heart as he pulled her so very close, and she had no idea if it was real or the peace of death.

But at that particular moment, either one was fine with her.

CHAPTER THIRTY-SEVEN

The bedroom door wasn't going to hold them back for very long, even though Squire had rammed a dresser from across the room up against it.

"Be sure to add this to the list of things that we're going to need to reimburse Remy for," the goblin said with a crooked smile.

"Fuck you," Mulvehill responded, hauling out the heavy wood drawers of the dresser and stacking them on top to give the obstruction a bit more height. It had grown quiet on the other side, the Bone Masters probably regrouping, trying to figure out how they were going to get through.

Squire stepped out of the closet with some heavy Samsonite suitcases. "Do you think he's gone?" He grunted as he tossed them on top of the drawers.

"Who, Assiel?" Mulvehill asked. He'd gone to the closet as well, coming back with two smaller cases. "Yeah, I think he is."

The pair stood back, admiring their work.

"It ain't the Great Wall, but it'll have to do," the goblin said.

Mulvehill went to the bed and stared at the figures upon it, deep in the grip of unconsciousness.

"Maybe we should throw them up onto the barricade," Squire suggested. "Least that way, they'd be serving some purpose."

"They're serving a purpose," Mulvehill retorted, looking first at Ashley, then at Linda, and finally at Marlowe. "They have to be someplace . . . doing something."

"They're doing something, all right," Squire grumbled. "But it ain't doing squat for us."

"They're doing their thing, and we're doing ours," Mulvehill said. "It's what we agreed to."

"Do you think they're actually helping him?" Squire asked, motioning with his chin to Remy lying in the center of the bed.

"Yeah," Mulvehill answered. "I do. I have to; it's the only positive thing I've got to hold on to."

"You've still got your health." Squire shrugged with another of his crooked smiles.

"Have I told you to go fuck yourself recent—"

There was a sudden pounding on the door, and the sound of splintering wood.

"Ah, showtime," Squire said, as he picked up the small battle-axe that he'd gotten from Francis' place.

Mulvehill checked the clip in his gun for what could have been the hundredth time, thinking how awesome it would have been if the ammunition fairy had been by to replenish his bullets, but no such luck. He still had less than a full clip remaining. Every shot was going to have to count.

Again something slammed against the door, and he could see the cracks through their makeshift barricade.

"You ready for this?" Mulvehill asked, his gaze now focused entirely upon the door.

Squire spun the axe in his hands. "Oh yeah, this type of bullshit has become old hat."

The door, and the things stacked in front of it, shook again, and Mulvehill could hear the sound of wood splintering and falling away. It wouldn't be long now.

The bangs and crashes were coming closer together now.

"Let me take the first crack at them," Squire said, hefting the axe. "If it looks like they're gonna get past me put a bullet in their eye. How's that sound?"

"Sounds good," Mulvehill said, feeling the tension in the room escalate with each new assault on the door. He was about to check his clip again, just to have something to do, when he heard the sound, a soft sigh of exhalation, and spun around to see. . . .

"They're awake," Mulvehill announced, going to the bed.

Ashley slowly sat up, looking around at the room, confusion on her face. "Where . . . ?" she began.

Something pounded savagely on the door, and one of the drawers crashed to the floor.

"Jesus Christ!" she exclaimed, eyes wide as the realization of the situation began to sink it.

"How are you doing?" Mulvehill asked her, wanting to make sure that she was all right but also wanting to keep an eye on the door situation.

Marlowe had awakened as well, and he appeared just as confused.

"We're good," Ashley said, patting the dog's head and looking over to the still-slumbering Linda, and, of course, Remy.

"Nice to see ya back, kid," Squire said. "I've got to go take my place near the door to hold back unwanted company."

"You do that," Ashley said.

Marlowe was sniffing at Remy and Linda.

"Did it work?" Mulvehill asked her.

Ashley looked at him and then back to Remy and Linda. "I really don't know what we did in there."

The door was being slowly hacked apart by their attackers, holes now appearing.

"So I'm guessing he won't be back," Mulvehill said, feeling a nearly overwhelming sadness envelop him. He hadn't realized how much hope he'd placed in the three saving Remy and somehow bringing him back.

"I don't think so," Ashley said, tears running from her eyes. "I don't know about her, either." She reached over to take hold of Linda's hand. "Maybe they're together."

Mulvehill wasn't about to let the sadness cripple him; he forced himself to replace his moroseness with a growing anger toward their aggressors. "That would be nice," he managed, then turned away to join Squire in front of the barricade.

The dresser slid forward, revealing the door, its wood broken away in strips. They could see their attackers on the other side. Squire stepped forward, battle-axe ready for first blood. Mulvehill's finger twitched upon the gun, eager to squeeze the trigger.

"I'm going to use this, okay?" said a voice from behind him.

He turned his head to see Ashley and Marlowe standing behind him. She was hefting a short sword.

"Yeah," he said. "Are you sure?"

She nodded. "I'm sure. . . . Where should I stand?"

Remy had found his love, snatching her up from the maelstrom and hugging her to him.

He had no idea how she could be where she was—in this place— but it did not change the fact that she was indeed there with him.

She trembled convulsively as he clutched her to his body, taking her away from a world in the midst of disarray. The reality below them had gradually come undone, as one reality was erased to be supplemented with another.

In the center of it all, he held Linda tightly, using the love he felt for her as his focus. *It would be so easy to let it all go,* he thought, his identity slowly dwindling as he infused himself into the very universe he was creating. No longer would he be only who he was.

He would be everything, and everything would be him.

"Remy." Linda whispered his name once more. He looked down at her and into her eyes.

"Is it really you?" she asked.

Feeling the tug of a universe upon him, he hesitated only briefly. "Yes, it's me," he said, pulling her up to him, and they kissed.

As a universe took shape around them.

Linda awoke with a gasp, having witnessed the birth of a universe.

For a moment she simply lay there, in a kind of shock, as she attempted to adjust to her new reality. Her body felt stiff, achy, and she rolled over on the bed, onto the body of her lover, who was incredibly still.

And cold to her touch.

She couldn't find the words as she looked at him, the memories of what she had done and why rushing back to her now.

"Oh, Remy," she said, bringing a hand to her mouth to stifle the flow of emotion.

It was the sound of a single gunshot that brought her fully back to the moment at hand. She looked away from the body of her lover to the front of the room, staring in abject horror at the sight of her friends as they attempted to keep monsters from forcing their way in.

She looked back to Remy, saying a silent good-bye before bounding from the bed to help her friends. Having just witnessed the birth of a universe, she was filled with a sense of wonder the likes of which she had never experienced before, and was not yet ready to surrender.

Desperate to hold on to the life that still remained for her.

Floating in the midst of creation, Remy began to truly understand how God worked.

For great things to happen there is always a catalyst, something that jump-starts the process of change, a spark struck to the gasoline.

Unification was to be the start of something glorious, the next phase of something amazing that began with creation itself.

But for that next chapter to begin, for the new to be ushered in, the imperfections in the old plan must be found.

The flaws—those nasty bugs—those annoying defects that seemed to arise whenever the process of change began.

They had to be driven into the open, drawn from the shadows, and once exposed . . . destroyed.

As dramatic as it all was, as reality took shape around him, Remy understood the method to God's madness.

And his place at the head of the asylum.

CHAPTER THIRTY-EIGHT

Mulvehill's bullets were gone, but that didn't mean the gun was useless.

Holding the .45 by the barrel, he used the weapon as a bludgeon, cracking skulls and faces and any other appendages that might be broken with a solid strike from the gun's grip.

He was painfully aware of the direness of their situation; it wouldn't be long at all until they were overrun. He couldn't speak for the others, but he could feel himself growing tired, his brain becoming fuzzy, his response time slowing. He chanced a quick glance at Ashley, seeing her stab the short sword into the throat of a Bone Master that was attempting to crawl into the room between the legs of another. It went down gasping, clutching at its throat, but still managed to make its way farther into the room. Marlowe leapt upon it, pinning the demon to the floor, and then Linda stepped forward, jamming the sharp end of a broken drawer into the Bone Master's eye, taking it out for good.

It was good to see her back as well. If only Remy . . .

Mulvehill pushed the sad thought aside, returning to the moment at hand. They were like a well-oiled machine, he thought, watching a blood-soaked Squire hack limbs away with abandon, but he, too, looked as though he might be slowing down.

But he couldn't think like that. They had to keep fighting—fighting for Remy.

He chanced another look over his shoulder to the bed, where his friend lay, wishing that he would miraculously wake up and save the day, but he knew that wasn't about to happen.

About to turn back to the battle at hand, something caught his eye, and he hesitated. A shadow passed before the window in the corner of the room that looked over the small backyard. Mulvehill's addled brain immediately began to search for what it could be: a bird, a piece of trash blown by the wind, a cloud formation drifting past . . .

The shadow was back, and it was larger now; then it crashed through the window in a shower of glass and wood.

"Fuck," Mulvehill screamed, already on the move. "I've got this," he announced to the others, who more than had their hands full.

He raced around the bed as the Bone Master assassin rose to its full height, a cord tied about its waist that it'd used to swing in from atop the roof. Their eyes met, and the killer smiled as it drew the six-inch blade from a scabbard on its leg and turned its attention to the unconscious Remy.

Mulvehill knew this killer. He'd spoken with it in the kitchen, before the siege on the Beacon Hill brownstone had begun.

And Mulvehill also knew that this one was here to finish the job.

It was absolute chaos, and it took everything Linda had to hold on. The room was filled with the stink of blood, piss, and shit, and the floor of the bedroom where there had only been the most lovely of memories—lovemaking, lazy Sundays reading the newspaper and sipping coffee—was now slippery with the blood of demons.

She was exhausted and not sure how much longer she could hang on.

The demons that managed to get by Squire and Ashley and Marlowe were her responsibility, the jagged piece of pine proving to be far more effective than she had thought it could be. She stabbed it into bodies again and again, even going so far as to grip the leg of one of the demons as it attempted to slither back out the door and drag it back, jamming the wooden spear into the back of its pale neck until it no longer moved.

A tiny, scared voice in the back of her head asked, *What are you doing?* Another, louder and far scarier, voice answered, *Surviving any way that I can.*

It was like being in a dream, things seeming to move in slow motion. Looking up from her kill, she was ready for whatever would come at her next, and she glanced toward the broken door. Most of the panels were missing; only the actual framework remained. She looked into the hallway and saw with horror that there were still far more killers out there than there were already dead in the bedroom, and it seemed that more were heading up the stairs.

"Shit," Squire said, obviously seeing what she did.

But the strangest thing happened. The Bone Masters at the door began to yell in some strange foreign language and turned their attentions—their fury—upon the newcomers.

"What's happening?" Ashley asked, her pretty face spattered with blood. "What's going on?"

Linda didn't answer, transfixed by what was happening outside the door. The newcomers that she had mistook as Bone Master reinforcements were not that at all. In fact, they were attacking the Bone Masters with knives, guns, and clubs.

But who were these mysterious saviors?

Were they friends?

Or were they some new foe?

Mulvehill threw his empty gun, the spinning projectile connecting with the demon's face and causing it to stumble back. Taking the opportunity, he dove, tackling the monster and driving it away from the bed.

The Bone Master still held the knife, and Mulvehill put all his attention on that arm, taking it in his hands and using his waning strength to bend it back and away. But the demon was stronger, and Mulvehill felt the arm begin to come around. The detective reacted in the only way he knew how, driving his forehead down into the demon's face. He saw stars from the blow, and felt a gash open in his face, but he did it again, and then again. For a moment, he thought he might have had an advantage, but that was short-lived as the Bone Master yanked its arm free, driving its elbow into Mulvehill's throat.

The homicide cop began to choke, reaching up to his neck as he tried to catch his breath. His legs suddenly went out from beneath him, and he sat down hard upon the wooden floor. The blood from his head wound streamed down his face, obscuring his vision. Through a scarlet haze, he saw that the assassin had recovered and was making its way toward the unconscious Remy, knife still in hand.

Mulvehill tried to cry out to the others, but his voice was little more than a croak, and besides, his friends were already a bit busy. His eyes fell on the cord that trailed in from the broken window, the cord that was attached to the killer's waist. He leapt on it, pulling the assassin back and away from its prey.

The Bone Master turned with a look upon its grotesque face that said it all. If the Bone Masters could kill with their eyes, Mulvehill would have died at least ten times over from the intensity of that gaze.

The assassin sliced at the cord as Mulvehill threw himself at it. The two collided head-on, flying backward onto the bed, where Remy lay. Mulvehill wildly threw punches, desperate to gain the upper hand, but the assassin ducked its head, then surged up, sending Mulvehill flying backward to the foot of the bed.

Mulvehill watched in horror as the assassin climbed upon Remy's prone figure and raised the dagger high, about to finally silence Remy's heart. Reacting totally on instinct, Mulvehill reached for Remy's legs, pulling his still form from underneath the Bone Master just as the blade stabbed into the mattress.

Screaming something unintelligible, the demon turned, but Mulvehill was already throwing himself upon the assassin and attempting to wrestle the blade from its hand. As far as he was concerned, the only place that knife was going was up the Bone Master's ass.

The killer managed to wriggle out from beneath him, and as Mulvehill reached to grab for it again, he was stabbed. The blade was sharp, and he really didn't even realize that it had gone in until he saw the Bone Master smile and felt the warm rush of blood as it cascaded from the wound in his side.

"Aw, shit," Mulvehill managed, his hand immediately going to the wound to try to stop the bleeding.

The assassin chuckled, then stabbed him again in the stomach.

Mulvehill tried to grab hold of the monster's neck in a last-ditch effort—in a show of preternatural strength—but his gore-covered hand just brushed against the killer's pale skin, leaving bloody streaks like war paint on one side of its face.

The Bone Master simply pushed Mulvehill's body aside, making a show of licking the blade clean of his blood. "All for naught," the assassin said, holding up the knife as it returned its attention to the unconscious Remy.

Steven Mulvehill wasn't sure where he found the strength—an unknown reserve stored away in the human body for just such an occasion. And he didn't really know what he was doing or why, but he managed to fling his bloody body across the bed, landing atop his friend, looking down upon his gray face.

"If there's any chance of you waking up," he said, blood dripping from his mouth, "I strongly suggest you do it now."

Lost in the creation of a universe, Remy Chandler smiled, for he saw how it all fit together, and the part he would play in maintaining its order.

He was in control now.

He was the Creator, and this belonged to Him.

There was so much He had to do, so many details that had to be just right in order for . . .

He felt it at His back, a gentle caress of a cosmic wind. It captured His attention, distracting Him from His prodigious chores, and the being that had once been Remy Chandler turned away from the reality He was shaping to see something that reminded Him of what he was—*who he was*—and it drew him back from the brink of Godhood.

He saw a world that had been his home, a world that had provided him with so much.

A world that made him who he was and showed him the unlimited wealth of true humanity.

Remy closed his eyes, letting the remembrances of his time there and those who had helped him become . . .

His eyes opened wide, a raw, ragged vision of an ungodly act he did not understand slicing its way into his view of the world he'd been taken from.

"Steven," Remy said, feeling the spatter of warm rain upon his face.

Something was wrong; he could feel it—a disturbing tremor in the ether. And feeling only a hint of guilt, he turned his back upon Godhood and all that it entailed.

To begin his journey home.

CHAPTER THIRTY-NINE

The strangers appeared like a swarm.

Squire had no idea who they were, why they were there, or where they'd come from, but he did not like what he saw.

They'd come loaded for bear, and shotguns and pistols blasted at the demon Bone Masters. And here he'd thought the place had been total chaos before.

The hobgoblin made his way out into the hallway, Linda, Ashley, and Marlowe close behind him, and they joined with the strangers in the chaos against the demons. *The enemy of my enemy is my friend's brother's half sister with the incredible ass, or something to that effect,* Squire thought, believing for a moment that they might actually survive all this.

But his hope could have been a bit premature. A Bone Master demon that appeared to be wearing some sort of protective gear suddenly appeared on the stairs, lugging what looked like some sort of bazooka.

"Get the fuck out of here," Squire screamed to Linda, Ash, and the dog, pushing them down the hall toward the guest room. He heard the rush of air as the projectile was fired, and then the hallway exploded in a rush of smoke and flames.

Squire and the girls were thrown to the floor at the end of the hall, but many of their strange allies didn't fare as well, their bodies and pieces of their bodies littering the hallway.

"You guys all right?" Squire shouted over the beeping of smoke detectors. He quickly looked them all over to be sure they weren't bleeding. Even the dog looked to be all right, but they had lost their position outside the bedroom, and now all he could think of was Remy and Mulvehill. "Gotta get back to the room."

He fished for his axe on the floor and was starting down the hallway when he noticed the next wave ascending the staircase through the thick, writhing smoke.

"Any chance you guys want to lay low?" he asked, motioning with his chin toward the guest room behind them.

"Not a one," Linda said, readying her improvised spear.

Ashley still had her sword and was staring straight ahead at the shapes moving in the thick gray clouds of smoke. She didn't answer his question per se, but she didn't have to; her attitude said it all. Even Marlowe had decided to stick it out, lowering himself to a crouch and growling menacingly.

Squire guessed that it was now or never and started down the hallway, using the smoke as cover. They were going to need all the help they could get if they were going to get back to the master bedroom.

The noise from the first floor was thunderous, and for a minute Squire thought the Bone Masters had found another piece of heavy artillery, but he quickly realized that what he was hearing was a voice—a scream, really: a bellow of rage.

And it was coming closer.

Squire held out a hand, stopping Linda and Ash. The banister had been destroyed in the explosion from the bazooka, and they were careful not to fall over the side as they peered down at the first floor.

Whatever was coming—*who*ever was coming—was causing quite the commotion; everyone, Bone Masters included, was focused on the staircase.

A large and powerful figure appeared in the downstairs hallway. Bone Master assassins hung from his back and arms, and the enormous figure plucked them from his body, smashing them to the floor and against the staircase wall as if they were only a minor inconvenience.

"This is interesting," Squire muttered as he watched the bellowing giant ascend the steps.

The assassins began to fire their weapons, but they didn't seem to have any effect upon the bear of a man, who quickened his pace to reach them. He roared as he grabbed hold of one and swung it around by the leg, using it as a weapon against the others. From where Squire was standing, they didn't have a fucking chance.

The behemoth with the long, flowing hair and thick beard was an unstoppable force no matter what the remains of the Bone Master assassins threw at him. And behind him, racing up the steps, were even more unknown allies, cleaning up the stragglers with rapid gunfire.

The giant finished off the last of his attackers, throwing one over the side of the staircase while nearly breaking the other in two by slamming it savagely over his knee.

Squire kept his back to Linda and Ashley, trying to protect them, as the large man stood still and looked around. And then the hobgoblin noticed the man's eyes and the milky film that covered them.

He was blind.

"I know you're there," the giant roared, craning his head ever so slightly, listening. "I can hear the three of you"—his shaggy head tilted in the other direction—"four of you breathing."

"Not bad for a blind guy," Squire said. "Can you guess our weights, too?"

The big man stared for a moment and then started to laugh. It was as big and loud as he was.

"You've got to be one of Chandler's friends," he said. "The guy always seems to surround himself with wiseasses."

"Who the fuck are you people?"

A dark-skinned man suddenly appeared from around the giant, assault weapon in hand.

"We're friends," he said. "Sent here to help with Remy's . . . assassin problem." The man came forward, extending his hand. "I'm Lazarus," he said. "And the big guy is Samson."

"Of course he is," Squire said. "And them?" He nodded toward the heavily armed men who had made short work of the remaining Bone Masters.

"Them? They're Samson's children."

"Lazarus and Samson?" Linda questioned, a trace of hysteria in her voice. "As in *the* Lazarus and *the* Samson?"

"Our reputations precede us," the big man said as he poked at a bloody bullet hole in his shoulder, squeezing the wound like a zit until the bullet popped out.

"You've got to be shitting me," Linda said, and she seemed to sway a bit.

"Where is he?" Lazarus asked. "I heard he was in a pretty bad way, and . . ."

The scream was sudden and earsplitting, emanating from the room at the end of the hallway.

"Let me guess," Samson said, turning toward the sound.

Squire pushed past them, rushing down the corridor, doing his damnedest not to trip over the bodies of the dead felled in their little war.

Desperate to reach the mournful wails coming from the end of the hall.

Ripper of Souls grabbed hold of the expiring human and carelessly flipped him from atop its prey.

The Bone Master positioned itself over the angel and stifled the urge to spit in his pale, comatose face. This was merely business, it reminded itself, a nasty bit of business that cost the lives of many young and, yes, it would have to admit, inexperienced assassins, but it was still a contract that they'd agreed to fulfill.

And a Bone Master always fulfilled a contract.

It raised its knife, ready to finally complete the job that had cost them so much.

Not even Heaven itself could stop them.

It thought of all the places the blade could enter its prey; directly into the heart would kill the angel instantly, whereas a slight deviation would nick the muscular organ, and although it would eventually produce the same outcome, it would most definitely cause more pain.

Such thoughts were not permitted to Bone Masters. All feelings—all emotions—were supposed to be suppressed, tapped down so far that only one focus remained: to extinguish life, fulfilling a contract.

But in some instances, emotions did manage to rise to the surface, their buoyancy providing a little more pleasure to the task at hand.

This was one of those times. To think of so much life lost to one assignment.

Ripper of Souls studied its prey. Was the life of one divine being worth so much? The answer, of course, was yes—but Ripper of Souls still had its doubts.

It imagined its journey back to the home world, when it would have to explain to all the mothers and fathers that their children had met their end attempting to complete a contract for which they were not yet prepared.

One did not send the uninitiated to deal with an angel of Heaven, but that had not been Ripper of Souls' decision. It would be the Broker who bore the brunt of that decision.

It decided to be merciful, bringing the blade down directly into the angel's heart. But the point of the blade had barely broken the angel's skin when the fire erupted from his body. And then it all happened in an instant: a powerful hand suddenly clutched about its throat, alive with flaming divinity, the orange fire hungrily consuming the flesh of its face.

The assassin screamed, a song of agony announcing the angel's return to the waking world.

The burning demon flailed in his grasp, but as soon Remy saw Steven's body lying bloody and still upon the floor, he tossed the shrieking killer across the room and went to his friend.

"Steven," Remy cried, his voice dry and cracking. He recalled the divine fires as he carefully pulled Steven's injured body into his arms. "Steven—it's me. Hey . . . I'm back. Please . . . please say something. . . . Please be all right."

Remy could feel his friend's life force dwindling away. He placed a hand against one of the wounds to stifle the flow of blood, but it continued to pool on the floor beneath him. He remembered what it had been like to be God, knowing that then he'd had the power to stop this—to keep his friend from dying.

Steven's eyes were barely slits, and Remy couldn't tell if he was even conscious. He thought of all the things he might try to save his friend's life, but knew that every single one would fail.

It was too late.

Steven Mulvehill was about to die, and there wasn't a damn thing that Remy could do about it.

There had been another time very much like this one, when a homicide investigation had crossed paths with a missing persons case in the parking garage at Logan International Airport. The young detective had ended up gut shot and was fading fast. The private investigator who had found him, believing that the cop wouldn't survive, had done only what he felt he should—he'd revealed his true identity as an angel of Heaven and helped the man to understand that there was nothing to fear from death.

That homicide detective had survived, and a powerful, long-lasting friendship had been forged.

A friendship that was drawing to a close.

Linda pushed past them all, climbing over bodies of dead assassins as she made her way into the bedroom.

She was met with the horrific sight of one of their attackers, its face melting as it burned. It picked itself up from the floor of the bedroom and threw itself through the front window. She wasn't sure if it was attempting escape or ending its life, and she really didn't care.

Remy was awake. He was awake.

He was kneeling on the floor at the foot of the bed, cradling something folded into his arms. She was so overwhelmed by the sight of him, by the idea that he was alive, that her brain didn't process what was going on.

She ran toward him, an attempt at calling out his name ending as a mere cry, followed by tears as her brain caught up to her eyes and she saw.

She really saw.

"Steven," she gasped, as she realized that Remy was cradling the body of his friend. She dropped to her knees near them as she heard the others charging into the room, ready for a fight.

But the fighting was over.

And one of their own had paid the price.

*　　*　　*

Remy closed his eyes and imagined them in a place where they could talk.

Where they could say good-bye.

"I don't know what to say," he said to Steven Mulvehill.

The detective didn't look dead here, his clothes relatively clean, although wrinkled as hell, as they often were.

"Then don't say anything," Steven replied.

"I should have been there to . . ."

Mulvehill shook his head slowly. "No, you were where you needed to be." He looked around. It was a place of nothing. . . . Nothing as far as the eye could see. "I understand that now—although I didn't at first. I thought you were going to die."

"I thought I had," Remy answered him. "I was sent to see some things . . . things that might be . . . that could happen here."

Mulvehill nodded, reaching into the pocket of his rumpled sports jacket and removing a pack of cigarettes. "Yeah, I get that now." He put one in his mouth, then found a lighter and lit up. "You've still got some shit to clean up here."

"Yeah, I know," Remy agreed.

Mulvehill looked around again. "So, is this it?"

Remy stared at him numbly.

"Is this Heaven?" Mulvehill specified as he took a drag on his cigarette.

Remy shook his head. "No, this is just something I did so we could . . ."

"Say good-bye?"

"Yeah."

Mulvehill seemed to be okay with that. "Good, 'cause I was gonna say, this is pretty fucking disappointing."

Remy chuckled. "I guarantee you, it's better than this."

"Good." Mulvehill puffed on his cigarette some more, seeming to really enjoy it. "Guess I won't have to quit now," he said, and smiled.

Remy was seriously going to miss that smile.

"Are you in any pain?" he asked.

Mulvehill shook his head. "I don't feel a thing, really."

Remy considered what he was about to say, debating on whether he would, but the words tumbled from his mouth before he could stop them.

"I could . . . There's a chance that I might be able to . . ."

"No," Mulvehill said firmly. "Let me go."

"What if I don't want to?" Remy asked with a touch of anger.

Mulvehill laughed, smoke streaming from his nose. "When has this ever been about you?"

Remy thought for a moment and then smiled as well. "You've got a point there."

They were quiet for awhile, Remy not wanting to say anything to spoil what little time they had left.

Mulvehill was looking around again at the nothing, but it was almost as if he could see *something*.

"What is it?" Remy asked.

"It's going to be something special," Mulvehill said.

Remy wasn't sure what he was talking about.

"Unification," Mulvehill explained. "It's going to be something special . . . if it happens."

"What do you mean, 'if it happens'?"

"You saw what happened in the other place," Mulvehill said as he pulled on his cigarette. "A real fucking mess."

"You know about that?"

He nodded. "I know lots of stuff now." He took another drag. "You have to stop him from setting things in motion . . . the forever man."

Remy listened, slowly nodding—remembering that other place and who was responsible.

"Can you handle it?"

Remy smiled, but it quickly went away when he noticed the tall, dark figure standing off in the distance.

Waiting.

Mulvehill noticed the change in his expression and turned.

"Looks like my ride's here," he said, turning back.

The Angel of Death, Israfil, waited patiently.

"He'll wait a bit," Remy said. "He owes me."

Mulvehill finished his smoke and flicked the filter toward the ground at their feet, but it never reached it, disappearing before it could become litter. "So this is it." He seemed suddenly uncomfortable.

"Guess so."

"I was going to have another smoke, but why bother? Might as well get it over with."

Remy said nothing, dreading the inevitable.

"Hey, I'm okay with this," Mulvehill said. "Seriously, I am. Sure, I would have liked to have hung around for a few more years. Y'know, retire from the force, get fatter than I am, and then go out someday drinking a good scotch while listening to the Sox play on the radio." The homicide cop smiled. "That'd be something, wouldn't it?"

"Heaven," Remy said.

"Yeah," his friend agreed.

They stood there for a moment longer, all the words that Remy thought he would say at a time such as this meaningless.

"You take care of yourself, Remy Chandler," Mulvehill said as he stuck out his hand.

"You, too, Steven Mulvehill." And Remy took his hand in his and gently squeezed it, then pulled his friend to him in a powerful embrace. "And thank you."

"For what?" Mulvehill asked as he hugged him back.

"I couldn't have asked for a better friend," Remy said, squeezing him tight, not wanting to let go but knowing that he had very little say in the matter.

"You're right about that," Mulvehill said as he pulled away. He was smiling again, though there was a tinge of sadness in it.

He turned toward the dark figure still waiting patiently.

"Okay, then," he said as he looked down at himself, attempting to smooth away the wrinkles. "Do I look all right?" he asked over his shoulder.

Remy laughed. "Gorgeous."

Mulvehill chuckled as he began to stroll toward death.

"Take care of things for me, Remy."

"I will."

"Love ya, pal."

"I love you, too."

*　　*　　*

Remy opened his eyes to find that his wings had unfurled, closing up tightly around himself and his departed friend.

He studied the still features of Steven Mulvehill and saw a peace there that made letting go just a little bit easier.

Just a little bit.

He opened his wings and gently lifted his friend, laying him carefully on the bed. It took him a moment to realize that he wasn't alone. He furled his wings as he stood on bare, trembling legs, taking a moment to process, the other place—what had slowly become *the* reality for him for what seemed like a very long time—gradually receding into the background of his mind as another reality—*his* reality—slid back in to retake its place.

"I'm back," he said, his voice sounding weak and old.

Linda came at him in a rush, but Marlowe, barking insanely, beat her, nearly knocking Remy to the floor in his excitement. He bent down, allowing the dog to frantically lick his face, before he was roughly pulled into Linda's arms.

Her embrace was invigorating, life-affirming, and he found himself growing stronger the longer he held her.

"I thought I would never see you again," she whispered in his ear.

"But here I am," he answered, squeezing her tightly.

"Yes, here you are," she said, her lips warm against his neck.

He looked over his shoulder to see the others there, amidst the remains of great violence.

"Thank you," he said. "Thank you all for fighting for me."

Ashley ran to embrace him as Linda had. Marlowe continued to circle around them excitedly, tail wagging, barking happily.

Squire stood off to the side, twirling a bloodstained axe in one hand.

"Do you want to get in on this?" Remy asked.

"Naw," the goblin answered. "I'm good."

Samson had been blocking the doorway with his mass, and Remy could see his children behind him. But he was surprised when another figure squeezed past the Biblical strongman to enter the room.

"You," Remy said, feeling his anger surge.

Linda and Ashley let go of Remy, feeling the change in his body, as he strode to stand before the man called Lazarus.

"I thought you died," Remy said.

Lazarus stared at the floor, shaking his head. "No," he said softly, a tremble in his reply. "For what I did . . . for what I tried to do . . . I didn't deserve it."

"You tried to end the world. Damn right you didn't deserve it," Remy said, barely holding his anger in check.

"I know I did wrong, but I've been working to make amends," Lazarus said. He held out a hand as if to ward something off, as if the fury radiating from Remy were a physical thing. "I've been helping God with Unification . . . watching . . . making sure that the other one . . ."

"The other one . . . ?" Remy questioned.

"Simeon," Lazarus said, finally looking up into Remy's eyes.

"He has to be stopped," Remy said, feeling the divine fires inside him surge to life.

"I know where he is," Lazarus said. "I can take you to him."

CHAPTER FORTY

Meg Miller had a feeling.

She'd opened her eyes that morning and had a sense that something was going to happen. It wasn't a bad feeling, like that sense of dread, waiting for the other shoe to drop.

No, something wonderful was coming, and she knew it right down in the core of her soul.

Meg wasn't a religious person in the least, but what she experienced that morning as she rolled out of bed, preparing for work as a paralegal at Fragomen, Del Rey, Bernsen & Loewy, could only be described as spiritual.

And whatever it was, it affected her deep to the core of her being, lifting her up and making her feel as though what was coming was going to change everything.

Change the world.

She walked across the cold tile floor and stood at the kitchen window of her North End condo, looking up into an unusually blue sky.

Meg smiled. She was ready.

Joe knew he was going to die.

He'd known as soon as they'd admitted to him the nursing home that that was probably it for him. But he was okay with that. At ninety-three, he'd lived a good and long life.

His heart hadn't been right for years, and it finally was giving out on him. Fluid, the docs had said. They'd offered surgery but then said he probably wouldn't make it anyway. *"Then why bother?"* he'd asked them, and they'd just nodded their heads.

His kids were torn, but they understood. His time was just running down.

They'd been with him since he got there, standing by his bedside, holding his hand and telling him how much they loved him. It was nice; he appreciated them being there, but he knew his time was close, and truth to tell, he wanted to do it alone.

He'd practically cheered when they'd gone for coffee, even though he hadn't been able to do much of anything, having been pretty much unresponsive since the ambulance had brought him in.

Yeah, he hated to do it to them, but it was something he strongly felt he should do alone. What was it his father used to say? *"I came into this world alone, and I plan on going out the same way."* And his dad had done just that, dropping dead of a heart attack after taking a shower when he got home from working third shift. When Joe's mother got to him, Dad was long gone.

Joe could feel his heart slowing down, the beats becoming more irregular. Yeah, it wouldn't be long now.

Within the darkness of his closed eyes, he saw a flash and focused on the warm light. And suddenly from the light there was a vision unlike anything he'd ever seen before. It was as if his eyes were open and he was looking out the window of some grand villa somewhere like where he'd been stationed during World War II. The sky was filled with what appeared to be a city . . . a city unlike anything he had ever seen before. It was everywhere he looked—all-encompassing—but he had a sense that it was not whole.

That it was somehow incomplete.

But something was about to happen, something that would make this city—*Heaven*; suddenly he knew the city was Heaven—whole for the first time in a very long time.

And he was going to be there to see it.

Joe smiled as his heart slowed, the beats of the once powerful muscle coming less and less until they were so infrequent that his body shut down, and Joe left the world to travel to another, to witness something.

Incredible.

Syed Hamza had planned to do evil this day.

He'd planned to strap a device loaded with explosives to his chest and walk into a crowded marketplace in Pakistan and detonate it.

At one time not too long ago—hours, really—he'd believed that he was doing such a terrible thing in the name of his God, but now . . .

Syed sat upon the floor of his tiny apartment, the murderous device lying unassembled upon a towel in front of him, and cried.

For God had sent him a vision. And there would be no acts of violence perpetrated in His name on this day, or any day forward.

God was about to touch the world, and any who would do evil in His name would suffer greatly.

It would be a time of great celebration.

It would be a time of something wondrous.

The demon sat nestled in the darkness at the back of Methuselah's, a wall of empty glasses stacked before him, ready to add another to the fortification.

He was angry, angry at the sensations he was experiencing as the divine being—the so-called Creator of the universe—prepared for something of great magnitude.

And he knew, as he studied the faces of various beings that inhabited the saloon as he did, that he wasn't the only who felt it. Some wore disgusting expressions of bliss, while others—such as himself—wanted to scream and perform acts of extreme violence in response to this coming cosmic event.

His race had always had an aversion to the divine.

The demon finished his drink, enjoying the dull buzz that he was experiencing behind his pointed ears. It was helping to drown out the sensations being broadcast through the ether, but the demon still felt it in the center of his brain, like an annoying itch that he couldn't scratch.

Yes, the drinking helped, but also the recollection of the act he had perpetrated upon one of the divine beings who most assuredly would have some part to play in the Heavenly pageant unfolding within the universe.

The demon smiled, remembering how angry he had been in this very establishment, when an angel of Heaven had insulted him as only the arrogant messengers of God were capable of. This one—this Remy Chandler—had looked upon him as nothing, a stain upon the fabric of reality.

The waitress brought him another round, and he grunted his thanks as she placed the liquor before him. Gathering up the empties and placing them upon her tray, she left him with a better view of the bar and its patrons.

If only they were aware of what he had done. He had struck back against the arrogance of Heaven, and the slights heaped upon his species. He had ordered a contract on the angel who'd slighted him, this Remy Chandler.

The demon smiled. The Bone Masters never failed. He wished he could have been there to see it for himself, but he took great joy in the knowledge that he had been responsible for the Seraphim's death.

He drank deeply from his latest beverage, allowing the effects to wash over him, and suddenly, he could no longer keep it to himself.

The demon stood abruptly, his chair shrieking behind him as it skidded across the floor. A part of his brain tried to warn him to be quiet, but he ignored it. He had to make them aware of what he had done.

He felt multiple sets of eyes upon him, especially the minotaur at the front door. Even the golem owner behind the bar had stopped making drinks and was watching him suspiciously.

He should have sat back down, but he couldn't hold it back.

He wanted them all to know that a force of darkness sometimes won over the light.

Raising his glass, he looked around at all who watched him. "To Remy Chandler," the demon announced. "One less flaming jewel in the Almighty's crown." And then he downed what was left of his drink and smiled at those watching him.

"Drinks for everyone," the demon ordered. "In honor of an angel fallen too soon." And then he began to laugh, sitting back down in his pocket of darkness, the attention of the tavern upon him.

That's it, he thought. *Look at me. Look at me and wonder: Was I responsible for the death of an angel of the Lord?*

The demon smiled so widely that it nearly split his face.

Remy stepped out into the dusk on Pinckney Street. It was strangely quiet on the Hill, the carnage that he had left behind in the apartment like another world entirely.

Linda and Marlowe joined him, standing behind him as he gazed off into the ether, feeling the call of Heaven.

"What is that?" Linda asked, slipping her warm hand into his.

"You can feel it?" he asked.

"Yes," she said, searching the sky for something she could not see.

"It's something that has been a long time coming," Remy told her. Marlowe sniffed around the base of a tree near the front of the brownstone, then lifted his leg, watering it with a spray of urine.

"What did you call it?" she asked him. "Unification?"

"That's it," he said. "Heaven moving to be whole again . . . and the start of something new."

Others on the Hill had come out of their homes, to go to work the night shift, or walk the dog, or go for a run. And they stopped as well, as if hearing something pleasant off in the distance.

"They're hearing it, too," Linda said.

"Some are more sensitive than others," Remy answered. "Most will just get a feeling that something is about to be different."

He could sense the others behind him now.

"We cleaned up the best we could," Samson said.

"The shadow beasts will be eating good for quite some time," Squire added, the goblin's use of shadows to travel to other worlds where hungry beasts resided perfect for the disposal of the Bone Master assassins' bodies.

"I want to thank you all for what you've done," Remy said, turning to them. "Seriously, I can't thank you enough."

Samson laughed, and his children smiled.

"When the Morningstar contacts you personally and requests your services, who are we to say no?"

Remy found himself rankled by the mention of the fallen son of

Heaven, but reminded himself that soon Lucifer, the son of the Morning, would be back in the good graces of Heaven.

"I took care of that favor," Squire said, giving Remy the nod.

He had asked Squire to take Steven's body back to his apartment.

"Thank you, Squire."

Lazarus was the last to leave the brownstone.

"Are we ready?" Remy asked.

The dark-skinned man nodded.

"Show me." Remy unfurled his wings, inviting Lazarus to step inside.

"Take me to the forever man."

Francis stood in front of his dresser mirror and straightened the knot of his tie. Staring at his reflection, he again attempted to recall something that nibbled aggressively at the back of his mind. Something that he had been doing—of great importance, he believed—but now . . .

He had other things to concern himself with now, things of great cosmic significance. His employer was being welcomed back into the fold, as was he, and all the others who had fallen during, and after, the Great War in Heaven.

It was a day that he'd truly never thought he'd see.

Stepping back, he got a better look at himself in the mirror.

Looking good, he thought, bringing his hand down the front of his suit jacket, smoothing away any potential wrinkles. He wanted to look his best; after all, one did not get welcomed back to Heaven every day. Checking himself from every angle, Francis decided that he looked all right. He stepped away from the mirror and went out to the living room, where the golden Pitiless pistol waited for him atop the coffee table.

Can't go anywhere without this, he thought as he picked up the gun. With little thought to his actions, Francis flipped open the cylinder, then reached into the front pocket of his shirt and removed a single bullet.

The bullet throbbed with incredible power—the power to create or to destroy—but Francis did not think of such things as he loaded it into the chamber and flipped the cylinder closed with a loud snap. The Pitiless then disappeared into an inside pocket of his suit coat.

He could feel it there, silently thrumming, almost like a small animal purring contentedly.

Unbuttoning his jacket, he sat down in his favorite leather recliner and waited. He glanced at his watch for no good reason; there had never been a time mentioned. It would happen when it happened.

But he could sense that things were moving in the ether, sliding into position. His eyes drifted to the closet door, where an entrance to the Hell prison, Tartarus, had once existed, but no more. Once Lucifer had returned to power, he'd torn down the prison and reconfigured Hell to a realm that could rival Heaven in its awesomeness. Things had really changed for his boss.

He glanced at his watch again and was considering getting up to check his reflection again just in case, when he felt the sudden change in the atmosphere of the room. Francis' eyes shot immediately to the closet door; an eerie greenish light poured out from beneath it.

They're opening the gateway again, he thought as he stood.

He buttoned his jacket, then ran a hand down the front of his suit as the closet door swung open to reveal an entrance to Lucifer's new Hell.

Impressive, he thought as he slowly approached the opening, the Pitiless against his chest, pulsing with life.

And with the potential for death.

The Archangel Michael stood upon the edge of the Garden as it hurtled through the curtains of reality, on its way back to where it had originated.

Called home by the Father of creation.

Michael smiled, as did his faithful legions, for they had been successful in cleansing the Garden of something infernal in its design.

The Shaitan waited in the dirt of Eden, untouched by the archangels, rendered invisible to the divine warriors by the words of the human, Simeon.

The Lord God had assigned them a task, and they had met it with great success. The Garden of Eden would return, to become part of

Heaven once again, as it had been so long ago when the universe was young and uncomplicated. Michael kept his thoughts to himself, still believing that this—this Unification—was the worst of ideas, but he hoped that he would be proven wrong—

The human Simeon had said that they shared a common hatred, an abhorrence of the Almighty and the kingdom that He presided over. Simeon had told them he would give them what they most desired— what he most desired—and in so doing they would be responsible for the fall of Heaven. The Shaitan found no downside to this and agreed to the human's proposal.

But deep down, in the core of his being, Michael suspected that he wasn't wrong. The Morningstar could not be trusted, for he would bring ruin to Heaven.

Now the Shaitan would wait, nestled in the soil of the Garden, biding their time until their arrival at the steps of Heaven.

CHAPTER FORTY-ONE

Simeon missed not having a magick user at his disposal; he so hated getting his hands dirty.

From a bowl made from the skull of one of the world's most powerful clairvoyants, he took a pinch of the yellowish powder and sprinkled it into the foul-smelling contents of a cauldron bubbling nearby.

The powder was the ground bones of angels from the host, Grigori, also known as the Watchers. Their bones, mixed with a number of rare ingredients that he'd acquired over the countless centuries he had lived, would temporarily give him access to a talent necessary for his plan.

The pulverized bones reacted with the substances boiling within the cauldron almost immediately, creating a scarlet mist that writhed up before him. Simeon leaned into the red vapor, letting the thick steam coat his face, leaving his eyes wide-open so that the strange fog could cover them as well.

The pain was instantaneous, and he reared back, stifling a scream as he stumbled around his sanctum for a place to recover. Dropping heavily into a leather wingback chair, Simeon waited, allowing the spell to wash over him—change him. Again he wished that he still had a magick user in his employ.

The world had gone black, but he quite enjoyed the darkness. It reminded him of something similar and comforting on the day he had died, before the Son of God chose to wrench him back from the cusp of Paradise, to suffer the indignities of the mortal world forever.

The accumulated anger was always there for him, an endless reservoir of fuel that had propelled his engine of wrath to this very moment.

From the blackness there came vision.

At first he could barely comprehend what he was seeing, his all-too-human brain trying to understand what only the divine were meant to see.

Simeon was now looking through the eyes of the Archangel Michael as he performed his function in the process of Unification. It was the angel's job to escort the newly cleansed Garden of Eden back to its original home—to reunite this piece of Paradise with Heaven. Through the archangel's eyes Simeon saw the Garden's journey and smiled with the thought of the surprise that it had in store for the Creator and His kingdom.

And the final act of vengeance that would follow.

He couldn't wait to see it.

Remy appeared in the tunnel leading down to where his secret enemy hid. He furled his wings and adjusted his eyes to the darkness of the descending corridor. According to Lazarus, Simeon had these hidey-holes all over the world, workshops for the nefarious schemes that he'd been plotting for thousands of years.

He was surprised that he'd never encountered this forever man before, but then remembered that Simeon possessed the rings of Solomon. Perhaps he had met him before but was ordered to forget.

The memory of his alternate self's past had started to grow less defined—more foggy—the longer he was back. But he would never forget the horror of his actions in that other universe. Those memories were still strong, like raised scars upon the surface of his brain.

He would see that those same actions never came to fruition here.

Remy entered the main chamber to find it lit by multiple jars stationed strategically about the underground room. Inside the jars were glowing spheres of ethereal energy that he at once recognized as souls. He could hear—*feel*—them screaming from within their traps, begging to be set free.

Rounding a thick circular pillar made from skulls stacked upon skulls, Remy saw his enemy. He reclined within the embrace of a chocolate-colored leather wingback. There was a look of absolute joy upon the pale-skinned man's features, his red-tinted eyes unusually wide and unblinking.

And suddenly the anger that had pooled inside the Seraphim, collected as a seething, black miasma at the center of his being, seemed to develop a life of its own, taking control of the divine fire and causing it to surge forward. A fire fueled by the rage at this person—this soulless thing—for what another version of him had done to another world and what he intended to do to this one.

The anger was stupid and rash, and its actions alerted his foe to his presence. Simeon leapt up from his chair. Remy could see the rings upon each hand and knew that the words—the commands—were about to be uttered. Fearing what was to come, he had no qualms about unleashing the fires of divinity that churned angrily inside of him. The fire leapt hungrily upon the forever man, wrapping him in a seething blanket of reds and yellows, the flames so intense that the leather chair caught fire as well, filling the air of the underground chamber with a blinding, choking smoke.

Remy watched his enemy burn, feeling no sense of guilt or pity as Simeon collapsed to the floor, his body lost within the divine inferno. The flames burned savagely, and Remy knew that it was only a matter of time before there was nothing left to burn.

But a voice, ragged and raw, shrieked from within the conflagration. "Pull . . . back . . . the . . . fire!"

Remy felt the words upon him—the power of Solomon's ring—and was compelled to obey, wrangling the living flames and returning the divine power to where it belonged, inside of him. His wings exploded from his back as he prepared to leap into action, but the burned man—the forever man—was quicker.

"Stop right there," he hissed through blackened lips.

And Remy froze, his wings extended and ready.

Simeon chuckled as he and his leather chair, and a nearby table covered with books and scrolls, continued to burn.

"Is that who I think it is?" Simeon asked through a cracking voice seared by the fire.

The forever man blinked his oozing eyes, and Remy could see that despite the fire that still covered his body, he was healing: a blessing and a curse for those who have been touched by the power of Heaven.

"I do believe it is." Simeon haltingly stepped closer, away from the flames that continued to spread behind him. The farther he removed himself from the hungry conflagration, the more quickly his flesh seemed to be returning to health.

"Remy Chandler," the man hissed, and he attempted to smile, the charred skin cracking and oozing.

It reminded Remy of another man, a better man, who had aided him on a previous mission. A man who was gone now—gone like the reality in which he'd lived.

"I had plans for you, Seraphim," Simeon said, his voice sounding stronger. Flakes of blackened flesh had begun to crumble from his face, exposing bloody new flesh beneath. "You were to be my final affront, the cherry on top of the sundae, the pièce de résistance."

But that man had a counterpart, another version of himself, still very much alive and just as eager to make amends for his sins.

"I was going to make you God's killer." Simeon's eyes twinkled wetly with the revelation. "Can you just imagine that? You would have been responsible for it all falling down." Simeon's ravaged face twisted with disgust. "But then you had to go and get yourself nearly killed and screw up all my plans."

He paused for a moment, and Remy wanted to hurl himself upon the forever man and rip him limb from limb, but he was unable to act upon the violent impulse.

"But I didn't let it get to me," Simeon said slyly. "Oh no, I just acquired another pawn."

He was standing no farther than three feet away, and Remy could easily have reached out and crushed his skull in his hands, but he did not. The magick of the ring prevented it.

"It's a good thing that you have friends," Simeon continued. "Ready to step up in a pinch."

"Yes," Remy agreed, and he couldn't help but smile. "It is good to have friends."

There was a flurry of movement behind the forever man. A single figure leapt out from the shadows, running through the smoke and flames, a glint of something metal—something deadly—in his hands. Simeon began to turn, and Remy could see the rings still on the blackened fingers of his hands, ready to be used.

Lazarus screamed and raised his sword as he lunged at Simeon. His clothing had caught fire as he'd come through the voracious flames, but that didn't stop him.

"Stop!" Simeon cried, attempting to use the powers of the rings.

But they were useless against another forever man.

And Lazarus brought the blade down, cleanly severing both hands at Simeon's wrists.

Remy roared with freedom, surging forward to grab hold of the stunned Simeon. "How dare you!" the Seraphim raged as divine fire once again took hold of the forever man.

Simeon tried to speak, lifting his trembling arms to look upon the bleeding stumps where his hands had once been. "What did you do?" he screeched.

"Isn't it obvious?" Remy asked, letting go of him. "We've taken away your advantage."

Simeon's body had already begun to repair itself, and Remy knew it wouldn't be long before two new hands replaced the old. But he would have none of that.

He willed a pool of Heavenly fire into the palm of each hand, and before the forever man had a chance to react, he firmly took hold of each stump. There came the sound of sizzling flesh, followed by the overwhelming aroma of cooking meat.

And Simeon screamed.

Remy roughly threw the man to the floor, wanting no more than to tear him apart, watch him heal, and then tear him apart all over again. For here was a man who wanted to kill God—who actually had in another, twisted reality. He was far too dangerous to live.

Remy reached down to the trembling Simeon with bloodlust in his eyes. Who knew what he would have done then, if it weren't for the voice of Lazarus?

"Remy. Stop."

Remy had lifted Simeon up by the front of his burned and tattered shirt, his feet dangling inches from the floor.

"If you could only have seen what he was responsible for," Remy said, his mind filled with staccato images of a world where God had been murdered.

Lazarus had been badly burned by the fire and leaned heavily upon his sword. "I know," he said wearily. "But this isn't what *He* wants."

The angel knew Lazarus was right. God didn't want this man maimed for all eternity; He had other plans for the forever man. Reluctantly, Remy drew back upon his rage, but it was hard. Made even harder when Simeon began to laugh.

"What's so damn funny?" Remy demanded, pulling the man closer so they were nose to nose. The stink of burned meat still lingered on the forever man's body.

"All this fury." Simeon giggled. "Such a waste of perfectly good anger."

Remy shook the man. "What are you talking about?"

"It's all for nothing," Simeon said. "It's all been put in place . . . all been set in motion." He was laughing hysterically now, waving the blackened stumps at the ends of his arms as if conducting a silent orchestra. "It's a done deal. Whether I'm around or not, it's all coming down."

Simeon smiled hideously. "Unification will fail, and Heaven is going to come crashing down around your ears."

"*He* knows," Remy said quietly, allowing a smile of his own to form, watching the madman's eyes as an understanding of the words slowly began to sink in.

Simeon's expression went from one of pleasure to surprise—blending into rage. "How? He can't know. . . . That's impossible! My plans—"

"Your plans will be stopped," Remy interrupted the forever man, his voice booming in the underground chamber. It took all he had not to break the man in two and burn his remains to ash, but that wasn't His way. God's way.

God had a plan for Simeon.

"Give me the rings," Remy said to Lazarus.

And his friend complied, pulling the rings from the fingers of the dismembered hands lying on the floor in a puddle of congealing blood.

"What are you going to do with them?" Simeon asked as Lazarus placed them in the palm of Remy's hand.

"That would be telling," Remy said, spreading his wings to their full span and then closing them around himself and his foe.

They had places to be if they were going to put a stop to the fall of Heaven and the end of the world.

Lazarus envied Simeon. To be allowed to see . . . to experience what he was about to.

The pain was incredible, stealing away his strength, and he fell to his knees, the sword that he'd been using as a support clattering away across the floor. But he didn't mind; it was a good pain.

A constant pain.

A pain that told him he was no longer healing.

He smiled, and it was excruciating, but he could not hold back his happiness. *Is it possible?* he wondered. *Can this actually be it?*

Can this really be the end?

He managed to drag himself across the chamber floor and propped himself against an ancient bookcase stuffed to the gills with all manner of books and swollen journals. For a brief moment he admired Simeon; he had done something incredible with his longevity—even if it was meant to cause the death of God and the fall of Heaven.

Lazarus slowly lifted his hand. It was burned, but the liver spots marking the passage of time—of age—were definitely there.

And they appeared to be multiplying.

He practically cried with joy, laying his head back and resting it upon a shelf.

The pain was worse, too, and that was good. Normally, he would have started to heal by now, the agony lessening as bones knitted and flesh filled in. But that wasn't happening now. The pain just went on and on, growing more intense, like a symphony building to a crescendo.

What a wonderful song.

He, too, had lived a long life. He had done some good, but in retrospect, he should have done so much more. Although eternal life was hard, and sometimes a torture, and it twisted some in such subtle ways that they didn't notice.

Lazarus was sure that Simeon was very aware of what he had become, but Lazarus, all he knew was that he was done with life and wanted to die.

And a desire such as that, a desire so strong, had made him selfish and susceptible to the wants of others—the promise of death making him do some awful things.

And for that, he had been punished, physically battered and broken and allowed to heal, mentally tormented with the memory of what he had done.

For a brief instant, Lazarus panicked, no longer feeling the symphony of pain, but he quickly realized that he had just grown numb. He managed to lift his hand again and saw that the wounds were still there, his skin blackened, blistered, and seeping.

He sighed, realizing that it was still happening.

That he was dying.

Lazarus knew that he deserved to live forever, especially after what he had done in almost bringing about the Apocalypse.

But the Lord God had taken pity on him and had given him a chance to make amends. And Lazarus had taken that chance without question, never really knowing when or if his actions would be enough.

Never knowing when or if he might be forgiven.

But now, he knew his time was coming. He could feel it slowly happening: All the parts of him that had kept him going over the long centuries were shutting down. It was a strange feeling, and somewhat frightening.

Lazarus gurgled a laugh. After wanting to die for so very long, here he was, afraid. How insane was that?

But then he realized that he was no longer alone.

He knew who it was who now stood over him, for he'd been waiting a long, long time to meet him again.

"Nice to see you," he managed, looking up into the kindly face of the Angel of Death.

And Israfil smiled, offering his hand.

CHAPTER FORTY-TWO

Simeon struggled pathetically in his grasp, and Remy was tempted to let him go. He couldn't think of a better fate for one so vile than to be released into the void, to live and die repeatedly for all eternity.

It would be a Hell that the forever man deserved.

But Remy had made a promise to the Lord and would see it through to the end.

"I've watched you, Remy Chandler," Simeon said, finally ceasing his struggles. "Or should I call you Remiel?"

Remy did not respond.

"Since the first time I laid eyes on you, I've known you were something special . . . someone to watch."

Simeon's words were like serpents, wriggling into his ears, his brain. But Remy continued to ignore him, focusing instead on their journey.

"I believe your Lord God feels the very same way, allowing you this life—this human existence. Permitting you to believe that you are free."

Remy could feel the forever man's eyes on him, probing for weakness, a chink in his armor.

"But you've never truly been free, Remiel," Simeon cooed. "He's always known exactly where you've been, winding you up and putting you in motion when needed."

"Shut up," Remy ordered through clenched teeth, regretting the words as soon as he said them. He'd allowed the man under his skin.

"You've always been there on His earthly plane to keep things in order for Him. Such a good little soldier. He must be so appreciative."

"I said shut up," Remy yelled, squeezing the forever man just tight enough that he felt the bones creak, on the verge of breaking.

Simeon grunted in pain, but it didn't stop him. "How does He repay you for your hard work, this loving God of yours? . . . Oh yes, that's right. He took your wife from you."

It was all that Remy could stand. His rage bubbled up in a scream and surge of divine fire. "Silence!" he cried, now more Seraphim than man, more angel than human.

And Simeon wailed in agony, his flesh once again burned by the fires of Heaven. Reveling in the screams of the forever man, Remy unfurled his wings in the darkness of the void between where they had been and where they were going.

"I should leave you here to burn for all eternity, a candle of wickedness to light the darkness of the void."

"Do it!" Simeon croaked. "Nothing can be worse than what I've already endured! Do it!"

The raw emotion in Simeon's voice caught Remy off guard, and he suddenly felt an odd sense of compassion. He reined in the fire, briefly considering that Simeon might actually have been punished enough.

And with that merciful contemplation, the darkness became consumed by light. Remy grabbed hold of his smoldering foe and turned toward the source of the imposing illumination, his gaze resting on the most wondrous of sights.

Something that would never be seen again.

Unification.

Remy was speechless as he beheld the mechanizations that would reunify Heaven and bring the world of man that much closer to God. It was like looking at the workings of some great cosmic machine. The stuff of Heaven, Pandemonium, and Eden gradually moving toward one another, each of the enormous masses changing—reconfiguring— to join with the core that was Heaven and the Golden City.

Remy managed to tear his gaze away from the wonder of it all, to look upon the forever man, who stared with eyes wide, tears streaming down his blistered cheeks. Holding Simeon tighter, Remy flapped his wings, allowing them to soar closer to the magnificent happenings.

"Look at it," Remy commanded him. "This is what you wanted to stop."

Simeon struggled but soon relented, allowing the awe-inspiring sights to wash over him.

The air was filled with the music of the chorus of the divine, singing out in joy.

But that sound was rudely interrupted with the sound of screams, bellows of rage suddenly rising up from the green of Eden.

The Garden was in the midst of returning to whence it had come, tendrils of thick root already reaching out to entwine about the base of the Golden City. But from its earth, monsters emerged, monsters that were very familiar to Remy. They were the Shaitan, and they would see Heaven dragged from the sky.

The Archangel Michael and his soldiers stood at the Garden's edge, entranced by the transformation before them but seemingly unaware of the scene transpiring behind them.

Simeon looked at Remy then and smiled; the cruel creature that the years of immortality had forged returned. "And so it begins," he said, laughing, enjoying the nightmare that was about to unfold.

Remy released him then, tossing the man away from him as if repulsed. The forever man spun through the air, drifting toward the center, which was the Kingdom of Heaven.

The Shaitan had launched themselves into the air above the Garden of Eden, a swarm of the abominable, intent only on evil forged from God's rejection.

Remy knew what he must do. From his pocket, he removed the rings of Solomon and without a moment's hesitation slid the rings upon his fingers.

Countless millennia hidden beneath the soil of the Garden had twisted the Shaitan, who were once considered as the Almighty's messengers and servants, before the creation of the angels. No longer were they divine in nature.

But demonic.

And it was time that Remy informed them of this.

"Hold, demon spawn!" he announced, feeling the power of Solomon's ring flow through him.

The Shaitan shuddered en masse, their pale forms in flight above the Garden beginning to fly in a circular motion, creating a kind of demonic cyclone.

"You will do no harm this day."

The Shaitan fought him, screaming and attempting to break from their spiral configuration, but they were held in place by the power of the ring.

Remy then turned his attention to the Archangel Michael and his troops, still blissfully standing at attention, totally unaware of the evil that had arisen behind them.

"Michael," Remy called as he hovered above the archangels.

He saw Michael's eyes clear, realization gradually turning to fury.

"Remiel," he spat in recognition.

Again, Remy felt the power of the rings, this time allowing him to command his own kind.

"Archangels of Heaven, behind you is a threat that must be disposed of if Unification is to be carried out."

Michael and the others spun around, truly amazed at the sight of the Shaitan behind them, swirling above the Garden.

"What madness is this?" Michael asked, turning his angry stare to Remy.

"A madness that has been allowed to go on for far too long," Remy told him. "Dispose of it and be done."

It looked as though the archangel commander might argue with him, but he had no choice, and spread his powerful wings. The others did as their commander did, swords of fire igniting in their grasps. Michael let out an ululating cry before leading a flock of angels toward the maelstrom.

To at last purge a festering evil from Eden.

And allow it to return, pristine, to Heaven.

Remy turned from the massacre of evil to the spectacle before him as the Golden City and Hell's Pandemonium came together to create a thing of awe and beauty.

He flew toward the new city, a fascinating yet strange mixture of ornate citadels and spires that appeared to be forged from crystal, gold, and the rays of the sun, and towers and buildings that seemed as if they were chiseled from obsidian, marble, and arctic ice. It would be called simply "the Kingdom," and it would be breathtaking in its awesomeness.

Flying toward the center of the shifting and changing city, Remy was suddenly bathed in an unearthly light, and everything before him seemed to fade from view, revealing two figures standing upon a platform of gold that hovered in the air. He was compelled to go to it and touch down before the two figures.

"Hello, Remy," the Almighty said, wearing the guise of the old gentleman as he had before.

"Remy," Lucifer Morningstar said, a sly smirk upon his perfect features.

Remy furled his wings as he landed upon the platform, bowing his head and dropping to one knee.

"That's quite enough of that," the Almighty said, stepping forward to gently take Remy by the arm and force him to rise.

"I got here as soon as I could," Remy told him. His eyes then darted about nervously, catching Lucifer's attention.

"Lose something?" the Morningstar asked.

"Simeon," Remy answered. "I tossed him in this direction, but . . ."

"The forever man," Lucifer said, glancing to the Almighty beside him. "Your Son truly had no idea what He'd created in that one."

The Almighty smiled sadly and nodded his head. "To some it would have been a gift to truly experience everything that life had to offer as well as to use the knowledge acquired with this great longevity to benefit mankind itself."

"You would think," Lucifer commented. "But alas . . ."

"Alas," God repeated sadly. He gazed off into the distance, seeing something beyond the glowing white light of the void, something that Remy was not privy to. "So many realities . . . so much anger."

And Remy believed that he actually saw tears in the Almighty's eyes.

"Where is . . . ?" he started to ask, curious as to what had happened to the immortal called Simeon.

"He is being dealt with," Lucifer answered, looking directly at God, giving Remy the impression that he did not approve of whatever God's plan was for the forever man.

"Is there anything you'd like me to do?" Remy asked.

God smiled at him, reaching out to rest a liver-spotted hand upon Remy's shoulder. "You've done quite enough, my son."

"There is one thing," Lucifer said. "We need a witness." He extended a hand toward the Creator.

"A witness to the act of Unification," God added, turning toward the Morningstar.

And Remy did as was asked of him, watching as God took hold of the First of the Fallen's hand. The two shook fiercely, and Remy waited for something . . . more: a choir of angels singing hosannas, perhaps.

Something to signify the importance of what had just occurred.

"You look disappointed," Lucifer said as he released his Father's hand.

"I thought there would be more to it."

"What, like a parade?" Lucifer chided.

"I love a good parade," God said with a cheery smile.

"So Unification is done?" Remy asked.

God turned ever so slightly to the glowing void behind him, and the white of nothing turned to reflect the glorious new Kingdom of Heaven.

"And there's this," God said.

"Impressive," Lucifer Morningstar said, standing beside him.

It was as if they'd forgotten him, chatting back and forth about the new city that had come to be. Remy saw that the Garden of Eden had now joined to become part of the Kingdom, miles and miles of lush plant life, and flowering vines entwined about the towering structures, adding a touch of green—of life—to the amalgam of two great cities.

It was truly a sight to behold.

He seemed to come out of nowhere, like a storm with the potential for great destruction.

Francis.

The Pitiless pistol—*the Godkiller*—was clutched in his hand, its shining golden surface reflecting the lights from the Kingdom. He was coming up behind them, behind God and the Morningstar, and Remy was too far away to stop him.

But then he remembered what he still wore upon his fingers.

"Francis, stop!" Remy cried, his voice echoing powerfully off the sprawling city before him.

Francis was behind the Almighty, the barrel of the golden pistol pointed at the back of God's head. Remy wasn't sure if his friend had heard the words, and his mind was filled with the imaginings of the gunshot, the roar of thunder, the screams of another world, another reality, as it began to die.

But the sound did not come.

God turned to face the fallen Guardian angel and pushed the barrel of the weapon aside with His hand.

"That might've turned out badly," Lucifer said, taking the gun from Francis. That seemed to snap the fallen angel out of a kind of fugue state, and he looked around, confused.

"What the fuck?" he asked, eyeing Remy and then the Almighty and Lucifer. "Oh crap, what did I do?"

God smiled again and shook his head. "You did nothing but bring this to a close."

Lucifer opened the pistol and fished for the special bullet.

"Ah, there you are," God said as Lucifer held it out to him. He closed His hand around the bullet and the light of creation streamed from between his fingers. "It's good to have you back."

"The rings," Lucifer said, extending his hand toward Remy.

Remy hesitated a moment, then reminded himself that things were different now.

"Would somebody mind telling me what's going on?" Francis asked.

"It's a new day," Remy said simply, dropping the pair of rings into the center of Lucifer's palm.

The Morningstar smiled that beautiful smile, then returned to God's side. He held out the golden Pitiless pistol and the rings as the All Father raised His still-glowing fist toward them. There was a white flash as the Almighty opened His hand, unleashing the power that He held there. The rings and the pistol were gone, but a glowing sphere now hung between the two former adversaries.

They both seemed pleased with the sphere as it continued to grow, glowing brighter with each passing moment.

"It is done," God said.

"What's done?" Francis whispered to Remy. "What is it?"

"The end of this," God answered as the sphere began to rise.

"The grand finale," Lucifer added, watching the ball of light grow as it climbed higher.

"A new star will shine in the firmament," God said, "its light touching the new Kingdom and all those who live within it."

The glowing sphere climbed higher, and higher still, its size and luminosity becoming larger and more vibrant as it took its place in the blackness of the void.

"Did you get that?" Francis asked Remy, his eyes affixed to the object shining above them. "It's a star."

"I got it," Remy said, just as the sphere seemed to explode in a flash of brilliance that consumed the darkness around them.

Filling it with light.

Simeon seethed.

All the anger and fury contained within his body threatened to explode. And he wished that he could, the intensity of his rage most assuredly capable of obliterating the Heavens and all that existed within them.

The Seraphim had tossed him away, abandoning him—to where?

Simeon floated in a sea of darkness. He had drifted toward the changing landscape of Heaven when there came a blinding flash, and then there was nothing.

Darkness.

He extended his arms to either side, feeling nothing in the pitch black.

Was this his punishment? Had the Lord God Almighty banished him to live eternally in a place of perpetual shadow? It would be just like that merciless being to do such a thing. To want to torture him further.

Now not only would he live on and on, but he would do it alone, and in total darkness.

A fitting punishment for one who hated God with every fiber of his being. Maybe the Lord expected him to reflect upon his evil, to realize the error of his ways, and to repent his sins.

Simeon wouldn't dream of it.

Instead he would spend eternity thinking of ways to escape the endless night of this prison, and the awful things he would do to God and those He favored.

"As long as there is life in this body," Simeon snarled as he floated in a sea of black, "I will never forgive."

Never.

It was as if something—some*body*—was listening.

The darkness was gone, and Simeon was . . .

He did not recognize his surroundings at first, the faces of those who hung over him as he lay.

But then it came to him. How long had it been since he last thought of them? His family . . . his wife, daughter, and son. His very first family . . . the family that he'd had in the life before his death.

Before he had been brought back.

They were sitting at his bedside, within the tiny desert hut that had been his home then. They were praying for him between their tears. He wanted to scream at them to stop . . . that the God they prayed to was a monster.

But he was too weak, too tired from the sickness that had ravaged his body.

Was this further torture from the God that hated him? To relive the moment when he'd first bid farewell to the family that loved him so? To finally be released from the sickness and pain?

To die, and know the joy of spiritual bliss as his soul returned to the stuff of creation?

Was that how he would now be punished?

Simeon glanced up again at the family that he had loved so very much. To see them again was something special, for he had nearly forgotten their loving faces.

But now there was another face—an older man whom Simeon did not recognize, standing beside the foot of the bed.

Who?

But as the old man looked at him, Simeon knew.

His eyes overflowed with hate as he glared at the stranger. *Torture me all you like,* he wanted to scream, *but I will never forgive you.*

The old man stepped closer, reaching out to place a cool hand upon

Simeon's feverish brow, and all the anger and hate that had fueled his purpose for countless millennia left him.

"For all the pain," the old man spoke, *"I give you release."*

And the rage that had become so much a part of him was gone, burned away like the morning fog.

Simeon lay there as he had so very, very long ago, tired from the sickness that ravaged him, ready to go on. Looking up into the face of the old man.

Looking into the eyes of God, Simeon told Him that he was ready.

God whispered how sorry He was, leaning forward to place a gentle kiss upon his dampened brow.

With his last breath, Simeon forgave Him.

And lived no more.

EPILOGUE

The demon sat in his web of darkness, drowning his sorrows in drink after drink.

The angel was alive.

He had hired the greatest of assassins, and the Bone Masters had failed. The Seraphim still lived.

The demon grabbed his glass and drained it, slamming the empty down upon the wooden tabletop loud enough for the waitress to hear. He looked around but did not see her—in fact, the bar seemed to be empty.

"Waitress!" he bellowed.

He hoped that the golem heard him, heard the anger in his voice, and fired the bitch for not serving him properly. But he didn't see the golem, either. The demon's eyes ticked to the entrance of the establishment and saw that even the minotaur doorman wasn't in his usual place.

What's going on? he wondered. He grabbed the empties that surrounded him, tossing them back, hoping for one more sip from each, as he waited for someone to serve him.

But the bar remained empty.

The demon was about to get up and explore, when he at last saw somebody come out from the back. "About fucking time," he hissed, holding up one of his empties and giving it a shake.

The figure did not seem to take note of his need, walking toward where he'd taken up residence for the last five hours or so.

"A drink!" he screamed at the figure, who still did not stop.

It was then that he noticed the figure wore a heavy, hooded cloak, similar to the ones worn by . . .

"They're all dead," the figure said, slowly removing the covering around his head to reveal the pale guise of a Bone Master assassin.

"What?" the demon squawked. "Who's dead?"

The Bone Master remained silent, staring at him with eyes that burned with unquenchable hatred.

The demon was unable to hold his tongue. "Well, I'll tell you who's not dead: the guy I paid my life savings to have killed, that's who's not dead."

"It is all because of you that we are no more. Except for me, Ripper of Souls, the Bone Masters are extinct. And it is all because of you."

The demon jumped up, sending his heavy wooden chair flipping to the floor. "I don't know what you're going on about, but I want what I paid for," he snarled. "I don't care what happened to the other Bone Masters. . . . I don't care that you're the last one; I expect you to deliver what I was promised."

"And would that be a hit on an angel by the name of Remy Chandler?" A human in a dark suit emerged from a patch of darkness across the bar and strode over to join them.

"What's it to you?" The demon bared his rows of razor-sharp teeth.

"I need to be sure," the stranger explained.

"So what if I did?" the demon asked. "He a friend of yours or something?"

The human smiled and unbuttoned his jacket. "As a matter of fact, he is." From the inside pocket of his suit coat the man removed a pouch, heavy with its contents. He hefted the leather purse and then tossed it on the table top with a clatter.

"That's good enough for me," the man addressed the Bone Master, adjusting the black, horn-rimmed glasses on his face.

"What's that?" the demon asked, his clawed fingers reaching for the pouch.

The assassin's movements were a blur as he pinned the demon's hand to the table with a knife. The demon screamed and tried to pry the blade up, but it was imbedded, too, in the wood of the table.

"That's his payment," the stranger said.

The demon didn't understand. "Payment? Payment for what?"

The stranger smiled again. "Payment for the murder of the piece of shit that tried to have my friend put down."

The demon's eyes widened, and his survival instincts kicked into high gear. He pulled his hand up from the table. The pain was excruciating, but he knew what was to come would be much worse.

And all too final.

With a wet, ripping sound, his hand came free, and he stumbled backward, tripping over his overturned chair and landing on the floor.

The Bone Master loomed above him. "All dead, because of you," the assassin said mournfully. His hands emerged from within his cloak, clutching a weapon of bone.

The demon didn't even have a chance to beg for his life before he was dead.

Loose ends.

Francis hated them more than just about anything else. They prevented him from thinking clearly, from focusing on the future. No matter how hard he'd tried to let go, no matter that his friend had survived, that Heaven and the universe had managed to pull through once again, it didn't change the fact that someone—some*thing*—had put a contract out on Remy Chandler and had nearly killed him.

That didn't sit well with the Guardian angel Francis.

Guardian angel.

It still gave him quite a kick that he had been returned to his full status as a Guardian, that his penance had been counted and he'd been absolved of his sins, and he'd been given back his title and all that it entailed. Yes, he still worked for the Morningstar, but since Unification, that was no longer such a dirty thing.

Francis watched the Bone Master as he stood over his prey, his living weapon of bone, cartilage, and sinew dangling from his hand.

Loose ends still dangling in the breeze. It was time to wrap them up once and for all.

He'd never expected to hear from Methuselah. The golem bar owner tried to keep mum on his clientele and their doings, but having one of his demon regulars flapping his gums about Chandler must not have sat well with him, and he'd made the call.

Originally Francis had planned to do it himself, but then he'd realized that would take care of only one of the loose ends.

And there were two.

He'd thought that all the Bone Masters had been destroyed in one way or another, but he learned through the grapevine that one had survived—driven nearly insane by the murder of his species and hell-bent on discovering who was responsible. But if a Bone Master assassin still lived . . .

"You do good work," Francis complimented.

The Bone Master just stood there, staring at the dead demon, who had already begun to rot and stink up the joint. "I perform the function that I was born for . . . and what I am paid to do."

"The Bone Master assassins," Francis said. "The most proficient killers in existence, I hear. . . . Well, they used to be."

The Bone Master turned his dark gaze upon him.

"I hear that you're the last of them," Francis added. "Is that true?"

The assassin seemed visibly shaken. "The entire guild, even the uninitiated, have been killed."

"Wow, that really sucks," Francis said. "And this is the piece of shit that was responsible for making that happen?" He pointed to the dead demon on the floor of the bar.

The Bone Master looked back to the corpse and snarled. "This one hired us to slay an angel of Heaven who had offended him."

"And what, it didn't go so well?" Francis asked curiously.

"The angel did not die, and when my brothers attempted to complete the contract . . ."

"Let me guess—his friends didn't take too kindly to that."

The demon assassin glared at him, eyes shiny and dark with madness.

"His friends," the Bone Master said with a snarl.

"So because you Bone Master types wouldn't pull back on a contract put out by this asshole"—Francis pointed to the dead demon again—"your entire species, except for you, has been wiped out."

The demon assassin trembled with repressed fury.

"And the contract, as it stands now?" Francis asked.

"Still unfulfilled."

"So let me get this straight," Francis said. "Even with the guy who took out the contract dead at your feet, and only one of you Bone Masters left alive, you're still planning on carrying out that contract?"

The Bone Master puffed out his chest proudly. "As the last, it is my responsibility to . . ."

"Thanks; that's all I needed to hear." In one fluid movement, Francis pulled the revolver from inside his jacket and fired a single shot into the killer's forehead.

The Bone Master's eyes went wide in death, as if not believing what had just occurred. His body fell backward, landing splayed across one of the wooden tables.

"Stupid son of a bitch," Francis said, returning the pistol to the inside of his jacket. "And here I was going to let you live."

He'd hoped the assassin would have been smarter, to realize that the idea of fulfilling the contract on Remy Chandler just wasn't worth it anymore.

So much for common sense.

"So are we done here or what?" asked a voice from across the bar.

Francis looked up to see Squire entering from the kitchen. He was being followed by the sorcerer Angus Heath, who was the cook at Methuselah's; the minotaur, Phil; and the establishment's owner, Methuselah himself.

"Yeah," Francis said, satisfied that all the dangling threads had been snipped away. "I think we're good."

Squire came to stand with him. The goblin was holding a plate of chicken wings in one hand and eating them with the other.

"So you had to kill him?" Squire asked about the Bone Master.

"Yeah," Francis said. "He was still planning on going after Remy."

The goblin shook his head as he had another wing, sucking the bone clean of meat in a matter of seconds. "You'd think he would have quit while he was ahead."

"I suppose it must have something to do with honor," Francis said as he stared at the cooling corpse of the killer atop the wooden table.

"Something to do with being fucking stupid, if you ask me," Squire added his two cents.

"We've got to clean up," Francis said, going to Bone Master's corpse. "Help me with the other one."

"I'm eating," Squire complained.

"You're always eating," Francis said, hauling the corpse up from the table and slinging it over his shoulder with a grunt.

"And you're very hurtful," Squire retorted, setting his plate on another table and taking the legs of the dead demon.

Francis headed to the front of the bar.

"Sorry about the mess," he apologized to Methuselah.

"No worries," the golem said as he went to his place behind the bar. "Nothing that a mop and a bucket of soapy water can't take care of . . . Right, Phil?"

The minotaur snorted by the front door.

"As if I don't have enough to do," he said, picking up a magazine of crossword puzzles.

Francis pulled from his pocket the satchel of coins he'd used to pay the now-dead assassin and tossed them onto the bar with a heavy jingle.

"For your troubles."

"You're too kind," Methuselah responded, his great stone fingers closing around the purse and making it disappear somewhere beneath the bar.

"Could probably do up a pretty good stew with those two," Heath said, wiping his hands on the stained apron that covered his protruding belly.

"Sorry, they've already been promised to a hungry lady," Francis said, moving past the sorcerer/head chef and into the kitchen, heading for the back exit.

"Pardon me?" Heath questioned as Squire followed, dragging the demon by the legs. "Is this somebody special?"

"Oh, she's special all right," Squire answered, maneuvering the corpse around the corner and into the kitchen behind Francis. "In fact, I don't know if I've ever seen anything quite like her."

"Sounds mysterious," Heath said with a laugh from outside the kitchen.

Francis waited at the screen door for Squire, holding it open with his shoulder as Squire dragged the demon corpse behind him.

In Methuselah's back alley, a beautiful black 1960 Lincoln Continental purred.

The door slammed closed behind them with a clatter as they made their way to the front of the car to deposit their goods.

"Here ya go, sweetheart," Francis said, dropping the body down in front of Leona. "Eat up."

Squire dragged the demon's body alongside the Bone Master's and dropped his legs.

"You might want to step back," Francis said, just as the car lunged forward with a roar of its engine, the front grill opening wide with the metallic screech of rending metal, and began to feed upon the corpses before it.

"Ain't that a sight," Squire said.

"Isn't it, though?" Francis said.

The bodies were gone in less than a minute, and Francis knew that it was time to go.

"So, where to now?" Squire asked, climbing into the passenger seat and slamming the door closed.

"I've got to go to work," Francis said, putting the car in drive.

"Matters of the newly formed Kingdom, is it?" Squire asked with a grin. "Must be kind of exciting with everything being all shiny and new."

Francis held on to the steering wheel but didn't really need to do anything at all. Leona knew the way.

"I guess," he said with a shrug. "Shiny and new, but there's still plenty of darkness there, which is why I still have a job."

Squire was silent.

"Are they hiring?" he asked suddenly.

"What? Are you looking for a job?"

The goblin gave him a shit-eating grin. "Sure," he shrugged. "I could use the dough, and I've got a talent or two that could be beneficial."

"Insatiable hunger? Don't really see the use for that."

"Fuck you," Squire squawked. "Seriously, if I got a job there, maybe we could be partners."

"Oh no."

"Yeah, think of it," Squire said.

"No thanks."

"We could be like Cagney and Lacey."

"Who?"

"Simon and Simon?"

"I have no idea what you're talking about."

"Jake and the Fatman?"

"I think you can get out here," Francis said, nothing but perpetual darkness outside the car as they traveled through the fabric of reality.

"Anyplace to eat out there?" Squire asked. "I'm fucking starved."

Remy sat on his rooftop deck, snoring dog by his chair, and gazed up into the Heavens at the new star blazing in the sky. He missed his friend.

It was on nights like this, with summer just around the corner, when he knew that he would miss him the most.

Remy reached for the bottle of Glenlivet and poured himself two fingers of the fine scotch.

"Toasting Steven again?" asked a voice from nearby.

He turned in his chair to see Linda leaning in the doorway. The sight of her made him smile, and it was almost enough to take the sad edge off.

Almost.

She came to sit in his lap, throwing her arms around his neck. Marlowe lifted his big head and studied her momentarily before dropping it back down to the deck, snoring again in seconds.

"Where is it again?" she asked, taking the smallest of sips from his glass of scotch.

"The new star? Right there." He raised his hand and pointed to a particular place in the heavens. "It burns just a little bit brighter than all the rest; can you see it?"

"Yeah," she said. "Now I can."

The world wasn't that much different since Unification had come to pass. Those more sensitive to the preternatural could feel that something wonderful had occurred somewhere out there in the ether, but just about everybody else simply went on with their lives as they had before.

Even though Heaven was watching more closely now.

Linda had some more of his scotch before giving the glass back to Remy. "There weren't any stories about him on the news tonight," she said.

He knew exactly what she was talking about. Law enforcement was still on the hunt for a killer, or killers, who'd slain Boston Police detective Steven Mulvehill in his Somerville home. The search had been relentless, and even Remy had been questioned repeatedly. He wished that he could have shared the truth with them, but the truth was just too much.

Even with the Unification, the world was just not ready to know the reality of what existed around them, and Remy wasn't really sure if they ever would be.

"It's old news now," he said, sadly swirling the golden liquid around in his glass. "Eventually, it'll even be forgotten."

"Steven will never be forgotten," Linda said, leaning her cheek against his head.

"No, never."

"I think I'm going to bed," she said, and kissed him gently on the cheek. "Are you coming down?"

"I think I'm going to sit here a little bit longer, if that's all right."

"That's fine," she said getting up from his lap. "Feel free to wake me when you get in."

He held her hand and kissed it before letting go.

She smiled at him, and he felt that oh-so-human flutter in the pit of his belly that reminded him how lucky he had been to find her.

"Come on, Marlowe," she said to the dog. "Let's go to bed."

The dog looked at him first.

"Go on," he told the beast. "I'm just going to sit here, think for a while, and drink."

The Labrador climbed to his feet and stretched before trotting off to join Linda.

Alone, Remy closed his eyes and listened to the prayers of the world. The voices were much clearer since Unification, and he allowed them to wash over him.

But one prayer seemed to separate itself from all the others. It wasn't that it was more important, it just stood out, as if it wanted to make sure that he heard it.

To know of it.

Curious, Remy focused on the pleas of a young woman in the throes of childbirth. She was praying to the Holy Father for her child—her son—to be healthy, and brave, and smart, and a leader whom others would look up to in times of need.

That he would be a good person.

Remy thought that was a lovely sentiment for her to want for her newborn child, but he could not understand why this plea—this prayer—was coming across so very strong, nearly drowning out all the other prayers of the world.

As if he was being told to pay attention.

Used to the mysterious machinations of his Holy Father, Remy did what he thought he should, putting all his focus on this new mother as she was about to bring life into the world.

Maybe she was in danger of some kind, he thought.

He set his glass down upon the table and stood, tilting his head in such a way as to listen beyond the woman's silent pleas for her child's future.

The screams of childbirth were bloodcurdling, but nothing out of the ordinary, soon followed by the wails of the newly born.

Satisfied that mother and child were safe, he attempted to pull away, to disconnect from the moment and return his hearing to normal, but he found that he couldn't.

He became focused on the cries of the child as the baby became acclimated to the world, hearing something in those noises, a language that only an angel could understand.

Normally, they were purely instinctual—*I'm hungry, I'm cold, I'm afraid*—but this baby's cries . . . this baby's voice . . .

Remy gasped, stumbling back and bumping into the table. And then he realized that he wasn't alone, catching a glimpse of a familiar old man standing at the other end of the rooftop, looking out over the city. The old man turned and smiled. But before Remy could ask what it was that He wanted, He was gone.

The baby continued to cry, and it called to Remy.

It took only a moment to unfurl his wings, and he was soaring through the Boston sky, touching down upon the rooftop of Brigham and Women's Hospital, in the center of the helipad.

Not wanting to be seen, he wished himself invisible as he crossed the rooftop, going to the door that would take him down into the hospital.

The prayers of the sick, dying, and thankful were particularly loud here, but a baby's cries—*this baby's cries*—were all that Remy could focus upon.

It did not take him long to find them: mother, child, and father. They were all together in a recovery room, overjoyed with the moment, overjoyed that they were now a family.

The baby was silent now upon his mother's breast, lulled to sleep by the familiar sound of her beating heart.

Remy slowly approached the young family, stopping beside the bed as the new parents huddled together lovingly. They could not stop looking at their child.

Their new baby boy.

And neither could Remy.

He leaned in close to the mother to see the child's face.

"Is that you?" he asked the sleeping babe. The child yawned, his tiny hands fussing at his face before disappearing beneath the blankets. And in that moment, taking in the sight of him, taking in the smell of his newness, Remy knew the answer.

He'd known it as soon as he'd heard the newborn baby boy proclaim through his cries, *I am an old soul.*

Remy could only surmise why the old man had come to him on the rooftop, that perhaps this was His way of saying thanks. But who really knew?

"What should we name him?" the baby's father asked, reaching out to lovingly stroke the child's ruddy cheek with his finger.

He did most certainly move in mysterious ways.

The mother did not answer, and Remy knew that she was thinking—searching for that sudden inspiration that would tell her what her son should be called.

Remy could not resist, leaning in close to whisper in her ear, knowing that no other name would be right for the old soul she held in her arms.

"Steven."

It would be comforting to have this soul in the world again.

The woman smiled. "I have just the name," she said, leaning down to kiss the top of the baby boy's head.

"His name is Steven."

Read on for a special preview of the
first book in a new series from *New York Times*
bestselling author Thomas E Sniegoski,

THE DEMONISTS

Coming in April 2016 from Roc

At first glance, the house at 145 Westview Lane in Pittsburg, Pennsylvania, was nothing special. It was a typical ranch-style home built in the early seventies on a plot of land where an old farmhouse once stood before it burned down in 1961.

"Got anything?" John asked his wife.

Theodora stood silently beside him in the near darkness of the living room, using her special gift—her enhanced senses—to find and touch any residual spirit energies left by the home's previous occupants.

"Nope, same as the last time you asked me—nada. The place is strangely, pardon the expression, dead."

"Nice," John said dryly. "I'm surprised you didn't save that one for the viewers."

"Only the best for you, snookums," she gushed, and although it was too dark to see it, John imagined that special twinkle in her icy blue eyes accompanied by a smile that could melt the stoutest of hearts.

"Hey, Jackson, how are we doing for time?" John asked the cameraman behind them. They were in the midst of a commercial break on their live show on the Spirit Network.

Jackson touched his earpiece and listened for a moment. "Two minutes twenty," the man replied, hefting the night-vision camera back onto his shoulder.

"Think we'll take a look at the stain next," John said. He clicked on his flashlight and moved the beam over the hardwood floor. They'd seen it earlier when they were doing their prebroadcast walk-through. Supposedly it was blood, but John had his doubts.

"That stain is gross," Theodora said.

"Gross is good for Halloween," John answered.

"We're back in ten," Jackson warned. "Nine . . . eight . . . seven . . ."

John and Theodora positioned themselves near the stain and waited to be told they were live.

"Showtime," the cameraman whispered, and John launched into his spiel.

"We're back with this special live Halloween broadcast of *Spirit Chasers*," he said, staring at the tiny red light on the night-vision camera that Jackson was pointing directly at him. "For those of you just tuning in, I'm John Fogg, and I'm here with my wife, Theodora Knight, and members of my *Spirit Chaser* team, investigating a home in rural Pennsylvania. We've dubbed it the House of Torment, because throughout its history, its many residents have almost all been victims of troubled lives."

John moved through the inky black, flicking his penlight across the floor as he walked. "Right now Theo and I are checking out a strange stain that, according to the current owner, Fritz, grows more pronounced when paranormal events in the home begin to escalate."

He shined the beam of the flashlight on the living room floor, illuminating a dark stain shaped like the state of Florida. "Jackson, can you show this to the folks at home, please?"

John continued as he watched the red light on the infrared camera turn away from him and down toward the floor. "If you remember, Fritz believes this is a bloodstain left when the previous owner murdered his wife, supposedly on this very spot."

"Just one of the many disturbing events that have transpired in this seemingly accursed home, and part of the reason why Fritz refuses to live here anymore," added Theodora as the couple knelt to examine the darkened spot.

"Right," John agreed. "Once he began renovating the place, he began to notice strange sounds and smells, and he reports seeing shadow figures from the corners of his eyes."

"John, why don't you get some EMF readings while I get out the blood test kit?"

The sound of Theo going through her things could be heard, and the red light on the camera again faced John. He removed a cell phone–sized device from his pocket and held it over the spot, slowly moving it around the area of the stain. As he did so, he reminded the folks at home that he was looking for high electromagnetic fields supposedly emitted by ghostly beings, and expressed disappointment that the device remained perfectly silent, as it had throughout the evening's investigation.

John felt his wife poke his arm in the darkness.

"Here's the kit, hon."

He reached for the offered items and again knelt before the stain. "In this bottle is a hydrogen peroxide mixture that will react to a chemical found in blood called catalase. If this really is blood," John said as he removed the cover on the plastic bottle and squirted some solution onto the tip of a cotton swab, "then the liquid should start to bubble."

He knew it wouldn't, but he had to go through the motions for the live show. Again the camera panned down to the stain. He could imagine the viewers at home, sitting on the edges of their seats, eyes glued to the screen, hoping that John would confirm a bloodstain.

"And as you can see," he said, rubbing the saturated swab across the stain, "no bubbles, indicating that this stain is definitely not blood."

"I'm guessing some sort of petroleum product, maybe," Theo said as she squatted next to her husband. She placed the tip of a well-manicured finger on the center of the dark spot and gently rubbed at it. "Whatever it is, it's saturated the wood. It could be that it reacts differently to the temperature in the house during the change of seasons, and that's what leads the homeowner to believe that it's indicating paranormal activity."

John's walkie-talkie squawked and he removed it from his belt, hoping that it was something good to save the show—maybe some disembodied footsteps, or better yet, a creepy voice recording from the EVP session Phil Carnagin and Becky were conducting in the basement.

"Go for John," he said into the device.

"John, it's Phil. Think we might've found something you're going to want to see."

"We'll be right down," John said, forcing himself not to sigh in relief. "How we doing for time?" he asked Jackson.

"Commercial coming up," the cameraman replied.

"Excellent," John said. "We'll take a little break, and when we return—"

"The basement, with Phil and Becky," Theodora finished.

"And we're into commercial," Jackson announced, lowering the camera.

"To the basement, then," John said, clicking on his flashlight to illuminate their way.

"Where our ratings are going to be if something doesn't happen soon," Theodora replied, turning on her own flashlight.

"You've done it now," John warned, already heading toward the kitchen, where the door to the basement awaited them. "Now all hell is going to break loose."

"We can only hope," Theodora said.

John chuckled. He had to agree with her. They'd researched this place pretty thoroughly, even sending in a preinvestigation team that had garnered good results—EMF spikes, interesting electronic voice phenomena, or EVP, and shadow entities. The place had seemed perfect for their Halloween broadcast. Hell, it had won out over a Scottish castle!

So why is it now so silent? John wondered as they crossed the kitchen and headed down the stairs. "Let's hope for something good," he said aloud. "Or next Halloween, we'll be at home, handing out candy."

"Full-size?" Theo asked.

"Excuse me?"

"Will we be the house that gives out full-size candy bars, or the minibites?"

"If we lose the Halloween show, we'll have no choice but to go cheap—bite-size all the way."

Theodora descended into the basement carefully, following the beam from her flashlight. She again attempted to reach out to the home, to rouse dormant energies of those who had once resided there.

But still there was nothing.

It wasn't unusual to come up dry in newer homes, as the more recent structures often did not yet have the ability to collect the residuals of life and death. Although sometimes the land would hold something.

Something that would want to communicate with her.

But this place, a genuinely old house, built upon land that had seen a lot of living and dying, offered nothing.

It just wasn't right.

"We're back in one and a half," Jackson announced from behind them, clumping heavily down the wooden stairs.

John had reached the bottom, where some old apple crates had been stacked, and his flashlight beam played over the dirty, cobwebbed surface of the containers.

"Phil!" he called, walking around the crates. "Becky!"

"Back here!" Phil yelled.

The cellar went farther back than Theodora had expected, probably extending beyond the house and under the backyard. She followed her husband, hearing Jackson behind her, as they negotiated the darkness, skirting rusted old bikes and farm tools. She allowed her defenses to remain down, hoping to pick up on anything the house could offer.

And still there was nothing.

They finally came upon Phil and Becky in a tiny room where the products of fall canning probably had been stored on shelves for the winter. Now the shelves were empty of everything but a thick coating of dust, as was the rest of the room. All except for a sealed jar on the floor in the center of the room.

"What is it?" Theodora asked from the doorway, feeling Jackson trying to move around her for a better shot.

"Less than a minute," he announced as he pushed past her.

"We'll pick up with a discussion of this," John said, his flashlight beam on the jar.

Theodora couldn't take her eyes from the object. There was something about it that didn't seem right.

Jackson gave John the signal to begin.

"Welcome back to the live *Spirit Chasers* Halloween show," he said. "Thanks again for joining us. Just before the break, Phil and Becky called, asking us to join them in the basement, where they found this." He squatted and moved the light across the bronzed surface of the jar, revealing fine cracks in the glass.

He continued to talk, but Theodora was only vaguely aware of the words leaving his mouth. Her eyes were transfixed by the surface of the container.

The sound was faint, like that of ice cracking as it was warmed by the afternoon sun, and that was when she saw it. As the flashlight beam caressed the rounded contours of the jar, it began to appear upon the jar's smooth surface.

Theodora's breath caught in her throat as her highly attuned pre-ternatural senses were suddenly bombarded. Her head was filled with staccato images—images of heinous acts committed here in this house, in this basement.

"Where did you find it?" she gasped, interrupting her husband's monologue. She felt the eyes of the team fall upon her, but she couldn't take hers from the jar on the floor. More spiderweb cracks appeared on its surface.

"Tell me!" she screamed. "Where did you find it?"

Jackson was pointing the night-vision camera in her direction. It was a live show and this kind of thing was great for ratings, but ratings were the farthest thing from Theodora's mind.

"Theo, are you—," John began.

"In here," Phil said quickly. "It was over in that corner, on its side."

"So you touched it?" Theodora asked. "You touched it to place it here?"

She saw the image of a small girl falling on a staircase, and felt her pain as her baby teeth smacked the edge of a step, gouging the wood as they were knocked from her mouth. Theodora's stomach roiled as she struggled to raise her psychic defenses against whatever was seep-ing from the container.

"Something's happening," she heard Becky say from across the room. Theo had always suspected that Becky was a bit psychic as well.

"Would someone care to fill me in?" John asked cheerily, although his wife could hear the edge to his voice.

"Did you drop it?" she asked Phil and Becky, ignoring her husband's question.

"No. We just moved it to the center of the room so we could see it better. What—"

Phil was interrupted by a louder crack. Another wave of images poured over Theodora as their EMF detectors began to beep frantically.

Theodora was witness to more pain. She tried desperately to block it out, but the events were coming so fast and furious now that she could barely discern what she was seeing. All she knew was that it was horrible and that death was always the outcome.

"You touched it," she said breathlessly. "You shouldn't have—"

More, even louder cracks came from the jar, and she pushed back the surge of panic that threatened to overtake her. "We need to leave," she managed, her eyes still glued to the object. "We have to get out of here before—"

"Theo, what's going on?" John demanded, reaching out to grasp her arms.

The container shuddered; then, with a whiplike snap, a dense mist began to seep from the growing fissures.

"I know why the house was so quiet," Theo said. She gazed at the vapor filling the small room, and at the glowing white sigils that were beginning to manifest on the walls. "How stupid could I be?" She tried to pull away from John. "It wasn't that they weren't here. . . . They were silenced."

The beeping of the EMF detector suddenly stopped, its batteries drained by . . .

"This," Theo said, pointing to the cracking jar. Images were pounding at her skull, demanding that she look at them.

. . . To see what was about to be released into the world.

"Oh God," she cried, a new image worming its way onto the screen of her mind's eye. She saw Fritz. . . . She saw Fritz as well as others dressed in bloodred robes, painting the symbols upon the walls.

Symbols that would silence the voices of the home.

Silence the spirits so they could not warn the investigators.

Theo fell against her husband.

"That's enough," John said, holding her tightly. "Go to commercial," he ordered Jackson, but the man kept right on filming.

Theodora managed to focus her eyes on Jackson, and what she saw filled her with absolute dread. He had not done what was asked of him because he was no longer in control. She could see the spirits around him manipulating him, bending him to their will.

While at first the small room had been empty, it was now filled— filled with the dead, and with something more.

"It's too late," Theo said as the atmosphere in the room became even more oppressive.

"That's it for me," Phil suddenly announced. "I'm getting the fuck out of here while—"

Before he could utter another word or take a step, Phil's body was blown apart. Shreds of clothing, blood, and skin covered the ceiling and walls of the tiny room.

And Theo could see what it was that had done this to their friend.

Within the mist that had leaked from the container, there were terrible things, demonic things.

Harbingers of something larger, and far more terrible.